Travel & Mayhem

Angela Pearse

CLAMP.PUB

First paperback edition September 2021
Published by Clamp Ltd

Set in Junicode, Aristelle Script and Aristelle Sans Condensed
Cover Art by Estella Vukovic

ISBN 978-1-914531-96-5 ePUB
ISBN 978-1-914531-97-2 Paperback (IngramSpark)
ISBN 978-1-914531-98-9 Paperback (KDP)
ISBN 978-1-914531-99-6 Hardback

angelapearse.pub
clamp.pub

For my family

CONTENTS

Chapter 1: The Workshop

Dammit, she was going to be late! As soon as the bus lurched to a stop, Jane leapt off and made a mad dash along Princes Street—or tried to. The Fringe Festival was on and Edinburgh's main thoroughfare was chock-a-block with tourists and festivalgoers enjoying the balmy Sunday evening. And they all seemed to be going in the opposite direction she was.

Fighting her way upstream, Jane was nearly at Charlotte Street when her phone started vibrating in the back pocket of her jeans.

'Ambs, I'm two minutes away. It's bonkers out here!'

'I'm really sorry, Janie, I'm going to have to bail. I've got a hot date with a Jamie lookalike.'

Jane was well aware of Amber's obsession with Outlander, but this wasn't the time to make jokes. She was having heart palpitations about attending the travel writing workshop as it was.

'Ha ha, very funny. I'm just turning into Charlotte Street now.'

Then Amber said, 'You know I wouldn't do this to you normally,' and sounded so remorseful, that Jane realised she wasn't joking.

'Oh my God ... I can't go on my own!' Jane's power-walking pace slowed to a stroll, then stopped altogether. She pressed the phone tightly against her ear, her stomach starting to churn.

'Aye, you can! It'll be great, you might even meet someone. I know, I'm a shocker. He's just invited me to a stand-up at the Assembly Rooms at eight. We can catch up with you afterwards for a wee drinkie?'

'But …'

Amber had agreed to go along with her to the workshop for moral support. However, the city was overflowing with Scottish men from near and far at the moment, and Jane assumed Amber had been 'oot and aboot', as she put it, to take advantage of the fact. The guy she'd met, whoever he was, had obviously fit the Jamie bill closely enough to make this an exceptional circumstance.

Sighing, she grudgingly agreed to meet up with her for a drink, then forced herself to keep walking towards the hotel in Charlotte Square. Stop being such a wimp, she thought, it's just three hours out of your life.

When she finally reached the boardroom, breathless and slightly manic, the twelve other participants were standing about in twos and threes chatting stiltedly, waiting for things to kick off. Notepads, pens and downturned water glasses lay atop an oval, mahogany conference table. Her stomach flip-flopped with nerves. Now Amber wasn't coming, maybe she should just pull a no-show too?

Then a stoutish young woman with springing blonde curls and an air of confidence sat down at the head of the table and gestured for everyone to take their seats. Jane assumed it was Gemma Bickerton, the travel writer who was running the workshop. Now or never, she thought, and slunk into the room unnoticed, sliding into the closest empty chair.

As soon as she sat down, her nerves mysteriously disappeared. It was typical of her; she tended to work herself into knots about things that weren't even scary at all. Remembering what Amber had said about meeting someone, Jane scanned the table expectantly. Her hopes were soon dashed when she saw there were only three males, and none of them were exactly boyfriend material.

One was an elf-like man with a balding head and greying whiskers; another was a fresh-faced boy who looked barely old enough to vote; lastly, there was a sandy-haired guy with a groomed beard and glasses who was nearer her age, twenty-four, but who wore a T-shirt declaring "I'm So Gay I Can't Think Straight". The rest were women of varying shapes, heights and ages. The lack of potential talent was disheartening but probably for the best. The last thing she needed was to be distracted now she'd actually made it into the room.

Everyone turned to Gemma at the top of the table who smiled encouragingly. 'Hello and welcome! Just in case you're not sure what this is, or if you meant to sign up for something entirely different'—she paused, eliciting polite chuckles from the group—'you're about to embark on a three-hour travel writing workshop. Whether you're a writer who travels, or a traveller who writes, you should get something out of it. I'll share a few of my favourite techniques, and we'll also do some writing here so you can get feedback on your own work, which is one of the best ways to learn. Now let's get to know each other better!'

Gemma went on to tell them more about her background in her soft Scottish burr. She was an Edinburgh local, had been a travel writer for ten years, and listed an impressive array of local and overseas publications for which she'd written. At least she knows what she's talking about, Jane thought.

Then they went around the group and each person shared something about themselves and what had brought them to the workshop. Despite hating this kind of thing, Jane couldn't help but be interested in some of the stories. There was a woman from Stockbridge who had met a Frenchman last year and had travelled from Edinburgh to Paris so often she'd lost count. She'd started a blog to write about their romantic encounters, most of which involved copious amounts of red wine and four-star hotel rooms, but all very PG she hastened to add.

The elf-like man was from Corstorphine and told them his wife had recently passed away. They'd had one last epic three-month trip around Africa, so he wanted to write about their experiences for his family before he 'lost his marbles'. He chuckled as if this was some way off down the track, but then proceeded to tell the entire story over again. Everyone smiled tentatively.

Finally, it was Jane's turn. They all looked at her and her mind went blank. Damn, she should've rehearsed something inspiring at home.

'Um, well, I'm here because I'd love to be a travel writer, I guess. I currently work with accountants, which is hardly exciting.' There were a few titters and she hoped no one in the group actually *was* an accountant. What else should she say? 'Uh, I've started writing stories for my blog about wacky things that happen when I go away. I've got around twenty posts so far.'

Gemma looked impressed. 'Sounds like a good start. You're right, travel has a way of throwing situations at us out of left field, and an element of humour always makes for a fun read. Good, thank you, Jane.' She moved on to the next person and Jane heaved a sigh of relief that she didn't have to say too much else.

She'd shared the fact that she worked with accountants but failed to mention that she was a receptionist and she *detested* it— that she scanned online job adverts every day, had applied for over a dozen positions in the last month alone, and received a callback for only one interview. She hadn't been offered the job.

Since it was August, and the Fringe, she'd reduced her job hunting efforts somewhat, but she still checked her email notifications daily for anything she could apply for. However, there was one glaring omission in her CV that was making it difficult, if not impossible, to secure a better job: she'd been kicked out of her Accounting and Finance degree at Edinburgh uni.

She'd scraped through the first year but then failed so many papers in her second year that she couldn't complete the third and fourth ones. Now she was without a degree and even low-paying entry-level jobs seemed to want a university qualification.

The video chat she'd had with her parents to break the news about being kicked out was traumatic. Her mother had cried and her father just sat there, mute with shock. Jane felt terrible but at least she'd told them the truth. She'd heard of students who nabbed the tuition money, went on holiday and produced a fake online certificate. She knew her parents cared about her, but they donated regularly to several charities too. So they were probably also mourning the fact that the huge amount of money they'd wasted on her could've been donated to a worthy cause.

Anyway, *she* was the one who was now paying the price for her inability to complete a stupid accounting degree. Working as a temp at an accountancy practice to help pay for living costs in her second year had inexplicably turned into a full-time job.

The day she'd found out she didn't have enough credits to do her third year was the same day Melissa, the receptionist, had applied for two years' maternity leave. Officially she was only entitled to one year, but she'd asked for an extra twelve months, and was delighted when the owner agreed. Of course, Melissa had immediately handed in her notice. The owner encouraged Jane to put herself forward for the role, since she was already working there, and then had immediately hired her. She wasn't surprised.

Her life was officially a nightmare, so why not rub a little more lemon juice in the wound?

After two years of working at the practice Jane yearned to leave. On really bad days she fantasised about just quitting spontaneously and taking off to be a travel writer, but knew realistically it was a pipe dream. She couldn't quite see how it would earn her enough money to pay rent or buy food. If she couldn't get another job, she supposed she could go back to university. But the thought of asking her parents for more money to redo the failed year or study something else wasn't appealing. The idea of using her entire savings to study was even less attractive.

Besides, for the last couple of months she'd started dipping into her account to take advantage of cheap weekend deals to Spain. Feigning illness, she packed a carry-on bag and headed to Edinburgh Airport at the crack of dawn on Friday morning. She arrived in Majorca within three hours, enjoyed a lovely sunny weekend and flew back late Sunday night. She wore sunscreen so she didn't get too much of a tan and the dark circles under her eyes helped reinforce her story that she'd been ill all weekend. No one would have guessed she'd been drinking sangria at late night cafes and practising her Spanish on the locals instead.

At first, Jane felt guilty about the deception, but no one really did anything on Fridays anyway. The three accountants at the practice all had long, boozy lunches at the local pub and knocked off around three in the afternoon. If there was the odd client who wanted to schedule a meeting, they could use the online booking system. She justified it as a type of mental health break anyway to keep from going slowly insane. Unfortunately, surreptitious getaways and applying for jobs that she had no hope of getting weren't helping to further her career, whatever that ended up being. All she had to show for the last few months were a pile of rejection emails and hangovers from drinking too much cheap sangria.

After the introductions, Gemma handed round some sheets of paper with a snippet of travel writing that she pronounced 'pretty dire' and asked them to have a go at improving it. She gave them her own version of it and Jane got her first glimpse at how good a writer Gemma actually was. She gulped, reminding herself that Gemma had been doing this for ten years not ten minutes like her.

Then they had to write a descriptive paragraph featuring an inanimate object—hers was, of all things, a lamp post. But Edinburgh *was* inundated with atmospheric lamp posts, so she got carried away writing a spooky thing about bodies being dug up in Greyfriars Kirkyard for medical purposes and being transported under the cover of lamplight and haar fog.

After she nervously read it out to the class, the "I'm So Gay" guy gave her an appraising glance, which made her wonder if he actually swung both ways. Or, maybe he just liked hanging out in graveyards?

Next, Gemma talked about "hook techniques"—ways of grabbing the reader at the start of an article. She asked them to pair up with the person on their left, and interview each other about a personal travel experience for ten minutes. They then had thirty minutes to write a short, descriptive story using a hook technique.

Jane initially felt bad that the elf-like man had to pair up with Gemma because Amber hadn't come, but she figured he'd get more interesting material from an experienced traveller. Amber liked to travel but, more often than not, her trips involved simple pleasures, like hillwalking and whisky distilleries.

She was lucky that her own subject, Fiona, a forty-something housewife from Inverkeithing, was an avid traveller and a talker. She told her a funny story about her family's trip to Malaga. Apparently the five-star hotel they'd stayed at had an issue with the plumbing and the toilet kept overflowing. She, her husband and their two kids were moved to at least half a dozen different rooms, with the same issue happening in each, before eventually being upgraded to a deluxe family suite with a sea view.

'Did the toilet overflow in there?' wondered Jane.

'Yes, but the suite was so amazing we put up with it. Besides, we had two bathrooms, so we just rotated between them. They only charged us for the first room too. Best holiday ever!'

Jane laughed, her brain spinning into action. This type of situation was right up her alley. She started her story with one of the kids sitting on the toilet and screaming blue murder because it was gushing everywhere. Then Fiona running around in a panic to mop up the floor, with the husband on the phone giving the hotel staff an earbashing and demanding an upgrade. She was half-giggling to herself as she wrote it.

After a ten-minute break, Gemma said the person they interviewed would read their story to the class and she, and the other class members, would give them feedback.

When it came time for Fiona to read out her story, Jane was nervous about how it would go, but it turned out Fiona had a flair for the dramatic. With her thick burr, she played up her rolling r's for her husband's dialogue and put on funny voices for the hotel staff, which made everyone laugh. At the end, there was even a clap. Jane blushed with pleasure, though she was sure most of it was down to Fiona's acting.

When the workshop eventually wrapped up, she was about to leave, but Gemma approached her.

'Hey, thanks for coming, I hope you enjoyed it?'

'Definitely!' enthused Jane, pleased to be singled out.

'Your story was really great,' Gemma said. 'You got right to the heart of the action and teased out the humour of the situation. There were no boring bits that made everyone's eyes glaze over.'

Jane laughed. 'Well, Fiona did make it easy for me with a story like that. If I didn't even get a chuckle, I'd be disappointed.' She glanced over at Fiona, who was chatting with another woman; she waved at Jane.

'Aye, true.' Gemma paused, as if weighing up something.

'Hey, I don't know if you have time with your job and all but I might be able to throw some writing work your way if you were interested in doing it on the side.' Before Jane could say anything, she produced a business card and gave it to her. 'Have a think anyway and let me know. I'd like to read your blog too. Well, nice to meet you and keep in touch!'

Then she turned to the couple of students who'd been hovering patiently, waiting to quiz her, no doubt, about their own writing. Jane looked at the card. It was plain white with swirly black writing, and pronounced that Gemma Bickerton was a Freelance Travel Writer, and gave her email and social media handles. A small thrill went through her that she'd actually made an impression on Gemma.

Amber had texted to say she was at the Rose & Crown, so Jane headed in that direction. The sun had only just set and the streets were still crowded and lively in the twilight. The entrance to George Street thronged with people and from up the road she could hear the bagpipes and cheers of a ceilidh in full joyous swing.

To bypass the bedlam, she turned right into the narrow alleyway of Rose Street instead. It felt weird having been to a Book Festival event when the Fringe was on but now, feeling the smooth edge of Gemma's card in her pocket, she was mightily glad she hadn't pulled a no-show. The cool night air was sharp with the tang of hops, and Jane felt a tingle of hope. She couldn't remember the last time she'd been optimistic about anything.

Tugging the pub door open, she was hit by a wave of noise, followed by a fug of warmth and whisky fumes. She pushed her way in through the jam-packed pub and immediately heard her name shouted: 'Janie, over here!' Amber was in a booth with three other people she didn't know, a girl and two guys. One of the guys jumped up and asked her what she wanted. 'Oh, just a G&T, thanks,' she replied. Judging from the nearly empty glasses on the table, Jane could see they'd already had one round.

She plonked herself down in the leather seat beside Amber. 'How was the stand-up?' She sneaked a look at the guy across from them to see if this was Amber's date. By the way he had his arm draped across another girl's shoulders and was nuzzling her ear, she figured not.

'Och, it was one of those ones where you have high expectations for it to be brilliant. Great reviews, third Fringe appearance, sold out shows—has to be good, eh?'

'Well, you'd hope so.'

'It was a fizzer. Maybe he had an off night, but the jokes really weren't funny. Or maybe I just wasn't in the right mood. Everyone else was laughing though.'

Jane looked around. 'And—your date, what did he think?'

'He thought it was great. That's him, Colin, getting yer drink, by the way.'

'Ah!' said Jane. Amber nodded towards the couple. 'That's Moira and Kenneth, his pals. I'll introduce you when he gets back. They're a wee bit busy right now.' Jane surveyed the snogging couple and agreed they may not want to be interrupted.

Colin arrived then with her G&T and another round of drinks for the others. She started to get her purse out but he said to her, 'Nae bother! It's half-price drinks after 9:30 so it was cheap.'

Jane smiled and thanked him. He was roughly handsome, with a pleasant face, stubbled cheeks and curly brown hair with a reddish tint. About thirty, perhaps, she guessed. She was no good with ages. He did have more than a touch of Outlander-Jamie about him, so she would give Amber that. She raised an eyebrow at her friend, and Amber grinned impishly. 'Just a wee bit,' she said, reading Jane's mind.

'Colin, Jane—Jane, Colin,' said Amber, waving a hand towards each of them. She picked up her drink: 'Sláinte!' The couple stopped snogging long enough to clink glasses, say 'hi' to Jane and then continue with their own private conversation.

Colin grimaced. 'Sorry about them: newlyweds. So how was the workshop?' he asked Jane.

'I told him I was meant to be there with you and not at that godawful show with him,' Amber explained.

'It was actually great. It's made me want to be a travel writer even more.'

'Thank God,' said Amber. 'Then I won't have to hear you moan about your job anymore.' She squeezed Jane's arm to let her know she was only joking. 'I'm glad you liked it,' she whispered to her.

'What's your day job then?' asked Colin.

'I work at a chartered accountancy practice on Dalkeith Road.'

'Och, that must be good money though; travel writing seems a step down?' he queried.

Jane glanced at Amber. 'I'm not an accountant, I'm a receptionist.' She felt her face burn and sighed inwardly, waiting for the sneer.

'Oh, thank the Lord,' said Colin. 'I thought I was going to have to wax lyrical about how enjoyable it is to do ma taxes. It's not, by the way.'

Jane relaxed. Why did she always think people would look down on her when she told them what she did? She sipped her drink.

'What do you do then?'

'I'm a self-employed builder. Working on a contract out at Ratho at the moment for a new housing estate. Keeps me busy. Rather be seeing gigs at the Fringe though.'

He smiled at Amber, who blushed prettily, her long, glossy black hair softly framing her heart-shaped face. Jane was used to Amber getting attention from guys; the two had flatted together last year and had since become friends.

Petite, with an hour-glass figure kept trim by working out regularly in her local gym, Amber *bounced* with health. Not that Jane wasn't in good shape; she walked a lot, drank kale smoothies and went easy on the chocolate. She also knew there was nothing wrong with the way she looked: taller than average, naturally slim (though that meant less than she would've liked in the boob department), blue-grey eyes, a small nose and straight, shoulder-length, dark-blonde hair. Her peaches-and-cream complexion didn't need tons of makeup to cover any obvious flaws, and she only got the odd spot. A guy she'd been out on a date with had even told her she had luscious lips, which she'd been pleased about, even if he hadn't stuck around to try them out.

To be honest, she did get her fair share of male attention when Amber wasn't around. But lately she didn't feel particularly radiant; instead, she felt tired, even though she got at least seven hours of sleep a night. She had a sneaking suspicion her job (and her clandestine visits to Spain) were wearing her down.

'Speaking of jobs, I should head off. Monday tomorrow and all that.'

'Och, stay and have another,' Amber beseeched. 'It's the Fringe.'

Jane laughed. 'It's still the Fringe next week. Aren't we going to something Tuesday night?'

'Aye, another English stand-up. Hopefully this one's better.'

Jane finished her drink, said she owed Colin one, hugged Amber and headed back out into the street. The chill night air felt like a slap in the face after the warmth of the pub. 'Cheer up, love. It might never happen,' said one of the lurking smokers, catching sight of her expression. It's Monday tomorrow, thought Jane darkly, as she strode down to Princes Street to catch a bus home. And that means work is most definitely happening.

Chapter 2: James

Not pessimistic by nature, Jane had racked her brain to come up with some redeeming features of her job. But she'd struggled. She could only think of two good things: it was a mere ten-minute walk from her flat, and she got paid. That's where the positive factors ended. She knew plenty of people hated their jobs but, for them, the drudgery was made bearable by their colleagues. A bunch of people you could go to the pub and moan about work with. Being a receptionist to three accountants meant she didn't have that luxury. After all, they were the ones who had hired her, so she'd be moaning about them to their faces. Another thing she found hard to deal with was that all three accountants had maddening personalities.

The owner, Alistair McDowd, was fiftyish, lived in the West End and was prone to bouts of OCD. He'd get his tie in a tangle if the files in his office weren't in pristine order. So she had to take them out of the cabinet, colour code them and then place them back, making sure the spines lined up perfectly. This happened at least once a month. He liked the leaves of his potted plants dusted every second day too.

Craig McKenna, in his mid-thirties and also from Edinburgh,

was contradictory. He created impeccable spreadsheets but left his office in a complete mess, and it fell to Jane to tidy it up each afternoon. Some days were worse than others. She knew he was particularly stressed when he ate a ridiculous amount of pistachio nuts. The accountants didn't employ a cleaner, as they felt it should be part of the receptionist's duties. So not only did she have to pick up stray pistachio shells and chocolate wrappers from under his desk but wash up everyone's dirty teacups in the communal kitchen too.

The other accountant, Sylvia Johns, originally from Sussex, was bordering on forty and doing her damnedest (with Botox) to look twenty. She was Jane's least favourite. One minute Sylvia would be as nice as pie, then without warning she'd ignore her, making Jane think she'd said or done something terribly wrong. Over the last two years she'd learnt to manage all their various quirks and habits to some extent, but if she never saw them again she wouldn't lose sleep over it.

On Monday morning, she pushed open the front door of McDowd's Chartered Accountants—even the name sounded grim—and dropped off her bag behind the reception desk. The accountancy practice was housed in a Georgian building, like so many of the small businesses in central Edinburgh. Formerly someone's home, it had been repurposed into a commercial space in the late nineties. The ground-floor reception area with its light-grey walls, snow-white cornicing and dark wooden floorboards, had once been the drawing room. A tall, narrow window directly to the right of the front door let in, on occasion, a sliver of afternoon sun, and sometimes it also lit up the intricate stained-glass panel at the top. On those days, watching the coloured lights playing over the floor made her feel a tad more cheerful.

The budget for office furniture had been limited when Alistair had leased the place. Jane's desk was from a second-hand store, a seventies Formica thing placed at the back of the room facing the door. It had too many drawers and a low, unnecessary shelf that banged against her shins if she scooted her chair in too quickly.

Upstairs on the first floor, Craig had furnished his office—formerly the guest bedroom—from his mother's flat, so the overall look was a hodgepodge of mismatched antique pieces he called 'shabby chic'. He did, however, have a very nice green velvet chaise longue that Jane had tried out on more than one occasion when she was tidying in there. Alistair and Sylvia's offices were next to Craig's—the former master and guest bedrooms respectively—and decked out marginally better. They'd relied heavily on IKEA sales, so at least everything was from the same era.

This particular Monday morning started innocuously enough. Jane did a tea round for the accountants, printed some letters, and made a few calls to confirm bookings for later in the week. She was just settling into some transcription when the buzzer for the entrance door sounded.

Jane released the lock, thinking it was a courier, but a young guy opened the door and came into reception. She hadn't seen any client bookings for this morning on the system, unless this was a private meeting she didn't know about.

At first glance, she noticed he was tallish with dark-brown, glossy hair cropped close at the sides with a longer floppy fringe. He wore faded jeans and a black T-shirt with a white Vans logo. From the way he was dressed she gathered he wasn't a corporate, not one that worked in an office anyway.

'Hello, can I help you?' she asked.

The guy came over to the desk.

'Hello, aye. I haven't made an appointment but I ... I need some help with ma taxes, they're a wee bit of a mess.'

He was certainly Scottish, though he sounded slightly different to the other Edinburgh locals she knew. Along with the dark floppy hair he had smooth, clear, creamy skin, refined features and a pair of intense brown eyes that were now surveying her. Whoa, Jane thought, he's cute.

'Taxes can be tricky,' she replied, staring up at him.

He flashed her a grin and she couldn't help but smile back. God, he was hot. She could feel herself starting to blush.

'I dinnae suppose I could see someone this morning?' he prompted.

'Ah, yes, of course.' Jane composed herself and tried to act more professional. She gestured to the couch.

'Please have a seat and I'll see who's available. Can I just take your name?'

'Aye. It's James. James McAvoy.'

'Right.' Seriously? Jane's mouth twitched and he caught sight of it as he sat down.

'You're actually the first person I've met who hasn't asked me if I'm related to him,' he commented.

'Do you get that a lot?'

'Aye,' he said, rolling his eyes. 'Luckily for me I dinnae look anything like him, otherwise I'd have to fight off adoring fans wherever I go. I'm thinking of changing ma name by deed poll.'

Jane gazed at him, amused. Not only was he hot, he had a sense of humour too; she liked that. He glanced over at her, a smile playing around his lips, which she noted were full, soft and looked extremely kissable ... yikes, she thought, starting to feel flustered, she had to get a grip. 'Right. Yes, well, I'll just check to see if anyone can see you.' She tried Craig, who she knew didn't have a client until two.

'Yes, Jane?'

'Craig, can I send a walk-in up to see you? He doesn't have an appointment.'

Craig hemmed and hawed in her ear. She just *knew* he was eyeing up the green chaise longue, invitingly bathed in morning sun, and was planning to be on it shortly reading the Scottish Times. 'I'm a wee bit busy,' he said. 'Perhaps Sylvia can do it?' Grrr, bloody Craig!

So she phoned Sylvia, trying not to look at James, who she knew was listening to every word. When Sylvia answered, she tried a different tack.

'Sylvia, there's a James McAvoy here who doesn't have an appointment. Can I send him up?'

There was a sharp intake of breath down the line. 'James McAvoy? Well, don't keep him waiting, tell him I'll see him now.'

'Of course,' said Jane, trying to keep a straight face. She told James to go up to the first floor and turn left at the top of the stairs.

'The blue door. Sylvia Johns will see you.'

Without a doubt, there was quick-fire lipstick application and hair fluffing taking place right about now. James *was* exceptionally good-looking, Sylvia was just expecting his famous namesake.

Jane wondered what it would be like to have the same name as a celebrity. It probably did open doors on occasion, but she didn't know if she could personally deal with the constant looks of disappointment.

⊕

The following evening, she was with Amber at the Voodoo Rooms having a post-show drink. The stand-up comic they'd seen hadn't been too dire, thankfully. One year she'd come here, a man dressed as a gorilla had sat in a rocking chair and rocked backwards and forwards for an hour. She still didn't know what *that* was supposed to be about.

Jane had just finished relaying the story of what had happened with James, and Amber was having a giggling fit.

'Sylvia was pretty miffed afterwards. She was like, "Why didn't you tell me?!"'

Amber wiped her eyes with a tissue. 'But he was sitting right there! What were you supposed to say? "Oh, by the way it's not the *real* James McAvoy; he's an imposter." For heaven's sake.' She rolled her eyes.

'I know,' said Jane. 'She's a bit much. I would've loved to have been a fly on the wall though, just to see her face.'

Her phone beeped with an incoming text. She glanced at it, and then quickly turned it over on the table. Amber missed nothing, even after two and a half glasses of Pinot Grigio.

'What's with the secrecy?' she asked curiously.

Jane pretended not to hear, sipped her G&T and gazed around. 'I love coming here, it's so ornate. Look at the ceiling.' The neo-baroque bar had been packed when they arrived for the show, but it was slowly emptying out since it was getting on for 10:30pm. She yawned but Amber wasn't that easily deterred.

'Is it a guy?'

Jane relented. 'James may have asked for my number.'

Amber whooped. 'Mr McAvoy?'

'Yes, him.' Jane felt funny talking about it. James had paused by her desk on his way out and asked for it quite naturally, like he was used to doing that kind of thing. Feeling surprised and flattered, she'd quickly written it on the back of one of Sylvia's business cards for him. Since then, he'd sent one text yesterday afternoon to confirm the number, which she'd replied to with a thumbs up emoji, and now another tonight. That was it. She didn't want Amber to get all excited in case nothing happened, then they'd both be disappointed.

'Come on, what did he say?'

To humour her, Jane checked the text properly; her stomach flipped. 'He's asked me out for a coffee on Saturday morning.'

'Score!' crowed Amber. Then she frowned. 'Hang on, are you allowed to go out with clients?'

'Well ... there's nothing in my contract about it. I'm not an accountant *and* he's not my client. So, I can't see a problem.'

'Cool, cool. Just asking, keep your hair on. Is he cute?'

Jane blushed and didn't say anything.

'He must be if you're rendered speechless. On a scale of one to ten?'

'He's a twelve.'

Amber whistled. 'I don't think I've ever heard you say that about anyone.'

'Anyway, speaking of Jameses, what about you and the Jamie lookalike?' enquired Jane to change the subject.

Amber wrinkled her nose. 'Oh, he has a *child,*' she said, her tone indicating that "child" was tantamount to leprosy.

'Oh, well, it could be worse; there could be an ex-wife hanging around,' said Jane. Amber didn't say anything and took a big gulp of wine. 'Ok, there *is* an ex-wife hanging around. How do you know all this?'

Amber sighed. 'They visited the centre with Hector today. That's the child; he's three. They want to drop him off during the week as the ex-wife is going back to work.'

Jane winced. Despite appearances, Amber loved kids and worked at a day care centre in Bruntsfield. But looking after the son of the man you were dating and making small talk with the ex-wife who was in the dark about said dating was awkward, to say the least.

'That's bad timing,' sympathised Jane.

'Or good timing,' countered Amber. 'I was thinking of applying for a job at Claremont Park in Leith. It's closer to my flat and there's a vacancy going.'

'Perfect! So, I guess Colin is in the doghouse for not mentioning Hector?'

'Well, to be fair, we'd only been on one date so it's not like he needed to put all his cards on the table. It's just fast-forwarded things, to say the least. Now I know I would be dating a man with a child, which is a whole different kettle of fish.'

'Weird how they chose the exact nursery you work at,' said

Jane. 'What's Hector like?'

'Cute—blond, curly hair and a snub nose. A chatterbox.'

'And the ex-wife?'

'Nice enough, very Morningside, groomed. Colin was a deer-in-the-headlights when he saw me. He kept saying "my ex-wife this" and my "ex-wife that" so I could be in no doubt about their relationship. I couldn't even look at him, I just spoke to her. It was all quite surreal.'

'Have you heard from him since?'

'Yes, he sent a text wanting to meet up, but I haven't replied yet.'

Jane didn't think Amber would ditch him completely, it was probably just a shock. She patted her hand.

'Poor you. So much for the Jamie fantasy.'

'I know,' said Amber despondently. 'More like the Jamie reality when Claire discovered he was married …'

Chapter 3: Costa Coffee

Jane lived in Newington, a thin strip of neighbourhood sandwiched between The Meadows and Arthur's Seat. It housed mainly student flats, Airbnbs and owner-occupier couples before they had children and moved out to Portobello. She liked the area because Clerk Street, the street she lived on, had an abundance of practical shops, and was close to work. It was also near, but not right on top of, the Royal Mile and Princes Street, which were usually overrun with tourists.

She flatted with two other girls, Aimee and Rebecca, both students completing the final year of their degrees. Aimee, from Glasgow, was studying nursing, and had an affable face that matched her nature. Her long, curly brown hair tended to frizz because she refused to wear hair product; she also trimmed it herself because she balked at paying for a haircut. The men she went out with were ones from online dating sites that no one else would touch with a barge pole. She'd come back to the flat after a date and tell Jane things that made her cry with laughter.

'Naw he had dead long legs and a wee short body, he looked like a feckin' grasshopper,' or;

'Ugh, he wiz a steamin' gibbering eejit after two pints, he had tae keep goin' fer a pish,' or the most recent;

'He wiz slabberin' all over ma breests and I wiz like, "Get aff me ya bastard!"'

Jane usually had to leave the room, she couldn't handle it.

Rebecca was studying something in the sciences, and didn't date as far as Jane knew. She had straight, brown hair that she tied back in a severe ponytail, wore glasses and went round with a serious expression most of the time. Her favourite pastime was buying secondhand clothes from the British Heart Foundation, and she clomped around the flat in her purple Doc Martens, which drove Jane nuts.

Rebecca was from London, like her, so they had that in common. But she was very studious and always in the lab or at lectures, hanging out with her science friends or tapping on her MacBook in a cafe or her room. Jane noticed she only ever seemed to eat pot noodles, apart from Sunday nights, when she clomped into the kitchen to take advantage of Aimee's elaborate roasts with all the trimmings.

It must be nice to actually enjoy what you're studying, thought Jane somewhat wistfully the next morning at work as she made the first of many rounds of tea. She couldn't say she'd enjoyed one single thing about any of the papers she'd taken, and it was probably why she'd slacked off and failed so many. Unfortunately, she'd been good at maths, accounting and economics at school and her parents had decided that she'd make an excellent accountant. The fact that accountants were paid a decent salary was the basis of their argument.

'Darling, once you're qualified, you'll be able to afford your own flat, even in London,' her mother had purred. Both her parents were ex-lawyers, so they could be quite persuasive when they joined forces. Her older sister, Kath, was a doctor, and lived in Richmond with her husband, Xavier, also a doctor. This fact had been reiterated several times throughout the conversation, as if she should take note. The inference being that one accountant in the family was good. But if she could manage to snare a husband in that profession, two accountants were even better. In the end, she hadn't known what else to study, and since she couldn't get into Oxford, she'd applied to Edinburgh uni and was accepted. That was the first big lesson she'd learned in her life: don't let your parents choose your degree!

Aimee had heard the story over several cups of tea and a packet of Hobnobs and didn't judge. She was a big believer in things working out for the best. Rebecca had clomped in when the story was being told and nodded affirmingly in the right places, then clomped out again. She had asked Jane later, 'Why don't you just study something you want to now?' and didn't press it when Jane said it wasn't really an option.

Truthfully, she wasn't that keen on doing a degree, anyway. She was tired of studying—she wanted to travel, have experiences and write about them. Sitting in a lecture theatre and listening to a professor drone on didn't appeal. Besides, she'd become too used to working full-time and getting paid monthly. She didn't fancy being a poor student like Rebecca, riffling through secondhand clothes at charity shops and eating pot noodles for dinner. Though she doubted travel writers pulled in six-figure salaries.

Her mind flicked to Gemma's offer. She'd transferred her card to her purse, so she didn't lose it, and she could feel it in there, burning a hole. It had been two days since the workshop. Gemma might retract her offer if she didn't get in touch with her soon. She knew she was hesitating, stalling even, because she so desperately wanted something life-changing to come from it, and that was a lot of pressure to put on one email.

Surprisingly, the rest of the week passed quickly and before she knew it, she was due to meet James at the Costa Coffee near her flat at ten on Saturday. She was a tad late because she'd tried on half a dozen outfits, all of which seemed too overdressed for a cafe meetup. In the end, she just threw on some jeans and a white T-shirt, hastily applied some lip gloss, grabbed her phone and purse, and hotfooted it out the door.

It was a fresh, sunny morning and the air was a cleansing tonic as she walked towards the cafe. She breathed deeply and tried to calm down. Her palms were sweating, and her stomach was somersaulting like crazy. James was hot, and his intense gaze unnerved her. What would they even talk about?

She reviewed her list of failsafe topics: the weather, work, travel, movies, hobbies and as a last resort, favourite foods, if the conversation had well and truly stalled.

When she walked in, she spied him sitting by the window, leaning back with his legs crossed at the ankle, reading something on his phone. Her stomach did a slow back flip. God, what was it about him? He just oozed sex appeal. No wonder Sylvia was so flustered after their meeting. She'd been in a small room with him for close to an hour; how did she even manage to talk about taxes?

James was wearing the same faded jeans and a T-shirt—a dark-blue one this time—and immediately sat up when she came over. His dark hair flopped over his forehead. He pushed it back out of his eyes automatically and looked up at her with a grin. Maybe it was his eyes, she thought, staring at him; when he smiled, they were mesmerising.

'Hey! There you are,' he said.

Jane sat down hastily, her heart hammering.

'Um, hey!' she managed, horrified that she was blushing madly. 'Sorry I'm late.' She ducked her face.

'Nae bother, I was early. Can I get you a coffee?'

'Uh, sure. A cappuccino, thanks.' James went off to order; she took a breath and tried to relax. After a short while he was back with the coffees.

'Do you want…?' She reached for her purse.

'Nae, you're all right.'

They sipped their coffee. Jane's mind went blank. The weather, she thought desperately, talk about the weather.

'So, great weather we're having at the moment,' she said nonchalantly, looking out at the sky.

'Aye.' He nodded. Silence. All her other failsafe conversation starters flew out the window. But James, as if sensing her awkwardness, took the reins.

'How's Sylvia? Not too snowed under, I hope? With the amount of receipts I sent her the other day, she'll still be sorting out ma taxes by Christmas.'

Jane laughed. She'd forgotten he was easy to talk to, and his chattiness instantly made her feel more relaxed. 'She did mutter something about a problematic client the other day,' she retorted.

'At least I'm paying her for the pain of dealing with me.' He grinned cheekily, and it drew her in, like they were sharing a private joke.

'Where are you from?' she asked curiously. 'You don't sound like a local.'

James looked surprised. 'You've got a good ear for accents. I'm from Galashiels, near the border.'

'I think I've been there. My friend Amber and I did a day trip to Hadrian's Wall a few months ago, and we stopped off for a pub lunch. It's pretty.' She'd even written a blog post about it. Amber got into a fight with the pub owner about serving overpriced whisky and the whole thing had been quite hilarious. But she didn't mention that.

'You're not a local either,' he said. 'London?'

'Yes.'

'Hmm, well, you can't help being English ...' he teased.

Jane laughed. 'I guess not. So, what do you do that requires so many receipts?' she asked.

'Oh, sorry, I thought Sylvia would've said. I'm a freelance web designer.'

'I don't see clients' accounts or anything like that,' she explained. 'I just answer the phones and confirm appointments, mainly. Perhaps the odd bit of filing, and ... er ... tidying.' She grimaced, thinking of Craig's pistachio shells.

'How long have you been there?'

'Two years. I was studying accounting at Edinburgh uni but that ... didn't go so well. So now I'm working with accountants instead.' She screwed up her nose.

James grinned at her. 'You hate it, don't you?'

Jane shifted uncomfortably. 'It's fine. For now.'

'Go on. What do you really want to do?'

He seemed genuinely interested, so Jane ended up telling him about how she'd failed her degree, the secret trips to Spain and even the late night sangria drinking, which he thought was funny. She also mentioned the travel writing workshop, Gemma, and her offer to throw some work her way.

James raised an eyebrow. 'That's decent of her. Look, anyone can be a freelancer if you have ok writing skills, or even if you don't. You'd be surprised at the amount of bad content writers out there who manage to scrape together a living.'

Jane felt slightly offended at that.

'I'm not saying you'll be one of them,' James said hurriedly, 'but it's a gig economy. Freelancing gives you flexibility and you can call the shots. Don't like a client? Then don't work with that client. It's better than being stuck in a 9 to 5 job with a wanker of a boss.'

Or *three* bosses, thought Jane bitterly.

'You make it sound easy,' she said. 'But I doubt I can do travel writing full-time and make a living.' She couldn't believe she was telling him this stuff, but he didn't seem to mind, and she valued the opinion of someone working as a freelancer.

James waved a hand as if to brush aside her concerns. 'Och, people do, though. You've got savings, haven't you?'

'Yes,' said Jane warily, wondering where this was going.

'If I were you, I'd start saving even more, see what Gemma wants to give you and perhaps look into doing an online marketing course, so you've got a digital qualification for your CV. I can send you some links to some good ones if you want. I've got a mate in Bangkok who owns a content writing agency specialising in travel. I could probably hook you up with him. I dinnae think he pays much, but it would be something. And you'll need a website ...' He leaned back in his chair as if realising he was being too intense.

'Anyway,' he continued more calmly. 'Once you make the transition from employee to freelancer, trust me, you won't look back. Just make sure you can sort out your accounts yourself or get a good accountant, like Sylvia.' He grinned at her.

'Yes, well, I should be fine with that side of things, at least.' Jane smiled, feeling slightly overwhelmed. 'But thanks. Hearing all that makes it rather real. I guess I can't keep sticking my head in the sand forever. I'm just worried that if I quit my job, I'm going to end up in a cardboard box on the street.'

'Where do your parents live?'

'In London, in the Barbican.'

James whistled. 'I'm sure you won't end up in a cardboard box.'

'I can't ask them for handouts, not after the last time. They threw away nearly thirty thousand pounds on me. I doubt they'll want to give me a penny more. Especially since travel writing isn't exactly what they had in mind as a professional career.'

'I was thinking more of you crashing in their spare room or on their couch if you can't afford rent here. What about siblings?'

'An older sister, Kath. She's a doctor. So's her husband. They live in Richmond.'

'Do they have a baby?'

'Yes.'

'Hmm, not ideal if you need to work. Nothing's more

creativity-zapping than a screaming baby. Though you could go out to a cafe or co-working space,' he mused.

Jane stared at him and it dawned on her that perhaps she could be a freelance travel writer. Other people were doing it. She just needed to change her mindset. Thanks to her parents, she'd been way too focused on needing a university degree to be successful.

'The hard part is figuring out how to make the leap. Once you've done that, you can just start having fun!' continued James, finishing the last of his coffee and wiping his mouth with a napkin.

'Fun?' she echoed.

'Don't you think working should be fun? Especially when you have to do it seven hours a day, forty-eight weeks a year?' he asked.

'Well, when you put it like that, yes, I guess. Do you have ... er ... fun?'

It sounded suggestive when she said it, and she felt herself blushing again. At this rate, he was going to think she was permanently beetroot-coloured.

'Aye. Sorting out ma taxes does ma head in but having the freedom to do what I want, when I want, is dead brilliant.' He picked up his phone and flicked through some messages. 'Speaking of fun, I've got an extra ticket to a stand-up show tonight, if you're interested? It's at the Tron, I'm just going with a few of my friends.'

'Oh ...' She hesitated so as not to appear overly eager, but her brain was spasming. He wanted to see her again!

'Look, nae bother,' said James, taking her hesitation for reluctance. 'I can always find someone else if you don't fancy it.'

'Who's the comic?' she asked swiftly.

'A guy from London. Supposed to be good, so the reviews say.'

Jane laughed. 'Another English stand-up. I've seen a few! But ok, count me in. If he's terrible, then I'll hold you personally responsible.'

James grinned and held out his hand for her to shake, which she did, melting at the touch of his warm hand.

'Deal,' he said, gazing at her, and that was it; she was a goner.

CHAPTER 4: THE TRON

Jane tended to be wary of superhot guys. This was because the ones she'd met had acted like they were God's gift. But strangely, James didn't seem to be like that. He appeared quite down to earth and oblivious of the effect he had on women. Maybe that's why he was so chatty, she thought, he did it to knock the drooling on the head, otherwise he'd never be able to have a normal conversation. And what with his dark hair, sexy eyes, and the irresistible grin, he was definitely droolworthy in her book. Plus, he exuded an aura of confidence and knew so much about freelancing. His conviction that she could do it too was inspiring.

Being a hopeless romantic, she knew she'd start overthinking it. So, after the Costa Coffee meetup, she went back to her flat and deliberately concentrated on practical tasks, like cleaning the bathroom and putting on a load of washing.

Then, unable to resist, she texted Amber: *He has a good handshake Jx*—and waited, laughing to herself. Amber couldn't stand men with limp, fish-like handshakes and it was the first thing she always asked her when she'd been out with someone new.

Her phone beeped two minutes later: *Bodes well :) :) Did Mr 12 ask you out again? Ax.*

Jane grinned and typed: *Yup. Fringe show tonight with his friends.*

Amber texted back: *Pity not a 1-2-1 but still good. Have fun. Seeing Colin tonight. Wish me luck xx.*

Jane sent the requisite good luck text and thought about Amber's comment. She was right; an invite to a Fringe show with James's friends wasn't a date. She couldn't realistically read romance into a coffee meetup or a handshake either, but he was definitely giving off signals. She sat on her bed thinking about their conversation, how he'd looked at her, and the touch of his hand ... then despite herself, she started imagining what would happen tonight. In the darkened basement of The Tron, he'd lean over and whisper something like 'Having a good time?' in her ear and she'd whisper back 'You're here, aren't you?' And then he'd tilt her chin up and kiss her slowly and expertly until things started getting so steamy it was prudent to just come back to her flat immediately ...

Ten minutes before seven, Jane was in the kitchen wearing low-rise, tight blue jeans, a nude-coloured bra and a white silk camisole; simultaneously wolfing down tuna pasta and ironing her favourite hot-pink cotton top. Aimee hovered in the background, offering to help, but just as Jane thrust the iron at her, the buzzer went. 'Hell, he's early. Can you let him in? I'll be out in a sec!' They'd arranged that James would collect her at seven, since he was coming from Mayfield Road and it was on his way, but she figured he must be a fast walker or have caught an earlier bus.

She flew off to her bedroom with the three-quarter-ironed top, chewing furiously on a mouthful of pasta spirals. After all the illicit daydreaming, her brain was completely addled at the thought of seeing him for real. Annoyed that she was getting into a state, she rolled some lavender aromatherapy oil on her wrist and took a deep breath. Better. She had to keep it together or she'd look like a ditzy blonde, and she didn't want him to think that.

Hastily she donned the top, put on her low-heeled black boots, brushed her hair madly, grabbed her good black jacket, as well as her phone and purse, then checked her makeup. No smears of mascara or clown-like lipstick: good. With no time to brush her teeth, she swigged some water and swished, then bared her teeth in the mirror like a crazed chimpanzee. No food stuck, good: breathe!

James was talking to Aimee and had his back to her in the lounge when she walked in, outwardly serene but inwardly a bundle of nerves. He turned around and Jane swallowed hard. The daytime casual look was gone, and he was wearing dark-blue jeans and a black shirt with the cuffs rolled up. His hair was different too—gelled or something—so it wasn't as floppy. The fact that he'd put in some effort made him even more attractive; though to be honest, he could've been wearing a bin bag and she'd still be salivating.

'Hey, ready to go?' He smiled at her and she felt a twang of desire. God, maybe they should just stay here and forget about the show altogether. Aimee was watching them and saw Jane's goo-goo eyes.

She cheekily mouthed behind his back—'hot!'—and made a swooning face. Horrified that James might see, Jane ushered him down the stairs and out the door. She nearly laughed out loud. Bloody Aimee!

The Tron was ten minutes away, and the temperature had dropped, so they walked quickly to keep warm. 'Your flatmate Aimee seems nice. What does she do?' asked James conversationally, then a stream of people came surging between them. It seemed the whole of Edinburgh was out tonight.

'She's studying to be a nurse,' Jane told him, when they were walking together again, 'and she makes a mean roast.'

James laughed. 'Always a good skill to have. I'm more of a microwave man, but I have been known to whip up the odd lasagne.'

Jane glanced up at him. He was taller than she'd initially thought now they were side by side. She was five foot seven and he was a good head above her. He wasn't gangly either; she got the impression that his body was more on the muscular side, like he worked out.

'So, who's this comic? Have you seen him before?' she asked as they turned into Hunter Square.

'Aye, I saw him last year,' replied James, grasping her elbow to manoeuvre them around an overflowing rubbish bin.

'Watch your step. He was brilliant. Very politically incorrect but hilarious.'

'Now I have high expectations,' said Jane, following him into The Tron, an understated corner pub with grey and white painted columns on its façade. The place was packed to the gunnels, and a wave of talk and laughter assaulted her ears. She kept her eyes trained on James's bobbing head as he forced a path through. He showed their tickets on his phone to a young guy by the stairs.

'We can go down now and meet the others if you like?'

She nodded, and they went through an internal door and clomped down some narrow wooden steps. The walls were lined with old Fringe posters that were tattered and peeling.

At the bottom was a dimly lit, cave-like area with concrete columns holding up the floor of the pub above and set up with benches, chairs and tables facing a small stage. James scanned the room and nodded towards a small group of three guys near the back. 'That's them,' he told her. They headed over. Then there was a short burst of commotion and 'McAvoy!' and shoulder clapping.

Jane hung back, feeling shy, but James pulled her forward and introduced her. There was Angus, tall and skinny with red hair and freckles; Brian, blonde and stocky; and Pete, dark and pale-skinned like James but a less attractive version. Everyone shuffled around to make room, and an extra chair was fetched. There was still a good twenty minutes until the show started so James went off to buy drinks from the bar, leaving her with the three guys.

'You'll be safe, they dinnae bite. Well, not much!' he threw over his shoulder as he disappeared into the crowd.

'So, Jane, where are you from?' asked Angus since she was sitting next to him. He had a pleasant, resonating burr.

'Oh, London. I've been living here for four years.'

'So's our wee Brian here. Clapham, eh, Bri?'

Brian nodded. 'Which part are you from then?' he asked.

'Ah, my parents live in the City now, but I grew up in Richmond.'

'Nice,' said Brian, raising his eyebrows.

Please don't ask me what I do, she prayed.

'What do you do in Edinburgh?' he asked.

Just then James came over with their drinks, and there was more shuffling and rearranging, so she was saved from answering. 'Och, that was feckin' extortion. The barmaid charged me practically twenty quid. I ken it's the second-to-last night and all but they're making a killing!'

Jane thanked him and said she'd get the next round. With all the G&Ts she'd been drinking lately, it was surprising she wasn't permanently hungover. Speaking of which, she needed to use the ladies'. She asked James, and he pointed to the door next to the bar. Jane headed in that direction, hoping there wasn't too much of a queue. Another girl was waiting outside the door for the one and only ladies' loo. She was about her height with long, flowing chestnut hair and smooth olive skin. Jane couldn't help glancing at her lilac crop top, the crossover neckline barely containing her ample breasts. Were they real, Jane wondered? Teamed with painted-on black, leather pants and nude stilettos, the outfit would have been bordering on slapper for anyone else but somehow, she made it look classy. To Jane's surprise she spoke to her.

'Hi, I'm Kistella,' she said, flicking back her hair. Her voice was rich and velvety with a slight French accent.

'Jane. Nice to meet you.'

'Having a good night?' enquired Kistella, taking a compact out of her purse.

'So far,' said Jane, leaning against the wall. She thought about James and smiled. Kistella checked her makeup and said something that ended with '… James.'

'Sorry, what?'

'I said, so you know James?'

Jane was taken aback. 'Uh yes, through work. Why? Do you know him too?'

Kistella smiled, showing perfectly even white teeth. She stared at Jane, and her green almond eyes narrowed imperceptibly. 'Oh yes, you could say I know James.'

The door to the loo opened, and the occupant came out; Kistella waltzed in without saying anything else, or even goodbye. Jane was discomforted and didn't know what to think. She waited for a while but then didn't particularly want to be there when Kistella came out, so made her way back to the table. James and Angus were having a discussion about a software program, so she sat and sipped her drink thoughtfully. Something about the way

Kistella had looked at her and spoken about James was strange and unsettling. It was like she was trying to provoke her.

James nudged her with his elbow. 'Show's starting soon. You all right?'

'Yeah, just something weird happened outside the loo. This girl said she knew you and was ... dramatic ... about it.'

'What girl?'

'She said her name was Kistella.'

James swore under his breath, and Jane felt him tense up. He put his drink back on the table and she noticed his knuckles were white. He glanced around the room. 'In the ladies', aye?'

'Yes, she went in before me.' Jane scanned the crowd too. 'I can't see her now.'

James scowled. 'That's good.'

Jane was perplexed. 'Who is she? An ex?' she asked curiously.

'It's a long story, but let's just say I'd prefer not to bump into her.' Jane felt unnerved, but he gave her a smile and said, 'It's ok. Nothing to worry about,' and she relaxed. Then the lights went down, and the show started.

The hour passed quickly. James was right—the comic was hilarious, and his derisive wit had the audience in the palm of his hand. However, how James had reacted to Kistella was still bothering her. Her attention wandered and she kept searching the crowd trying to spot her. When it was over and the lights came on, Jane was relieved. Amber had texted saying she and Colin were at the World's End in Royal Mile if they wanted to join them. But

James was looking tense again as they made their way upstairs to the noisy bar area, so she didn't mention the invite. His three friends were discussing the show and seemed keen to stay for another round of drinks. Just then, the throng parted, and there was Kistella. She was standing with two men, laughing at something one of them had said. His hand moved to rest lightly on her hip as she leaned towards him.

'Is that …?' questioned Brian peering at her.

'Aye,' said James tersely. Jane glanced at him, alarmed to see his face flushed, and his eyebrows drawn together in an angry scowl. 'I'll catch you guys later,' he said abruptly and walked out. Brian looked uncomfortable and exchanged glances with Angus and Pete.

'Let's all go,' said Pete. Jane had no choice but to trail after them.

When they got outside, she saw James pacing around nearby and flexing his hand as if he were getting ready to punch someone. His friends called their goodbyes, awkwardly said "Nice to meet you" to Jane and walked away together down to Cowgate. James didn't seem to notice.

'What just happened?' asked Jane, going over to him.

James sighed and stopped flexing. 'Sorry about that. I just had to get out. I didn't want to order you to come with me if you wanted to stay with the others.'

'Don't be daft,' said Jane. 'I came here with you, not them. Look, do you want to go to the World's End? My friend Amber and her man Colin are there. We can have a quiet drink and just chill out.'

'That sounds great,' said James, attempting a smile, 'but I dinnae think I'm in the right mood for it. I'll just head home.'

He didn't offer any explanation about Kistella, and Jane didn't ask. She figured it was none of her business and he'd tell her if he wanted to. James accompanied her to South Bridge and then gave her a curt 'see you later' and sauntered off down the road, presumably to catch a bus or walk all the way home.

As she strolled down High Street to the pub, Jane felt disappointed and confused. Who was Kistella and why had she ruined a perfectly good evening for everyone? She had half a mind to go back to The Tron and ask the woman herself, but it seemed overly interfering under the circumstances.

At the World's End, she spied Amber and Colin in a corner nook and headed over. The place wasn't too crowded. She wished James had decided to come too.

'Hello, love,' said Amber, scooting over to make room on the buttoned booth seat. She looked over Jane's shoulder. 'Where's Mr McAvoy?'

'Hi Amber—Colin.' Jane sat down and removed her jacket and bag before answering. 'Uh, he decided to go home,' she said evenly.

Amber arched a perfectly formed disbelieving eyebrow. 'He went home before nine on a Saturday night?'

Jane sighed. 'There was an ... incident at the pub.'

'Huh? What, like with the police?'

'No, no—nothing like that. Oh, I don't know. It was all just really weird.' She slumped back in her seat, feeling dejected. Colin tactfully decided to get some drinks leaving them alone.

Amber watched him go up to the bar, 'I do like that man's sense of timing,' she said, then switched into girlfriend mode. 'Now, quickly, tell me what happened, from the beginning.'

Jane told her about bumping into Kistella by the loo, James's reaction and his abrupt exit from the pub after seeing her upstairs. 'He walked off leaving me with his three mates.'

'Och, strange,' said Amber. 'Then what happened?'

'So, I went outside, and James was still there but all het up, pacing around and acting like he wanted to punch someone.'

'Aw, noo! Then?'

'Then I asked him if he wanted to come here, and he said no, he didn't feel like it, and he was going home. That's it.'

'Has he texted since?'

Jane checked her phone. 'No.'

Colin came back then with a round of whiskies.

'Glenfiddich. Purely medicinal,' he said, 'You looked like you might need it.' Jane wasn't a big fan of whisky, but she sipped hers gratefully, the tingling warmth pervading her body.

'Thanks, Colin. I really do owe you a round.'

'Nae bother. Got a wee bit of man trouble?' he asked. Amber gave him a poke with her elbow.

Jane managed a smile. 'It's ok, you can tell him.'

So, Amber gave him the shortened version.

'Hmm, sounds like he's had a bad breakup. You dinnae want to get tangled up in that,' said Colin, swirling his whisky.

Amber looked at Jane sympathetically. 'He seemed so nice.'

'He's still nice!' protested Jane. 'If she did the dirty on him or something, it's not his fault.'

'Aye, but if he hasn't dealt with it then he's going to be emotionally encumbered,' said Amber, putting on her "I know what men are like" expression. 'He might take out his issues on you. What's it called? Transference or projection, I forget which.'

'Transference sounds right,' said Colin. 'Look, I'm not a head doctor, but it sounds like he's got emotional baggage. Plenty more fish in the sea and all that.'

Jane downed the rest of her whisky and gave a shudder as the alcohol burned her throat. 'Yeah,' she muttered softly.

Amber gave her an awkward half-hug and started talking about the show they'd seen to liven the mood. They'd been in a shipping container in George Street seeing a gay male duo perform snippets of Shakespeare's plays with song and dance.

'It was hilarious,' said Amber, and Colin nodded.

'I wasn't sure about the prancing about wearing tights, but it was pretty funny.'

Amber patted his knee. 'Aw, you loved it!'

Jane was glad Amber and Colin seemed to be getting on well, despite her earlier misgivings about the ex-wife and child on the scene. James's ex-girlfriend might also turn out to be just a blip and nothing to stress about, she thought hopefully. The whisky started to do its trick and she cheered up. 'Anyone want another drink?' she asked, getting out her purse. 'It's my round.'

Chapter 5: Coffee and Cake

Sunday was a write-off, as Jane had a G&T and then Colin had bought them another couple of whiskies. After three drams she'd started to feel disconnected from her body but managed to make it home in one piece when the pub kicked them out around twelve. But it meant she snoozed in an alcohol-induced slumber until mid-morning.

James still hadn't messaged, so she gave up fixating on her phone and cooked some bacon and eggs instead. She was on her second bit of toast when Aimee came into the kitchen, puffing and red-faced. She'd been doing a running circuit around Arthur's Seat lately.

'You're keen,' said Jane, munching her buttered toast. 'What's it like out there?'

'It's feckin' roastin'. It must be aboot sixteen degrees,' gasped Aimee, gulping down a glass of water and splashing some on her neck and face. 'Have ya just got up lazy bones?'

Jane nodded affirmatively, her ponytail bobbing. Aimee wiped her dripping face with her hand and grinned. 'Did yer hot pal stay over? Is he still here?'

'If he was, do you think I'd be eating bacon and eggs by

myself?'

'Aw, right, aye. No man can resist bacon n' eggs, even if he says he's vegan. Is he vegan?' she queried.

'No, he cooks lasagne.' Jane dumped her plate in the sink with a clatter.

Aimee stared at her, noting the tense line of her lips. 'Did yer date no go weil?'

'It's nothing,' said Jane. 'I just need to sort my life out, and he's not really helping. Well, he is, but he's confusing things too.'

'Feckin' men,' sniffed Aimee. 'Jist go for a walk to clear yer heid. I'll cook us a nice roast tonight and you can tell me all aboot it.'

Feeling somewhat comforted, Jane did as she was told and by mid-afternoon she was back in a good headspace. James hadn't messaged, but that was fine—ideal, in fact, as she didn't have anything to say to him. Maybe what had happened was a blessing in disguise, and she'd dodged a figurative bullet.

By the time Monday morning rolled around, she was seriously thinking about emailing Gemma and doing something about starting a freelance career. She'd just got into work when Alistair rang down and asked if she could come upstairs for a chat.

Jane's stomach lurched. That sounded ominous. She went upstairs and knocked on his oak panel door. 'Come in,' Alistair intoned. Grey-haired and bespectacled, he was sitting behind his glass desk, and Sylvia was also there, perched on a grey two-seater couch off to the left-hand side of the room. 'Good morning Jane, please take a seat.' There wasn't any room on the couch as Sylvia was sitting in the middle, so she sat in the seat directly in front of him like a client.

'Now, how long have you been working here, Jane?' asked Alistair, looking at her thoughtfully.

'Around two years, I think,' she said, knowing exactly how long it was. She glanced at Sylvia, trying to gauge what this was about. Had she made some kind of mistake? Sylvia's blank, botoxed expression didn't give her a clue.

'Och, that long? How time flies. Well, as you know, Melissa has been on maternity leave, but she called me first thing this morning to let me know she's ready to come back on the ninth of September. It seems they've put their wee 'un into day care already. So, I'm afraid we have to let you go from reception, and I'm sorry about that.'

'Oh,' said Jane, her mind whirling, 'I understand. That's perfectly ok.' Damn—she knew Melissa's leave was nearly up, but no one had said anything, and she'd assumed she wouldn't come back at all, like many women when they started popping sprogs.

'But there's a silver lining,' continued Alistair. He nodded in Sylvia's direction. 'I'll let Sylvia fill you in.'

Jane turned to Sylvia, who shook her blonde hair away from

her unnaturally wrinkle-free face and gave a minuscule smile.

'We know you were studying accounting at university but didn't quite complete your degree. Is that right?'

Jane flushed. 'Er ... yes, I didn't finish it.'

'Well, Alistair and I had a discussion, and we would be happy to pay for you to do the AAT Foundation Certificate if you worked here as my assistant in the meantime. We'd pay your fees and a living wage, of course, until you received your qualification. Then we could look at a suitable pay rise. There's a small box room that's being used for cleaning equipment at present, but we could turn it into an office for you. I have quite a large workload at the moment, so I'd be happy to give you a few of my easier clients, and you'd be working under my supervision, of course.'

Jane was silent. It was certainly a step up from being a receptionist. But the thought of training for a job she hated and working under Sylvia from a glorified broom closet made her balk.

She licked her lips which were suddenly dry. 'Thank you for thinking of me,' she said carefully. 'It's certainly not what I expected.'

Sylvia gave a passing resemblance of a smile and nodded. 'I know, it was my idea. It came to me when Alistair told me about Melissa. I thought it was the perfect win-win solution.'

Perfect solution for *her*, thought Jane. She got a dogsbody to offload her work onto while she swanned off for a round of Botox.

Sylvia hadn't finished. 'There would be a condition, however.

We'd need to put a clause in your contract about staying for at least two years or paying the course fee back, but I'm sure that won't be an issue. You've demonstrated that you're a very stable employee.'

Jane bristled; it just got better and better. Alistair and Sylvia looked at her and she realised they were waiting for an answer.

'I really appreciate the offer. Would ... would it be ok if I thought about it and got back to you?'

'Aye, of course, Jane,' said Alistair, glancing at his computer to see what his first appointment of the day was. 'We appreciate it's a lot to think about. If we could have your answer by the end of the week though that would be ideal. Sylvia and I will discuss it further now.'

She was dismissed. As soon as she was out the door, Jane ran for the stairs in a panic. She sat at her desk and put her hands over her mouth and moaned softly. Oh God. This was a disaster. What the hell was she going to do? A small voice suddenly popped into her head. 'Email Gemma' it said firmly. Without pausing to think about it, she grabbed the business card out of her purse, logged into her personal account and dashed off an impromptu message to Gemma saying she was open to anything she might throw her way. She added a link to her blog. Done. Now it was in the hands of the Universe.

⊕

As the week dragged on and Friday loomed closer without any reply from Gemma, Jane became increasingly stressed. Did she say yes to Alistair and Sylvia or say no and sign up for the unemployment benefit? Neither was what she wanted. Her mind went back and forth like a yo-yo and at night she tossed and turned sleeplessly, not knowing what to do.

Late Thursday afternoon she was in Craig's office on her hands and knees under his desk picking up pistachio shells. Someone came up behind her and went 'pssst' and she got the fright of her life and banged the top of her head.

She backed out rubbing her scalp and frowning, to find James, larger than life, right there in Craig's office.

'Whoops, sorry,' he said, smiling at her. 'I didn't mean to scare you.'

She stared at him warily, unwilling to be lured in again by his good looks in case he had some more skeletons rattling around in the closet.

'What are you doing here?' It came out frostier than she'd intended, and she immediately felt bad when she saw his smile fade.

'I just wanted to say hi. I had a meeting with Sylvia, and I caught a glimpse of you in here when I came out.'

'Oh, well, hi,' said Jane, dumping the shells in the bin. 'How was the meeting?'

'Och, fine. Sylvia's almost finished getting ma tax return sorted. She mentioned something about having an assistant soon, so I gather I could be dealing with them next time.'

Jane groaned and sat down heavily on the green chaise longue.

'What's the matter?' James said, concerned. 'Are you ill?'

'I'm the assistant she's talking about! They offered to pay for my accountancy training, but in return I have to be Sylvia's assistant in the meanwhile. I haven't agreed to it yet. I'm to give them an answer tomorrow.'

'What happens if you say no?' asked James, walking over to sit beside her.

'Then I'm out on my ear in two weeks. Melissa, the girl I took over from, is coming back from maternity leave.'

'Ah, that's pretty shite,' said James sympathetically. 'Doesn't leave you with a lot of options … except ...'

'I emailed Gemma. She hasn't replied, so I'm not hopeful of getting any help there.'

'I'm sure she'll get back to you—' James cleared his throat. 'Look, I feel I owe you an explanation about what happened on Saturday.'

'You don't,' said Jane, standing up smartly and brushing her skirt of pistachio remnants. 'It's none of my business.'

'But I want to,' said James beseechingly. 'Please, let's just go somewhere and get a coffee and talk.'

She sighed. Great, now she had to hear all about Kistella. 'Fine. I was about to head off anyway. Maybe meet me outside. If anyone catches us coming out together ... well, it won't look good.'

When she came out, James steered her to a nearby cafe with some scrumptious cakes displayed in the window. Her stomach growled; she'd hardly eaten any lunch because she was so stressed. Hmm, was he trying to soften her up with sugar?

Jane went up to order and came back with the coffees since she owed him one. Then the cheerful young waitress brought over a two-tiered flowered platter piled with an assortment of cakes. James's eyes widened.

'I was hungry,' Jane confessed. 'But I didn't think there'd be so many. You'll have to help.'

'With pleasure,' said James. He picked out a chocolate frosted cupcake and bit into it enthusiastically, smearing icing all over his nose. She opened her mouth to tell him but then shut it again. She took a piece of shortbread and waited.

He took a breath. 'So, you were right. Kistella is my ex-girlfriend.'

Jane nibbled on her shortbread and said nothing.

'She's a marketing assistant for an agency in the West End, and the company I was contracting with at the time hired them to do some branding work. We hit it off and went out for around six months after the contract ended. For a while it was great, perfect even—she was beautiful and ... I ... I thought I was in love ...' He trailed off.

Jane felt an urge to kick him. 'Cool, thanks for telling me.'

James rubbed his nose and looked surprised when he saw icing on his finger. He licked it off. 'And then I found out through a friend she was seeing someone else, actually quite a few someone elses.'

She winced, despite herself. That must've hurt like the dickens. She'd sensed Kistella was trouble just from that one encounter.

'Oh no—I'm sorry,' Jane said, genuinely sympathetic.

Feeling hungry all of a sudden, she helped herself to the piece of carrot cake with cream cheese icing.

'That's not the end of the story. The friend also told me she'd been spreading rumours I'd roughed her up.'

Jane swallowed a mouthful of cake. 'Really?'

'Aye, it was all utter shite. God knows how many people now think I'm a girlfriend beater.' He ran his hand through his hair and frowned. 'The irony is that it makes me so mad I *do* feel like punching someone.'

'What did you do?'

'I called her out on it, and she didn't deny it. So, I just packed ma bags and stormed out. She didn't even try to stop me. Probably glad I wasn't cramping her style anymore.'

'Packed your bags—so you were living with her?' Wow, ok, she thought, it was quite serious then.

'Aye, maybe it was a wee bit soon, but things were going well. Plus, she needed help with the rent. I felt like a right eejit when I left, as I had nowhere to go. So, I stayed in a cheap hotel in Haymarket, in a windowless room. And the air conditioning broke, so it was sweltering. Not a fun time.'

'When did you break up?' asked Jane slowly.

'July,' said James, avoiding her gaze.

'Like last month?'

'Aye.'

'So, you're not over her,' she stated flatly.

'I wouldn't say that. I'm moving on.'

'Is that why you asked me out, to "move on"?' Great, she thought. I'm the rebound.

'I guess,' said James. 'Obviously I'm not completely there yet, otherwise I wouldn't have reacted like I did the other night. But that was the first time I'd seen her since it happened, and it just hit me all over again.'

'Wow, she sounds like a right piece of work, poor you.'

James took a swig of his coffee. 'I'm better than I was. It took ages to find a flat as it was right before the Fringe started. Everyone wanted to rent theirs out on Airbnb to make a mint. I was lucky a friend was subletting his, so I didnae have to deal with agents or anything. I just moved in and worked out of the flat. Days were ok as I had work to keep me busy, but at night it was just me greeting alone into ma microwave curry.'

'I'm sorry,' she said again, not knowing what else to say.

'Och, it's fine, it's better I found out when I did. Anyway, enough about me. Have you decided what you're going to do?'

'Oh … um … not a clue. Unless Gemma offers me some amazing travel writing job and makes it easy for me. But it would be a miracle if that happened.'

'But you would leave if she did?'

'Like a shot.'

James looked at her thoughtfully. 'I've got this idea—you might think it's crazy but hear me out.'

'What is it?'

'Well, I thought I might do some travel, probably just around Europe. Why don't you come with me?'

Of all the things he might have said, she wasn't expecting that. She sat back in her chair, confused and giddy from all the sugar.

'Huh?' she said dazedly.

'I've been thinking about our conversation at the cafe. You want to travel. You hate your job and now you have to leave. I need to get some space from *the situation*, and ma mate is coming back and needs his flat. It's perfect timing. What do you think?'

I think you're *really hot* and *really messed up*, and I shouldn't even be in a cafe with you, let alone a European city. But she didn't say that.

'I don't know—I'd have to think about it.'

'Of course, it's completely up to you. I know we've only just met but you seem cool, and it's more fun travelling with someone than by yourself. Besides, it doesn't have to get complicated.'

'What do you mean?'

'Like we can stay in twin rooms or hostels with male and female dorms or something.'

She didn't say anything, realising that Colin was right. He had enough emotional baggage to fill a luggage carousel and she should walk away right now.

Yet, despite that, the thought of travelling with him was incredibly tempting. Her mind flicked ahead, imagining them walking through a cobbled alleyway at sunset, their hands accidentally brushing ... or James watching her get undressed and saying, 'My twin bed is big enough for two ...' Damn, she thought, feeling her expectations rise, this actually *could* get complicated.

After her cafe meetup with James, Jane went straight back to the flat and instigated an emergency heart-to-heart with Aimee. They were now ensconced at the kitchen table, with cups of tea and a packet of Hobnobs. She'd filled her in about Kistella and the spontaneous travel invite.

'Do you think it's mad?'

'You really like him, eh?'

Jane nodded.

'But he's no ready for a relationship.'

'No.'

'I dinnae need to tell you that going travelling with him is risky.'

Jane sniffed. 'No.'

Aimee bit into a Hobnob and chewed it slowly. 'So, as I see it, you have four options. One: you can stay at McDowd's and they'll pay for your accountancy trainin', but you have to work as Sylvia's dogsbody.'

Jane wrinkled her nose.

'Two: you can go on the unemployment benefit while you look for another job.'

Jane shook her head.

'Three: you can go travellin' by yerself.'

'That's a possibility.'

'Four: you can go travellin' with a dead hot guy yer've only just met who's gettin' over another woman.'

Jane reached for a Hobnob.

'As you can see, my life is officially a mess!'

'Och, it's not that bad,' said Aimee, soothingly. 'At least you have options.'

'What would you do?'

'Me? Probably no go travellin' with the hot guy so I get ma heart broken.'

'Oh.'

'But if you do, ye'll find out sooner rather than later if he has any turnoffs or disgusting habits.'

'Like…?'

'I dinnae ken, like ... back hair ... hoikin' in public or pickin' his nose and eatin' it? … oooh, no givin' spare change to homeless people, that's a big turnoff in ma book.'

Chapter 6: The Barbican

Two weeks later

Jane was beginning to wish she'd accepted James's offer to help. Her upper arm muscles strained with the effort of lifting her bulging day pack into the overhead locker. She was also now regretting packing books, an extra two pairs of shoes, and a travel hairdryer in her wheelie bag that was now in the hold.

With the pack finally stowed away, she slumped into her seat with relief and glanced at James in the window seat. He'd slid in, carry-on bag free, with just his phone and a bottle of water. He was also halfway through the inflight magazine, and they hadn't even taken off yet.

'Anything interesting in there?' she asked, reaching for the menu card to peruse the options. Their Saturday flight to London was leaving at noon and she'd been too nervous to eat much for breakfast, so now she was starving.

'Just an article on places to stay in Berlin. Maybe we should add it to the list?' He pointed to a photo of a hotel room with quirky decor and a hammock swing in the window. 'It overlooks the zoo, so you can lie in bed and hear the lions roar.' Another photo showed a jungle-themed rooftop bar and a glasshouse restaurant with 180-degree views of the city.

'Hmm, that would be cool,' she said, quickly pushing aside a mental image of James lying in bed with his T-shirt off. 'But that hotel does look expensive.'

'Aye, what's the plan again, Ms Accountant? Only visit cheap countries and stay in hostels?'

Jane sighed, turning her attention back to the menu card. 'I wish you wouldn't call me that. I failed my degree, you know.'

'Aye, but you did two years of it, *and* you worked with three accountants for another two years. So, I know you must have some skills, even through osmosis. Besides, I'm shite at financial stuff, as you know.'

Jane had been trying not to think of McDowd's, but as the plane moved off down the runway, lifted into the air and banked sharply over Edinburgh, she couldn't help feeling sentimental. Everyone had been very understanding about her decision to leave, though Sylvia had raised an eyebrow, or tried to, when she said she was going travelling for three months.

'Like, backpacking?' she'd said, sounding aghast. 'Or one of those Contiki bus tours?' like it was the worst way to travel. Jane couldn't help laughing to herself whenever she thought about it. She hadn't given out too many details, as she was worried James's name might slip out. All they needed to know was that she was going to Europe with a "friend".

Amber had thought travelling with him was a bad idea but once she'd heard the whole story about Kistella, and had met James properly, she'd come round. Besides, she was now loved up with Colin, so she wanted everyone else to be too. Jane was under strict instructions to tell her every detail of what happened this weekend.

Suddenly, the decision she'd made to freelance and travel with James felt very real, and her parents had no clue about any of it. Rather than tell them on the phone or by video chat that she'd quit her job and was going off with a guy she hardly knew, she'd suggested they make a pit stop in London before heading to the Continent. Which was why they were staying at her parents' apartment tonight before catching a cheap flight to Barcelona on Sunday evening.

She sneaked a peek at James who was trying to get a last glimpse of the city before they flew into the clouds. 'So, are you ready to meet the parents?' she asked.

James screwed up his nose. 'Let's just say it's not what I'd choose for the first stop on the itinerary.'

'I know. But not telling them in person just seemed wrong, and they'll worry if they haven't seen for themselves that you're not some psycho creep.'

'How do you know I'm not? I might be a wee Scottish murderer,' he said, rolling his r's and poking her in the ribs.

'Oy, stop that,' she said, giggling. 'Well, just be your usual charming self and I'm sure they'll adore you.'

'Oh, so you think I'm charming, do you?'

The stewardess rolled up then with her trolley and asked if they wanted anything to eat, and Jane was saved from answering.

Truth be told, she thought he was incredibly charming. Over the last couple of weeks, they'd spent quite a bit of time together and she, slightly worried about Kistella's accusation of him being a girlfriend beater, had scrutinised his behaviour, looking for any signs of underlying aggression. But the more she got to know him, the more she thought it was a load of old codswallop. He was kind, a good listener and always ready to give her advice if she was stressing out about freelancing. He'd even helped her set up a website.

Unfortunately, along with the initial attraction, it meant that she now liked him more than ever. It was strange. Sometimes she could talk and laugh with him and feel completely at ease. At other times she was so intensely attracted to him it caught her off guard.

A few nights ago, when they were alone in her kitchen talking about the trip, there was a definite *moment* between them. He'd given her one of his cheeky grins and she'd felt a strong compulsion to sweep off the empty teacups and make out on the kitchen table.

Luckily it had passed, but later, when he'd gone home, she got cold feet and wondered if going on the unemployment benefit was the smarter move. But she was in too deep now; plus she was looking forward to it. As Aimee had pointed out, it was the one path that opened an endless array of possibilities. One of them, she hoped, involved her and James getting together at some distant point in the future. Well, within the next three months anyway!

The short flight had them touching down in Gatwick around 1:30pm and, after grabbing their hold luggage, they took the Gatwick Express to Victoria, then the Circle line to Barbican. By the time they came out of the stuffy, crowded Tube into Barbican Station it was close to 3:30pm. Jane felt exhausted from the crowds, the heat and a lack of sleep.

Luckily, Lauderdale Tower was across the road from the Tube, so it was just a one-minute walk. She looked over at James who had donned a pair of aviator sunglasses. With his backpack, blue T-shirt and khaki cargo shorts, he was in tourist mode but still managing to attract glances from female passersby, and a few males as well.

'Ok?' she asked. He nodded, and she adjusted her pack on her shoulder and wiped the sweat from her upper lip. Jane was glad she'd thought to layer a white tank top under her turquoise cardigan, which was now tied around her waist, but was regretting the skinny black jeans. She pointed over to the tower block on the right. 'We're going in there.'

Her mother buzzed them in at the main entrance and Jane pressed the button marked "39" in the lift—there were 42 floors.

'Christ, that's high up,' commented James. 'Almost the penthouse!'

'Ah ... it is the penthouse,' said Jane, dumping her pack on the floor of the lift and rubbing her shoulder. 'It's split over three levels.'

James didn't say anything.

'You're ok with heights, aren't you?' she asked.

He nodded soberly. 'You said your parents lived in the Barbican, but you didn't mention it was in a penthouse. You could have warned me they were loaded.'

'They're not multi-millionaires or anything just … comfortable,' said Jane. She hadn't thought where her parents lived would be an issue. 'Plus, they've been here about ten years. It cost a lot less when they bought it.'

'How much does it cost now?'

'I'm not entirely sure. I can ask them for you if you like.'

'God, no,' said James quickly. 'Forget I said anything.'

Jane laughed. 'Don't worry, they're not royalty or anything. Just retired lawyers.'

The lift slowed to a stop and Jane clattered out into the foyer with her wheelie bag. She was thinking about ditching some stuff at her parents' place, when the door opposite opened and her blonde-haired mother came out, swathed in a cloud of flowery perfume. She was tanned and summery in a cornflower-blue flowing top and white capris.

'Darling, there you are! I thought I heard luggage noises. Was the flight all right? Did you have lunch? And is this James?'

Jane chuckled and hugged her. 'Yes, to all three questions!'

Her mother smiled. 'Excellent! Well, come in, come in, your father's upstairs. Kath and co. aren't here yet.'

They were bundled through to an airy open-plan kitchen and dining room that ran almost the length of the building. Through the floor-to-ceiling windows, she caught a glimpse of the squat grey concrete fortress of the Barbican, and beyond that the London skyline shimmering like a mirage in the summer heat. She noticed James giving the room a once-over but trying to be subtle about it.

When she'd emailed, she hadn't really explained anything to her mother, just that she was coming to London with a "friend" called James and could they stay for the weekend before heading to Barcelona? She planned to explain their travel intentions at some point during the visit. Though by the way her mother was gazing at James approvingly, maybe she should have reiterated the "friend" part.

'Just leave your bags there,' said her mother, waving a hand. 'We'll sort them out later. Come and have a cold drink, it's sweltering today.'

She ushered them up a narrow internal stairwell and into a lounge area half the size of the one below, with bi-fold doors opening out onto a sizeable concrete terrace to the left of the room. This lounge was bordered on the right-hand side by her parents' bedroom and their ensuite, plus an adjoining guest bedroom with another separate ensuite. The lounge they'd just come from downstairs had another smaller guest bedroom, which was used as a study, and a bathroom at the far end. Jane was always curious about who cleaned all the bedrooms and bathrooms in the place, but she never asked.

Her father was relaxing on the couch reading The Times when

they came in but immediately folded the paper and stood up to hug Jane and shake James's hand. He was a tall man, clean-shaven with wire-frame spectacles and hair the same colour as Jane's, but closely cropped and thinning on top. Her mother did the introductions.

'Darling, this is Jane's friend, James ...? Sorry, dear, Jane neglected to tell me your last name.'

James looked at Jane who was trying not to laugh.

'It's James McAvoy, Mrs Aitken.'

She saw her mother visibly melt when she heard the accent.

'Oh! No relation to…?'

James smiled and shook his head. 'I'm afraid not. Not even a distant cousin, as far as I'm aware.'

'Well, never mind, and please, call me Yvette. Now what will you have to drink? We can sit outside. We've had the shade sail up all day, so it won't be too roasting out there.'

Jane saw they'd set up deck chairs and a drinks table on the terrace, with the requisite jug of Pimms and a half-empty bottle of Beefeater London Dry and mixer; there was even a bucket of ice and a jar filled with slices of lemon, so it was all very civilised.

'Looks like we're settling in for the afternoon,' Jane commented. 'G&T for me, please.'

'James? We have Pimms in the jug or some beer in the fridge downstairs if you prefer,' said her father.

'Pimms is fine with me, Mr Aitken,' James told him. He collapsed in a deck chair and plucked his T-shirt away from his chest. 'Phew, is it always this hot in London in summer?'

'Please—call me Theo,' her father replied, busying himself at the drinks table. 'And yes, if there's a heatwave. I think it's due to break either tonight or tomorrow. So, you might have a wet trip to the airport on Sunday.'

Jane was about to sit down too, but her mother asked her to help with the food. She went dutifully, leaving her father and James discussing the safe topic of London weather.

'I'm going to do a cheeseboard,' her mother announced as they entered the downstairs kitchen. She opened one of the doors of the towering silver fridge, plucked a dozen or so cheese packages from the depths and piled them on the counter.

'Gosh, are a load of French people coming over?' enquired Jane, amused.

'Well, you know how Xavier likes cheese. Does James?'

'I have no idea,' said Jane, helping herself to some grapes that were now being added to the selection. 'He may be allergic, for all I know.'

'Oh dear!' said her mother, pausing mid-swing, a carton of dip and hummus in each hand. 'I do wish you'd told me.'

'What—that he may be allergic to cheese, so don't buy any?' scoffed Jane, popping a couple more grapes in her mouth.

'Stop eating those,' her mother chided. She handed her a wooden board. 'Now, I've put you two in the bedroom down here. I'm not sure if the others are staying, as Emma's been restless lately, but if they do, they can go upstairs, as it has more room for the cot.'

Jane stopped her cheese arranging. Blow, she really *should* have reiterated the "friend" part. 'Ah, does it have two single beds?'

'No, dear, just a double, but it should be quite comfortable—what?' she asked, since Jane was staring at her with a pained expression.

'I told you, Mum, we're not together.'

Realising her mistake, her mother frowned, 'Sorry, I thought "friend" was a euphemism for something else.'

'Well, in this case it's not,' said Jane, continuing to stack cheese for Africa and feeling a tad annoyed.

'The gym!' exclaimed her mother after a moment's silence, during which she'd been thinking rapidly.

'Huh?'

'The gym on the top floor is practically empty. Your father's been selling off equipment since he doesn't use it. James can go up there. I think there's one treadmill so he can even have a run if he likes. The bathroom's rather tiny but I'm sure he'll manage. We'll get the camping mats out later. It'll be fun.'

Jane relaxed, somewhat mollified. It was her fault anyway that she hadn't explained. 'Thanks, Mum, sorry for the confusion. It's ... complicated.' Her mother looked as if she wanted to say something, but decided not to.

The buzzer rang just as they were about to head upstairs with the food. 'That'll be Kath,' said her mother, precariously balancing two small bowls of dip and a plate of carrot sticks in her left hand in order to lift the handset with her right. 'You go on up. I'll let them in.'

Upstairs, Jane deposited the cheeseboard on the coffee table, assembled a large piece of brie on a cracker and went outside. The topic of discussion, from what she could gather, had moved onto James's work. She collected her G&T from the drinks table, added more ice and collapsed into a deck chair.

'There's food in the lounge,' she said as she caught James eyeing her snack. Her mother appeared with the dips and the rest of the finger foods, along with Kath, her sister, whom she hadn't seen since April, just after Emma was born. Bringing up the rear was her brother-in-law, Xavier, with her niece fast asleep in a carrycot.

More introductions were made, hands were shaken, and there were hugs for Jane from Kath, more drinks were poured and chairs shuffled. Jane could feel herself fading, so she closed her eyes and listened to the familiar commotion of her family. Then a piercing cry shattered her reverie; Emma was awake. She must've zoned out again, as when she opened her eyes James was bouncing her niece on his knee and making goo-goo sounds. Six-month-old Emma reached out her hands to him, gurgled and blew bubbles.

Kath beamed. 'Look, Jane, she adores him, and she usually hates strangers.'

'Um ... that's great,' said Jane, trying to ignore the fact that now everyone would think James was destined to be the father of her unborn children.

'Let me have a turn,' she said to James.

Emma sat on Jane's knee, docile enough then, without any qualms, reached out to James again and everyone laughed.

'Doh, rejected Jane!' called Xavier from the lounge where he'd stationed himself by the coffee table. 'Come and have some cheese instead, before it's all gone.' She handed Emma back to James and went inside.

She saw Xavier was making inroads into the cheeseboard single-handedly. He was half French and loved cheese with a passion so Jane wasn't surprised. Xavier's mother was from Bordeaux, and he'd been born there. But he'd lived in London since the age of thirteen with his English father until he went to Oxford University to study medicine and met Kath. He was dark-haired and olive-skinned in contrast to Kath's lighter colouring.

She looked over at Kath now, sitting next to her mother. The two of them could be sisters with their honey-blonde hair and lightly tanned skin. They had similar personalities as well—bright and breezy, confident that they'd be liked by everyone they met. Jane felt she was the washed-out version. Like Pete was next to James.

Xavier gave her a plate piled with cheese and crackers. He nodded at James who was playing peek-a-boo with Emma. 'Seems like a good sort. So, how did you meet him?' Xavier's accent was perfect Oxford English though he did speak fluent French.

'Oh, just through work,' said Jane, biting into a Jacob's cracker topped with salty blue cheese.

'Serious?' asked Xavier, cutting off a generous hunk of camembert.

'God, no,' spluttered Jane. 'We're just ... er ... friends.'

Xavier arched an eyebrow. 'Yet here he is, meeting the family?'

Jane sighed. 'There's a reason for that, but I was going to wait until you got here to tell them what's happening.'

'Better make it quick,' advised Xavier sagely as there was a squeal of laughter from Emma. 'I think there's a potential Daddy in the house.'

Chapter 7: Eton Mess

She finally managed to get James alone after everyone had gone off to relax before dinner. Xavier and Kath had decided to stay after all, so they were sorting themselves out on the second floor and James was relegated to the gym on the third floor. He didn't seem to mind though.

Jane had given him a couple of self-inflating camping mats to use as a makeshift bed. She didn't mention this was plan B and that her mother had assumed they'd be in the same room. James was inflating one of the mats, and she was doing the other. 'Do they actually use these for camping?' he asked.

'I think they did once on a glamping weekend but that was about five years ago,' said Jane. She poked the one she was inflating to see how full it was. 'Will you be ok with them? They feel pretty comfy, and I don't think they're that cheap.'

'Och, don't worry about me. This is luxury compared to some of the couches I've slept on,' he said cheerfully.

When the mats were inflated, they stacked them against the back wall. She'd brought up some sheets, a summer duvet and pillows, and dumped them on top so he could make the bed later. The small bathroom had a narrow shower and was stocked with soap, toothpaste and toilet paper; all the essentials a man needed.

Her mother was right. There was indeed just one treadmill, and James said he was looking forward to going for a morning run. He seemed pretty content with the whole set-up.

'Do we have to go to Barcelona?' he teased. 'I think I'm getting used to living at the Barbican.'

'I'm afraid so since we've booked our flights and all. Besides, I don't think my parents want a Scottish boarder at the minute.'

'So, are you going to let the cat out of the bag at dinner then?' he asked, sitting gingerly on the mats as if they were going to explode. Jane sat on the floor cross-legged.

'I don't know. I guess I'll just judge the moment and see if it feels right. If it does, I'll say something. If it doesn't, I won't.'

James frowned. 'I thought that was the reason we came here, so they could meet me before you told them about going travelling?'

'Well, that, and because we had a day in between our flights,' she said, gnawing on the edge of a fingernail. 'Everyone's having a nice time and getting on well. I don't want to be the fly in the ointment. You know, the harbinger of doom and all that.'

'They seem pretty easygoing. Are you sure they'll care that much that you've quit your job, have no prospects and are on the run with an older man of twenty-nine?'

Jane giggled. 'Well, when you put it like that ... I guess I just don't want them to think I'm a failure.'

'You're young. You're allowed to experiment a wee bit. I had a gap year in Asia when I was your age,' said James.

Jane smirked. 'You're only five years older. You make it sound like you're ancient. Asia, huh, were you sowing your wild oats or something?'

His cheeks reddened slightly. 'Let's just say I got cheap Asian travel out of my system. Anyway, the point I'm trying to make is that if you were forty-five and still aimlessly mooning around, I'd be worried. But you're not forty-five, so I'm not worried, if that makes sense.'

'Yeah, thanks, I get it. Twenty years to sort my life out. That should be enough time.'

'Have you heard from Gemma yet?'

'No, nothing. It's been three weeks. I've kind of given up on that.'

'I'd send her a follow-up email, just in case she didn't get the first one or it went to spam.'

'Can't hurt, I guess.'

James frowned at her lackadaisical tone. 'You have to put in some effort if you want ...'

Jane pulled a face. 'I know, I know—I was lucky she even said anything to me. I'll follow up tonight.'

'Good lass.'

Jane took a long, lukewarm shower before dinner and then, wrapped in a towel, rummaged through the guest bathroom cupboard, searching for moisturiser. She found some Jo Malone body lotion and slathered a generous amount on her legs and arms, enjoying the fresh scent of lime, basil and mandarin. In her room she changed into a white cotton mini skirt and a forest-green cami top, adding the delicate gold-chain necklace she normally wore. It was still sweltering, and even after the shower, she soon felt hot again. Now that she was acclimatised to the weather in Edinburgh, any temperature over fifteen degrees now felt positively tropical. Jane was glad they were going to Spain when it was cooler. Once she'd been in July and it was unbearable.

Idly, she brushed her hair and thought about James. What exactly had he got up to in Asia? She was sorely tempted to ask, but wasn't sure if she wanted to hear the answer, or even if he'd tell her. Hastily she yanked her hair up and twisted it into a messy bun, then firmly poked in a heap of bobby pins to get her mind out of the gutter.

Jane turned towards the door to leave and saw her laptop sitting on the bed. Buoyed by a sudden bolt of determination, and James's insistence that she follow up, she typed another short email to Gemma, saying she was off to Barcelona for a week tomorrow, and that she'd left her job to pursue freelancing and was open to any travel writing gigs. She added a link to her blog again and sent it. Hopefully her overactive imagination could be put to better use as a travel writer. She was likely to conjure up almost anything where James was concerned.

It was nearly time for dinner, so Jane walked through the dining room to the kitchen, the black-and-grey speckled marble tile cool on her bare feet. The long, polished oak table had been laid for six people, and the floor-to-ceiling windows were shaded by partly lowered blinds like a row of half-winking eyes. Her stomach clenched when she thought of telling her parents she was now unemployed.

Her sister came down the stairs just then and smiled at her. 'Hello! You look nice. Very chic.'

Jane patted her hair. 'It was roasting with it down. Yours is shorter.'

'Yes,' said Kath. 'I've got Mummy hair now. No time to fuss around with it in the morning.'

'Speaking of which, where's Emma? Not with James again?'

Kath chuckled. 'No, she's in her cot. I gave her some dinner earlier and set her down for a short nap. I don't know where he is.'

She linked her arm in Jane's and they went out to the kitchen where their mother was at the oven door checking the lamb in a flurry of steam. Her face was the same shade as the red apron she'd donned. Jane wasn't sure why she was cooking a roast in this weather, but she religiously produced one whenever there was a family get-together.

'Do you know where James is?' Jane asked her, leaning against the bench.

'Almost done! Kath, can you microwave that veg?' Her mother shut the oven with a decisive bang. 'James? Oh, your father took him and Xavier out to see the gardens. James mentioned he was keen, and Xavier has never seen them properly.'

'Ah yes, the exclusive gardens of the Barbican,' said Kath, winking at Jane. 'Only those with a resident's key can enter. It'll be nice and cool in there at least with all the fountains going. I assume Dad will be in his element playing tour guide?'

'Well, it does have a fascinating history, darling,' said her mother, pouring greeny-brown mint sauce into a jug from a jar. 'Remember that architecture tour we all went on when we first moved in?'

'Vaguely,' said Jane wrinkling her nose. 'Afternoon tea in the conservatory afterwards was the highlight though; mmm those tiny cakes were delicious!'

'You ate so many you were nearly sick,' said Kath. 'I had to use my newly acquired medical training to assist.'

'What, you told me to put my head between my legs? You don't need a medical degree for *that*!'

'Speaking of degrees,' interjected her mother, stirring the mint sauce vigorously, 'do you think you'll have another go at yours, Janie?'

James, Xavier and her father came in just then and the topic was dropped. Jane let out the breath she hadn't realised she was holding. Good timing!

'Is there anything I can do to help?' she asked, taking advantage of the interruption to change the subject.

She and James were seated at the widest length of the dining table facing the windows. The blinds had been raised and they could see, across the horizon, dark, billowing clouds gathering in the sky above London.

'There's your storm,' said her father, glancing outside. 'It's coming closer. Looks like it could be quite a show.'

'How were the gardens, by the way?' asked Jane, taking a sip of red wine, a zingy little number from Australia.

'Dead brilliant,' said James 'It's like a private oasis down there.'

'Did you see the conservatory?' enquired Kath. 'They do afternoon teas in there.' She caught Jane's eye and smirked. Jane stuck out her tongue.

James looked at them slightly confused but smiled. 'Nae, we just went through the park at the bottom of the tower and along the middle bit with the ponds and the fountains. Och, and we saw the waterfall at the end. And a guy in one of the apartments was painting. I wouldnae like that. It's a goldfish bowl where everyone can see what you're up to.'

Her mother came through with the last of the platters. 'Right, help yourselves! It should be cooler soon. The air con's going full blast.'

'Thank God for that,' grumbled Kath. 'I don't know why you didn't turn it on sooner.'

'Should we wait for Xavier?' asked Jane, handing James the

roast potatoes.

'He's bathing Emma, so he might be awhile. I'll save him a plate.' Kath poured herself some more wine. 'So, tell us about your trip. Where is it you're going—Barcelona?'

'Uh ... yes,' said Jane, swallowing a chunk of potato. 'We're flying out tomorrow evening from Gatwick.'

'How much time are you taking off work?' interjected her mother. 'A week? I guess two weeks is pushing it, but Spain is lovely this time of year. We're thinking of going to the Costa del Sol at the beginning of October.'

Jane paused, a forkful of tender lamb halfway to her mouth. She lowered her fork and took a gulp of wine instead. Here we go, she thought.

'So, the thing is, we're travelling for longer than a week, or even two weeks, actually. I ... I've left my job to be a freelance travel writer.' No one said anything and the word *freelance* seemed to hover above the table like a UFO.

She waited, but weirdly there was no fallout. Her mother kept eating and didn't say anything, though her lips had tightened. Kath intervened by starting to talk about the house renovations they were doing.

Jane gave James a sideways glance, and he shrugged as if to say, see, that wasn't so bad. She wasn't convinced she was going to get off that easily and took another fortifying gulp of wine.

'What about your flat?' her mother questioned suddenly. She'd stopped eating, knife and fork poised, and was frowning.

'I've sublet it, Mum, to a friend of Aimee's. She's happy to take on the lease for three months.'

'Three months! That's quite a holiday.'

'Well, I will be working too, hopefully, so it's not really a holiday,' said Jane, rapidly losing her appetite. She poked at a piece of cold uneaten lamb with her knife.

'What will you do for money if you don't? It all sounds terribly pie in the sky.'

'I've got some savings.'

'I thought you were going to use that to redo your second year?'

'I never said that.'

Kath's head was swivelling backwards and forwards between the two of them like she was at a Wimbledon tennis match.

'If you enrolled now, you could have it finished by this time next year.'

'But I don't want to be an accountant. Besides, even if I did want to, I don't need to have a degree. They were happy enough for me to start with the AAT Foundation Certificate.'

'Who was?'

'Er ... Alistair and Sylvia at McDowd's. Melissa was coming back from maternity leave, so they didn't need me for reception. They offered to pay for the certificate so I could continue to work there as Sylvia's assistant.'

'And you turned it down?' Her father now joined in the discussion.

Great, now the two of them were ganging up on her. It was always like this.

Jane took a breath and tried to stay calm. 'Yes, I did, because it's not what I want to do.'

'So, what you want to do,' he said, 'is swan off to the Continent, and be a digital nomad? In other words—a glorified layabout. No offence James.'

'None taken,' said James, sounding amused.

Jane's heart sank. They didn't understand. They were still hoping she'd get a degree and then a professional career and work in it until the day she retired or died, whichever came sooner.

'Who's being a glorified layabout?' asked Xavier, choosing that moment to make an appearance. He was carrying a pink baby monitor that he handed to Kath. 'She's out for the count. We're good for a few hours at least, I'd say.' He didn't seem to notice the frosty atmosphere, which had the effect of thawing it out marginally.

'Yours is in the oven,' said Kath. 'We're pretty much finished.'

'So, what'd I miss?' enquired Xavier after retrieving his dinner.

'Well,' said Kath, raising an eyebrow since no one else was saying anything, 'Jane has quit her job at the accountancy practice and is heading off to the Continent with James to be a digital nomad, or as Dad so delicately put it, a "glorified layabout".'

'Good for you, Jane,' said Xavier, digging into his lamb with gusto. 'I'm surprised you lasted as long as you did. This is delicious, Yvette. Is there any more wine?'

Her mother pursed her lips, muttered something about dessert, and left the table.

Jane looked at James, who was staring at his clean plate with a blank expression. She couldn't tell what he was thinking. Probably wishing he'd never suggested going away with her. Just then, a searing white light flashed into the room, making everyone jump in their seats.

'Whoa, wait for it,' said Kath quietly, and a few seconds later an ominous rumble sounded almost directly overhead.

Jane leaned closer to James and was relieved when he touched her shoulder with his. 'Scared?' he whispered.

She shook her head. 'Mum's ten times scarier when she gets like this. Well, at least that's over with. C'est la vie,' she whispered back. There was another flash of lightning and ensuing rumble of thunder. She shivered, and James gave her a sympathetic look.

Kath started gathering up empty plates to make some room on the table for dessert. Her mother was coming back to the table carrying a large, delicate crystal bowl full of Eton Mess when there was a crack of thunder that sounded like a gunshot. She shrieked and threw her arms up instinctively. Jane saw it happening in slow motion—the bowl sailing up into the air, flipping over and over gracefully then plummeting down onto the hard marble tile and exploding into a million tiny crystal splinters.

The effect was shocking but oddly satisfying as well.

A melange of cream, meringue and strawberries splattered all over the tile and up the walls. But the majority went over her mother. Jane was reminded of the movie *Carrie*, except it was white cream and pieces of strawberry instead of bright-red pig's blood, that dripped down over her face and clothes. Her mother's face was affixed in a fitting imitation of Edvard Munch's *The Scream*.

No one moved. Then everyone did in a rush, wanting to know if she was ok, crunching crystal shards underfoot, skidding on cream and mushing strawberries. James skirted the edge of the mess to get to the kitchen, presumably to get a cloth or paper towels; Kath and her father were trying to help her mother out of a puddle of cream and crystal; while Xavier stood licking bits of strawberry and drops of cream off his hand. Watching it all, Jane had an uncontrollable urge to burst out laughing. She caught Xavier's eye and he mouthed 'yum' and her mouth twitched. It took a herculean effort, but she held it in.

The baby monitor cackled to life with a piercing shriek and a whimper.

'Christ, that's all we need!' exclaimed Kath, sounding stressed. She stepped out of the puddle of cream, wiped her feet on a paper towel James handed her, and headed towards the stairs.

'I'll go with you,' said Jane, scraping back her chair, thankful to have an excuse to flee the chaos.

Chapter 8: Two Trains

The storm passed as quickly as it had come, leaving a gusty wind and a steady rain in its wake. Kath went back down to help with the clean-up, and Jane said she'd stay to make sure Emma was asleep. However, she was content to stand idly at the balcony door and stare down at passing cars churning up standing water on Aldersgate Street. She knew her mother was all right, and the red streaks were strawberries and not blood, but she was still smarting from the lack of understanding about her decision.

Her parents were from a different generation and so blinkered in their way of thinking. It was like their way was the only way, and she was tired of it. The world had changed. Maybe from now on she'd only tell them things on a need-to-know basis. If they never took her side or supported her, then what was the point in telling them more?

'You can come down,' whispered Kath, sticking her head round the door. 'The munchkin's out to it.' She nodded at Emma flat on her back with her thumb in her mouth.

'How's Mum?' asked Jane, turning to look at her.

'She's ok. She had a shower, and now she's resting. She feels pretty embarrassed ... about the whole dessert disaster.'

'Ah, right,' said Jane, returning to the view. 'Yeah, I'll be down in a minute.'

'You shouldn't take it personally, Jane.'

Jane felt a ripple of annoyance. 'So I shouldn't feel upset that my parents don't support me in what I want to do?' she whispered curtly. 'It's never any different. The only way I can make them happy is to be an accountant. Doesn't that seem a tad narrow-minded to you?'

'They just think it's a logical choice, since you got such high marks in accounting at school. They think you're wasting a perfectly good brain and you'll regret it later on ...' Kath's whisper trailed off as Jane frowned and walked over to her.

'But I want to do something that I actually *enjoy*!' Jane was getting het up at this point, and Emma stirred in her cot.

'Anyway,' she whispered again, glancing at Emma. 'They told you all this, did they?'

'Not in so many words, but I understand their reasoning. They just want you to be able to get a decent job so you don't have to worry about money. Look, I think it's cool that you want to do some travel and writing or whatever. I wish I could just take off and have no responsibilities for a while, and Xavier's mad jealous too. You're young. You should go and see the world before you settle down and start popping out sprogs.'

Jane gave a half-smile. 'So that's being decided for me too, is it? What if I don't want kids?'

'Then you'll be burnt at the stake.'

'Ha ha.'

Kath gave her a quick hug. 'It'll be ok. Now, come and help us clean cream from the furniture. Isn't that something you always wanted to do on a Saturday night?'

Jane chuckled. 'God, James will think I've abandoned him.'

'He's ok. Xavier's got him wiping the bookshelf. I think he was on the M's last time I looked.' Jane stifled a giggle and followed Kath downstairs.

By the time they'd righted the dining room, had a cup of tea and chatted about nothing in particular in the lounge, it was nearly time for bed. Her father said goodnight to everyone and Kath and Xavier decided to head up shortly afterwards too. This left Jane lying on one sofa and James on the other, sitting facing her, with his feet propped up on the coffee table.

Jane yawned. 'I don't think I'll be long out of bed myself. I'm knackered.'

James yawned too. 'Now you've got me started.'

'Hey, thanks for helping to clean up and everything. It's not always this dramatic.'

James arched an eyebrow. 'I thought you said your mother was an ex-lawyer. Are you sure she's not in the theatre?'

Jane chuckled. 'Perish the thought. Though I think she did do drama at high school before she went to uni.'

'Did she like being a lawyer?'

Jane shrugged. She sipped the dregs of her tea and pulled a face at the taste. 'I guess so. I never heard her complain about it. She gave it up for about five years when she had me and Kath but she went back to it, so it can't have been too terrible. Besides, she was working locally in Richmond. She wasn't a big city lawyer like Dad was.'

'Who looked after you when she went back to work?' asked James curiously.

'We had a full-time nanny until I was old enough to go to boarding school. Then I guess she was let go; I didn't see her again.'

'You went to boarding school?' James sounded surprised.

'Um ... yes, why?'

'You just seem so ... normal.'

Jane laughed. 'Are you sure about that?' she said, and pretended she had a nervous twitch. 'It was ok. I had a nice group of friends, and we had a laugh. I didn't mind the teachers either.'

James raised his eyebrows slightly, and didn't say anything.

'Why, where did you go to school?' she asked.

'Och, just the one in Galashiels. I had a great graphics teacher, and she encouraged me to get into web design. It has a few claims to fame too, like Darren Ritchie.'

'Who's he then?'

'The Scottish long jump record holder.'

Jane giggled. 'I don't know who Queenswood's are but I'm sure there are some.'

'Did you have midnight feasts?'

'Not really. We were too well fed during the day. Why?'

'Uh, when I was living at home, I was scrounging for something to read and Ma had these old boarding school books. I only read one. It was all midnight feasts, lacrosse and slapping each other.'

Jane chortled at that. '*Slapping* each other?'

'Aye, this girl was being a right bitch, so this other girl who had a bad temper slapped her one. That was the highlight. It was all downhill from there.'

'God, that sounds mad. Everyone was really into Harry Potter when I was at school, so it was all capes and wands and pretending to be Hermione.'

'Me too—not Hermione, of course—but just a general wizarding person.'

Jane yawned loudly. 'Sorry, you're not boring me. But I think I'm going to have to go to bed soon.'

James didn't say anything, and her eyelids grew heavy so she shut them momentarily, tired after the long eventful day. After a while, feeling a weird tension, she opened them and discovered him watching her unabashedly. He gave her a lazy grin and she flushed, though she wasn't sure why. He was the one who was staring at her!

Clearing her throat to break the silence, she said, 'So you'll be ok upstairs?' and the corner of his mouth lifted in a smile that set her heart thudding. Dammit, now he knew she'd been thinking about the sleeping arrangements.

'Aye, I should be ok, but I'll text you if I get scared of the dark,' he said lightly. She swallowed. That was definitely flirtatious. So much for not getting complicated, she thought.

Shortly afterwards, James said goodnight and headed upstairs. Jane went round turning out the lights, then collapsed into bed.

The next morning, she awoke to a beam of sunlight hitting her full in the face. She'd been so tired last night she hadn't even pulled the curtains properly. Groaning, she squinted and rolled over groggily to grab her phone and check her messages; there was no text from James during the night inviting her up for a midnight rendezvous. She wasn't sure whether she was relieved or disappointed. However, there was a text from Amber wishing her bon voyage and, more surprisingly, an email from Gemma. Jane quickly sat up and scanned the brief message. Apparently there was a hotel review article in the pipeline that Gemma could give her a trial run on. She'd let her know in the next few days if it was a go.

Jane let out a scream and bounced up and down on the bed excitedly. She had to tell James! Grabbing her black silk kimono robe from her bag, she hastily tied it and sprinted up two flights of stairs to the third floor, only to pull up short when she arrived at the top. James was running on the single treadmill against the far wall, wearing just a pair of shorts and trainers. He had headphones on, so he hadn't heard her come up the stairs. Her eyes travelled slowly over his muscular back, which was glistening under a light sheen of sweat. The graceful, steady rhythm of his feet pounding on the belt, each step accentuated by a heavy breath, was strangely mesmerising. Reluctantly, after a few minutes of unadulterated ogling, she realised that if he happened to look around he'd catch her lurking like a pervert. Awkward.

Slowly Jane backed down the stairs, one foot at a time, trying not to overbalance. When she made it to the second level, she turned tail and ran back down to the main floor as if a pack of hounds were after her. She arrived back in her bedroom and collapsed on the bed, giggling to herself. You eejit, she thought. Oh well, at least now she knew he didn't have back hair.

After showering and getting dressed, it was almost eight. She went out to the kitchen, and everyone was at the table already having breakfast, including James, now in a T-shirt and shorts, and decidedly unsweaty. He looked completely at home munching on muesli and reading a section of her father's Times.

'Good afternoon,' he said, glancing at his watch as she sat down.

'Ha ha.'

'Morning, sleepyhead,' said her father, handing her a bowl. Jane sat in the empty chair next to her mother and grabbed the packet of muesli.

'How are you, Mum?' she asked, pouring on some soy milk.

'I'm fine, darling. Thank you. I just needed a good night's sleep. Your grandmother's bowl is a goner though.'

The charged atmosphere from last night seemed to have

dissipated entirely. She didn't feel any animosity, and neither did her parents, it appeared. Agreeing to disagree was always their fallback position.

'Don't worry about that, as long as you're all right. I'd rather pick tiny pieces of crystal out of the potted plants than spend the night at the hospital,' she quipped.

Kath stopped feeding Emma mashed banana and peered at her suspiciously. 'Why are you so perky? You usually hate mornings.'

Jane had a mental flash of James's naked, sweaty back and blushed. 'Ah, no reason. It's just a gorgeous day.' She dipped her head to avoid Kath's gaze and took a mouthful of cereal.

Emma saw Jane eating and waved her hands and squawked, so Kath thankfully dropped the Spanish Inquisition and resumed feeding her.

'It is indeed,' said her mother. 'What are the plans for today then?'

'Oh, I'm not sure. We haven't talked about it. I guess we've got a whole day to kill before we have to go to Gatwick this evening.'

James was staring at her over the top of the paper, and her mind went blank. Xavier came to the rescue with the suggestion that they go to Hyde Park to enjoy the sun and to let Emma play in the Princess Diana fountain. It was on their way to Richmond, so they'd just go home after that, and the two of them could make their way back to the Barbican by Tube and do some sightseeing if they wanted.

'Ooh, yes, you could stop off at the Tate Modern,' suggested Kath enthusiastically, wiping yellow sticky goo from Emma's mouth.

'Is that ok with you, James?' Jane asked. 'We can do something else if you want.'

'Anything that involves being out in the sun is fine with me. Gotta get some kind of tan going for Barcelona.'

Jane gulped. Did that mean the T-shirt was coming off again?

'What about you?' she asked her mother quickly.

'Don't mind us, dear, we're just going to relax here. I don't really feel like gallivanting about London after last night. We might go out to the gardens, but we'll be here when you get back in the afternoon.'

'Ok then, sounds like a plan.'

They spent a mellow morning at Hyde Park, splashing about in the fountain with Emma before it got so busy with toddlers and parents that Kath and Xavier decided to head off back to Richmond. Jane and James caught the Tube to Blackfriars and walked across the bridge to the Tate Modern. But upon seeing people sitting outside in the sun, James suggested they have some lunch at the Founder's Arms first.

After ordering a couple of Ploughman's lunches and soft drinks, Jane used the ladies' to freshen up. She came out to find their drinks had been served, but the table empty and James standing by the railing, looking at the Thames.

Jane went over and nudged his arm. 'Hello? Anyone home?'

'I can't go,' James muttered.

'Huh? That's ok we don't have to. I'm not that into art anyway.'

'No, to Barcelona.' He groaned and smacked the heel of his hand against his forehead. 'Eejit!'

'What's going on?' Jane asked him, trying to remain calm. 'Has something happened?'

He thrust his phone at her. 'Read it.'

She took the phone, which had an opened email message. It was from Kistella, stating that she was pregnant, and James *might* be the father, but she wanted to make sure by doing a paternity test. She'd added the website and contact details of a DNA-collection clinic in New Town and wanted him to make an appointment *asap* so they could collect his sample.

Jane felt like she'd been kicked in the guts.

'What are you going to do?'

James looked ill. 'I don't really have a choice, do I? I guess I'll have to try and get back to Edinburgh tonight.'

'But, what about the trip?' asked Jane in a small voice.

'Shite. Look, it's best if you just go to Barcelona as planned and I'll let you know what's going on as soon as I know. Hopefully it's some other poor bastard's.'

'And if it is yours?'

'God, I dinnae ken. I'll cross that bridge when I get to it.'

Jane didn't know what to say. She felt slightly dazed and kept opening her mouth and shutting it again, like a freshly caught fish. Out of the corner of her eye she saw the waiter bringing their lunch over to the table.

'Look, let's just have something to eat.'

James rubbed his eyes with the heels of his hands leaving them red and watery. 'Aye, good idea. I'm starving.'

In the end, Jane could only nibble at her sandwich; she felt queasy and overwhelmed. Tears started welling and she quickly swiped at her eyes. Oh God, she was going to start blubbering. How embarrassing.

James glanced at her 'Are you ok?'

'I'm …,' She tried to breathe. 'It's just a bit of a shock.'

James reached over the table and grabbed her hand. His warm touch was like an instant balm, reassuring and solid. It simultaneously calmed her down and made her feel even more sorry for herself because he was being kind. They sat for a while like that, with him looking at her, concerned, and Jane with a lump in her throat, trying not to cry.

Finally, she pulled herself together. There was no point getting emotional. She had to think practically; plus, it might not even be his.

She took a deep breath. 'Can you even do a paternity test when it's still in the womb?'

James gave her hand a squeeze and let it go when he saw she

was ok. He sighed. 'Yeah, that was my first thought too. But I Googled it when you were in the loo—apparently eight weeks is the earliest.'

'Eight weeks! So, she's only just found out or she's only just decided to do something about it?'

'I dinnae ken.'

Jane thought back to that evening in The Tron and the way Kistella had said, 'Oh yes, you could say I know James.' She shivered. Kistella would've been pregnant then. It was like she'd somehow planned the whole thing.

'Well, at least she wants to do a paternity test. She could've just said it's yours.'

'Hmph, she knows I'd ask for one, especially after all the lies she told about me. She's not stupid.'

Jane took a shaky sip of Diet Coke, wondering how to broach her next question delicately. 'Er ... this might be a bit personal but did you not use...?'

'She said she was!'

'Right.'

'I trusted her. More fool me.' He looked mournful.

'So, what next?' asked Jane, trying to sound positive.

'Check the flights, trains and buses, I guess. See what's available and book a hotel in Edinburgh.'

Then Jane remembered Gemma's email and thought she may as well mention it. 'I forgot to tell you, but I heard back from

Gemma. She's considering giving me a trial run on an article.'

'Och, that's good news. It makes me feel better about leaving you in the lurch.'

Jane nodded miserably. It looked like she'd have to get used to the idea of travelling by herself, and the possibility that James might soon be fathering a child. Was this seriously happening?

Chapter 9: Barcelona

At Gatwick check-in, Jane scanned the departures board. Her 8:10pm flight was now apparently delayed until 9:20pm. She swore under her breath. Swiftly calculating the journey duration and time zone difference, she knew it meant getting into Barcelona sometime after midnight. This day was rapidly turning into a nightmare.

Right about now, James was pulling out of King's Cross station for a five-hour train ride to Edinburgh Waverley, or technically Haymarket, where he was staying. Jane didn't like to think of him having to go through this alone. Perhaps she should've gone with him? She shook herself mentally. It wasn't her problem; it was his decision to go and face up to the music.

They hadn't mentioned to her parents that they were parting ways at Barbican Tube station with James heading to King's Cross and her heading to Victoria. She didn't want to worry them or cause more undue stress about her situation.

After lunch they'd hotfooted it back to the Barbican. James excused himself, saying he had to send a work email, and had raced upstairs for a spot of quick-fire travel arranging on his laptop. There were no spare seats on any flights to Edinburgh, but he'd managed to get one of the last tickets on the 6:15pm train, and also book a windowless room at the same cheap Haymarket hotel he'd stayed before—with no issues. Almost like it was meant to be, thought Jane despondently.

Then they'd had a cup of tea with her parents, chatted about their day and pretended everything was normal. Even though she was dying inside.

One thing she made sure to do before she left for the airport was to email her interest to Gemma and tell her she was flying to Barcelona tonight; she mentioned her travel plans were flexible. She wasn't sure why she'd said that, as she and James had created a spreadsheet itinerary with the various cities they were visiting in the next three months. All she had to do was keep to the plan. But James had gone off-piste, so why couldn't she?

After check-in she went through Departures, walked for miles through Duty Free and attempted to find a seat in the general waiting area, but there weren't any. She sighed. Every man and his dog seemed to be flying out of Gatwick tonight. She was tempted to pay for a lounge since she had two hours to wait, but figured she should save her money.

She leaned against a wall and sent James a text: *Flight delayed, in Departures twiddling thumbs. Where you at?*

He replied almost immediately: *Train on time, just passed Stevenage. Wish I was there, instead of here.*

She texted back: *Me too. Might go to bar and have a drink*

(or two) to drown sorrows. She added a sad face emoji and couple of wine glass emojis.

He replied: *Ok. Don't get too sozzled.* And a vomiting face emoji.

She laughed and texted: *Will try not to.* And a thumbs up emoji.

Jane felt a bit brighter after that exchange, and that she had a plan, even if it involved drowning her sorrows. She headed to Wetherspoons and ordered a G&T. She thought about messaging Amber but wasn't sure what to say. In the end she just texted: *Hiya, weekend went well. Now at airport waiting for flight, delayed, but all good. Jx.*

She sipped her G&T and relaxed. Amber's text came five minutes later: *Bummer about flight! Glad weekend went well. Did you share a bed? Ax.*

Jane smiled wanly and typed: *Lol, no! Separate rooms. Keeping it casual, remember? Jx.*

Amber's reply said: *He seems to really like you? Ax.*

She wasn't sure what to say to that, but eventually typed: *Time will tell. I'll msg you in Barcelona. Jx.*

Two hours, four G&Ts and a burger and fries later, Jane was feeling slightly sloshed. In the toilets near the gate, she peered at her heavy-lidded expression in the mirror. Drunk biddy, she told herself, now pull yourself together so they let you on the flight.

She used the toilet and splashed cold water on her face, which helped. Luckily she'd emailed Gemma earlier when she was sober, otherwise who knows what her message would've said.

Hi Gemma! I'm unemployed, my parents are about to disown me, the guy I like may be having a baby with his manipulative (but exceedingly beautiful) ex-girlfriend and I'm travelling solo to a city I've never been to. Oh, and I'm drunk. Love Jane.

She shuddered.

Her flight finally touched down in Barcelona ahead of schedule, but it was still nearly one in the morning by the time she'd caught the train into the city and jumped off at Passeig de Gràcia. Hostel Valeria was on La Rambla, so it was just a ten-minute walk and one street over from the station. There were people around, so she didn't look too conspicuous, trundling her bag along. It was a warm night, and she felt grimy and sweaty from the airport. The buzz from the G&Ts earlier had long worn off and all she could think about was a cool shower and bed.

When she reached the hostel entrance, she pressed the buzzer for floor two, and waited. Nothing. She tried again and held her breath for an answering click, or voice. Nothing. Jane groaned and rubbed her tired, gritty eyes. Whose idea had it been to stay here?

Bloody James's, probably. She buzzed again. Not. A. Thing. She kicked the solid green wooden door and promptly burst into tears. What the hell was she going to do now? She sat down on her bag and tried to find a tissue, but she didn't have one, which made her cry harder.

'Hola, cuál es el problema?' asked a male voice. A pair of black pant legs stopped in front of her and she looked up blearily to find a Spanish guy about her age smartly dressed in a white shirt and black waistcoat. He had some kind of thin tie around his neck but had undone it, so the top of his shirt was open. Whoops, here we go, she thought, instantly on guard. She wiped her eyes. He smiled down at her and switched to heavily accented English. 'What's the problem?'

'Um … I can't get in.' She scrambled to her feet and gestured to the door. 'I'm supposed to be staying at this hostel tonight.'

'Ah, and they're not answering?'

'Si,' said Jane. She sighed. 'I guess they went to bed.'

The guy laughed. 'It's Sunday, so yes, maybe. I'm Miguel.' He held out his hand. Jane hesitated, then took it.

'Jane,' she said. 'Do you know of any other hostels around here?'

Miguel shook his head, and she noticed his dark hair was tied back in a short ponytail. 'Sorry, no. I work at a bar further down and it's just closed. I'm on my way home.'

Jane took out her phone and pulled herself together. She could handle this. All she had to do was find a cheap hotel with a twenty-four hour desk, stay there for one night and sort out the hostel in the morning. 'Thanks for stopping. I'm ok now, really.'

Miguel looked like he was going to leave then seemed to change his mind. 'I have an apartment where you can stay.'

'Oh! No, but thanks!' said Jane, attempting to get the internet to work but the connection kept dropping out.

'It's ok.' Miguel gestured to her phone. 'You may still be here tomorrow trying to find something. My friend Gabriella is in LA. I'm looking after her place for Airbnb. There's no one there tonight.'

Jane was torn. 'How far away?' she asked, thinking if it was way out in the suburbs she'd definitely say, 'No, gracias.'

'Just a ten-minute walk. Look, I'll even carry your bag.' He grabbed the handle.

'It has wheels,' said Jane, and then somehow found herself walking away from La Rambla with Miguel wheeling her bag efficiently beside her. It was risky but her instincts were judging him to be normal enough. If she detected anything even remotely dodgy, or he tried to make a move on her, then she'd run for the hills.

'Are you from England, Jane?' he asked conversationally.

'Yes, si, from London.' She was glad he spoke English so well. Jane knew some Spanish but trying to form a coherent sentence at this time of night was beyond her.

'I have friends there, and I've always wanted to visit but it's usually winter when I have time off. Winter in England isn't the same as here.'

'No, it's a lot colder,' agreed Jane.

'Is this your first time in Spain?'

'It's my first time in Barcelona but I've been to a few of the islands: Majorca, Ibiza, the Canaries.'

'Ibiza? To party?'

Jane laughed and shook her head. 'I'm not really into that.'

They were walking down a particularly quiet, dark alleyway and she breathed a sigh of relief when they popped out into a busier main street with the odd moped and people strolling past.

'Not much further,' Miguel reassured her.

Jane nodded. She felt like she was sleepwalking. After another five minutes, he turned up a side street with a slight incline and stopped at a tarnished wrought iron door inset with intricate swirls. He tapped a four-digit code on a keypad and the door opened with a click. He beckoned her into a small lobby, reaching to turn on a light switch she hadn't noticed was there.

'It's just one flight,' he said, and hefted her bag with his hand so he was carrying it by the handle and started up the stairs. She hesitated but followed him.

The apartment was the first on the left in a narrow corridor with bare white painted walls. Miguel fished in his pocket and produced a set of keys. He took one off and unlocked the door, then stood aside to let her go past him into the dark apartment. She felt a flicker of fear, and hesitated but Miguel simply switched on the light and put her bag inside the room. He didn't attempt to come in after her.

'There are towels in the cupboard in the bathroom. There's nothing in the fridge but there's a fruit and vegetable shop downstairs that also sells pastries. It should be open tomorrow morning about eight. The keypad code is 2424. Oh, and just one thing if you could, please.' He looked sheepish. 'Gabriella will kill me if I let her plants die. The cleaner always forgets, and I haven't watered them for a week ... could you?'

Jane smiled. 'Sure, I'll sort them out.'

'Gracias, Jane. I'll say goodnight now. You can stay until ten in the morning, that's when the cleaner is due. When you leave tomorrow, could you bring the key with you? I don't start work until 5:30pm, but I will meet you at the hostel to pick it up, at around five?'

He looked unsure, as if it suddenly struck him she could trash the place and steal the TV. Though when she looked around the small lounge, she couldn't actually see a TV.

'That's fine. Thanks so much, Miguel, for letting me stay here. I'll leave it clean and tidy.' She took out her phone. 'Should we swap numbers just in case?'

'Si, of course.'

After Miguel left, she locked the door securely behind her and felt the tension ease away. She was safe and off the streets. For tonight, at least.

Jane dumped her bag in the bedroom. It was bijou, but it had a double bed. She used the even tinier bathroom, climbed thankfully between the cool cotton sheets and was asleep in minutes.

The next morning, she woke up feeling disoriented. Part of her brain thought she was still in the Barbican and that James was upstairs. After a while, she got up, put on her robe, and padded to the kitchen for a large glass of water. The lounge had a pair of French doors that led onto a small balcony with a table and chairs and a row of wilted houseplants. She gave the droopy plants some of her water and sat out there, enjoying the morning sun.

There was a conversation taking place underneath the balcony, so she poked her head over. A man in the street was gesturing to another inside the store, and she caught the words 'fruta' and 'cara' which she translated as 'your fruit is expensive'. She returned to sunbathe on the chair until the rumbling of her empty stomach became unbearable.

Donning yesterday's clothes, she grabbed the key and headed downstairs to get a few supplies. Ten euros later for some fruit, pastries and a bottle of water, and she had to agree with the other customer. It seemed she was staying above the most "cara" fruit shop in Barcelona.

Now that it was daylight, she could check out the apartment in more detail. As per her first impressions, it was small, but immaculate. It had a neutral colour scheme with a hessian-covered double sofa, a couple of black-and-white framed photos of the Barcelona cityscape on the walls and a soft cream woven mat on the dark wooden floorboards. The kitchen was tucked in behind the lounge and had a hot plate, a small fridge and a pull-down table. Two steps down the hallway and the bathroom was on one side with just a shower and a sink; the bedroom was on the other, with a double bed and chest of drawers. The balcony was the saving grace as it added a few extra square metres to the lounge and let in cooling fresh air.

It was nearing nine after she'd eaten, showered and changed into clean clothes. Her weather app was showing seventeen degrees with a high of twenty-five; she had to sort out the hostel before it got too hot to think. She could ask Miguel about staying here, but even though it was small, she figured the apartment was going to cost more than the hostel.

So she put the sheets and towel in the hamper, gave the plants on the balcony some more water, and let herself out. Retracing her and Miguel's steps from the night before, eventually she ended up back outside the hostel. Déjà vu, she thought. Though everything looked brighter and less ominous than it had at one in the morning.

She raised her hand to the buzzer, but the door opened before she could push it. A couple of young Asian girls came out, almost barging into her. She managed to grab the door in their wake before it swung shut. An old-fashioned grille lift in the middle of the dimly lit lobby took her up to the second floor. When she got out, there was a sign on the wall saying "Hostel Valeria" and an arrow pointing to the left, so she headed in that direction. A heavy glass door led into a brightly lit, modern reception.

Slightly surprised, Jane glanced around. From the outside and the lift, she'd been expecting something rundown and poky. Yet there was a spacious lounge area with comfortable seating, pine wood walls and bookshelf stocked with travel guides. Out the window she spied an outdoor terrace with a row of empty sun loungers with black padded cushions. Ok, James, she thought, you're off the hook.

She headed over to the reception desk and waited for the young guy with a shock of dyed blond hair to look up from his tapping.

'Hola, can I help?' he asked, finally acknowledging her.

'Hola, yes, I'm Jane Aitken. I was meant to stay here last night but my flight was late, and no one answered the door when I arrived.'

'Oh, right. Yes, the buzzer doesn't work. We've been trying to get it fixed, but it's taking a while.' He flicked his fringe and looked at her accusingly, like she'd broken it. His eyes were a striking shade of green, but she thought he may have been wearing coloured contacts.

'Ah, ok. So how do people get in?' she asked, confused at the set-up.

'Well, they normally just ring reception on their mobile and someone goes down to let them in. Or ...' he continued, 'they just wait. Someone comes out or goes in, eventually.'

'Not ideal at one in the morning,' she said.

'No, but we wouldn't have been able to let you in, anyway. We go home at ten on Sundays.'

'Well, can I check in now?' asked Jane, starting to flag from the long-winded explanation.

'Oh, well, it's a bit early to check in, that's normally at two, but I can make an exception. Let me just see if your bed's still free.' She waited while he tip-tapped on his keyboard.

'Jane Aitken, you said? I can't find a booking for that name.'

'Oh, try James McAvoy. I think my friend booked it but for separate dorms.'

More tip-tapping took place, and she started to feel like she was slipping into an alternative reality.

'Ok, yes, I have that name,' said the guy suddenly, startling her out of her reverie. 'He booked a bed in a male dorm and a female dorm for a week.'

'That sounds like it. He's obviously not here. Long story.' She smiled, trying to be blasé.

But the guy just said, 'Ok, sure,' in a bored voice. 'So, you're in room eight, bed six. That's down the hallway over there and the last door on the right. It has an ensuite bathroom. The breakfast room is through there.' He pointed over her shoulder. 'It's a buffet, and that starts at 7:30 during the week and eight on weekends.'

He handed her a key, a towel and a slip of paper with the Wi-Fi code, and Jane gathered that was it for the spiel. She said thanks and went off to find her room. Welcome to hostel life, she thought, feeling sorry for herself.

Chapter 10: Miguel

After she'd found bed six in room eight, and deposited her bag in the provided locker, Jane checked her emails. There was one from James, and one from Gemma. Her heart started beating faster. From the former or the latter, she wasn't sure. James's first. He said he'd had the paternity test first thing this morning and now it was a four-day wait to find out the result. Either way, he said he'd fly to Barcelona to meet her immediately after.

Jane let out a whoop but then quickly realised she was celebrating prematurely. There was still a good chance he was going to be a daddy. And where did that leave her? If she got involved with him—a pseudo stepmother at twenty-four, that's where! Plus, there was always the possibility that he'd get back together with Kistella and play happy families. She doubted it, but stranger things had happened. Thinking about it all just made her feel depressed. It was always such an emotional rollercoaster with him.

She moved onto Gemma's email. It was entitled "Como" and had an attached a PDF; that was it. Jane clicked on the PDF, and discovered it was a promotional brochure for a swanky four-star hotel overlooking Lake Como. As she was scrolling through it, another email popped up from Gemma.

Hi Jane, I hope you got the PDF ok? It's background info for the trial article if you're still interested. I contacted the owner of the Bella Vista, a hotel in Como, a couple of weeks ago to ask if he wanted a review in exchange for a free stay. He's just agreed to it and said this week would be best. I'm flying to the US tomorrow so I can't do it and since you're just a short flight from Milan, I suggested you. I said you were a new writer I'd taken on board and (I hope you don't mind) sent them a couple of blog posts you wrote on the hotels where you stayed in Spain; and they liked them.

If you're keen, he's happy to give you a complimentary stay in the hotel for four nights in return for an in-depth feature article posted on my site with a link to their hotel booking page; they'll provide the photos. I'll also give you an author byline. I know it's short notice, but email me back asap if you want to do it. Then you can book your flight and train. You'll have to pay for them yourself, and your own food; but there may be a free dinner one night in the restaurant so you can write about it.

Jane let out an even louder whoop and started jumping up and down. She didn't care if anyone heard her.

After emailing Gemma immediately to confirm she was keen,

Jane spent some time searching for a return flight to Milan, making sure she got the best deal, since she had to pay for it out of her own pocket. Then she booked the train from Milan Centrale to Como, which was pretty cheap. Now all she had to do was cancel the hostel for the rest of the stay, try and wangle a refund and head out to Barcelona Airport tomorrow morning.

She was fizzing with excitement. The job had come up at the perfect time, and had neatly slotted it into the empty hole she'd found herself in by no fault of her own. Now she wasn't waiting for James like some pathetic hanger-on, she was working! It was going to be fine, she could cope without him …

Near noon she finally managed to escape outside and walk down La Rambla. The wide, tree-lined avenue flowed freely with strolling tourists and locals heading for their lunch breaks. There was plenty to look at but, for some reason, all she could see were young Spanish couples holding hands; sharing private jokes, gazing into each other's eyes or kissing. A flower vendor in a white T-shirt and jeans jogged past her; a gigantic bunch of blood-red roses bouncing softly on his shoulder. Their sweet perfume floated back to her on the breeze.

Jane groaned inwardly. Maybe she'd been a tad unrealistic about her coping abilities. She and James wouldn't have been walking down La Rambla holding hands, or kissing, but at least he'd be here to talk to and laugh with. Detouring into a side street to escape the loved-up couples, she found a quiet café, bought some lunch and sat outside under an umbrella.

On a whim, she decided to call James. She took a big bite of her mozzarella and tomato sandwich, not expecting him to pick up right away, but he answered on the second ring.

'Hey, everything ok?'

Jane managed to chew and speak at the same time. 'Umph, yes, I'm fine. It was just quicker to call, and I've been on my computer all morning so I needed a break,' she could hear herself starting to gabble. She took a gulp of Diet Coke to wash down the bread and steady her nerves. 'I got your email about the test. How was it?'

'Aye, it was all right. Just a throat swab. And then they'll contact me when the results are ready in four days. I'm just glad it's done so I'll know one way or the other.'

'Have you seen Kistella?' she blurted.

'I'm not sure if I will or want to. I guess I'll see how I feel once I get the results.'

Jane didn't say anything.

'I'm sorry all this happened.'

'It's not your fault.'

'Well, it is partly ma fault. I think I just need to stay away from pretty lasses from now on,' he said wryly.

Jane gave a nervous laugh. 'Are you going to take a vow of chastity?'

'Aye, I'm thinking of getting myself a monk's habit and shaving a bald patch on ma head.'

'That would be a shame,' she said, 'Because you … er, have nice hair.'

James laughed. 'Anyway, how's Barcelona? How was your first night in the hostel?'

'Um, it was fine. I got in quite late so just, you know, hit the hay.' Jane took another gulp of Diet Coke, deciding not to mention Miguel. 'Listen, I'm actually flying to Milan tomorrow. Gemma just emailed about a free stay in a hotel in Como in exchange for an article, and I get to have a byline so I can link to my blog. I've just got to pay for my flight and train, oh and my f—' Jane held the phone away from her ear, laughing. James's whoop was even louder than hers had been. 'I know. Great, isn't it?'

'Great? That's an understatement. It's dead brilliant!'

'Well, as they say, it's who you know,' she said casually. 'In this case, knowing Gemma is definitely helping me.'

'So, I'll have to cancel the rest of my stay at the hostel for this week,' she continued, 'but I'll try to get them to refund you. What day are you planning on arriving?'

'Uh, Saturday, fingers crossed. I'm hoping to get the test result on Thursday, Friday at the latest. I cannae book another flight until I hear, though, in case it turns out to be later. Why, what day are you back?'

'Early Saturday evening,' she told him.

'It's perfect timing.'

'I know! It's like fate or something.'

'Nae, it's just networking.'

Jane laughed hollowly. 'Networking, right! So, I guess we just play it by ear until we know what's happening your end.'

'Aye, probably the best thing to do at the moment. I'll book somewhere to stay when I find out the results.'

La Rambla was emptying as she wandered back to the hostel, the heat driving people indoors for their siestas. Shops were also shutting and wouldn't open again until late afternoon. Jane yawned feeling hot and dozy; she could do with a siesta herself. Luckily the main door of Hostel Valeria was off the catch, so she didn't have to go through the rigmarole of ringing reception. When she came in through the glass door, there was no one there, anyway. She'd have to sort out the cancellation later. She yawned again and headed to her dorm to take a nap.

Jane was unceremoniously woken by girlish giggles. The dorm room seemed to be inundated with young Asian women. She counted at least half a dozen, either running in and out of the bathroom in skimpy robes or rummaging in their lockers. She recognised another two girls sitting chatting in the bunk opposite as the ones who'd nearly bumped into her this morning. Jane smiled, but they just looked at her and didn't respond, returning to their conversation, which she couldn't understand.

It was getting on for five and she had to meet Miguel, so she got her makeup bag from the locker and took advantage of a break in the bathroom activity. But when she went in, she discovered it was dripping wet from floor to ceiling, like a giant bucket of water had been sloshed around the room. She picked her way carefully across the slick tile in her bare feet, glad she was only here for one night.

After applying some mascara and rose-pink lipstick, she brushed her hair until it was smooth and glossy. She sensed an air of tension outside the bathroom, as if there were more human tsunamis waiting to come in and throw water around, so she left them to it. As long as they didn't wet her stuff, she didn't care what they did in there.

Her phone was beeping when she got back to the bunk. Miguel had just texted to say he was on his way to collect the key, so she quickly got changed, stowed her laptop securely in the locker and went to meet him.

As she was leaving, Jane saw a girl stationed at reception so she asked her to cancel the rest of her stay and refund James. The girl wasn't happy about it but eventually agreed. She made a mental note to tell James to book somewhere else for Saturday night as this hostel was getting on her nerves. Jane laughed at herself going down in the lift; she hadn't even spent *one* night here and she was already over hostels. The Airbnb apartment last night had spoiled her.

When she came outside, blinking in the late afternoon sunlight, she saw Miguel leaning up against a tree. He was wearing his bartender's uniform with the necktie done up this time. His black hair was pulled back neatly in a ponytail, and he was freshly shaved.

'Hola, Jane,' he said and greeted her with a kiss on each cheek, and she caught a whiff of musky aftershave.

'Hola!' she returned, smiling at him. She fished the apartment key out of her bag and handed it over.

'There you go. Thank you again for letting me stay at your friend's Airbnb. You really were a lifesaver.'

'El gusto es mío. I was glad I could help ... ah, I was wondering, do you have plans right now?' He glanced at her, and she noticed his brown eyes were fringed with long, dark lashes. Women would kill for those, she thought.

'Oh no, not really. I might go to the market on La Rambla and perhaps try to see the Magic Fountain later.'

'Sí, Mercado de La Boqueria? It is open now but the fountain doesn't work on Mondays,' he said.

'Really? Wow, ok, that's bad planning on my part.'

'You can go tomorrow.'

'Hmm, no, I'm actually flying out tomorrow to Italy.'

Miguel looked surprised but said, 'Do you want to walk with me down La Rambla? My bar is just a small distance?'

'Sure.'

It was just the right temperature for a stroll, and since Miguel was in his uniform, she was glad she'd changed into a light-blue summer wrap dress and black flats, rather than jeans and a T-shirt. The sunlight dappled the pavement through the leafy trees ahead of them and the street was slowly starting to come to life again. There was a delicious aroma of roasted chicken wafting from one of the sidewalk vendors.

'So tomorrow you're leaving, but you just arrived yesterday? Is Barcelona that bad?'

Jane smiled at him. 'No, not at all. I just have some work to do in Italy, but I'll be back on Saturday.'

'Ah, I see.'

They reached a glass door inset into one of the concrete buildings and Miguel stopped. 'This is my bar. Would you like to come in for a drink and some tapas before the market? It's usually quite empty at this time so I'll probably just be wiping glasses.'

Jane shrugged. 'Sure, if that's ok.'

She followed him into the bar which was dimly lit and decked out with polished concrete floors and copper piping. It was industrial but homely with bright modern artworks on the wall and squat wooden tables with round stools. It was, as he said, practically empty with just a couple cosied up at the back of the room. The entire right wall was stocked with bottles of wine, liqueurs and spirits, while along the left side was a narrow serving counter and another barman.

Miguel steered her to a table on the right-hand side near the entrance. Jane sat down and put her small handbag on the table and looked at the menu. The list of tapas was extensive. Sensing her alarm, Miguel said he'd bring over a selection. Was she vegetarian? She shook her head. Did she like sangria? She nodded vigorously. He laughed and went behind the bar.

Jane pretended to study the menu and out of the corner of her eye saw the other barman glance at her and say something to

Miguel, who shook his head. He said something rapidly back in Spanish and she caught the word 'amiga'. She relaxed. It was good that he was saying she was a friend. Jane hadn't assumed it was a date, especially since her "date" was working behind the bar, but after all, coffee didn't always mean coffee. She'd learned that pretty quickly on her first trip to Spain.

Miguel soon brought over her sangria and a small plate of tapas, and pointed to each in turn, saying 'croquetas, bombas and montaditos'. She took a sip of the frosty sangria and her taste buds tingled. It was fruity, tangy and refreshing all at once. 'Gracias, Miguel. I'll pay, of course.'

'Please don't worry about it, you're here as my guest.'

'Are you sure?'

'Si, si! Enjoy! Unfortunately, I have to work but come and see me before you go?'

Jane nodded and indicated her phone. 'Is it ok if I make a quick call?'

'Of course.'

'Ok, muchas gracias again.'

When Miguel had disappeared out the back to do something, Jane speared a croqueta with her fork and dialled Amber. She knew she was off work early on Mondays.

'Hello?'

'Hola cómo estás?'

'Hola hola! Where are you?'

'Sitting in a bar in La Rambla, drinking sangria and being fed tapas by a dishy Spanish guy,' Jane said in a husky whisper.

Amber screamed. 'No way! You hussy!'

Jane hurriedly turned down the volume. 'Yes way. Well, not the hussy bit, it's all very civilised. I'm at the table and he's working behind the bar,' she said in a low voice, peeking to make sure Miguel was still out the back.

'You picked up a barman? You've only been there one day!'

Jane laughed. 'I'm a fast worker. No, he's just a guy I met when I arrived. I couldn't get into my hostel last night, so he kindly let me stay in his friend's Airbnb apartment.'

'Hang on. So where was James last night? Where *is* James now?'

Uh oh, thought Jane, here we go.

'James is in Edinburgh.'

'Edinburgh! What the hell is he doing in Edinburgh?' squawked Amber, her Scottish rolling r's reverberating out of the phone loudly. Jane lowered the volume some more. Perhaps ringing Amber wasn't such a good idea. At this rate, the whole bar would know the story.

'He's coming back on Saturday. He just had something personal he needed to take care of,' she said, choosing her words carefully.

'What—like a dentist appointment?' Amber scoffed.

'Er, a little more personal than that ... a paternity test.' Jane turned the volume way down and held the phone away from her ear as Amber let loose. When she'd finished, she tentatively turned up the volume again.

All she could hear was deep breathing.

'Are you still there?' she asked.

'Aye.'

'Are you ok?'

'Me? What about you? The wee eejit has possibly got someone up the duff and you seem very calm and collected about it!'

'Not just someone—Kistella.'

'Aw, nooo,' breathed Amber. 'That bitch!'

Jane had to laugh, though she hadn't felt like laughing about it at all since it had happened.

'So, he abandoned you to go off back to his fancy woman.'

'Not quite. He's had the test, and he's flying back on Saturday, no matter what the results.'

Amber sniffed. 'Sure, he says that now. If he learns the bairn's his then it might be a different story.'

'I don't think he's just going to fall into Kistella's arms. He doesn't trust her as far as he can throw her.'

'So how would you feel if it turns out it's his?'

'I really don't know. I mean, I guess she could always decide not to keep it, but since she's probably making all the potential fathers have tests, it seems likely she's thinking of keeping it.'

'What? So, he's just one of many who could be the father?'

'Yes, that's the reason for the paternity test. She's not sure whose it is!'

'Oh, my Lord. She's a piece of work, that one.'

'Si,' sighed Jane, finishing the last montadito, which was topped with cured tuna and tangy cheese.

'Anyway, there's not much I can do about it, so I'm just going with the flow. Besides, I'm off to Italy tomorrow. I got my first travel writing job!'

'Och, it's all happening!' said Amber. 'I want details. But first tell me about this barman; is he cute?'

Jane surreptitiously checked out Miguel behind the bar. 'He's definitely cute, but the ponytail doesn't really do it for me. He seems like a nice guy, though. Why—are you looking? What about Outlander-Colin?'

'It's going ok, but I still feel weird that his child is at the centre and his ex-wife is picking him up every day. Anyway, it is what it is. Tell me about Italy.'

Jane quickly filled her in on the details, with Amber oohing and ahhing at the appropriate moments. After she got off the phone, she realised her quick call was more like a half-hour marathon. Thanks to cheap roaming, she was now officially one of *those* people who talked on their phone in bars.

No one seemed to care though, so she finished what was left of her sangria, grabbed her bag and went over say goodbye to Miguel. The bar had filled up since she'd come in, so he was busy making cocktails, and a pale pink concoction was whirring away in a blender. He looked up as she approached and switched off the machine. She watched as he poured the frothy drink into a tall glass and added a garnish of mint.

'Looks good,' she said, indicating the cocktail.

'It's the house specialty—Pink Panther Passion, a secret recipe.' He leaned towards her conspiratorially. 'I could tell you what's in it, but then I'd have to kill you.' He grinned and plonked in a cocktail umbrella.

'Ha ha,' said Jane, knowing he was joking but thinking that's *not* the sort of comment you make to a woman you've only just met.

'So, gracias, Miguel. I'll head off now.'

She took a step towards the door. Suddenly she wanted to be out in the fresh air and looking forward to her trip to Italy without any obligations.

'No hay problema, Jane. Perhaps we can see you when you come back on Saturday?'

'Perhaps, yes. I'm not sure what I'm doing yet,' she hedged. 'Just ... er ... text me.'

'Ok, hasta luego!' he farewelled her cheerfully. The other barman smiled at her and gave her a nod. So she smiled back and said 'gracias' to him, too.

Dammit, thought Jane when she was back out in the sunshine and walking towards the market. She was grateful to Miguel for helping her out with the apartment, but now he'd also given her free food and drink. It made her feel like she owed him something for his generosity. She wished he'd let her pay and be done with it. Oh well, he probably wouldn't text her anyway, so she was getting her knickers in a twist over nothing.

Chapter 11: The Girl on the Train

Jane had an uneventful night and managed to get a decent seven hour's sleep. Not even stirring when various girls tiptoed around with their phone torches in the wee hours and started rummaging in lockers and plastic bags.

Since it was still earlyish she didn't feel the need to get up just yet so she lay there contentedly in her bunk dozing. It was good to be back on track again after the drama of the last few days. And doubly good to know she'd be staying in a four-star hotel for the rest of the week.

She was just beginning to drift off again when a waterfall of water came gushing down the side of the bunk all over her bedding. 'What the hell?' she screeched. Remarkably, no one else in the dorm woke up to find out why she was shouting. Jane got out and poked her head into the top bunk to demand an explanation. No one was there, but a tall plastic water bottle without a cap seemed to have overbalanced spilling its contents. Why it had chosen to do so at that particular moment, or where the owner of the bottle was, remained a mystery.

Great, she thought, surveying the large wet patch that was slowly spreading across her bedding. She flicked back the drenched sheets and duvet to reveal an equally sodden mattress. Her Zen-like reverie ruined, she left the mess, grabbed some clothes and her towel, and headed to the bathroom to have a shower. Jane thanked her lucky stars she was leaving today, the hostel could sort it out.

By the time she'd dressed, packed her bag, and collected her laptop from the locker, there was a general stirring of bodies. She was still bemused by the fact they hadn't woken up when she'd shouted. Maybe they were all wearing ear plugs or just remarkably sound sleepers? Too bad if she were being murdered, she'd just have to fend for herself.

All packed, Jane headed to reception to check out, thinking she'd grab some breakfast at the airport. She didn't really want to spend another moment here if she could help it—even if the breakfast was free.

The same guy who had checked her in was manning reception. He looked surprised when she trundled up to the counter. It was still quite early, and Barcelona was a party city, so he probably didn't usually expect to see anyone until late morning.

'Hola!' she said brightly 'I'd like to check out please. Room eight, bed six,' she handed over her key. 'Oh, and there was an accident. The girl above me left her water bottle cap off and it tipped over spilling water onto my bed.'

'Sure, right, that's ok.' He shrugged, nonplussed as if it happened every day.

'It was a full two litre bottle,' she insisted, trying to get some kind of reaction. 'The duvet, sheets and mattress are soaked!'

'That's ok,' he replied airily, turning back to his computer and dismissing her.

Wow he really doesn't give a monkey's, thought Jane pushing open the hostel door. She hoped it *was* sorted so the next occupant didn't have to sleep in a sopping bed. That's if they could even get in through the front door in the first place!

Once she was out in the fresh air, she relaxed and tried to focus on what she had to do, namely get to the airport and fly to Milan. It felt like ages since she'd flown in but it had only been two days.

Forty-five minutes later she was entering the massive hangar-like structure of Barcelona Airport. She checked the departure board and breathed a sigh of relief when she saw her flight to Milan was on time. The hotel in Como wasn't expecting her until the afternoon but she didn't want any more travel dramas for a while, just everything to go smoothly and run like clockwork.

After checking in her luggage, she went through security and into the departure lounge. Her flight didn't have a gate yet so she found a vacant seat, got out her laptop and logged into the free Wi-Fi. She wanted to have a proper look at the hotel's website to check out the location, rooms and services.

The hotel was larger and grander than she'd first thought. Perched on the western bank of Lake Como, it commanded sweeping views of the water. There were a range of rooms, in different sizes, the largest a corner suite of thirty square metres. According to the website most rooms were lake facing and had balcony terraces. It looked like the website's copy had been translated from Italian into English. One room was described as 'furnished that seem designed to make you feel good' which made her wince.

The hotel had an on-site restaurant, an outdoor bar, and organised guest services and activities, such as driving a Ferrari, having tea in a countess's mansion or, if you really felt you needed one, a personal butler.

There was a welcome message from the hotel owner, Roberto Gianni, expounding on the hotel's merits and how guests loved it so much they returned every year. The accompanying headshot was an Italian man in his fifties, extremely tanned, with very white teeth. On closer inspection, Jane was positive black hair dye was involved. Gemma had said Roberto was her point of contact, so at least she now knew what he looked like.

A bit later, as she was waiting in line to board, she felt her phone vibrate. Miguel had sent a text saying: *Buen viaje Jane!* And a smiley face emoji. It was her turn at the counter, so she quickly brought up the airline's app with her e-ticket and got beeped through. She walked down the air bridge and her phone went again. Another text from Miguel, this time a bunch of emojis and some question marks. She frowned, disconcerted. The first one made sense, the second was kind of random.

Since she was preoccupied with getting on board and finding her seat, she didn't look at the text again until she was settled in. Miguel had sent a black triangle, a white triangle and another black triangle, then three question marks. She stared at it blankly. It didn't compute at all. If she wanted to read anything into it, it looked like he was asking if she were into threesomes. But surely he wouldn't ask her that?

Her mind flicked to the bar; the conversation between Miguel and the other barman, and his 'perhaps *we* can see you' when she left ... bloody hell, maybe he was? Jane hastily switched her phone to airplane mode. Hopefully he wouldn't text her again if she didn't reply. She had enough going on without Spanish bartenders wanting to hook up for a threesome.

The ninety-minute flight to Milan was smooth until they were coming into land. A strong wind buffeted the plane making it constantly sway and dip suddenly. Jane grasped the armrests and closed her eyes until she felt the wheels touch the tarmac and the plane started taxiing to the gate. She wasn't a nervous flyer normally but she hated turbulence.

After navigating her way through the airport and collecting her luggage, she followed the signage to the Malpensa Express. A train to Milano Centrale was due in five minutes so she bought a ticket at the self-service machine and jumped on board when it arrived. It took just under an hour to get to Milano Centrale and the Wi-Fi wasn't great, so she just looked out the window and checked Google Maps for the train's progress for most of it. She located Como on the map just under five miles from the Swiss Border, which was gouged into the top of Italy like a giant, jagged U-shape.

All the towns up in that area were a confusing mish mash; ones with Italian-sounding names were ensconced in Switzerland, while Lake Lugano was sliced in half with one part in each country. It would be weird living so close to another country, Jane mused. She started thinking about James, growing up in Galashiels near the English border. Feeling a sudden compulsion to talk to him she got out her phone to send a text, but the train was approaching the station. She'd send him a photo of the hotel later.

Disembarking in the middle of the lunchtime rush with people crossing her path left, right and center, Jane was initially dazed and confused, then shook herself and checked her phone—she had thirteen minutes to find her train! She marched purposefully towards the departure board and scanned the list of trains, looking for Chiasso or Como. There, platform five. She was at platform twelve now so she started walking fast down the row of trains, and then broke into a slight jog, trying to avoid barging into anyone.

Why was it, she wondered, that you always had hours to kill when getting somewhere, then all of a sudden it turned into a mad panic at the other end? Finally reaching platform five, she saw the train waiting and heard its engine running. She checked her phone, still four minutes to go—heaps of time. Then she saw a conductor with a whistle in his mouth stick his head out one of the carriage doors further down, and look both ways, as if to check that no one else was boarding. So she sped up again and wrenched open the handle of the closest carriage.

A slim, tanned hand reached down, so she grabbed it gratefully and was practically lifted into the train in a jumble of luggage. She straightened up, laughing, blowing hair out of her face and making sure she had all her belongings.

'Cutting it a bit fine aren't you, mate?' questioned the girl who had heaved her into the carriage. The train jolted and started moving.

'I guess so,' answered Jane. 'Thanks for that. I thought I had enough time.'

The girl smiled and nodded. 'No worries. Are you going to Chiasso?' she asked. Jane tried to place her accent.

'No, Como. Are you Australian?'

'Yep, I'm from Sydney.'

'Oh, you're a long way from home.'

'Yeah,' said the girl, biting a nail. She was leaning up against the wall alongside a large navy backpack.

Jane looked through the interior carriage window; the seats all seemed to be full. 'Do you have a seat? I think I'm meant to be further up the train.'

'Nah, I just jumped on so I don't have a seat.'

'So you haven't paid?'

The girl laughed. 'Don't look so shocked. If someone asks me to cough up I'll pay. If they don't, well, that's not my fault.'

Jane thought about her carefully researched-and-paid-for ticket sitting on her phone. It hadn't even crossed her mind to try her luck at a free ride.

She looked at the girl curiously. She was around her age, perhaps a year or two older, medium height, with short, straight hair dyed bright auburn, a small snub nose and a sprinkling of freckles across high tan cheekbones. The rest of her was very tanned too, as if she'd been sunbathing on the beach for the last two weeks. Jane noticed the girl subtly checking out her clothes and her luggage.

'Are you going to Como or Chiasso?' Jane asked. She moved her bags to one side and leaned on the opposite wall. The train was picking up speed as it left the city and the carriage was swaying.

'Como,' answered the girl. 'I don't want to cross over into Switzerland just yet as I'm on a Schengen visa.'

'What's that?' enquired Jane.

'Since I'm from Aussie I can only stay in a European country for ninety days. Then I've got to take off to another country in the Schengen zone. I've got a few more days to go for Italy, so I'm staying near the border.'

'Oh,' said Jane. 'That sounds complicated. Are you working or on holiday?'

'Kinda both. I do social media management but since it's mainly scheduling posts I can do it wherever. I'm not going to get rich from it but the money is ok. I can't afford Gucci but I can buy gelato.'

Jane laughed. 'Yes, Italy isn't really known for being cheap. That's why I usually go to Spain.'

'Hablas español?'

'Si, a little español, especially "sangría por favor"'.

The girl grinned, her white teeth flashing against her tan. 'That's all you need really. Or maybe "Dónde está el baño?"'

'Ha, yes. Everyone I've ever met in Spain speaks English anyway.' Jane thought of Miguel with his long eyelashes and ponytail making pink cocktails in the bar. She still couldn't believe he'd sent her that text. Surely, he didn't really expect her to agree to it? What was she supposed to say: *Si, I'm into threes* with a thumbs up emoji? She shook her head.

'So why are you in Italy then if you usually go to Spain?' the girl was asking.

'Oh, well, it's a long story. I was meant to be travelling to Barcelona with a friend, but he got … waylaid. So I went alone, then I got some freelance work in Como, so I flew here today. It's just for four days, then I'm flying back to Barcelona on Saturday to meet him.'

'Sounds fun,' said the girl, 'spur of the moment, I like it.'

'Yes,' agreed Jane, realising she'd had more excitement in the last two days than she'd had in the two years she'd been an accountant's receptionist.

The girl held out her hand. 'I'm Natalie, by the way, but everyone calls me Nat. Do you want to meet up for a few coldies in Como?'

Chapter 12: Bella Vista Hotel

Jane exchanged numbers with Natalie, agreeing to meet up for a drink before she left. When they arrived in Como, she helped her put on her oversized pack. Then Natalie walked off into town to find the hostel she was staying at, saying she'd text her later.

Taking a taxi to the hotel seemed easier than trying to figure out the buses. It was a short but scenic ride, and the road hugged the shoreline, giving her a clear view right across the blue, glistening waters of Lake Como. Lowering the taxi window, she took in a lungful of crisp autumn air and felt the sun on her skin. The foliage around the edge of the lake was a vibrant mix of red and gold. Suddenly, it didn't matter what happened with James or if she could earn enough money to support herself—she had made a new friend and she was staying in an amazing hotel tonight. Carpe diem, she thought.

The taxi pulled up in front of the Bella Vista in a swoosh of crunching gravel. Jane paid the driver, and he retrieved her bag from the boot. She was glad she'd worn her slim-fitting pearl-grey office dress, slightly creased though it was; the hotel looked like it was used to hosting the rich and famous. In fact, she wouldn't be surprised if a few celebrities were staying here now.

She went through the main entrance and into the reception area. An attractive Italian girl with tawny hair pulled back into a bun and impeccable eyebrows, gave her a welcoming smile as she approached the front desk. 'Buon giorno. May I help you?'

'Hi, I'm Jane Aitken. I'm here to meet with Roberto Gianni,' she said, trying not to be intimidated.

'Ciao Jane, we've been expecting you! I'm Francesca. Please, come with me and I'll take you to Roberto.' She got up from the desk and strode off swiftly on thin-heeled black stilettos, her pinstripe tailored dress accentuating her statuesque figure. Francesca was tall and had very long legs so Jane had to trot to keep up with her. 'Roberto's been in meetings all morning, so he'll be glad of the diversion.'

I'm evidently not counted as a meeting; I'm more of a coffee break, she thought, amused.

Francesca knocked twice sharply on an oak-panelled door, listened with her head cocked for a reply, then beckoned Jane to follow her in. Roberto Gianni was seated behind an oversized desk that had a laptop, a glass bottle of sparkling water and a small cactus. He was talking on his mobile in rapid Italian but finished up with an abrupt 'ciao!' when they came into the room. He leapt to his feet and grasped her hand in both of his.

'Buon giorno. Jane, is it? Welcome to Como and of course Bella Vista.' He spoke English just as well as Francesca and Jane relaxed, glad she didn't have to try and use her pidgin Spanish as a workaround for his pidgin English.

'Thank you; I mean, grazie,' she said. He beamed and gestured to one of the two easy chairs positioned facing inwards at the front of his desk.

'Now, where did you fly from? Barcelona, was it?'

Jane nodded. 'Yes.'

'It's a pity that Gemma couldn't make it this week. I was interested in her writing a review for us, as she has a large number of followers, but if we can still have an excellent article published on her website, that's the next best thing.'

No pressure, thought Jane.

'I must apologise if our English section of the website makes your research difficult. We recently hired an Italian writer who said they spoke perfect English. As you may have seen, this wasn't the case, and we have to get it all redone ...' He pulled a face, and then realised the other girl was still standing by the door listening.

'Grazie, Francesca, che sarà tutto.'

'Forse vorrebbe del tè?' countered Francesca staring stonily at Roberto, then said to Jane, 'I'll bring you some tea and biscotti.'

'That would be wonderful, grazie,' said Jane. Francesca smiled at her, gave Roberto a dirty look and whisked herself out of the room.

Roberto sighed and sat down in the other chair opposite Jane.

'Forgive my wife. She gets a little jealous if I pay the slightest attention to another attractive woman. I tell her I only have eyes for her, but she refuses to believe me,' he said with a casual smile.

'Y ... your wife?' Jane spluttered.

'Yes, Francesca and I have been married for around three years now. I suppose it is strange that we're colleagues?'

'No, no. That's great that you work together.'

She looked at Roberto more closely. Yes, he was definitely in his fifties, maybe even older, and very tanned; she assumed his pink silk shirt and dark-blue suit were by Armani, Prada, or some other famous Italian designer, since they were close to Milan. He wasn't in bad shape, though a little portly round the middle. Her guess about the hair dye had been spot on too. He'd probably had women falling all over themselves back in the day. But Francesca looked like she'd stepped off a catwalk, and was at the most twenty-five, so there was a huge age difference. The funniest thing was that, according to Roberto, this gorgeous creature seemed to be jealous of her! She felt a hysterical giggle threatening to let loose and took a deep breath to quell it.

'Your hotel is lovely, Mr Gianni,' she said to change the subject. 'How long have you owned it?'

'Please, call me Roberto ... let me see, I think three years now? We spent the first year renovating all the rooms and we were very pleased with the result. The guest reviews have been very positive. I will give you a tour after you've had your tea and show you to your room.'

Francesca arrived back carrying a tray laid with a linen cloth upon which was a cup of tea, some paper strips of sugar, a small jug of milk and some rock hard biscuits. She mimed dunking them in the tea when she saw Jane tap one with a finger and frown.

'Grazie, Francesca,' said Roberto pointedly, raising an eyebrow. She saw one of his hands twitch as if he wanted to shoo her away. Jane concentrated on pouring milk into her tea and tried not to stare.

'Now, tell me, Jane,' said Roberto after Francesca had left. 'How was your flight and your trip here? The scenery is beautiful, no?'

They spent a pleasant ten or so minutes chatting about this and that while Jane sipped her tea and crunched biscotti and tried not to crack a filling. Roberto was easy to talk to and attentive, so she saw how Francesca may have been charmed by him. She still couldn't understand why she'd married someone so much older but maybe Italian men were like fine wine: better with age.

Eventually, to her relief, as she was starting to fade, Roberto said he'd show her to her room. They went back out into the foyer where Francesca had already checked her in and readied a key card for her. Jane "grazied" her.

'The Wi-Fi code is on the first page of the guest book,' said Francesca. 'If there's anything you need, please let me know. I hope we can meet tomorrow morning and talk more about the hotel for your article? Roberto, did you mention that?'

'I didn't, but all in good time. I'll show Jane to her room now and give her a little tour so she can find the breakfast room tomorrow.'

Jane felt sorry for Francesca and told her that tomorrow morning was fine to meet up. Would after breakfast suit?

Francesca brightened and told her to come and find her at reception. Then Jane followed Roberto to the lifts, and they went up to the first floor.

'Your room is on the second floor, but this is where the restaurant is,' he said as they entered a bright spacious room with picture windows giving sweeping views of the lake. A dozen or so tables were set with crisp, white linen cloths and silver cutlery. French doors at one end led out onto a raised terrace where there was an outdoor bar.

'The restaurant doubles as the breakfast room. In the morning, we serve a buffet with both continental and cooked options,' explained Roberto. 'Then in the evening we offer an à la carte menu. I would be honoured if you would join me for dinner in the restaurant, perhaps tomorrow night? It would be included as part of the stay so you could write about it for your article. You may want to mention we have a newly acquired Michelin-star chef.'

'Of course,' said Jane, taking in the scene. 'This room is amazing. I love the floor.' She gestured to the green and white marble tiles laid in an intricate geometric pattern.

'Si!' said Roberto, beaming. 'The floor is our pride and joy. Many of the tiles were cracked and stained when we arrived, and it took months to restore them to their original state.'

After Jane had oohed and ahhed some more, they went back to the lifts and up to the second floor. The doors opened to reveal royal purple plush carpet, and cream wallpaper with a delicate black feather pattern; the hallway was lit with golden wall sconces. All the elegance was slightly overwhelming. She wasn't sure if she was the only guest staying here or if everyone was out exploring Como, but it seemed quite devoid of people.

'Many of our guests take excursions out onto the lake or visit nearby wineries during the day,' said Roberto, as if reading her thoughts. 'You'll see more people around in the evening. In the shoulder season we are quieter, but it picks up again for Christmas.'

Jane had her key card ready for room number three which turned out to be the second room on the right. She held her breath as she inserted the card into the electronic lock and Roberto swung open the door. The first thing she noticed was the size of the room; it was enormous. The next thing she saw were French doors opening out from the lounge area onto a sunny terrace overlooking the lake, complete with two white sun loungers.

'This is one of our junior suites. It's a popular choice with couples but I thought you'd enjoy the extra space. I hope it's not too big? We have a deluxe that's smaller if you'd prefer.'

'No, it's perfect,' said Jane quickly. She checked out the cream décor and flowing sheer curtains. Pride of place was a king-sized bed with a black velvet headboard, snow-white duvet and numerous plump purple sateen pillows. She was itching to take some photos, but she politely waited for Roberto to continue with his spiel.

'The furnishings are genuine velvet and we have Beautyrest mattresses on all our beds. As you can see, you have your own private terrace if you want to sunbathe. Please, come with me.'

He opened a door on the right to show her the bathroom. It had a sunken Jacuzzi bathtub with shiny, gold taps, a separate shower with a rainforest head and was decked out from floor to ceiling in black-and-white marble. 'Whoa!' exclaimed Jane. 'That's impressive!'

Roberto puffed out his chest at her comment. 'Carrara marble. We refurbished all the bathrooms in the hotel with it. It cost, how you say, an arm and a foot, but it was worth it.'

'Arm and a leg,' said Jane automatically, staring at the Jacuzzi bathtub and wondering if it would be impolite to say she needed to take a bath right this second. Again, Roberto seemed to be in tune with her thoughts.

'I will leave you now to get settled in and relax. If you need anything, please ring reception and let Francesca know. We have a room service menu if you'd like to order something for dinner. It would be good for you to try that out ...'

'For the article, yes, of course.'

Roberto smiled dazzlingly, his white teeth flashing against his tan. 'Thank you, Jane. I hope you will enjoy your stay. Oh, and please help yourself to complimentary snacks and drinks in the minibar. Arrivederci!'

And with that, he left the room and she was finally and wonderfully alone. Fifteen minutes later she was lying in a warm bath with the jets going, bubbles floating around her ears and swigging from a small bottle of Prosecco from the minibar. What the hell, she thought—why not toast Roberto since it's free?

She'd left the door to the bathroom ajar so she could see the terrace, and beyond that, the sublime view. The gauzy curtains in the bedroom swirled and fluttered in the breeze. She felt like an A-list movie star, escaping the trials and tribulations of Hollywood to chill out in Italy.

God, that last movie really took it out of me, darling. I'll have my mobile, so leave a message if you must get hold of me. But expect not hear back for a while, I have some serious relaxing planned.

Jane closed her eyes as the bubbles pummelled her body. It was hard to believe that last night she'd slept in an eight-bed dorm, and now she was in a room the size of a small apartment. It was taking some mental adjustment. Much later, when the water had begun to cool, and the Prosecco was long gone, she sighed and heaved herself out. She dried off with a large, white, fluffy towel and slipped into one of the complimentary white cotton robes hanging behind the door. Matching slippers were tucked into the pockets, but they were humongous, so she went barefoot.

Tying the belt, she went out the French doors and wandered over to the railing and took in the magnificent view stretching for miles across the lake. A soft, fragrant breeze lightly fingered the back of her damp neck. She'd been in the bath so long the sun was starting to go down. The lawn and promenade that skirted the front of the hotel were in shadow.

Some guests were sitting outside on the terrace below having an aperitif and she felt like calling down and waving. Perhaps they were famous? Jane peered at them, trying to see, and laughed; one small bottle of Prosecco and she was behaving like a nutter. Food, that's what she needed. There was still some heat in the sun, so she fetched the room service menu card and stretched out on one of the loungers to see what was on offer. Everything looked amazing but eye-wateringly expensive. She knew she had to foot the bill for it, so decided on the Caesar salad and an entree of the local pasta specialty. If she got hungry later, there were always the minibar snacks.

Jane lay there enjoying the soft sunlight on her arms and legs until shade started to creep across the terrace. The light was now fading quickly, and the outside lamps of the hotel had flickered on. A chill in the air was making her shiver, so she went back inside to the warmth to order dinner. After doing so, she sat on the bed for a while in the darkening room, listening to the water slap against the shoreline and the odd duck quacking as it paddled nearby.

A knock on the door made her jump. She tightened her robe and turned on the main light to answer the door. A waiter was there with a food tray, so she said 'ciao' and 'come in' and stood back as he busied himself setting it down on the table by the window. Afterwards he paused momentarily, looking at her, and she realised that maybe he expected a tip, then the moment passed and he gave a slight nod and said 'buon appetito' and left. Jane checked her phone for the time: just before six. No text from Natalie. Probably having too much fun in the hostel, she thought. Nothing from James either; she'd sent him a photo of the room and one of the view from the terrace. She felt strangely disconnected from everyone, but not lonely. Like she could exist this way and be perfectly happy about it for an extended length of time. Though it would be nice to have someone wonder, eventually, how she was getting on.

The local pasta turned out to be large, soft tubes covered in a creamy tomato sauce mixed with pieces of delicate fish and the requisite sprinkling of parmesan cheese. After polishing off the delicious, but small, meal in about two minutes flat, she realised she probably should've ordered the main. Ah well, there was still the salad and an incredibly crunchy bread roll that threatened, again, to crack a filling. You really needed dental insurance before coming to Italy, she thought, tearing off a chunk of the bread to mop up the leftover sauce.

After finishing the salad, Jane was still hungry so she rummaged in the minibar for some snacks. Then grabbed the remote and flicked on the large flatscreen TV and went through the channels. Most of them seemed to be in Italian apart from one that had CNN, so she sat in bed and watched for a while, munching black truffle crisps, breaking off pieces of Kit Kat and swigging from a bottle of Diet Coke. Hopefully they'd restock the minibar tomorrow, as at this rate she'd soon be out of snacks.

The king-sized bed was soft and comfortable, so she got up briefly to clean her teeth, then turned off the TV and drifted asleep.

CHAPTER 13: EMERGENCY EXIT

Jane woke with a start some hours later, disturbed by her phone flashing and beeping with a series of texts on the nightstand. It was pitch black in the room and for a moment she lay there, completely at a loss as to where she was. Then she remembered: Lake Como, junior suite, Prosecco ... it wasn't just a nice dream.

Feeling thirsty, she got up and gulped water from a plastic cup in the bathroom. Her reflection stared back at her groggily with mussed hair and puffy eyes. A real A-lister look, she thought. Refilling the cup to put on the nightstand, she went back to bed and checked the time on her phone: 2:37am. Who the hell was texting her at this hour?

She found out soon enough. Natalie had obviously had a few and decided to say hello to her new friend with a 'wassup gurl' and something that looked like 'fancy schmancy hotel' and something else that was spelled so badly Jane couldn't even understand it. She had mentioned she was staying here, and Natalie must've looked it up.

Jane shook her head. She was about to turn off her phone and go back to sleep when another text came through that made her sit bolt upright: *Soz dumb auto be @ yours in ten in taxi hostel sux.*

An alarm bell went off in her head as she read this. From the state of the texting Natalie sounded pretty drunk and Jane immediately imagined various scenarios. Natalie staggering in and demanding loudly that the night porter ring her friend Jane's room. Or worse, getting thrown out of reception and saying Jane was a friend of hers. Not a good look. He was sure to tell Francesca and then Roberto, too, would find out. She doubted he'd be so keen for her to stay in the junior suite if he thought she was inviting friends over to take advantage of his hospitality.

Racing to her bag, she pulled out a pair of jeans and a sweatshirt. She didn't bother with underwear, not enough time. Somehow, she had to head Natalie off at the pass and put her back in the taxi before she made it into the foyer. But how? Her glance fell on the guest folder on the sideboard and she remembered from looking at it that afternoon that it had a hotel floor plan.

She quickly flicked through the laminated pages to the plan and scanned the ground floor to locate a side entrance—there, next to the bathrooms, was an "uscita di emergenza" door that opened out onto the roadside.

Jane grabbed her phone and key card, tucking both into the back pocket of her jeans, and walked swiftly out the room. She bypassed the lifts and took the stairs instead, the concrete icy cold on her bare feet. When she reached the ground floor, she cautiously poked her head out into the foyer. The night porter was sitting at the front desk but with his back to her, so all she had to do was tiptoe around the corner to the hallway and head to the exit door. It had been ten minutes already; she had to go now. Taking a deep breath and letting it out slowly, Jane gently opened the door and slipped sideways into the hallway, trying not to make a sound. She nearly kicked an oversized brass urn holding a dwarf palm tree but managed to circumvent it at the last minute.

Padding down the hallway silently hugging the walls, she felt like a cat burglar. A cat burglar who was more than a little annoyed. Bloody Natalie; it was a bit of a cheek coming here in the middle of the night. She was expecting to meet up with her for a civilised drink, not have her turn up drunk at the hotel.

Jane reached the emergency exit door and pushed down on the panic bar. It didn't open. In desperation she pushed down harder, putting her shoulder to it and giving it a hard shove. The thing flew open, catapulting her outside, and an ear piercing alarm sounded. Crap, now the whole hotel was going to wake up!

She started running up the road to the entrance with her hands over her ears, just in time to see a figure with a handbag clumsily getting out of a taxi and weaving unsteadily towards the hotel. The taxi driver was yelling something out the window that didn't sound very complimentary and Natalie gave him the finger. Damn, thought Jane, realising that putting her quietly back in the taxi wasn't going to be an option.

Slowing to a fast walk and ignoring the pain of the gravel on her bare feet, Jane grabbed Natalie's arm, said, 'This way, Nat,' and steered her off towards a darkened path lined with trees.

The taxi driver was gunning his engine in annoyance, and the shrill alarm was prompting lights to flicker on in the hotel rooms. But Natalie was oblivious.

'Jaaane!' she slurred, finally recognising her. 'I was coming to see you.'

'I know, I know,' said Jane soothingly. 'We'll just hang out here for a while by these trees.'

'What's that noise?' asked Natalie, holding her hands over her ears. 'It's hurting my head.'

'Shhh,' said Jane, patting her shoulder and trying to see what was happening in the foyer. By this time the taxi driver had driven off in a squeal of tyres and people were now starting to appear in bathrobes and talk to the night porter behind the desk. She could see him throwing his hands around and getting agitated.

Jane quickly ran through her options. She could ring Natalie another taxi, but if the same guy turned up she doubted he'd take her. She could send Natalie off, but that felt irresponsible when she was drunk. They could wait out here until morning, but it was freezing and she had bare feet. Or she could smuggle her into the hotel. Out of all the options, it just seemed the most sensible.

Jane watched the porter carefully, knowing that if he went into the hallway, it was time for them to move.

'Natalie, we need to run soon. Can you do that with me?' Natalie shivered and nodded. The chilly night air was starting to sober her up.

'When I say go, we're going to run really fast into the hotel and we're going to climb some stairs to my room, ok?' Natalie nodded again. More people came into the foyer and were pointing to the hallway. The porter stood up, mouthing something. She could almost hear him saying, 'It's just an alarm, it will turn off soon,' but the guests were insistent and he had no choice but to leave the desk and try and do something about it.

'Go!' Jane grabbed Natalie's hand and yanked her out from the trees. They ran along the path swiftly and towards the hotel entrance. Luckily the front door wasn't locked, and she pushed it open, dragging Natalie with her.

By now, the small group of guests and the harassed night porter were all in the hallway trying to stop the ringing door, so they ran across the empty foyer and straight to the stairs by the lifts without anyone seeing them. They bumped into an elderly couple coming down in hastily tied bathrobes. 'Is there a fire? Should we go outside?' asked the man, sounding panicked; his voice had an American twang.

'I think it's all fine. It's just a false alarm,' said Jane, giving Natalie's arm a yank to keep her moving up. 'False alarm, y'all,' said Natalie, waving as they went by, leaving the confused couple hesitating on the stairwell.

There was no one in the hallway when they came out of the stairs on level two, so she gripped Natalie's elbow and walked her quickly to her room. She could still hear the ringing coming from below as she closed the door, and then it stopped. Finally! She heaved a sigh of relief. Jane didn't bother trying to extract any sense out of Natalie. She just got her a cup of water from the bathroom and helped her take her shoes off and get into bed. Minutes later she heard a tiny snore, so Jane turned off the light and lay there fully clothed, hoping sleep would overcome her too.

Eventually she dropped off into a fitful doze and woke up feeling like she'd been run over by a bus. Natalie was still out to it, breathing heavily on the other side of the bed. Luckily, they'd given her a room with a king-sized bed. If it were a single, Natalie would be sleeping in the bathtub.

Careful not to wake her, she got out of bed and headed to the bathroom to splash some cold water on her face. She sat on the toilet lid and massaged her temples. Her impromptu thinking last night had worked but now there was the problem of today. Natalie had to go; that was a no-brainer. She hadn't turned up with her pack, so Jane assumed it was still at the hostel. That was a good thing. It meant she could act like she was a guest and simply walk out to a waiting taxi without anyone suspecting anything.

Now she'd thought it through and couldn't see anything that was likely to go wrong, Jane felt better. After showering, and washing her hair with the complimentary shampoo and conditioner, she donned a robe and wrapped her hair up in a turban. She went back out into the bedroom, hoping Natalie was awake so she could tell her the plan. However, the bed was empty. Jane was momentarily confused. Had she gone already? Then she noticed the French doors were ajar. She padded outside onto the sun-drenched terrace and found Natalie stretched out on one of the loungers. She was wearing the robe that Jane had draped over a chair when she went to bed.

'Morning,' said Jane, sitting down on the other lounger.

Natalie grinned at her. 'Mate! Look at that view!'

'I know, it's gorgeous. Hey ... um ... so what happened last night? You were kind of out of it.'

Natalie laughed. 'Yeah, I was completely off my face, but thanks to you, now I'm here in the lap of luxury.'

'Was the hostel that bad?' asked Jane.

Natalie cringed. 'Let's just say I've stayed in some iffy hostels, but a windowless room full of snoring sheilas isn't my idea of a good time.'

'So, you went to a bar instead?'

'Nah, I had a bottle of grog in my bag, so I just sat in the courtyard and quaffed the lot.'

'Then you decided to come here?'

'Yeah. Sorry about that. I was munted.' She sounded genuinely apologetic and Jane softened.

'Well, it could've been worse. At least you didn't get beaten up by the taxi driver. He looked murderous. What happened with him?'

Natalie looked embarrassed. 'Ah, I may have left my purse at the hostel and skipped off without paying him.'

'Wow, ok, that would explain it.'

'Look, you must think I'm a right numbnuts. I just do things on the spur of the moment sometimes when I've had a few.'

'We all do stupid things when we're drunk, even me.'

'Really?' Natalie surveyed her with narrowed eyes, squinting in the sunlight.

'You sound surprised.'

'You just seem so …'

'What?'

'Conservative.'

'Looks can be deceiving. At the moment, I'm trying not to get emotionally involved with a guy who may or may not be having a kid with his ex-girlfriend. And there's this Spanish guy who's texted me something that I think means a threesome.'

'Oooh, let me see.'

Jane fished her phone out of her robe pocket and brought up Miguel's text. She showed it to Natalie.

'Yup, that means a threesome, mate.'

'Are you sure?'

'Defo.'

'How do you know?' asked Jane.

'Coz I got sent something like that in Milan.'

'Oh, right. What happened?'

'Nothing, like literally,' said Natalie 'I was up for it, but the two guys were more into each other than me. Threesomes are bloody boring, I reckon.'

Jane burst out laughing. She took her phone back, caught sight of the time, and swore. 'Look, I have to go down to breakfast, and

I'm meeting the owner's wife afterwards. Are you ok to order a taxi? Perhaps they'll let you swap rooms at the hostel or maybe you could stay somewhere else?'

'Yeah, no worries. I've got to take off and do some work, anyway. Thanks for putting me up for the night. It's an awesome hotel—I wish I could stay here.'

Jane laughed. 'I think they might wonder what was going on if I suddenly had an assistant.'

Natalie looked thoughtful. 'You could tell them you have a friend who'll do their social media in return for a couple of nights' free accommodation.'

Jane didn't want her thinking along those lines—it was getting complicated enough as it was.

'Hmm, probably not. I should go and get dressed and head down. You might be gone by the time I get back but grab something from the minibar if you're hungry.'

Natalie sighed and stretched out her tanned legs on the lounger. 'Sounds good. Oh mate, could you spare ten euros for the taxi since I don't have my purse? I'll pay you back.'

'Right, sure.'

After Jane had dressed and blow dried her hair in the bathroom, she came out to find Natalie in the exact same position she'd left her. It didn't look like she was in any hurry to leave, and Jane suspected she might be harder to shift than chewing gum on a flip flop.

Grumpily, she called out from the lounge that she was heading off now and the ten euros was on the side table. She got a hand wave and a 'have fun, mate' in return. Jane was trying her best to be cool, but she couldn't help feeling irritated. It seemed Natalie was now perfectly fine and relishing her good fortune. If she decided that four-star was preferable to hostel living and dug in her hooves like a stubborn donkey, what was she supposed to do: throw her off the balcony?

As she waited for the lift, she thought about ringing James and asking for his advice but she knew what he'd say—'Tell the wee madam to clear off. She's nae business being here, this is your job.' He was right. Jane was just going to have to be tough. But breakfast first; she needed a full stomach if she was going to have a barney.

A young female attendant, dressed in a smart black and maroon uniform, smiled at her when she approached the restaurant, which had morphed into a breakfast room.

'Buon giorno. La tua camera numero per favore?'

'Oh, uh número tres,' said Jane, figuring Italian was pretty close to Spanish.

'Tre, si, grazie.' The girl scrolled down the list and found her name and put a line through it. 'Allora, puoi andare,' she said cheerfully and waved her through.

The room was busy with guests either milling around the buffet or sitting at the tables eating and chatting. She noted that it was mainly older couples—no kids or millennials in sight—but she'd figured from last night's encounter that well-to-do empty nesters were the hotel's target audience.

Jane's eyes widened when she saw the buffet spread. It was enough to feed a small army. There were cakes, pastries, croissants, cereals, fruit, even slabs of white and dark chocolate. That's weird, she thought. Chocolate for breakfast? She was tempted to carve off a sizeable chunk but grabbed a plate and turned to the silver tureens instead, discovering they contained freshly scrambled eggs, glistening bacon, fried tomato and mushrooms. They must get plenty of British guests, she thought, piling her plate up. She poured an orange juice and took both over to a single table by the window.

After she'd polished that lot off, she went back up to the buffet and heaped up a small plate with some soft white bread rolls and collected some tiny jars of jam and some butter. She was just about to pour herself a coffee to feel more awake when she spied Francesca striding towards her, looking like she'd stepped out of a Gucci ad.

'Buon giorno, Jane, come stai?'

'Oh, hi, Francesca, I'm good, thanks.'

'I was just coming to find you since we should make a start on our meeting.' She looked pointedly at her watch.

Jane glanced at her plate piled with bread rolls and decided to forego the coffee.

'Of course—can I bring this with me?'

'Si, please. I can talk and you can eat.'

Francesca swivelled on a stiletto heel and walked rapidly back to the lifts, with Jane following, carrying her plate of carbs. Somehow, she didn't think Francesca chowed down on bread rolls for breakfast.

'How did you sleep? Well, I hope?' enquired Francesca politely as they waited.

'Yes, very well, thank you,' Jane lied.

'We had a minor incident with a security door near the main entrance last night. I hope it didn't disturb you. We're still trying to figure out what happened. The camera should tell us more.'

'The ... camera?'

'Yes, we have a small CCTV camera in the exit door sign. Roberto is going over the footage now on his laptop, I think.'

Jane's hand shook, her bread rolls wobbling dangerously around on the plate. Well, that's it, she thought, blinking rapidly as tears began to threaten. Her freelancing career was over before it had even begun! The lift dinged, and they went down to the ground floor. Jane looked around nervously. She was half expecting Roberto to be waiting at reception with a thunderous look on his face, but the foyer was empty.

'Please, take a seat,' said Francesca, gesturing to one of the two chairs behind the desk. 'I'll bring up the website and show you the rooms we want you to focus on. I can also give you some background information about the hotel. You can take notes.' She handed her a pad and pen.

Obediently Jane sat down and for the next twenty minutes or

so, Francesca talked rapidly about the hotel: details about the fixtures and fittings of the refurbished rooms, what guests could expect when they stayed and the activities they could arrange. Jane nodded and tried to take notes, while nibbling on jam-dunked bread and butter. The job was straightforward. She just needed to collect all the information she could and then produce something that showed them in the best possible light.

As if sensing her nerves, Francesca said reassuringly, 'I saw some of the hotel writing you did, and I liked it. It was very evoking. Is that the right word?'

'Evocative,' said Jane hollowly. She couldn't stop looking over at the hallway that led to Roberto's office. Any moment now he was going to come storming into reception, and she'd be out on her ear. Hopefully Natalie's hostel wasn't full as she was going to need a bed tonight. In the distance she heard a door slam and flinched. Here we go, she thought.

Sure enough, Roberto was coming over to them and he didn't look happy. She started to get up to explain everything but to her surprise it was Francesca he spoke to through gritted teeth.

'My dear, who was the person you hired to install the security camera?'

'It was my uncle. You know that, Roberto.'

'And is he a qualified electrical engineer?'

'Well, no, but he has years of experience. He rewired his own home. Perche?'

'Static,' hissed Roberto. 'All I see is static.'

'Static?' queried Francesca blankly.

'On the CCTV recording, woman! I can't see anything but static because your uncle didn't do his job properly,' spat Roberto.

Then he seemed to realise having a domestic in the foyer wasn't very professional and collected himself. 'Excuse me for my bad temper, Jane. It is just very frustrating. It looks like we'll never know if it was a guest who got lost or an attempted break-in.'

'I'm sorry to hear that,' said Jane evenly, trying not to sound too elated. The lift dinged and out of the corner of her eye, she saw Natalie come sashaying across the foyer wearing a tight black dress, black heels and bright red lipstick; with her faux black leather handbag slung over her shoulder.

Jane groaned inwardly as she recognised her expensive little black dress, the one Amber had talked her into buying, 'just in case things need heating up with James'. Worse, it looked like it was being stretched to capacity in Natalie's fuller figure!

Roberto turned and did a double take as Natalie smiled beguilingly at him, and deliberately ignored Jane. She waltzed out of the hotel and into a waiting taxi. When he turned back to Francesca, who looked like she'd eaten something nasty, he seemed to have forgotten their previous conversation.

'Who was that woman—is she famous?' questioned Roberto, looking bewildered. 'And why wasn't I told she was staying?' Francesca glanced at Jane and rolled her eyes.

Chapter 14: Second-Best Dress

After that, Roberto went back to his office and her meeting with Francesca seemed to be over. She couldn't help feeling sorry for her once again. Roberto seemed to treat her more like a servant than his wife. Still, her uncle's incompetence did mean Jane wasn't going to be found out. Smuggling a drunk friend into her hotel room wasn't the worst crime in the world, but it wasn't entirely professional either. She probably could've explained what had happened and Roberto may have been understanding, but she'd be on the back foot for the rest of her stay. Plus, she still had to do the job for Gemma if she wanted more work in the future.

Since she'd been given a second chance, she thought she better not waste it, so Jane said she'd go back to her room and start on the article. She felt it was the least she could do. Francesca smiled gratefully.

'Grazie, Jane. Please let me know if you need anything. Roberto will see you in the restaurant at seven for dinner.'

Damn, she forgot she was meant to be having dinner with Roberto tonight. Thanks to Natalie she wouldn't be wearing her little black designer dress either. But this was a minor problem after thinking she was going to get fired from the job and kicked out of the hotel. She headed back to her room feeling blessed.

Her good mood lasted until she opened the minibar to get a Diet Coke. It was completely empty. Not a bottle of tonic water or a chocolate bar in sight. Since she'd only had the Prosecco, Kit Kat, Diet Coke and crisps she knew there had been other goodies left. Great, so not only had Natalie used her makeup, taken her dress and heels, she'd also stuffed the rest of the minibar into her handbag, making Jane look like a scab. She texted Natalie and politely but firmly told her she needed to meet up with her to get her dress and shoes back.

Jane was beginning to wish she hadn't exchanged numbers with her. She hated feeling like that, but Natalie seemed to be causing chaos ever since she'd met her. Maybe next time she wouldn't give out her number so freely to a stranger or tell them where she was staying. It wasn't a nice way to think but she didn't want to go through last night's shenanigans ever again.

Luckily her laptop was still where she left it, so Jane logged in and started putting together an outline for the article from her notes and then wrote a rough draft. It felt good to use her brain to think about something other than Natalie. She still had the plate with some bread rolls and jam from breakfast too, so she was quite content.

Later on, she changed into her bikini, grabbed a towel and did a spot of sunbathing on the lounger while listening to her favourite playlist. It really was gorgeous autumn weather, warm but not too hot. From her position on the terrace, she could watch people scooting around on jet skis out the front of the hotel.

She even spotted a guy levitating into the air jerkily with a hydro backpack and flying over the water, a long hose trailed behind attached to a small, enclosed motorised boat. It looked like he was having fun, even if it was a little disturbing to witness.

When she'd thoroughly topped up her vitamin D levels, she went inside and riffled through her bag, trying to find something suitable for dinner. Luckily she had her second-best dress: a sage-green tailored number with short sleeves that she used to wear to work, and a pair of gold strappy high-heeled sandals; it would have to do.

She felt like messaging James and telling him, 'See, this is why I packed so much—for situations like this when my clothes get nicked!' There was still no reply from Natalie, which only served to irritate her immensely. She got dressed, put on some makeup and brushed her hair. Then, as it was too early to go down for dinner, she lay on the bed, closed her eyes and tried to think calming thoughts. But images of Natalie striding confidently across the foyer in her dress kept interrupting them.

Finally, it was time to leave, so she grabbed her key card and headed down to the first floor. She was beginning to feel cooped up in the hotel. Maybe she'd ask Roberto if he could recommend an excursion for tomorrow.

The man in question was spruced up in a black tuxedo and waiting for her at the entrance of the restaurant so she didn't have to walk in alone. He greeted her and smiled dashingly, then crooked an elbow for her to take so he could escort her in.

The room had morphed back into a restaurant and was softly lit, while the white linen tablecloths were set with silver cutlery and slim vases of artfully arranged flowers. Tanned waiters with freshly shaved jawlines and slicked back hair, swanned around holding trays, pouring drinks and generally being charming to guests. Delicate piano music tinkled in the background. Jane was instantly swept up in the occasion, feeling like a rich socialite, even though she was severely underdressed.

Roberto played the part of a gracious host, holding out her chair for her and summoning a nearby waiter.

'What would you like to drink?' he enquired once she was seated, and the waiter had flicked the linen napkin onto her lap with a flourish. 'We have a nice house Rosé, or a local Pinot Grigio?'

'Perhaps a Prosecco?' ventured Jane.

'Excellent choice! I chose this year's selection myself after a trip to Conegliano Valdobbiadene in Veneto. I'll order a bottle for us.' He nodded to the waiter, who obediently went off at once.

Roberto had steered them to a table right in the middle of the restaurant, so Jane felt slightly conspicuous but tried not to fidget. The drinks arrived, and she took a sip of the cool, crisp fizz of deliciousness.

'E' buono, no?' Roberto cocked his head at her. 'It pairs well with most of the dishes we're serving tonight. Speaking of which

...' He snapped his fingers twice and the same waiter came over, this time bearing dinner menus, which he handed to Roberto.

Jane watched, amused. She'd only ever seen that done in the movies. Roberto owned the hotel, so she guessed he could snap his fingers and order everyone around as much as he liked. He gave her a menu that was entirely in Italian.

'Some of our dishes sound strange when literally translated, so let me know if anything is unclear and I will explain.'

Jane nodded, thinking that it was all pretty unclear, but at least she recognised the words for "chicken" and "bread". Roberto pointed out several things she may like to try, each a 'speciality of the region' and in the end she just asked him to choose for her as she was getting hungry, and it was taking a while. How bad or weird could it be? she thought.

Luckily, he chose the most innocuous things on the menu. Some tooth-cracking bruschetta topped with olive oil, tomato and basil to start; then something that sounded fancy but turned out to be spaghetti bolognese, accompanied by a green mixed salad. She sighed in relief. A whole grilled baby octopus might not have gone down well, even if it had been cooked by a Michelin-star chef.

Jane did her best with the bruschetta, but even though the oil had softened it, she still wasn't overly fond of hard bread. So, by the time her main arrived, she was starving. Roberto offered her one of his oysters, but she politely declined. She'd never been partial to them, and privately likened it to swallowing a giant slug.

'We find our British guests to be conservative when it comes to Italian food, which is why we've added some familiar dishes to the menu. Germans are much more likely to try something different.'

'Ah,' said Jane, taking another sip of Prosecco. 'Well, I do love a good spag bol and this one is delicious.' To be honest, it could've been dire and she still would've eaten it.

'How is ... er ... yours?'

Roberto had ordered the Fisherman's Risotto, which had numerous pink prawns still in their shells, complete with black beady eyes and spindly legs, gently steaming atop a bed of wild rice. Roberto was attacking them with gusto, using a small tool to crack open the shells and scoop out the delicate innards with his fingers. It was turning her stomach a little, so she tried to ignore it. After finishing her meal, which she had thoroughly enjoyed, even with Roberto noisily sucking on shells, she dabbed at her mouth with her napkin.

'Can I offer you more Prosecco?' asked Roberto.

'Si, please.' He poured more of the bubbling gold liquid into her glass.

He topped up his own and took a long sip. Then without warning he started to study Jane intently.

'Do I have sauce on my face?' she asked, grabbing the edge of the napkin.

'No, no, your face is bella, perfetta. In fact, I would very much like to see it much closer, later on this evening.'

'Um, sorry. I don't understand.'

'I think you understand me perfectly, Jane. I am inviting myself to spend time in your suite after dinner.'

Whoa, ok, seriously? Jane looked down, away from his penetrating gaze, and into the beady eyes of dead crustaceans staring at her from his plate. Her recently eaten bolognese churned alarmingly in her stomach. Roberto seemed to be waiting for a reply. She opened her mouth, but no sound came out.

Finally, she choked out a quiet 'No, grazie.'

'Scusa?'

She cleared her throat and sat up straighter. 'No, grazie,' she said, louder this time.

'Perche no?' he asked, a querulous look on his face like he wasn't used to hearing such a response.

'I don't want that,' she said, thinking honesty was probably the best policy in this situation. She could make something up but honestly couldn't be bothered.

'Come now, Jane. You are young. I am sure you have ... desires.'

'No, Roberto, I don't. You have a beautiful wife waiting for you at home. Just go and spend time with her.'

Roberto arched an eyebrow. 'Francesca is well aware that I like to have an ... open relationship. I have told her she is welcome to do the same if she sees someone she would like.'

Jane was silent thinking, ugh, you creepy pervert.

'Maybe think about it over dessert? We have some wonderful chocolate bon bons this evening,' said Roberto, starting to look around for the waiter.

You can stick your bon bons where the sun don't shine, she thought. Feeling very weary all of a sudden, she removed her napkin from off her lap, folded it and carefully placed it on the table. Then she drained the last of her Prosecco, and stood up unsteadily. All she wanted to do now was go to her room, preferably without this man, who was old enough to be her father, following her up in the lift.

'Thank you for dinner. Goodnight, Roberto.'

'But it's early! I will order you a coffee liqueur.'

'No, Roberto! Didn't you hear me? I said, good night. Or perhaps you'll understand "buenas noches" better since it's closer to your own bloody language!'

Guests were looking over at them and whispering but she didn't care. Avoiding Roberto's glare, Jane picked up her key card and left, trying not to wobble on her high-heeled sandals as she walked across the restaurant. She felt hot and clammy, like she had a fever. He'd probably had the waiter drug the Prosecco or something. She knew she was being paranoid but seriously did think he had. Ugh, and double ugh!

Back in her room, she did regret the tone she'd used with him but did he honestly think she'd consider sleeping with him? And what about Francesca? She sat on the bed and took off her sandals; her feet ached. Her head ached.

Checking her phone, she saw there still wasn't a reply from Natalie. But there was a brief email from Gemma.

Hi Jane, just checking in to see how things are going at the hotel—is it as posh as it looks in the photos? No rush, but do you think you'll be able to finish the article by the end of the week? Drop me a line when you get a minute. Cheers, Gemma.

Wow, Gemma dodged a bullet, thought Jane, or maybe he wouldn't have tried it on with her. She got up and double locked the door just in case Roberto had a master key. Should she say something to Gemma? Her instincts said no in case Gemma thought she'd done something to provoke him, like wear a short skirt. Jane snorted and went into the bathroom to take off her makeup. She couldn't believe she was reverting to the age-old victim stance that women always took in these situations. Why couldn't she just say to Gemma, he did this, he was the one who was inappropriate? Why was it somehow her fault?

Kistella would've handled it differently, she thought, taking off her dress and kicking it out of the bathroom. She'd probably just sleep with him, then blackmail him to buy her diamond jewellery for not telling Francesca.

Chapter 15: The Sunflower Hostel

The next morning, after a good night's sleep, Jane felt better, but she still had an aura of unease. Ironically, this had been what she was trying to avoid in the first place by smuggling Natalie into her room, but it had sniffed her out anyway. She rolled over onto her back and stretched. Maybe some yoga on the terrace would help her unwind. Then she'd email Gemma and tell her ... what, exactly?

Everything's fine here in four-star land. I smuggled a drunken woman I met on the train into the hotel without being caught. She subsequently cleaned out the minibar and stole my dress and shoes, but it could have been worse! Oh, and Roberto is a lothario who tried to sleep with me behind his wife's back, but I escaped his clutches. Phew! Hope you have a good time in the US.

Another worry was James. She'd emailed him last night before she went to bed to find out if he'd booked a hotel for Barcelona, and just to see how he was in general. He'd replied tersely, saying he hadn't booked anything, he'd been busy working, and that the

Haymarket hotel was shite and several other negative-sounding things. She'd replied somewhat testily that if he was sure he was coming no matter what, then she was happy to book somewhere. She hadn't heard back and there was no reply this morning either.

It wasn't like him to be cold and unresponsive, so she figured he was probably stressed. Waiting to find out if he was going to have a kid with someone he didn't particularly like, or trust, was obviously testing the limits of his patience. Jane wasn't sure how things would pan out if the kid was his. She liked him a lot but didn't want to be an emotional crutch or get involved to the point where she became a pseudo stepmother.

How had her life become so complicated so quickly? She was barely a week into her trip, and things weren't going to plan at all. Jane had thought she and James would travel around for a few months, sightsee, and she'd try to pick up a few online jobs to prop up her savings, which wouldn't last forever, even though they were staying in budget accommodation. Getting this writing gig straight off the bat from Gemma had been a stroke of luck, and she could see it opening doors for her. But the shiny glow of the four-star hotel had dimmed since last night. She'd realised Roberto's initial attentiveness hadn't been simply because he was a good host. It had been part of a larger plan to seal the deal, so to speak, at dinner. The scowling look Francesca had given him when she'd left to get the tea flashed into her mind. She knew exactly what he was like, and was powerless to do anything about it. No wonder she'd been so keen to stick around in his office.

The phone on the nightstand let out a chirrup and jolted Jane out of her thoughts. She stretched out an arm for the receiver and said 'Hello?'

'Buon giorno, Jane. It's Francesca.'

Speak of the devil, thought Jane, immediately sitting upright. 'Ciao, Francesca, how are you?'

'Bene, grazie. Jane, Roberto has just asked me to ring you to say he wants to see you in his office for a chat this morning, first thing. It's nearly 8:30 now, so shall we say nine?'

'Oh, ok. Do you know what Roberto wants at all?' she asked warily.

'No, but it may be to arrange an activity,' came Francesca's reply over the line. 'He was talking the other day about a wine tasting tour that you might be able to join.'

'Oh,' said Jane, relaxing slightly. 'Yes, wine tasting. He did mention some local wineries last night.'

'Si, we have a few that we partner with for guest tasting tours,' Francesca said breezily. 'I must go now, Jane, but I'll see you later, ciao!'

'Ciao,' echoed Jane and replaced the receiver with a clatter. Roberto hadn't dropped any hints of a wine tasting tour at dinner, but maybe he'd forgotten all about last night and it was just business as usual?

She got out of bed and rummaged around in her bag for something to wear but everything was so creased. Sighing, she got out the iron and ironing board and quickly ironed a conservative grey wraparound top and her good pair of tailored black pants, and her black flats. She just had time to put her hair in a severe bun as it was getting on for ten to nine. Very nun-like, she thought soberly, surveying her appearance in the bathroom mirror.

Downstairs, Francesca was talking with a guest at reception but gave her nod and waved a hand towards the hallway to Roberto's office. Jane headed there with a knot in her stomach. When she reached the door, she imitated Francesca and gave a smart tap and waited for his 'vieni!' before entering. Roberto was on the phone again, but he pointed abruptly to the chair in front of the desk, so she sat down. He didn't seem to be in a hurry to get off like he had been when she'd arrived.

Eventually he rang off and swivelled in his chair to face her.

'Good morning, Jane. I trust you slept well,' he said with a smile that didn't quite reach his eyes.

She nodded, scanning his face for any hidden meaning in that statement but failed to find any.

'Excellent. Well, I have some bad news unfortunately. I've just had a large group booking come in this morning and we'll need your room to accommodate some of their party.'

'Oh, I see,' said Jane carefully, and she did see with crystal clarity. This was the price she was now going to pay for her rejection of him.

'Everyone is arriving this afternoon so you'll need to vacate by ten so we can clean and prepare the room. I know we agreed that you would stay until Saturday, but I hope you understand that it is out of our control?'

'Yes, of course,' replied Jane, doing her best to sound offhand. The bastard, she thought, now I really am going to have to stay in the hostel.

'Francesca tells me she's given you all the information, and you should have a good feel for what we offer by now, no?'

'Yes,' said Jane, trying to sound upbeat. 'She's been very helpful.'

'Excellent. Well, if you stop by the desk on the way out, Francesca will give you a small token to make up for the inconvenience. I'll call her now and let her know. Arrivederci Jane.'

And with that he picked up the phone and launched into a rapid stream of Italian with his wife. Jane sat there for a minute at a loss for words. She hadn't seen this coming but really, she was an idiot not to have. It wasn't hard to figure out why he'd sent her packing. He had a bruised ego, plus he didn't want her around in case she told Francesca, even though he'd said he was into an "open relationship". Francesca could probably be quite scary if she wanted to be. Jane certainly wouldn't want to get on the wrong side of her.

There wasn't much time to think about anything. She just went back to her room and haphazardly packed her bags, then took one last glance at the sun-drenched terrace with its accompanying loungers. It was easier this way, she consoled herself. There were only two more nights here anyway, and then it would've been even harder to leave. When she appeared at the front desk, ready to check out, she'd already ordered a taxi and the hostel, from her brief look online, seemed to have vacancies, so she thought she'd just turn up and try her luck.

Francesca was genuinely concerned. 'It's bad that we're throwing you out like this.'

'Don't worry, Francesca, it's all right. I'll get a room in town.' A windowless room with snoring sheilas, oh joy.

'Well, if you're sure.'

'It's perfectly fine, and I'll finish the article either today or tomorrow and send it to Gemma. She'll let you know when it's online.'

'Of course! And wait, please, before you go …'

Francesca opened the cash box drawer in the desk and pulled out a generous handful of euros in various notes and handed the cash to her. Jane pocketed it hastily, feeling like a call girl.

'Grazie, Francesca, I'll wait outside for my taxi. It's been lovely to meet you and thank you for everything.'

'Il piacere è tutto mio! I look forward to reading the article. We will stay in touch, yes?'

Jane said nothing. Taking her silence for acquiescence, Francesca whisked around from behind the desk and bent down to give her a kiss on each cheek in farewell. She really was a lovely girl, Jane thought; Roberto was an arse.

Dejectedly she stood outside the hotel with her luggage in a sorry heap. Finally, a white taxi showed up and slowed to a stop. A thickset man wearing a beaten leather jacket got out and helped her put her bags in the boot. He scrutinised her and she suddenly realised he was the driver who had dropped Natalie off the other night. The engine gunner. He must have dibs on this route; either that, or there was only one taxi in town. She kept her head down and slunk into the back seat. On the way to the hostel, she could see him watching her in the rear-view mirror, like he thought she was going to do a runner too. He pulled up outside the hostel and told her it was ten euros. Reaching into her purse she extracted a twenty euro note and handed it to him, saying 'Keep the change'. She hoped karma would be appeased. Now it was time to face Natalie, if she was even still here.

The Sunflower Hostel was inconspicuous in appearance. If it weren't for a small tile next to the door inscribed with the hostel's name, there was no other indication it was indeed one. Set right on the street front, it looked like a residential stone-block building, though it did have a faded yellow façade, in keeping with the sunflower theme. Jane pushed open the entrance door, which led into a reception room. The sunflower motif was more evident in here, she noted, due to the large poster of Tuscan sunflowers tacked to the wall. A wooden church pew against the lefthand wall also had several sunflower embroidered cushions propped up along its length.

A woman, who Jane took to be the hostel owner, was arranging pamphlets in a display stand. She looked up when Jane walked in. 'Ciao, I'm Bridget,' she said pleasantly. 'How can I help?'

Bridget was dressed in an interesting outfit of hot-pink tights, Birkenstocks, and a loose-fitting green T-shirt. Her curly brown hair was tied up in an orange scarf. The whole eclectic ensemble gave the impression she'd just come out of a meditation or yoga session, which would explain her chilled-out vibe, Jane thought.

'Uh, hi, I'm Jane. I don't have a booking I'm afraid. I'm just taking a chance you have a bed for a couple of nights.'

Bridget clacked over behind the desk and clicked the computer mouse to bring her screen to life.

'Well, you're in luck. We had a group check out early this morning, and the cleaner has already gone through their room.' Probably the same group that's checking into the Bella Vista, Jane thought snippily. 'So, I can put you in either a four-bed female dorm now, or there's a bed free in a mixed dorm later today. Which would you prefer?'

'Oh, definitely the four-bed, thanks,' said Jane, hoping it did actually have a window.

'You might have it all to yourself. I don't have anyone new checking in until tomorrow. Unless we get another random walk-in.'

She smiled at her amiably and Jane didn't take offence. Bridget checked her in, gave her a key card and a towel, then extracted various pieces of bedding from the locked cupboard behind the desk.

'You don't have anyone staying here called Natalie, do you, or Nat?' asked Jane casually.

Bridget hmm'd and put the bedding on the desk to check her computer. 'Natalie, that does sound familiar …' She tapped the screen with her finger. 'Yes, here she is. Natalie Janssen. I remember now, she was in a female dorm, but then she changed to a private room with twin beds. Australian. Is she a friend of yours?'

'You could say that,' said Jane. 'We're mainly online pen pals. She told me she was staying here, and how much she was enjoying it, so I decided to surprise her since I was in the area.'

'Oh, lovely,' said Bridget. 'Online relationships are necessary, of course, in this day and age, but I think it's so much nicer to meet in person. I'm sure Natalie will be glad to put a face to the name, finally.'

'Yes, I'm sure she'll be surprised,' said Jane, taking the bedding and key card Bridget handed her.

'You're in room seven; just choose whichever bed you like. Breakfast is from seven to nine and you can pay me now or when you leave, I don't mind. It's sixty euros for two nights.'

'I can pay you now.' Jane delved into her purse and grabbed a handful of Francesca's notes.

'Gosh, ok, lovely, thank you,' said Bridget, her face brightening as Jane handed over the cash. 'Well, enjoy your stay, Jane. We have a couple of bikes for guest use. You'll find them out the back of the courtyard in the laundry. There's a side gate you can go through. Just make sure to lock the bike if you leave it unattended. Perhaps you and Natalie might like to go for a ride along the lake shore? There's a lovely cycle path that goes right by the Bella Vista Hotel.'

'Yes, we might,' said Jane, thinking that biking in the other direction might be wiser. 'I'll mention it to her.'

Bridget gave her directions to her room, and she followed a narrow corridor that eventually opened out into an open-air courtyard planted with a few trees and raised flowerbeds, interspersed with chairs and tables. A couple of guests were sitting there with their laptops. A green door off the courtyard led to yet another corridor and a flight of concrete stairs, of which she had to climb two levels, lugging her bag. By the time she'd reached the door to room seven, Jane felt she'd had a thorough workout.

Upon entering, she saw the room had two single beds on the ground floor and two bunk beds directly above them at right angles. There was a small access ladder to climb up. The whole set-up looked precarious, and she was glad she had first dibs on the beds.

Dumping the bedding—sheet, pillowcase, duvet cover—on the bed nearest the window, she gazed out at the view beyond. In the immediate foreground there was a collection of square beige apartment buildings. Behind them, somewhat in the distance, rose the outline of a green scrubby hill with houses set into its base. There was no view of the lake from this direction. Neither, she realised, was there a bathroom. Bridget had failed to mention that.

She assumed there must be a shared one in the hallway.

It wasn't a junior suite, but she was grateful that at least she had the room to herself and there was a window letting in copious amounts of fresh air. God knows where Natalie had stayed that first night—somewhere in the basement, perhaps? She shook out the well-worn, cream cotton sheet and put it on the bed, tucking in the corners. Then she inserted the duvet and pillow into their respective faded blue covers and arranged everything neatly.

After she'd checked the Wi-Fi code worked, and stowed her bag in the locker, her stomach was letting her know it was time for lunch since she'd missed out on breakfast. Jane decided to go for a walk to find some food and come back and finish the hotel's article and get it off her plate. Then she could email Gemma and tell her the job was done and that was that. No detailed explanations of drunken women and lotharios needed.

Chapter 16: The Plan

Half an hour later, Jane was seated in the courtyard with her laptop, having just devoured a freshly grilled prosciutto and cheese panini from a nearby cafe. She was wiping her hands on a paper napkin and opening a bottle of frizzante mineral water when a familiar figure walked in, glanced over at her, and then did a double take.

Before she could scarper, Jane lifted a hand in greeting and Natalie had no choice but to walk slowly over. For her part, Jane was surprised to see that she'd bleached her hair. It was such a drastic change that the first words out of her mouth were 'You've dyed your hair!' and immediately regretted it when Natalie frowned.

'Nice to see you too, Jane,' she said, tight-lipped. 'What are you doing here?' Natalie sat down in the other chair and crossed her arms defensively.

The bleached-blonde hair didn't suit her, noted Jane somewhat cattily. It drained the colour from her tan and made her look ill. The white T-shirt paired with denim shorts wasn't helping things.

Jane took a sip of her water. 'Oh, yes, I'm staying here for a few nights.'

Natalie looked surprised. 'What about the hotel?' she asked.

'Things didn't go as planned and I had to leave, unfortunately.'

'Stink one. Hey, mate, I did mean to text you back, I just got busy. You know how it is.'

Jane nodded.

Just then, a guy, who also had bleached-blond hair but arranged in long dreadlocks, came in carrying a plastic shopping bag. Spotting them, he wandered over, and Natalie sat up straighter.

'Jane, this is Wazza. Wazza—Jane,' said Natalie as he reached the table. 'We've been hanging out together.' She shifted uncomfortably in her seat.

'G'day, mate. How's it going?' Wazza had an even stronger Australian accent than Natalie, along with tanned skin and rippling biceps. With his rainbow-coloured tank top sporting a Billabong logo and torn jean shorts, he looked like he'd be more at home surfing in Bondi than hobnobbing with the well-heeled in Lake Como.

He reached into the bag and handed Natalie a magenta bra and knickers with the tags still on. 'I saw you checking these out in town and reckoned I'd get them for you,' he said, pleased with himself.

Natalie's face went the colour of the underwear and she grabbed the items with a hurried 'Ta, mate,' and tucked them out of sight into her canvas shoulder bag.

Jane watched the little scene, amused. Natalie didn't waste much time. Now she had this poor schmuck running around after her.

'Did you find a better room to stay in, Nat?' she asked nonchalantly, pretending to look at her laptop.

'Uh, yeah, I'm staying in a twin. That other room sucked.' Natalie shuddered. 'Anyway'—she stood up abruptly, deciding the conversation was over—'we've got to go. Wazza wants to video chat some friends back home.'

She grabbed his arm and tugged him towards the door leading to the stairwell. 'We'll catch you later, Jane. Perhaps do a drink and pizza before you leave ...'

Wazza's voice drifted back to her as they walked away 'Huh? Did I say that?' and then the soft 'Shush!' of Natalie quashing his legitimate confusion.

Jane sat back in her chair and rubbed the back of her neck which had suddenly tensed up. She'd played that all wrong. Rather than waiting for Natalie to confess to taking her stuff and apologising, which she naively thought she'd do, she should've just questioned her openly. Wazza turning up had thrown her, and the whole underwear thing.

It was weird he'd had a plastic shopping bag, like the kind you'd get at a supermarket, but not a labelled lingerie bag. Surely he hadn't just lifted the stuff? But the more she churned it over in her mind, and then paired it with Natalie's reaction, she realised it was pretty likely that Wazza had indeed shoplifted lingerie for his new girlfriend. If the two of them were peas in a pod when it came to nicking things that weren't theirs, that made it all the more difficult for her. She decided to just concentrate on the Bella Vista article for now and worry about it later.

The rest of the afternoon passed uneventfully. Jane finished the article and sent Gemma an email saying that the hotel was wonderful (even better than the photos), Roberto was a gracious host and she was having a thoroughly excellent time. Lies, lies, lies. But at least two loose ends were now tied up.

The trailing thread of Natalie was proving more difficult to wind up and break off. While she'd been working on the article, she'd come up with a rough plan to get her dress and shoes back. It wasn't perfect, but it avoided actual confrontation and vehement denial on Natalie's part, both of which Jane didn't really want to deal with.

She wished she could just drop it, but it was an expensive dress and her favourite shoes. Plus, it was the *principle* of the thing. Also, she tended to be like a dog with a bone when someone did the dirty on her. Her mind went into overdrive and started hatching plots to get justice. Being the daughter of two lawyers, she figured it was probably in her DNA.

The first part of her plan involved finding out which room Natalie was in. To do that, she needed to carry on the facade about them being pen pals and ask Bridget. Jane couldn't see any other way around it unless she told Bridget what had happened. But then that really dragged Natalie's name through the mud, marking her as a drunk and a thief, and she didn't want to do that to her, even though she kind of deserved it. So lie she must.

Bridget was in reception, tapping on the computer keyboard, when Jane walked in. She looked up mid-tap and smiled in recognition, and Jane instantly felt guilty but she plastered on a smile.

'Hi, Bridget! I was wondering if I could ask you a favour?'

'Of course, Jane, how can I help?'

'Oh, great. Well, I haven't managed to make contact with Natalie yet and since I'm leaving on Saturday, it would be awesome to see her before I do. Are you able to tell me which room she's in, so I can put a note under her door?'

Bridget nodded and instantly started tapping again, studying the computer screen.

'That shouldn't be a problem. We don't normally give out other guests' room details but since you're a friend it would be a shame to miss each other because of a silly rule.'

She wrote something on a small pad with a pencil and handed it to Jane and whispered furtively, 'Destroy this note once you've read it.'

'Uh, ok.'

'I'm joking.'

Jane laughed. 'Right! Well, I will anyway, to be on the safe side. I wouldn't want you to get in trouble.'

'I hope you get to make contact. Haven't you got her mobile number?'

'Um, no, unfortunately. We just email usually. She knows I'm in Italy but I didn't tell her I was coming up north. When she said how beautiful it was and that she was staying here I thought it would be nice to, er …' Jane trailed off, feeling like the story was starting to sound convoluted. But Bridget didn't seem to notice.

'How lovely. Yes, the autumn foliage around the lakeside is just gorgeous. Most tourists come in summer, but I personally think this is the nicest season. Did you manage to find the bikes all right?'

'I haven't had a chance as I've been working but I'll go and do that now. Thank you for the room number.' She put the paper in her pocket.

'Oh dear, nothing too taxing, I hope?'

'Just some freelance work, nothing too strenuous …'

'Lovely. For a business here in Como?'

'Ah, yes, but I've finished now.' Jane forced a smile. She really had to get out of here, as she could sense that Bridget was gearing up to twenty questions about who she was working for, and she really didn't want her to ask outright if it was the Bella Vista.

'Well, anyway. I'll go and check out the bikes. Thanks again, Bridget.' She patted her pocket with the piece of paper and edged towards the hallway. Bridget got the hint but didn't seem to be offended.

'My pleasure, Jane. Enjoy the rest of your day.'

Well, that was simple, thought Jane, walking back to her room. She checked the piece of paper. Bridget had written 'number three but you didn't hear it from me' which made her smile. That meant Natalie was on the floor beneath her. Technically she could go and knock on her door right this second and demand her stuff back. But she had a hunch Natalie would simply shrug and close the door in her face. And if Wazza was there, he'd take Natalie's side. No, she had to be smarter about it.

The next day dawned fine and clear again. It was as if bad weather didn't exist in Como, Jane thought, sitting on her bed and dabbling her feet in the pool of morning sunshine on the floor. She wondered what James was up to and how he was feeling. There still hadn't been a reply to her email and her anxiety was starting to mount. Was he even going to come to Barcelona? Perhaps he'd completely gone off the whole idea? If he found out the baby was his, she couldn't imagine him wanting to do three months of carefree travel. It just didn't compute.

Luckily, she had other things to keep her mind off it, namely completing her first official freelance article and having it published on Gemma's site, which was exciting. Gemma had sent her a brief email saying that apart from a few edits to check for future reference, the article was great. It made up for all the other shite that was going on.

Jane had a few hours to kill before she could set up the next part of her plan, so decided to go for a cycle as Bridget suggested.

She checked out some bike maps online and discovered that the best route was up to Laglio on the western shore. Unfortunately, this went right past Bella Vista, but she figured if she wore a hat and sunglasses, kept her head down and pedalled fast, she wouldn't be recognised by Roberto or Francesca. And if she was, well, she had done nothing wrong.

She grabbed a ten euro note to buy something to eat and tucked it into her shorts pocket, along with her phone. Breakfast was included in the price of the hostel, but she didn't want to run the risk of bumping into Natalie and Wazza.

Remembering Bridget had said the bicycles were housed in the laundry, she headed down the stairs and into the courtyard. There was no one else about. She could hear the clinking of cutlery and chatter coming from the breakfast room, so she assumed anyone who was awake was in there.

The laundry room wasn't too hard to find, thanks to the big white L someone had painted on one of the side doors. Inside, two bikes with baskets were leaning up against the wall. Jane chose one and wheeled it out of the room. At the back of the courtyard, she spied a small black wrought iron gate laced with spiderwebs. Pushing it open, she found herself in an overgrown garden, with thigh-high weeds, a vegetable patch gone to seed, apple trees devoid of fruit and an upside-down wheelbarrow. She steered the bike along the path, trying to avoid green snaking tendrils.

Pity, she thought. With some care and attention, the garden could be transformed into an extra hangout space for the hostel.

You could string up a hammock, put in a water feature and decorate with some solar fairy lights. However, as soon as she found the other small gate that led out onto the road, she forgot all about tending the garden in the pleasure of being outside and riding along the street.

She knew from Google Maps there was a large Carrefour supermarket on the corner, across the road from a rectangular park, so she rode for a while until she saw the red-and-white signage.

Outside, she parked her bike in the metal grille, locked it and went in. The supermarket smelt of sour milk, which she took to be from the deli counter stacked high with cheeses. Mum would love this, she thought. After buying a couple of cream-filled pastries (one with custard, one with chocolate), some muesli bars, a bottle of water and some apples, she took her plastic bag out to the bike and placed it in the basket. Continuing on down to the lakefront, she rode alongside the park until she came to an imposing concrete tower with flags flying from the top.

Words had been chiselled into the front of it in Italian, and she assumed by the particular dates underneath that it was a WWI memorial. Continuing on with a stadium on her left, eventually she came out onto a small marina, with bobbing boats and a hangar that housed seaplanes. One was just being pulled out on a wooden trailer by a small orange tractor, so she stopped to watch and munched on the custard cream croissant.

Nearby, a group of Italian men in blue overalls, whom she

gathered were aircraft mechanics, were also watching the proceedings. They called out to her and pointed at the plane, then at her, and made flying motions with their arms. Laughing, she shook her head and pointed at the bike.

From there it was just a matter of following the path that hugged the lakeshore and the round blue cycleway sign. She realised that this was the road she'd been on with the taxi, initially to the hotel and then yesterday to the hostel. Everything seemed very different from the seat of a bike.

As she was cycling along, her mobile started vibrating in her shorts pocket, so she pulled over to check who was calling. James. She swiped to answer with a shaking hand. He must've found out the results of the paternity test.

'Hello' she said warily. She just wanted to know one way or the other but hoped to God the baby wasn't his.

'Ciao!' To her relief he sounded upbeat, not stressed out like his email had been.

'Ciao, yourself, how's Edinburgh?'

'Cold and dreich.'

Jane laughed. 'I probably shouldn't tell you I'm in shorts and a T-shirt right now.'

'I'm jealous. What's the temperature?'

'I think it's around sixteen or seventeen degrees.'

'You sound like you're outside.'

'Yeah, I'm cycling up the side of Lake Como,' she said, trying to talk with one hand and keep the bike from toppling over with the other.

'Och, now I'm really jealous. How's the hotel?' he asked.

'Oh—it was good. But I'm at a hostel now.'

'Eh? I thought you were at the hotel until Saturday?'

'It's a long story, but it's all ok. Just a slight hiccup,' she said.

'Well, you can tell me about it tomorrow.'

Her heart gave a leap. 'So, you got the results?'

'Aye, I got the results.'

'And?'

'It came back as 97.77777%.'

'What does that even mean?' she asked, confused. 'Is it yours or not?'

'It means it's inconclusive, so it's not definite that it's mine. It needs to be at least 99% to be definite.'

Jane let out a deep breath. 'Wow, ok. How do you feel?'

'Relieved, I guess. It really would've mucked things up.'

With me? she thought. Or just in general?

'Well, that's great news, then. So, you're coming to Barcelona?'

'Aye, I was just ringing to tell you. I booked my flight and a hotel. I'll email you the details.'

A burst of happiness flooded through her. She closed her eyes and tilted her face towards the sun and mouthed 'thank you'.

After she hung up from James, Jane hopped back on her bike and continued riding. She felt as free as a bird, now that the hideous paternity test was out of the way. What a bloody thing to have to go through. She felt sorry for herself, and sorry for James, and slightly sorry for Kistella, who *was* still pregnant, after all. But it meant that James was off the hook! Kistella couldn't pin it on him or extort money out of him for a single nappy. Even as she got closer to the Bella Vista, her good mood stuck. Eventually, she had to ride right past it. It was strange viewing the hotel from this angle rather than looking down from her balcony.

She couldn't resist sneaking a peek up at the second floor to check it out. All she could see from below was the top of a straw sunhat and the soles of a pair of bare feet. Someone was obviously making good use of the private terrace. She shrugged and looked away. It didn't matter. One more night and she would've been out of there, anyway. James was coming to Barcelona tomorrow; that's all she cared about.

Once she was well past the hotel, Jane pulled over to the side and leaned against the railing, looking out over the lake. It was time to text Natalie and ask her if she wanted to go out for a drink tonight, Jane's shout, of course. With free drinks on the cards, Natalie's immediate reply was: *Yeah, what time, mate?*

Chapter 17: Plans That Go Awry

That evening, Jane found herself leaning against a bar and ordering a round of Jägermeister shots. She'd sussed out a nearby enoteca that was open until late for them to have a drink. It seemed to be a popular local hangout with quite a few couples and groups chatting merrily in Italian while drinking aperitifs. They were lucky to find a free table.

Natalie was busy messaging someone on her phone, probably Wazza. The girl could drink. Which was why Jane was trying to hurry up the process with something more potent. They'd been there for an hour and three wines had been downed like water, so when she suggested doing some shots Natalie had agreed enthusiastically.

Jane was stone cold sober, sort of. She'd had a glass of wine, but then surreptitiously ordered grape juice for the next couple of rounds. She had to keep a clear head; there was no point doing this if both of them ended up sozzled.

She paid the bartender and carried the shots over to the table carefully. 'Cheers, mate,' said Natalie, and they clinked glasses. She chucked it back, and Jane did the same, shuddering as a rush of aniseed burned the back of her throat.

'Whoa!' exclaimed Natalie, shaking her head vigorously, her hair spraying out in all directions like bleached rat tails. 'That hit the spot!'

'I'll finish my glass of wine and get another round soon,' Jane said breezily.

Natalie looked surprised but pleased. 'Gee, thanks, doll. I didn't realise you were such a big drinker. You seemed kinda square at the hotel, but I guess I was wrong.'

'Oh, really?' Jane took a big gulp of grape juice to wash away the aniseed taste.

'Yeah, I said to Wazza, "That girl needs to chillax."'

'What did he say?' asked Jane, thinking this should be interesting.

'Oh, er, I really can't remember.' Natalie picked up her empty shot glass and upended it into her mouth to get at the dregs.

'Go on, I don't mind.'

Natalie paused. 'He said he wouldn't go there as his donger might get frostbite.'

Jane smiled thinly and didn't say anything. He should be so lucky, she thought, starting to kindle a dislike for him.

'What's Wazza short for, anyway? Surely it's not his real name?'

'Nah, it's Warren, but he suits Wazza better, I reckon.'

'Very fitting.' Jane finished her grape juice in a single gulp. 'Another round of shots?'

'Geez Louise, you won lotto or something?'

'I got paid some cash by the hotel. It's burning a hole in my purse.' Which was true; she'd started thinking of it as "Roberto's dirty money".

'What happened there, anyway?'

'Oh, there was a large group booking, and they needed my room,' said Jane, studying her fingernails.

'Bullshit. Did something happen with the owner? Perhaps his wife?'

'What makes you say that?' asked Jane, surprised.

Natalie shrugged. 'It's a logical explanation.'

Jane sighed. 'The owner wanted to sleep with me, and I turned him down. So, he kicked me out.'

'There you go,' said Natalie, grinning. 'So why didn't you?'

'Why didn't I what?'

'Sleep with him.'

Jane stared at her. 'Uh, because he was old enough to be my father and he's married!'

'Yeah, but at least you'd still be at the hotel,' Natalie said blithely, as if this was the most important takeaway from the situation.

Jane shook her head, not quite believing her ears. Natalie really was on a different planet. She didn't know what to say except: 'Another round of shots?'

A couple of hours later, to Jane's relief, they made their way back to the hostel. Her head was pounding, but she was still relatively sober, having managed to tip her Jägermeisters into a nearby plant while Natalie was downing hers. The girl in question had finally decided she'd had enough, and Jane was propping her up while they walked along the road, and trying to answer random questions thrown at her, such as 'Should I tell Wazza his feet stink?' and 'Where can I buy Vegemite?'

When they got to the hostel, she shepherded Natalie through the side gate and through the overgrown garden. There was a slight kerfuffle when Natalie tripped and nearly went face-first into a foul-smelling compost heap. But they made it into the courtyard, and Jane helped her up the steps to door number three. Natalie didn't ask how she knew her room number. She just fumbled in her bag for the key card, and they stumbled in together. Letting out a giggle and a yawn at the same time, Natalie dumped her bag on the chair and fell onto one of the twin beds face down. Within seconds, as Jane knew she would because she'd seen it firsthand at the hotel, she was fast asleep.

Even though her purse had been severely depleted, her plan had worked. Jane could hardly believe it. Now all she had to do was find her dress and her shoes and get the hell out of Dodge. She surveyed the room. The lamp on the nightstand had been left on, but the bulb was so dim she could only just make out a large freestanding wardrobe in the corner of the room.

Quickly she went across and opened the door. There were a bunch of clothes hanging up, but she couldn't tell if her dress was among them. Blindly she ran her fingertips over the various materials like she was trying to read braille. She felt something that may have been her dress and pulled it out to check but just then the door clicked open and Wazza came in. Yikes!

Jane shrank back into the corner, but it was too late; he switched on the main overhead light and the room blazed into view, putting her in centre stage left.

Wazza jumped back when he caught sight of her. 'Jane! You scared the bejesus out of me mate—what's that?' He was staring at the black dress dangling like a shroud from her hand.

'It's my dress,' she said, and bent down and scanned the bottom of the wardrobe to find her shoes lying in a jumble of other footwear. She yanked them out by the heels. 'And these are mine too.'

Wazza frowned and looked at Natalie prostrate on the bed, then at Jane holding the dress. His eyes narrowed in suspicion. 'Are you nicking her stuff?'

'It's *my* stuff,' said Jane, emphatically. 'Natalie borrowed it so I'm taking it back.' Wazza didn't look convinced. 'Maybe we should wake her up and ask her,' he said, giving Natalie's foot a prod. 'Why is she blotto?'

Jane was getting impatient. 'Look, trust me. It's my stuff.'

Wazza folded his arms and drew himself up to his full height, which wasn't much taller than her. 'Nah, sorry, mate. It looks fishy. I can't let you leave with them.'

'You're joking,' said Jane, feeling trapped. She eyed the door and wondered if she could push the blond surfer guard dog out of the way and make a run for it.

Unfortunately, even though Wazza wasn't tall, he had some muscle on him. She sighed, knowing she didn't have a choice. She inserted her dress back into the wardrobe on its hanger and put her shoes carefully back into the bottom.

'No hard feelings, mate. I'll talk to Natalie tomorrow.' Wazza moved aside from the door to let her pass. Jane mumbled good night and he shut the door smartly in her face. She stood there for a minute, and even thought about knocking on the door and trying to reason with him. But she remembered the clench of his jaw and the stubborn look in his eye, and doubted he'd change his mind. All that planning and money spent on drinks and she'd ended up being scuppered by bloody Wazza!

Slowly she walked upstairs to her room, and let herself in. It's just a dress and shoes, she told herself firmly. Let it go. She sat on the bed and opened her laptop. James had, as promised, emailed through his flight details and a link to the hotel he'd booked in Barcelona for two nights. She checked his flight arrival time—five in the afternoon—and realised that he was landing a few minutes after she was. That's funny, she thought, we should just meet at the airport then.

She clicked the hotel link and her jaw dropped. The place was five-star, a nineteenth-century mansion fitted out with mod cons and dripping with understated elegance, *and* just a stone's throw from the Sagrada Familia. She checked the room rate and nearly fainted—it cost a bomb! What was he thinking? He'd seriously gone off-piste this time.

It was late and Jane was tired, so she just typed a quick reply saying that she'd see him Saturday afternoon, did he want to meet at the airport, and was he sure he'd sent her the right hotel? She couldn't be bothered using the bathroom down the hall and fell into bed. But, unfortunately, even though she was exhausted, the Jägermeisters and the wine she'd drunk, along with her empty stomach, kept her awake.

It was well after midnight when she fell into a fitful sleep and dreamed she was in the overgrown garden, which was now lush, green and manicured, and sported a splashing fountain. Small birds flitted in and around the trees, which were laden with red apples. She felt at peace and happy. The gate at the end of the garden opened and James came in. He was carrying something in his arms. He smiled at her and bent down so she could see. It was a baby with short, blonde dreadlocks, and a full set of teeth. She watched as it grinned at her in a disarming way. Then it pointed its finger at her and began to scream until its face turned purple.

Jane woke at the crack of dawn feeling ill and dehydrated. It didn't take a genius to figure out the meaning of the dream. The whole thing with Natalie wasn't sitting well with her. She'd manipulated the situation to get her drunk so she could gain access to her room. She'd played the part of a defense lawyer, trying to win a case for the sake of winning. Somewhere along the way she'd lost the plot.

What she should've done (why hadn't she seen it before?), was to ask Natalie politely to her face to give her stuff back. If Natalie had refused or played dumb then she should've walked away, knowing she was in the right, but recognising and accepting the situation for what it was. That would've been the sensible and mature thing to do. Instead, she'd lowered herself to Natalie's level, and she'd been caught out by Wazza doing it. Now it seemed like *she* was a thief, as well as morally suspect for plying her with copious amounts of alcohol.

Jane groaned, the whole thing was getting out of hand. It was time to let it go and just move on. She'd have breakfast and head to Milan on the first train that was going there. Her ticket was for the 11:30am but at this point she didn't really care. She'd try to change the ticket, or buy a new one; either way, she'd rather leave early than remain at the hostel any longer than she had to. Dragging herself out of bed, she fetched her bag from the locker and started packing it again. She was dangerously low on clean clothes. It was probably a good idea to use the free laundry downstairs before she left.

After loading and setting the washing machine to its quickest cycle, Jane headed to the breakfast room. It was empty apart from a shambles of tables and oddly matched chairs. Breakfast consisted of boxed cereals, fruit, UHT milk, boiled eggs, packaged bread squares and a various assortment of jams. There was also a coffee machine.

She made herself a coffee and sat at a table near the door crunching slowly on bread and jam. The caffeine jolted her brain into action and she started to feel more herself again. Then Wazza strolled in. Damn! thought Jane, not the person I want to see right now. Since she was sitting in an alcove to the right of the door, he didn't notice her. Wazza walked over to the breakfast counter, took a cereal bowl and opened a package of cornflakes. When he turned the coffee machine on, Jane slowly got up from the table and edged her way to the door.

She reached the hallway without him knowing she was there. Jane decided it was safer to go back to her room and wait there for her washing to finish. When she got to Natalie's floor, she couldn't help taking a look down the corridor. The door to room three was ajar. Thinking back to the room from last night she realised that, like hers, it didn't have a private bathroom. She padded softly to the door and gently pushed it open to see if Natalie was there. The covers to both beds were tangled but there was no one in the room. Jane released the breath she'd been holding. Should she ... or just leave it? She wavered, agonising. Make a decision, she told herself, now before she comes back!

Fuck it, she thought, it's *my* dress. Her legs moved on their own accord. She marched into the room, went directly to the wardrobe, removed her dress from its hanger, collected her shoes and slipped out the door. Hardly daring to breathe, she reached the stairs and scampered up to her room.

Inside, she folded the dress and inserted it carefully into her bag, and laid the shoes on top, patting them fondly. Then she picked up her bag and pack and left the room, running swiftly down the stairs.

In the laundry room, the washing machine was winding down from the spin. Impatiently she had to wait for it to stop; it seemed to go on forever. When it finally did, it took ages for the light to go out so she could open the door.

Hands shaking, she gathered up her damp washing and shoved it into a spare plastic bag and put it on top of her shoes. Time to go, she thought. Walking down the hallway towards reception she felt like a criminal. Stop being so ridiculous, she told herself, it's your dress! But it had been in Natalie's possession so now, strangely, it didn't feel like hers anymore.

Just before she reached the doorway of the breakfast room, Wazza came strolling out, wiping his mouth with a napkin. Jane swore under her breath, she'd thought he'd be finished by now—he must be a slow eater. As he came towards her, he glanced at her, clocked her luggage and then continued on, his face devoid of emotion. Jane had to laugh. Usually she'd be bothered by that kind of thing, but right now she didn't give a flying fig. She wheeled her bag into reception and was glad to see that Bridget was there, tapping on the computer as usual.

'Ciao,' Jane said airily. 'I'm checking out today. Just dropping off the key card.' She placed the card firmly on the desk.

'Gosh, you're an early bird,' said Bridget, smiling at her. 'I hope you managed to meet up with Natalie, ok?'

'Ah, yes, I did,' said Jane. 'We went out for a drink last night. Unfortunately, I've got a train to catch so I can't stick around to see her before I go.'

'How disappointing,' said Bridget. 'Well, I'll make sure to tell her you said goodbye. She's leaving today too. It was lucky you asked me about her room number when you did.' This spurred Jane into action, thinking that the two of them could come walking into reception at any second. She started backing towards the door.

'Yes, thanks again, Bridget, probably no need to mention that to her though. Just tell her that it's been …'—she faltered, searching for the right word—'... real. Arrivederci!'

Chapter 18: Barcelona Take Two

Jane speed walked to the station, which was just ten-minutes from the hostel. It was nearing eight when she got there, and it was pretty much empty, apart from a woman behind a glass counter. She checked the departure board and was ecstatic to see that a train was leaving for Milan at 8:30am. She'd have a bit of time to kill before her flight. But that was preferable to hanging out at the hostel, where she might bump into the terrible twosome.

With everything that had happened, Jane was half expecting Natalie to come barrelling along at any minute, demanding to know why she'd been rummaging about in her room. Thinking she might try to change her ticket, Jane approached the woman at the ticketing desk, who immediately sprang to attention.

'Buon giorno. Posso aiutarla?'

'Er, buon giorno. Inglese?'

'Non, solo Italiano, mi dispiace.'

Great, thought Jane; this will be fun. She tried out the Spanish version of what she wanted, hoping that 'Cambiar boleto a Milano?' would do the trick.

The woman looked confused. 'Boleto?'

Jane showed her the ticket on her phone and pointed at the

11:30am time. The woman's frown increased. She still wasn't getting it.

Jane pointed at herself and made a motion with her hands like train wheels going round. Then pointed at the board. How the hell did you mime "now"? she wondered. Should she pull on her earlobe for "sounds like" as in charades?

But the woman wasn't frowning anymore. Jane saw her face clear; it was like watching a lightbulb click on above her head.

'Si, si Milano adesso alle otto e mezza. Vuoi cambiare il tuo biglietto?'

That sounded right. 'Yes, I mean, si por favor gracias.' Now she was totally speaking Spanish, but the woman didn't seem to mind. She busily checked her reservation number and tapped the number into her computer. Then printed off a ticket with the new time of 8:30am.

Jane sighed in relief. Spanish combined with hand signals was proving helpful after all. The train duly arrived, and she left Como feeling a lot worse for wear, even though it had been only a few days since she'd met Natalie and innocently exchanged numbers with her. She remembered the expectation of meeting up for a drink and felt remorseful. Why couldn't they just have had a pleasant time? Why did it have to descend into stolen goods and subterfuge? Jane felt the guilt of being directly involved in that herself.

The hotel was another story. She couldn't see any way that she could've avoided being kicked out. Should she have refused to have dinner with Roberto? Pleaded illness? But there was no way she could've known he was going to proposition her like that. Besides, it would've been terribly rude if she'd bailed on dinner. She would've risked offending Francesca, who may have said something to Gemma. The takeaway was that she'd managed to finish the job and stay in Francesca and Gemma's good books; they were the ones who mattered most in the whole sorry affair.

When she reached Milan Central, she didn't hang around and headed straight to the airport. It was too early to check in her luggage so, at a loose end, she sat on the floor leaning up against a window and wrote a review of Hostel Valeria for her blog. When she eventually checked in, she went through Departures and wandered around aimlessly, peering in duty-free shop windows at outfits, handbags and watches she couldn't afford. Did women actually buy two-thousand-euro handbags at the airport, she wondered?

She was starting to feel unhinged and fluttery, like she did before a visit to the dentist or a job interview. The fact that she was meeting up with James at the airport this afternoon probably had something to do with it. He'd sent a text while she was on the train, saying that he'd meet her by the arrivals entrance, and they'd catch a taxi to the hotel. And that yes, the hotel was the right one. It was weird the way he was completely ignoring their plan and booking fancy hotels and using taxis. Had he come into an unexpected inheritance or won Lotto?

Jane decided to do something productive while she waited to take her mind off James. So, she opened her laptop again and started writing an email to her parents, copying in Kath. She hadn't heard from any of them since leaving London, but that wasn't unusual. They weren't the kind of family that were constantly in each other's faces. Weeks could go by without having contact. It had been like that since she'd been at boarding school. When she'd had a problem, she usually figured out a solution herself. She didn't go running to Mummy or Daddy. They wouldn't have been much use even if she'd wanted to talk to them because her parents were always at work. Plus, they were dealing with issues much more important than hers.

Afterwards, living in Edinburgh had made her even more self-sufficient because of the distance. And because she knew they didn't really approve of what she was doing. Unfortunately, now it meant that she couldn't open up to them about the finer details of what went on in her life. But she figured she should send something just to let them know she was still alive.

Consequently, the email they received was the abridged version of events, including her brief time in Barcelona ... which skipped over the fact that James wasn't actually with her. That she'd flown to Milan to do a freelance job for a hotel in Lake Como ... but didn't mention that she'd been kicked out by the owner. Natalie, the drunken incident, the hostel and the stolen dress also didn't make the cut. Though she did say she'd been on a lovely bike ride along the lake and met some friendly locals— the sort of thing that they liked to hear.

After writing to her family, she also sent an email to Aimee to find out how she and Rebecca were getting on with their new flatmate. Hopefully not too well, she thought. She did want her room back at some point. Though how she was going to pay for the rent was gnawing at her. Writing gigs that offered a complimentary hotel stay were all well and good, but it wasn't actually money.

She'd considered James's suggestion to do an online marketing course and started researching the ones that would give her a qualification. There was also a popular freelance job platform that she'd signed up for that didn't cost anything to join. It was simply a matter of writing an enticing profile of what you could do, and bidding for jobs you liked the look of along with fifty other people. But she wasn't hired because she had no reviews or experience and she wanted too much money.

Some of the jobs had less than five applicants but there was a reason for that. Usually, they wanted product descriptions of sexy lingerie, articles about male erectile dysfunction or something equally seedy. One company had seemed to deal in cruises but when she asked for more information they said they were an escort agency.

So, she hadn't bothered applying for any more jobs on the

platform after that, figuring she'd wait until she had some articles published on Gemma's site that she could use as writing samples. If she ever heard from her again. There were no guarantees with anything if you were a freelancer; you had to be continuously self-motivated. Maybe James could set up a meeting for her with his content agency friend in Bangkok.

Eventually, after an age of waiting around, her flight was ready to board. It took just over an hour and a half to fly back to Barcelona, but it felt like a lot longer. She was looking forward to seeing James, but she was also nervous as hell. How were things going to pan out now? When she walked out of the arrivals hall after collecting her luggage, it was with some trepidation. The bright sunlight hit her straight in the eyes and she winced, pulling on her sunglasses. She glanced around but couldn't see James. His flight was due in five minutes after hers, so she parked her bag to the side of the main entrance to check her phone. Her hand was sweating so much she could hardly keep hold of it, and when a Scottish voice said, 'Hola' by her left ear she nearly dropped it altogether.

James looked perfectly normal (and sublimely gorgeous as usual), though somewhat weary and rumpled. What had she been expecting? Scowling with a bitter, twisted expression? Instead, he smiled benignly at her as if he hadn't just been on the verge of being an instant daddy. She couldn't believe he was standing in front of her.

'You're here,' she said, staring at him dumbly, and then promptly burst into tears.

'Hey, now,' he said, dumping his backpack on the ground and awkwardly giving her a one-armed hug. 'That's quite a welcome.'

She snuffled into his shoulder, feeling she could really let loose with a barrage of sobs, but with an effort she held herself together. She pulled away from him and wiped her eyes with her sleeve.

He fumbled in his jeans pocket. 'Sorry, I don't have a tissue.'

She gave him a watery smile. 'Welcome to Barcelona.'

'Thanks.' He was staring at her intently and she blushed. 'Are you ok?' he asked.

She dropped her gaze and nodded, feeling shy. He started to say something but stopped.

'What?' she asked.

'Um, shall we get out of here and go to the hotel?'

'Definitely, do you want to catch the train or …'

'Perhaps we should just grab a taxi,' he said, looking around.

'Uh, sure, though I think it costs like forty euros.'

'That's ok, come on.' He'd spotted a taxi sign and strode off in that direction. She had to walk fast to keep up with him.

'Have you got anything posh to wear in that luggage of yours?' he asked when she drew up alongside.

'Why's that?'

'I thought we could get dressed up and go out to dinner.'

Jane had to laugh. Should she take that as a sign that the

Universe was giving her the thumbs up for taking back what was hers?

'I've got the perfect little black dress for that,' she told him. 'Let's do it.'

A few hours later, they were sitting in the hotel's Michelin-star restaurant, poring over the menu. The dishes were outrageously expensive, so they didn't really want to risk ordering something weird and inedible.

'What's Mantequilla de Cabra?' asked James, frowning.

'Your guess is as good as mine,' Jane said. She did a quick Google search. 'Apparently it's goat butter.'

'Ah, and what about Lechon Iberico?'

'It's roasted baby pig!' Jane showed him a photo of a small, crispy piglet spread-eagled on a plate.

James shuddered. 'I'm not a veggie but that just looks so wrong. Do you think they have an English menu?' He looked around for the waiter.

'We'll be ok. We've got Google,' said Jane, nudging his foot under the table. 'Go on, ask me another one.'

'Parpatana andaluza?' he attempted, stumbling over the pronunciation.

'I think it's some kind of steak. Maybe tuna?' She showed him a photo of some squares of seared meat. 'But it looks safe enough.'

Eventually, after much deliberation, they managed to order a couple of dishes that they were confident they could actually eat. James had the seared meat and Jane had some fancy deconstructed paella. She had tried to pry some information out of the waiter with her rudimentary Spanish, but he was older and protested that he didn't speak English.

'They probably have a great old larf out the back when the unsuspecting tourist orders the baby pig,' scoffed James.

'Are you sure you want to eat here? We can always go find a Macca's or something. I think there's one in La Rambla.'

James shook his head 'I'm not taking you to McDonald's when you went to all that effort.' She caught him doing a subtle once-over at the dress.

Jane smiled to herself, hoping that after the rigmarole of getting her bloody dress back, it was finally going to earn its keep. She had to admit she'd scrubbed up ok, though *now* she was without any of her other clothes. Hanging up her damp underwear in the hotel bathroom meant James would see it and she didn't feel comfortable about that. So, she'd sorted something else out earlier on before dinner ...

After a short wait at the airport for a taxi, they'd pulled up outside the hotel and been ushered in by a smartly dressed doorman wearing spotless white gloves. They'd oohed and ahhed over the elegance of the lobby, and James had checked them in. Jane was still none the wiser why they were actually staying here but she wasn't complaining. Then they were pointed in the direction of the lift to take them to the fifth floor and eventually found their room down a maze of hallways and Masonic-pattern carpet.

The room was plush, with highly polished wood fixtures, ornate light fittings, and dark-blue velvet curtains. It had a super king-sized bed, which had been separated into two singles, each graced with at least half a dozen plump white pillows.

Jane tried to hide her disappointment at the twin bed setup by raving about the view out the window. Directly to the left (if you poked your head out), were the soaring unfinished spires of Sagrada Familia glinting in the rapidly diminishing rays of the afternoon sun. What did you expect? she told herself sternly. This was the arrangement!

While James was having a shower, she picked up the guest folder and quickly flicked through it to see what services the hotel offered. Sure enough, laundry was one of them. She dialled "0" on the landline and said she needed some washing done.

'Si, madam, of course. Please bring it down to reception,' was the reply.

There was a large white laundry bag in the wardrobe, so she dumped in everything she'd brought with her (apart from the black dress), including all her underwear, and heaved it down to reception.

The young male staff member she'd spoken to on the phone looked surprised at the amount of washing to be dealt with, but took it in his stride.

'What's the earliest I can get it back?' she asked.

'Sunday afternoon, madam.'

'Is there, er ... an express option?'

'I'm afraid not, madam. That's the quickest we can do.'

It couldn't be helped. She nodded, and he handed over a form for her to read and sign. It was a succinct statement, but all in Spanish.

'What's this?'

'We need your agreement that the appearance of your clothes after being laundered is not our responsibility.'

'Huh?' Was she going to end up with a bunch of rags?

'There may be mixing of black colours with the white colours,' he explained.

'Oh!'

'Si, some guests get upset when they find out their coloured items have been washed with white ones.' He leaned in conspiratorially. 'Once we were even sued.'

'Oh dear ... Americans?' He nodded, pinching his lips together.

'I understand.' She signed the form and watched him lug the bag out the back, wondering what kind of state her clothes were going to come back in.

When Jane returned to the room, James had finished in the shower and was dressed in a long-sleeved blue shirt and tight black Levis. With one hand he was reading something on his phone and leisurely towelling his hair with the other.

She stood in the doorway, drinking in his dark, tousled hair and tall, muscular frame. His shirt was slim fitting and clearly showed the outline of his biceps. Her gaze wandered over his chest and down to his hips where he'd hastily half-tucked his shirt into his jeans and a few of the lower buttons were undone. He moved slightly and she got a glimpse of his smooth, bare stomach … James glanced up at her, and Jane quickly looked away and made as if she just walked into the room.

'Hey, where've you been?'

'Oh, just had to drop off some laundry,' she said, depositing her key card on a wooden side table that had been polished to a high sheen.

'Ah, right. Are you hungry?'

'Starving!'

James chucked his phone on the bed, did up the rest of his buttons on his shirt and tucked it into his jeans. 'I thought we could get dinner in the hotel restaurant. I made a booking for seven, so you might want to get a wriggle on.'

So much for backpacking, she thought, amused, as she collected her dress and makeup bag and headed for the bathroom. Here they were in a five-star hotel and about to have dinner in a two-star Michelin restaurant. The budget seemed to have flown out the window, for tonight at least.

Chapter 19: Little Black Dress

Between bites of steak—it turned out to be tuna, after all—and various cubes of vegetables and dipping sauces, it came out that James was expecting a substantial payment from one of his clients for work he'd done during the last week. He told her how spending six nights in the Haymarket hotel, in a windowless room, had been hell. It was compounded by waiting for the paternity test result, but at least he'd had this particular job to focus on to keep his mind off things. When the paternity test had come through as inconclusive, he'd gone to town on his credit card to treat himself (and Jane, he said) to make up for the stress Kistella had put them through.

'But what about you? It's all been very hush-hush from your end. How was Como?' he asked, glancing at her curiously.

Jane took a sip of her wine, the most expensive bottle of Spanish red on the menu—it was rich and velvety with a slight hint of dark chocolate, and so delicious it had ruined all other red wines for her from now on.

'It was … busy. A lot of interaction with the owners and learning about the hotel,' she said vaguely, hoping he'd be satisfied with that amount of detail. She speared a juicy prawn and bit into the soft, succulent flesh. A hit of roasted garlic invaded her mouth.

'So how come you ended up in a hostel two days early?' James asked pointedly. Jane gave a slight jump as if she'd been caught out in a fib, but remembered she'd mentioned the hostel to him on the phone when she'd been cycling by the lake. She swallowed the rest of the prawn and sighed. There was no other way to say it.

'The hotel owner kicked me out because I wouldn't sleep with him,' she said. It sounded so sordid saying it out loud.

James stared at her. 'You're joking.'

'I'm not.'

'Who the feck does he think he is?!'

Jane was surprised to see a pink flush of annoyance creep up James's neck from under the collar of his blue shirt.

'I guess he's the owner, so he can do what he likes, or try to. I just felt sorry for his wife.' She toyed with her fork.

'His wife! He was married?! This just gets better and better.'

'Yeah, Francesca. She worked at the hotel on the front desk. She was like twenty-five and gorgeous, while he was old enough to be her father.'

James shook his head and reached for his water glass. He took a large gulp and wiped his hand across his mouth. 'So did she ken about all this?'

'No, I think that's why he kicked me out quick smart, so she didn't find out. He said they had an "open" relationship, but she may have missed the memo on that one.'

'I'm sorry.'

'Huh? Why are *you* sorry?' Jane wrinkled her nose, confused.

'That you had to go through that.'

'Ah, it's ok, I'm over it …' She trailed off—her phone was distracting her by flashing and vibrating on the table. Who the hell was calling? She picked it up and checked the screen: Miguel. Yikes! She quickly turned it over without answering it.

'Aren't you going to get that?'

'No, it's no one important.'

Meeting Miguel seemed like it had happened years ago, and to someone else entirely. Her phone stopped vibrating, and she took a sip of wine in relief. But it was short-lived. Her phone was now beeping madly as a series of texts came through. Oh great, she thought—he's texting to arrange the threesome. Not the best timing.

James looked at the phone—then at her. 'It sounds like someone really wants to get hold of you.'

Jane reluctantly checked it. The texts weren't from Miguel, but from Natalie. God, both of them hounding her at once! It was like her sketchy past catching up with her in one fell swoop.

The texts—there were three of them—were long and involved. She skim-read them rapidly. The gist of it was that Natalie had discovered the dress was missing when she packed her bag to leave the hostel. She'd gathered Jane had stolen it when she was in the shower. Wazza had also mentioned seeing her trying to take the dress the previous night and that he suspected she'd boozed her up with that intent. She thought she might have a chat with the local police about Jane's behaviour. Unless she saw fit to give her five hundred euros. If she did, then "Mum's the word, mate." Jane groaned audibly.

'Anything you want to share?'

'Not really.'

'Come on, what's that about?' He nodded at her phone. Jane hesitated, but knew she had to come clean.

'Fine. I've just been blackmailed by an Australian backpacker.'

James raised an eyebrow and said nothing, though his mouth was twitching. He began to methodically mop up the remnants of his meal with a wodge of crusty bread. Jane felt terrible, the illicit dress was suddenly burning on her skin. She was beginning to wish she'd never bought it.

'What are you thinking?' she asked worriedly.

James popped the bread in his mouth, chewed slowly, then washed it down with the last of his wine. 'I'm thinking that we should order another bottle and head back to the room. You've got some explaining to do.'

'Let me get this straight,' said James. He was sitting on one of the beds with three pillows behind him and a glass of duty-free Glenmorangie from Edinburgh Airport in his hand. Jane was in the easy chair at the bottom with her bare feet resting on the edge of the bed, cradling the bottle of red in her lap. She'd just finished giving him the rundown of what happened. The whole thing sounded convoluted even to her own ears, and she'd been there.

'So, this Australian, this Natalie girl, whom you'd just met randomly on the train, shows up drunk at the hotel at an ungodly hour and you smuggle her into your room—because it was the sensible option? Then, the next morning, she steals your dress and shoes from your hotel room, so she didnae arouse suspicion when she's leaving—a black dress and heels being what you wear in the middle of the day to not do that. Anyway, then you get kicked out of the hotel for not sleeping with the owner—what an arse. You book into the same hostel as Natalie, find out her room number from the owner, get her drunk again and try to take back the dress and shoes. But her new boyfriend Wazza—surely that's not his real name?—also Australian, catches you in the room and chucks you out. The next morning you're about to check out but happen to pass by her room. The door is unlocked, and the room is empty so you decide to take the dress and shoes—which are actually yours—then leave the hostel and Como. Several hours later, in Barcelona, you get a text from Natalie demanding a total of five hundred euros so she'll keep quiet about you getting her drunk, breaking into her room, and taking the dress and shoes—*again,* which are actually yours.'

Jane nodded. 'That's about it.'

James took a decent slurp of whisky and grimaced as it went down. He peered at her over the glass. 'You've had quite a week.'

Jane shifted uncomfortably. 'It's not like I *wanted* any of that stuff to happen. I was just there to do a job, which I did, thank you very much.'

'I'm not blaming you. It seems you've been the victim of circumstance to some extent.'

'Why only to "some extent"?' Jane queried. 'Are you saying I asked for it?'

'Well, you didnae have to aggravate the situation. I think you were blameless up until the point you got her drunk so you could get into her room.'

Jane sighed. 'I know; I kept telling myself to let it go but I couldn't.'

'Why not just ask her for your stuff?'

'I did! I texted her about it and she didn't reply.'

'Why not ask her again at the hostel?'

'I don't know. I guess I just played out the scenario in my mind and figured she'd act like she didn't know what I was talking about.'

'So, then you talk to the hostel owner, and see if she'll intervene.'

'I didn't want to involve her. I just thought it was easier if I managed it on my own. And I didn't want to have to explain about Natalie being drunk and a thief at the Bella Vista. Look, it's happened now. There's no point doing the "what if" thing. So, I don't give her any money, right? I mean that's extortion. Isn't the first rule of blackmail don't give the blackmailers the money?'

'It is in the movies,' said James, putting his empty glass on the nightstand. He unbuttoned his cuffs and rolled up his shirt sleeves and stretched out on the bed, propping up his head with a pillow. 'Look, I dinnae ken if they've got a case or not. I doubt the police would be very much interested, especially since you're not even in Italy anymore.'

Jane took a swig of wine. 'I know, right!'

'But you're still in the EU, and I think they have something called a European Arrest Warrant. Did you tell her you were going to Barcelona?'

'Uh, yes.'

James smiled reassuringly when he saw her worried face. 'Look, I'm sure you'll be fine ...'

He held out a hand to her and Jane crawled over and lay down beside him snuggling her head into his neck. It was the closest they'd ever been physically, and she felt hyper aware of everything about him: the warmth of his body, the steady, rhythmic thud of his heartbeat, the scent of whisky and soap. She closed her eyes hardly daring to breathe or move a muscle.

James lightly stroked her arm and whispered, 'Dinna fash. If you get put in prison for stealing your own clothes, then I'll bake you a cake with a spoon so you can hack out a tunnel like in *Shawshank Redemption*.'

Jane snorted and then they were both laughing at the ridiculousness of the whole situation. When she tried to stop, James made digging motions with his hands, which set her off again. Her side started hurting so much she had to get up and climb onto her own bed and burrow her head into the pillows until the hysteria had passed.

'I think I'm really tired,' she gasped when she eventually surfaced, wiping the tears from her eyes, 'and drunk.'

'Aye, me too,' agreed James. 'Maybe we should get some shut-eye.' And with that he reached out and flicked off the master light switch, instantly plunging the room into total darkness. They were both silent, then burst out laughing again.

'Wow, those are some blackout curtains,' said Jane. 'I can't even see my hand!' She heard a series of rustling noises coming from James's side of the room. 'What are you doing?'

'Erm ... taking off ma clothes.'

'Ah, right. Carry on then!'

'Aren't you?'

'I can't be bothered. I think I'll just sleep in my little black dress.'

She didn't mention that she also didn't have anything to sleep in since her entire wardrobe was currently being laundered God knew where.

'Fair enough, 'night then,' said James, making a harrumphing sound on the mattress as he turned over to get comfortable.

'—'night ...'

Jane didn't remember closing her eyes, but she must've done, as the next thing she knew there was a greyish quality to the light in the room. Her temples felt painful, and her mouth was dry like she'd been chewing on sawdust. So much for good-quality red wine, she thought. It still delivered the same kick to the head as the cheap stuff. James was fast asleep in the other bed. She could hear his deep breathing, which was comforting, if somewhat distracting, knowing he was so close.

She thought back to last night. Ok, so that was weird—she'd been wearing a sexy, erection inducing dress, they'd both had too much to drink and somehow James had decided to go to sleep! Jane knew it was against the "rules" but unlesss she was totally misreading the signals, the vibe for something to happen had definitely been there. Now she felt confused and hungover, and more than a little tempted to climb under the covers with James.

The little black dress had rucked up around her thighs, so she pulled it down—it was so bloody tight! Amber would kill herself laughing if she knew she'd slept in it. She was the one who had talked her into buying it in the first place. Jane had gone shopping with Amber, to buy sensible things like T-shirts and socks for the trip, when they walked past a designer dress shop in Thistle Street.

'Have you got a little black dress?'

Jane shook her head.

'Right, we're going in.'

'Why?'

'Because you're going to a stylish European city with a superhot guy—enough said, hen.' She flicked rapidly through the hangers. 'Here, try these on.'

Jane had tried on half a dozen black dresses, with Amber either screwing up her face or frowning at each, until the last one which had earned a wolf whistle.

'That's it!'

'Really? Isn't it too ... revealing?'

It was just above knee-length and body hugging, with tight-fitting three-quarter length sleeves. *Almost* something you could wear to the office, she thought—apart from the fact it had a neckline so plunging it was indecent. She twisted and turned in the mirror, trying to see the back.

'It's formal but sexy—and you don't have big boobs, so you won't fall out of it,' Amber proclaimed.

Jane laughed. 'Thanks for the confidence boost!' But she had to admit, it did make her feel ten times sexier, even if it cost a small fortune. She'd stowed the receipt in her box when she got back to the flat, in case she decided being able to afford food was preferable and needed to do a quick return ...

She suddenly tensed. Her receipt box! How could she have forgotten about that? She'd started keeping the receipts for every item she bought. It was a habit she'd gotten into when she'd tried to return a broken toaster and hadn't been able to because she'd thrown out the receipt.

Jane grabbed her phone and padded softly into the bathroom. She closed the door and turned on the light. It was 7:20am and, with any luck, Aimee would be either up for a shift at the hospital or coming off one. She answered on the third ring.

'Janie! Is everythin' ok?'

'Hi, Aimee, yes, everything's fine,' Jane replied, trying to speak quietly. 'Is now a good time to talk?'

'Aye, but shall we video chat instead? I'm just makin' breakfast.'

'Sure.'

They switched to video and Aimee's familiar face came into view with the kitchen behind her. 'Hello,' she said, then frowned as she tried to work out Jane's location. 'Where are you? It's feckin' early here.'

'I'm in Barcelona, in the bathroom of a hotel,' said Jane, turning her phone round so Aimee could see the white marble sinks and the tiled shower.

'Looks dead posh. So is James snorin' in the bedroom?' asked Aimee loudly as Jane turned it back to herself.

'Shhhhh,' whispered Jane hurriedly 'He's not snoring. I just need a favour.'

'Hmm,' said Aimee, pursing her lips. 'I'm not sure I believe you on the snorin', but ask away.'

'Can you get my receipt box and find the receipt for this dress? It should be at the top.'

'Where is it?'

'The box? Ah, it should be in the cupboard in the hallway.'

'Aye, hold on.' Aimee left the room, so Jane gazed at the side of a red saucepan, which she was using to make porridge, for a couple of minutes. Then Aimee was back.

'Is this it?' She showed Jane the lid of a blue shoe box.

'Yes! Now there should be a receipt in there.'

Aimee rummaged through the bits of paper, reading the contents 'Och mi gawd, there are so many feckin' receipts in here! Is it this one?' Aimee held it up to her phone so Jane could see it.

'That's it!' Jane gave her a thumbs up. 'Now can you take a photo of it and email it to me.'

'Aye,' said Aimee. 'But I'll have to hang up to do that.'

'Ok. Do you want to make your porridge and have a chat first, though?'

'Aye, just a wee one.' Aimee propped her phone on the bench and poured oats and water into the saucepan and set it on the hob. 'How's Mr McAvoy? Have you snogged 'im yet?'

'Nope.'

'Aw, nooo!'

'Shhh! It's a long story, but he's only just got here,' Jane whispered.

'Eh?'

'I flew over on my own. He had to go back to Edinburgh to do a paternity test. Kistella's pregnant and thought he might be the father.'

'The feckin' arsehole!' Jane hastily lowered the volume on her phone.

'It's not his—well, the test was inconclusive, so that's as good as a no, apparently,' she said.

'Aw, right,' said Aimee dubiously.

'Anyway, he's here now.'

Aimee poured her porridge into a waiting bowl. 'Do you mind if I eat this before it gets cold?'

'No, munch away. Did you get my email? How's everything working out with Johanna and my room?'

'Aye, I did, thanks. She's ok. I dinnae see too much of her since we're on opposite shifts at the moment.'

They chatted for a while longer about Aimee's work and study, and she didn't ask any more awkward questions about James. When she rang off, Jane waited impatiently, tapping her bare foot on the tile. Finally, she saw an email come through to her inbox from Aimee. Eagerly, she clicked on it and brought up the attachment. Sure enough, it was the receipt from the dress. She did a silent whoop. Natalie didn't have a leg to stand on. Jane had proof of the dress being hers, Bridget to back up her story of them being mates, and it was Natalie's word against hers that she'd "forced her" to drink copious amounts of alcohol. As she recalled it, Natalie's rubber arm had needed little twisting when she'd learned Jane was buying.

She quickly composed a text saying she wouldn't pay anything because she had proof the dress was hers, namely the original receipt, and that she was currently in discussion with a UK criminal defence lawyer. And by the way, did Natalie know that the punishment for blackmail in the EU was one year in jail? Of course, she had no intention of involving either her mother or father, but she figured it sounded good to have legal connections.

Jane switched off the bathroom light and went back into the bedroom. The curtains were open and James was lying on the bed with his legs crossed at the ankles, scrolling on his phone. He'd dressed and was wearing his faded jeans and blue T-shirt.

'Hey,' she said. 'You're awake.'

'Aye. Are you ok? You've been in there for ages.'

'Yes, just sorting out some legal issues.'

'Eh?'

'What do you think of this?' She came over and sat on the side of his bed and showed him the text. His eyes flicked over it and widened.

'You've still got the receipt?'

'Yep.' Jane showed him the photo Aimee had just sent through. 'So what's she going to do? Rock up to the police and say that I took back what was legally mine? Plus, there's the fact she's blackmailing me, which is a criminal offence.'

James looked at his watch. 'It's 7:45. I'm barely functioning after drinking too many whiskies last night, and you've been busily sorting out blackmailers in the bathroom.'

Jane laughed. 'Well, I got myself into this mess. What do you think—should I send it?'

'Aye, please send it so we can get your wee bitch off our backs and go and have some fun!'

Chapter 20: Gemma Calls

Colourful Park Guell was first on their sightseeing list. And then the Nativity Facade at Sagrada Familia, Antoni Gaudi's famous, unfinished cathedral. James had managed to nab the last couple of eye-wateringly expensive tickets for the lunchtime slot.

Now they were checking out the interior and Jane had given up on the audio guide, preferring to wander around without a voice chirruping in her ear.

'It's crazy and kind of creepy,' she said, craning her neck to take in the roof of the nave '—like spindly bones.'

'It's meant to represent the branches of trees,' said James, listening dutifully to the audio guide.

The cathedral was overwhelming for its scale and ambition, Jane thought, but there was something about it that didn't really feel like a church. Perhaps the construction work had chased off the holy spirit, or more likely the tourist throng had. Eventually they came out into the afternoon sun and Jane took a few shots of the Passion Facade but struggled to fit the mammoth structure in the shot.

'Do you want a photo of you in front of it?'

'Sure.' She handed James her phone and he went several paces away and crouched down to get her and the facade in the shot.

He took so long, turning her phone this way and that, that Jane started to get sore legs.

'How many did you take?' she asked when he handed her phone back.

'Ah, maybe fifteen.'

'Fifteen!'

'I tend to take more than necessary, so one of them should be ok.'

Jane flicked through the photos. 'But they're all good. I hate you and your expert photography skills.' James laughed.

'By the way,' he said casually, as they crossed the street to a small park, its shady trees giving some relief from the afternoon heat. 'Who's Miguel?'

Jane looked at James. 'How do you know about him?'

'You got a text when I was taking the photos. I couldn't help seeing who it was from. I didn't read it.'

Shite. Jane checked the text. It just said: *'Hola Jane! Are you back in Barcelona?* And a smiley face emoji. No threesome emojis, thank God.

'So?' prompted James. 'Who's he, then?'

'It's no one,' said Jane, evasively. 'Just a guy who helped me out.'

'You didn't mention him before,' pressed James.

'There was other stuff going on.'

'Why are you being so cagey?'

'I'm not. Look, do you mind if we sit down? I'm really hot.'

There were some park benches set back from the path, so Jane headed towards the nearest one with James following. She took out her water bottle and poured some into her cupped hand and wiped her sweaty face and neck. Then had a drink, wiping her hands on her shorts, feeling grimy from wearing yesterday's clothes.

She offered James her water bottle, but he shook his head sullenly. Jane sighed. She didn't really have any qualms about telling him about Miguel but why did she had to explain herself, when he hadn't exactly been forthcoming about Kistella? Had he seen her in Edinburgh?

'I met Miguel the night I first arrived. It was late, and I couldn't get into the hostel, so I was upset. He kindly said I could stay in his friend's Airbnb apartment, which he was looking after.'

'Uh ... ok,' said James, surprised. 'Where was that?'

'Just a ten-minute walk up the road,' said Jane.

'That was risky, wasn't it—what if he'd turned out to be a psycho?'

'I'm not stupid, I do know that. I trusted my instincts. It was fine.'

'Your—*instincts*?' James sounded incredulous. 'How many other girls have trusted their *instincts* and ended up dead in a suitcase?'

Jane sighed. 'And that's why I didn't say anything. I knew you'd react like this.'

'And for good reason!'

'Look, I made a choice, ok, and that's on me. Not every man I meet is going to murder me. If I thought that way, I'd have to start thinking that about you too!'

James shook his head. 'You still should've found a hotel to be on the safe side.'

'The internet wouldn't connect. Besides …'—Jane knew she was about to go into dark waters here, but she was getting riled up—'if you'd been there, I wouldn't have gone off with him, would I?'

James's jaw clenched. 'So, if you'd ended up dead, it would've been ma fault?'

'Pretty much.'

James said nothing, and they sat there in silence. Then, he got up.

'I think I'm going to head back to the hotel,' he mumbled. 'I'll see you later.'

As soon as he'd gone, Jane regretted what she'd said. She knew she'd been irrational, but him taking off back to Edinburgh right before their trip still felt raw.

Sighing, she looked at Miguel's text again. She had to get rid of him. He was going to keep ringing and texting her, and she didn't want James to think there was something going on when there wasn't.

So, she sent a brief text saying: *Hey Miguel, I'm back but I'm busy catching up with a friend. PS: I'm not into threesomes.* And a smiley face emoji.

A few minutes later she got back: *No es problema Jane, have fun!* Smiley face emoji.

Then another one straight after saying: *Lo siento! That other text was meant for someone else!* Embarrassed face emoji.

Jane followed in James's footsteps back to the hotel room. She found him sitting in the chair with a dram of whisky.

They both said, 'I'm sorry …' at the same time.

'You're right,' Jane said. 'It was dumb, and I'm lucky that he didn't turn out to be a psycho. I won't do it again.' Thank God she hadn't told him about Miguel's threesome text since it hadn't even been meant for her. She was willing to bet, after the Kistella business, that any mention of multiple men scenarios wouldn't go down well. Poor James. Hopefully he'd refused to meet up with her in Edinburgh. She glanced at the whisky bottle on the side table.

'Drowning your sorrows?'

'Perhaps. To be honest—I'm kind of stressed.' He rubbed his face and frowned. 'But it's no excuse. I shouldn't have stormed off like that.'

'I thought the stress was over,' said Jane, sitting on the bed and kicking off her shoes.

'Aye, the test result was brilliant news. But I've got a massive credit card bill coming up and I dinnae think I can cover it unless I get paid. But now ma client is ghosting me. He's a pain to get money out of. I charged him fifty percent upfront, but in hindsight I should've charged the total amount.'

'How much is on your credit card?' she asked curiously.

'Two thousand.'

Jane whistled. 'That client's definitely worth following up on then.'

'Aye.'

'Er ... as nice as it is, I don't think this hotel cost two thousand pounds for two nights, and the flight over can't have been that much. Have you been shopping for a Rolex or something?'

James seemed very interested in the material of the armchair all of a sudden.

'I may have also helped Kistella out with the bill for the paternity test—it was quite pricey.'

Her heart sank. 'Seriously? Why is that your problem?'

'It's not. I just met up with her and she mentioned the bill and that she was desperate for money. I guess I felt sorry for her ...'

At that moment the bedside phone rang, so Jane answered it. The receptionist said her washing had arrived back, and did she want to come and collect it? Good timing, she thought, not really wanting a blow-by-blow account of Kistella and her desperation.

She left James drinking his whisky and went down in the lift.

A grey malaise came over her. James had met up with Kistella and had even given her money! The whole thing was like a recurring nightmare she felt would never end. It would be years of Kistella constantly popping up, wanting something, and James never able to say no to her.

You could just leave after the weekend, a small voice whispered in her head. Cut your ties now; there's no obligation to him. He's not your boyfriend. Then another voice said, but you really like him and what if he really likes you? If you leave now, you'll never find out.

At reception, she handed over the ticket she'd been given and received a large, flat parcel in return, which she hugged to her chest in relief. Not having her clothes had been making her feel vulnerable. She was just walking out of reception when her mobile rang.

'Hello?'

'Hi, Jane, it's Gemma. Are you free to talk?'

'Hi! Sure, now's a good time.'

Jane sat down in a nearby chair and listened as Gemma outlined the brief for her next assignment.

Back in the room, Jane grabbed her bag out of the wardrobe and started to busily load it with her freshly washed and ironed clothes. They smelt delicious, like a mixture of lavender and cotton candy. From his chair, James watched the fevered packing warily.

'What's going on?'

'How would you feel about going to Budapest tomorrow?'

'Tomorrow! That's sudden.'

'I know. Gemma just rang me. It's for an article in conjunction with the Budapest tourism board. But she's paying me a cut this time and it actually works out. You're in damage control and we need somewhere to stay that's not five-star. I checked the flights briefly in the lobby, and they're dirt cheap because it's Monday. And there are heaps of budget hostels …' She screwed up her nose.

'What?' queried James. 'You had me at "budget hostels".'

'Well, from what I saw, some of them are more than just budget hostels—they're party hostels. Like, seriously hard partying. They don't let anyone stay there who's over thirty-five.'

James smirked. 'Och, we can handle it.'

'Ok, well if you're cool to come with, I'll let Gemma know I'll do it.'

'I'm in.'

'There's another thing,' said Jane, pausing in her packing. 'I'm going to lend you the money to pay off your credit card.'

'You dinnae have to do that,' said James quickly, frowning.

'I know I don't,' said Jane. 'I want to. It's just a loan, so you don't have to stress about it. You can pay me back when you get your money. Even if it takes a little while, that's ok.'

James let out a big sigh of relief. 'That would be amazing,

thanks so much.'

'Don't thank me yet. I want a favour in return.'

'Name it.'

'Could you get in touch with your friend? The one with the content writing agency in Bangkok?'

'Rick? Sure. Do you want me to set up a meeting?'

'Yes, I feel like I'm putting all my eggs in one basket with Gemma.'

'Sounds smart, networking—I like it,' said James, finishing off his whisky, and grabbing his phone. 'I'll get right onto that. Anything else?'

'Just some advice. Maybe don't give Kistella any more money.'

'But *you're* giving *me* money.'

'That's different, it's a loan. And I'm not your ex-girlfriend who you're trying to move on from.'

As soon as the words were out of her mouth she felt like the question "What am I then?" appeared and hung between them in shimmering silver letters. James looked at his phone and didn't say anything. Mortified, Jane stuffed the last of her washing into her bag and zipped it up. The last thing she wanted was to give him the impression she was fishing for some kind of clarification.

He cleared his throat. 'You're right. God knows I need to keep a clear head where she's concerned or I'll end up financing the kid's entire existence; I start off buying nappies, then before you know it, I'm funding his or her education. Ok, let me send a message to Rick to hook up a meeting and then we can look at booking flights.'

'Excellent,' said Jane, thankful that they were talking about practical things, and ignoring the elephant in the room. 'I like a man who takes action.'

'Action is ma middle name.'

'What *is* your middle name?'

'Hamish.'

Chapter 21: 24/7 Hostel

As soon as she gave Gemma the thumbs up to take on the job, they booked a flight to Budapest and a hostel immediately.

For Jane, it was a relief to be back on track with the budget and have some semblance of control. She knew James tended to get himself in a tangle with his finances. They had, after all, met at an accountancy practice. But he'd tried to mitigate the risk by charging half upfront. It wasn't his fault the client was ghosting him about the other half.

That was her reasoning anyway, as she transferred two thousand pounds into his account the same afternoon; it was a lot, and she had enough savings to do it, but if anything unexpected cropped up she'd be in the shite herself.

In an effort to keep expenses to a minimum, they'd booked one of the cheapest places to stay in Budapest: the 24/7 Hostel, based in the Pest side of the city. It was among the half a dozen hostels that they'd shortlisted, and James had immediately latched onto it. Not only because it was a notorious party hostel, but because he liked the fact it had mixed dorms, an on-site bar and seemed pretty lax about what people got up to in general.

Jane was steeling herself for the whiplash of going from a five-star hotel to a party hostel, but James had a romantic view of it all and saw it as "reliving his backpacking days", so she'd been caught up in his enthusiasm. How bad could it be?

Their late morning flight to Budapest took two and half hours, so there was plenty of time when they were aboard the plane to talk about the sightseeing they wanted to do. James was eager to visit a variety of WWII-themed sites, including one called "House of Terror", which Jane was less keen on, just from hearing the name.

'But you will come, though? It's an important part of history.'

'To learn about people that have been tortured and murdered right where you're standing. Hmm … sounds like a barrel of laughs. But yes, I'll go with you.'

Jane, instead, had been researching the city's bathhouses for Gemma's article, which was aimed at female travellers.

'Did you know Budapest is only one of three capital cities in the world that has hot springs? And there are a ton of Turkish baths.'

James immediately looked over. 'Should we go to some?'

'Sure, there's Széchenyi, but Gellert sounds good too and Rudas has a women-only day on Tuesdays, which is perfect for the article. I can go there tomorrow.'

'So, what am I supposed to do?'

'I'm sure you'll find something—'

'I might have to work, anyway.'

'Ah, yes. Do you think you'll be able to, in the hostel?'

'Apparently there's a common room, so I'll probably just perch in there. When's your chat with Rick?'

James had been as good as his word and had managed to get hold of his friend in Bangkok. Rick had been enthusiastic about meeting with her and had even sent through an official Google invite, so it was all set up.

'Tomorrow morning at eight; Budapest time.'

'Aye, he's five hours ahead of us. He said he's up north in the jungle at the moment, but back in Bangkok tomorrow. I dinnae ken how he can run a business from the jungle.'

'How do you know him again?'

'I used to work with him at a marketing company in London when I lived there for a year or so. We kept in touch through LinkedIn, and when I went freelance, he referred me to various clients, and I did the same for him when he ditched the nine-to-five. He always seemed very clean-cut, so aye, I can't imagine him roughing it in the jungle.'

'Do you fancy roughing it in the jungle?' asked Jane curiously.

'God no—I like my creature comforts too much; give me a bed, a pub and good Wi-Fi, and I'm happy. What about you?'

'I don't know—perhaps going off-grid and communing with elephants, or whatever he's been doing, has its merits. At least I wouldn't encounter dodgy hotel owners.'

James looked sympathetic. 'I'm sure that was just beginner's bad luck. You had a trial by fire, but you escaped unscathed.'

'Did I?'

'Aye, it's the Universe testing your mettle. If freelancing was easy, everyone would be doing it. This next job will be better.'

'I guess.'

'What about Miss Aussie Backpacker?'

Jane grunted. 'I haven't heard anything from Natalie since I sent her the text, so hopefully that's the end of it. She's like the killer in a horror movie. She keeps coming back to life.'

James patted her arm reassuringly and pointed out the window—the plane was turning to line up with the airport and as it dipped its wing, the Danube River came into view. She saw a sliver of blue water and ornate buildings lining the river's edge, and in the distance the Széchenyi Chain Bridge connecting the two towns—Buda and Pest—to create one unified city.

The connection from the airport to get into the city, however, wasn't as clear-cut since there was no direct train. So, they ended up catching a taxi to Keleti metro station. The metro ticket machine only took Hungarian forints so a hunt around for an ATM ensued, which gave them a single ten thousand forint note, the lowest amount it offered. When Jane attempted to feed the note into the machine to buy two single tickets, the machine let out an almighty shriek and spat it back out again, making them jump out of their skins.

'I guess it's too much money for it to handle. It only wants small change,' Jane said, looking around for a ticket counter.

Spying one near the station door, she left James with the

luggage and returned moments later with a pack of ten metro tickets instead. 'It was all they had. I'm sure we'll use them at some point,' she said, showing him. He agreed that they didn't have much choice in the matter. Then it was a case of riding the red line until Deák Ferenc tér then changing to the yellow line for Oktogon. From there it was a five-minute walk to the hostel.

'I wouldn't want to do that airport-metro trip into the city at night,' commented Jane as they walked along a wide tree-lined avenue in the direction of the hostel. 'What if the ticket counter wasn't manned?'

'You'd probably have to try and change the note somewhere,' mused James.

'In a seedy row of dimly lit shops,' said Jane shuddering.

'Not ideal, true.'

Speaking of seedy, she thought as they turned down a narrow side street. The grey stonework on the buildings they were passing may have once been quite lovely, but now chipped and weathered and daubed with graffiti—it just looked grim.

'Are you sure the hostel is down here?' she asked, fervently hoping it wasn't.

'Positive,' said James, checking Google Maps on his phone.

'Oh, ok.' Her heart sank.

A black-and-white sign for the 24/7 Hostel soon came into view. It hung lopsidedly above the entrance of the most dilapidated building in the street.

'It looks—atmospheric,' said Jane, eyeing the cracked

courtyard overgrown with weeds they could see through the archway. 'Tell me why we're staying here again?'

'It had great reviews, and it has cheap drinks,' said James. 'Come on, don't be a snob. It'll be fun. You can tell your grandkids you stayed in the notorious 24/7 Hostel, and they'll think you're a cool grannie.'

'I don't think this place will last five years, let alone fifty, from the looks of the crumbling walls, but I take your point. Ok, let's get this over with.'

They went through the archway and into the open-air courtyard that was much larger than it appeared from the street. There were rough-hewn tables and chairs set up around the perimeter occupied by several guests who were smoking and chatting. A few of them looked over when they came in and smiled. It seemed a friendly enough place, thought Jane, as they stopped in the middle, not sure where to go.

'I wonder where the front desk is,' mused James, looking around.

Sensing their confusion, one of the guests, a pretty girl with long, wavy, honey-coloured hair and big brown eyes, called out to them. 'Hey guys, if you want the front desk, it's through there!' She pointed to the back corner of the courtyard.

James flashed her a grin. 'Thanks!'

'No problem,' she said, staring at him openly a tad too long for Jane's liking. James didn't appear to notice though and headed off in the direction the girl had pointed. Sure enough, in the corner of the courtyard, there was an innocuous brown door that accessed the bowels of the building. James held the door open for her. 'After you.'

Jane gazed around the stark, white dormitory, stunned. It looked like something out of a psychiatric hospital. She'd been thinking four beds, six at the most. This had twelve metal-framed bunk beds, some with occupants still sleeping off the night before, though it was close to two in the afternoon. Other beds had tangled sheets, indicating they had owners who were out for the day. Some just had stained mattresses and yellowing pillows.

'Apparently they don't kick people out when the cleaners come round,' whispered James.

'Good to know,' Jane whispered back. 'So where are our bunks then?' She tried to ignore the state of the mattresses and pillows. She could feel her skin crawling at the thought of the thousands of bodies that had slept on them previously.

'They don't seem to be numbered or anything. I guess we just take the ones that aren't made up.'

James headed towards a couple of beds at the back by the window that weren't claimed, and she followed him reluctantly.

'Top or bottom?'

'Bottom,' she said automatically. 'Easier to escape.'

'You're not feeling this place, are you?' He looked disappointed and Jane forced a smile.

'It might grow on me,' she said quickly, putting her pillowcase on before she looked too closely at what was underneath. Either that or what was on the mattress would, she added silently. At least the bedding they'd been given seemed to be clean. 'I'm just hungry. Do you want to grab some food and do some sightseeing?' she said, trying not to be a downer.

'Sounds good. Can you just help me with this sheet?'

'Sure.'

After they'd made their beds and stowed their luggage in the provided lockers, being careful to be quiet, they went out, leaving the snorts and snores behind. This was so much worse than the hostel in Como, but she was determined to try to like it, for James's sake.

After a cheap sandwich lunch, they took in various attractions: the Shoes on the Danube, Buda Castle, Széchenyi Chain Bridge, the Dohány Street Synagogue ... and the House of Terror at James's insistence.

Jane had to keep stopping to type in her notes app, but James said he didn't mind as he wanted to take photos. They sat on the grass in a nearby park after the House of Terror, so she could type some more notes. James was playing around with the settings on his DSLR camera. She'd had a feeling he was being modest when he'd taken the photos of her at the Sagrada Familia, now her theory was proved correct; he knew exactly what he was doing. As she watched his long fingers deftly twiddling with the dials, she thought: lucky camera. She closed her eyes and couldn't help fantasising ...

'Earth to Jane.'

She opened her eyes to find James staring at her with an amused grin. 'Are you taking a nap?'

'Uh, no, just daydreaming.'

'Must've been good. You were heavy breathing.'

'I was not!'

He arched an eyebrow. 'Aye, you were. Come on, what were you daydreaming about?'

She gulped. There was no way in hell she was going to reveal what she'd just been imagining him doing to her.

'It's private,' she said primly.

James chuckled. 'Now I'm really curious. Maybe I should ...' Without warning he grabbed her round the waist. Worried that he'd tickle her mercilessly to extract some kind of confession, she hastily twisted out of his grasp and stood up before he could do anything.

He narrowed his eyes. 'A lucky escape.'

She laughed and poked out her tongue.

To her relief, he didn't ask her any more about it. And since the light had started fading, they headed back to the hostel, stopping off at a nearby grocery store to grab some supplies: cereal, snacks and fruit. When they arrived, there was a livelier feeling in the air. Hostellers were starting to emerge from their rooms, and congregate in the courtyard, like nocturnal animals sensing the onset of dusk.

James said he wanted to email the client who was ghosting him again, and she needed to organise her notes, so they grabbed their laptops and sat in the common room at one of the tables. It was a sizeable room, and it contained a kitchen with a communal fridge, microwave and kettle. Unlike the rest of the hostel, it had decent light to see by, even if several of the fluorescent lighting strips were flickering madly.

At check-in they'd been told they could help themselves to free tea and coffee, but Jane made sure she cleaned the cups thoroughly first and sniffed the milk to see if it was fresh; surprisingly it was. James was busily typing out yet another firmly worded email but smiled at her and said thanks when she handed him his tea.

It was nice to be here with someone, she thought—someone whom she trusted and could hang out with. It was like their own private bubble, protecting her from feeling alone in the midst of complete strangers. Although she had to admit, despite this place being shabby and dilapidated, it did have a positive vibe about it— a feeling of freedom, that you could be yourself, without judgement.

Speaking of judgement, she'd just finished organising her notes when she received an email from her mother. It was brief and to the point, which was typical of her mother who wasn't into writing long emails. Jane scanned it. It was mainly about their upcoming trip to the Costa del Sol, the dates they were planning on going and that she hoped Jane had enjoyed visiting Como: wasn't it gorgeous? It sounded as if her mother was coming round to the idea of her being a digital nomad, or perhaps that was just wishful thinking on her part.

Just then there was an ear-piercing, electronic squawk from the courtyard, a rhythmic pulse of bass and cheering. Jane looked at James and raised an eyebrow. 'I think the party just got started.'

'Do you want to check it out? I'm finished here.'

'Sure, I might just have a quick shower and get changed. I can take the laptops back to the room, if you like.'

'You look ok like that.'

Jane just smiled and shook her head. She'd been wearing the same clothes since yesterday, her hair felt oily and she wanted to look halfway decent, just in case … 'I won't be long. I'll find you.' She practically had to shout as the volume switched up a notch. The thump of the bass was so loud she could feel it reverberating through the floorboards.

James nodded and gave her his laptop, then headed off outside to see what was going on. Jane found her way back to the dorm room, nearly getting lost; all the corridors looked the same. She flicked on the light switch and wasn't surprised to see that the room was empty. It felt like she was the only person in the entire hostel who wasn't outside partying.

She stowed their laptops in the locker and got out her bag, thankful she had something clean to wear. They'd discovered earlier that there was a shower room just across the hallway, which meant either taking clothes with her or walking back to the room naked, wrapped in a towel. She chose the former, not wanting to tempt fate.

With her clothes, makeup bag and towel in her arms, she crossed the hallway. But when she opened the door to the shower room, she was disconcerted to see the other stall was occupied. Warm, moist billows of steam wafted around the room and the sodden orange shower curtain showed an impression of an elbow then a shoulder as the person moved behind it. Like the dorm room, the showers were also unisex, so whoever behind it was either male or female; take your pick. There were clothes on the slatted bench, but the pair of jeans and a T-shirt didn't give her a clue to the occupant's gender.

It felt weird getting naked with a complete stranger right next door, but she didn't really have a choice. So, she quickly took off her clothes behind the curtain, placed them on the bench and turned the shower knob round to hot. A blast of freezing cold water sprayed her and she screeched, hopping back out of the way. The warm slowly started coming through, and she stepped under, wetting her hair. There were pump dispensers of clear liquid soap and citrus shampoo affixed to the wall, so she soaped her body and washed her hair. She was just about to rinse out the shampoo when the water switched off abruptly.

'Well, that's bloody great!'

Shampoo was starting to run into her eyes, making them sting, so she closed them and groped blindly outside the shower curtain for her towel. Someone put it into her hand, and she wiped her eyes gratefully.

'Thanks! I thought it was closer … ' She opened her eyes gingerly and found herself peering through the steam at a lean, muscular torso, which was attached to a rather good-looking face—the occupant of the other shower. Thankfully he was wearing boxers.

'Ah, hi, there,' said Jane, clutching the towel, her hair dripping suds down the side of her face. She knew she was ogling him but couldn't help it.

'Hi, yourself,' said the guy. He grinned and gave her a nod. Jane's stomach flipped. She didn't think guys who looked like this stayed in cheap hostels. He'd combed his short flaxen hair back, but some longer strands escaped and fell forward in a wet heap around his chiseled face as he bent down to collect his clothes. The muscles in his smooth back rippled. Jane noticed he had a barbed wire tattoo encircling his left arm.

'Er … do you know if the hot water will come back on?' she asked. He straightened up to look at her and shrugged.

'Probably. I'd give it a try in a couple of minutes.' His gaze travelled down past her face, and he lifted his eyebrows slightly. He sounds British, she thought, staring at him, wondering where in the UK he was from. Suddenly Jane realised what he was looking at. The wet orange shower curtain was clinging to her body and her breasts were clearly visible. Bloody hell, she thought, horrified, and frantically tried to pluck it away from her skin without much success. The stupid thing refused to budge. She heard the guy laugh softly, and looked up just as he said, 'Catch ya later', and gave her a little salute on the way out.

Finally free of the shower curtain, Jane turned the knob off and then on again and warm water spouted out. She stuck her head under and quickly washed out the shampoo. So much for online dating, she thought, chuckling to herself. Unisex showers were definitely the way to go.

Chapter 22: Party Girl

Jane got out of the shower, dried off, and threw on her white mini skirt and a black cropped tank top. She attempted to rake some mascara through her eyelashes, wiping fruitlessly at the steamed-up bathroom mirror.

With no time to dry her hair, she just slicked it back and up into a high ponytail. Blusher, lipstick: done. She put on her trainers and headed back to the dorm room with her armful of clothes, makeup bag and wet towel. There was no sign of the cute guy, just a whiff of spice lingering in the colder air of the hallway. She checked her phone, but James hadn't texted so she had no idea where he was.

When she came into the courtyard, the full force of the thumping techno bass hit her like a shockwave. She stood there for a minute trying to adjust to the noise and the amount of people. A DJ was on a small stage at the far end, wearing headphones and pumping his fist. She scanned the mass of writhing bodies further in but couldn't see James. Upstairs there was a balcony with groups of people chatting and laughing but he didn't seem to be up there either.

Spying a makeshift bar set up on the left-hand side, she pushed her way through the stragglers at the back who were just bobbing about. As she got closer, she noticed two guys standing at the bar drinking beer. One of them leaned in and said something to his shorter friend, who laughed. He flicked his hair back, and she recognised the angular cheekbones, and poker-straight nose. It was him—the guy from the shower, now fully dressed in grey cargo pants and a tight black T-shirt that showed off his biceps.

Jane felt hot and cold at the same time. Like a deer caught in the headlights, she couldn't move. The guy glanced round and noticed her staring at him. He frowned for a moment and then his face cleared, and she saw that he'd clocked who she was. He said something to his friend who checked her out and smirked.

Oh God, she thought, cringing and making a beeline for the bar counter; I've only been here five minutes, and I've already got a reputation!

'Hi, shower girl,' said a voice by her elbow. Jane blushed and didn't say anything. She hated it when guys made fun of her, especially ones she didn't even know.

'Can I get you a drink?' the voice persisted. Jane turned around and found herself gazing up into a pair of amused slate-grey eyes.

'I guess—if you stop calling me shower girl,' she said, trying to sound haughty. He grinned. 'Sorry, I don't know your name. Maybe if you told me, I can call you that instead.'

'It's Jane.'

'Zeke.' He held out his hand. 'Pleased to meet you—with clothes on.'

Jane laughed and shook it. His grip was warm, and firm; a slight tingle went up her arm. She felt like she was supposed to say or do something next but wasn't sure what. So, she just stood there, staring at him blankly, somewhat dazed by how good-looking he was, and the music, which was so loud it was infiltrating her senses.

'I'll be back,' Zeke said and abruptly melted into the crowd. In a few minutes, he returned holding a glass swirled with pink froth, and a strawberry and lime wedge stuck on the rim. 'Here you go,' he said, handing it to her.

'Ah, er, thanks—what is it?' asked Jane; she sniffed it warily.

'A strawberry daiquiri. They're making cocktails further along.'

'Ah, I thought you were going to get something at the bar here. I'd love to but, you know ... roofie.'

'Oh.' He stared at her. 'I wouldn't do that.'

Jane was torn since he'd just bought her the drink and was about to take it, but James's reaction to Miguel was still fresh in her mind, so she just said 'Sorry.'

'Tell you what, you have this.' He gave her his half-finished beer, and took the pink concoction back. 'I'm hardly likely to roofie myself, am I?'

Jane sipped the sour, fizzy liquid and grimaced. 'Urgh, I got the short straw there.'

'Yep, it's some kind of Budapest craft beer. It tastes like dishwater strained through dirty socks. But it packs a punch.'

Zeke took a mouthful of strawberry daiquiri and turned to look at the coloured lights playing over the graffitied walls of the courtyard and the DJ encouraging the crowd. He glanced back around and caught her checking him out. She immediately averted her eyes, but he smiled at her, not bothered by it. 'Wanna go in?' He jerked his head towards the crowd.

'Ok.' She took another sip of her drink and then gladly deposited the beer bottle on the bar counter. He grabbed her hand and led her right into the thick of it, where the dancing was hot, heavy and going off. Within minutes, her skin was slicked with sweat, hers and other peoples, and she felt like she needed another shower.

At first she'd been scrutinising the crowd to find James and checking her phone. But Zeke kept distracting her by grabbing her round the waist and gyrating his hips against hers. Then he took off his T-shirt and hung it round his neck. Jane gawped openly, her attention now fully engaged. Zeke grinned.

After some energetic dancing, that involved her face being up close and personal with Zeke's sweaty chest, Jane managed to check her phone to see if James had texted. Actually, he'd sent quite a few messages, and she hadn't heard them. The latest one was: *Where are you? I'm upstairs*. She tilted her head back and scanned the balcony until she thought she saw his outline.

Quickly she texted: *Downstairs*.

His reply came back: *Come up for some pizza*.

Hmm, she was actually pretty hungry, pizza sounded good. She considered what to do.

Zeke had been watching her texting. He leaned in and called out over the music, 'Hey, who's that?'

'Just a friend,' she called back. 'He has pizza.' She pointed at the balcony. 'Up there.' Then, as it was only polite to ask, 'Do you want some?'

Zeke gave her the thumbs up, so she sent a text to James: *Ok be there in five*.

Jane wasn't sure how to even get upstairs, but Zeke elbowed his way through the crowd, with her following in his wake. He went over to an iron staircase she hadn't noticed set into the wall—he must've been here a few days, she thought, as he seemed to know his way around.

They climbed up to the balcony and then Jane took the lead, threading her way through the hordes. She knew the place had around ten dorm rooms, and even if they all had twelve beds in them that was only a hundred and twenty people. It felt like there was at least double that amount if not more. She was beginning to think this place was a gathering spot for a whole load of other hostels as well.

Eventually she spotted James leaning with his back against the railing, chatting with a small group. She noticed the girl who had directed them when they arrived was among them. No surprise there, thought Jane. There was a low table stocked with bottles of the cheap Budapest craft beer and water.

'Hey, I was wondering where you'd got to,' said James, looking relieved when he saw her. He gazed over her shoulder and raised an eyebrow when he saw Zeke, shirtless, behind her.

'This is Zeke,' she said, as he came up beside her and gave a wave to the group.

The others turned out to be Cara, the girl they'd met earlier, who was travelling with two friends, Shelley and Melany, and a guy, Mitchell, who was Melany's twin brother. He was off doing the pizza run apparently. They were all from the US—recent college graduates from Penn State. Everyone seemed to know who she was; James had obviously been talking about her. Mitchell turned up then with an armful of pizza boxes, so they were opened, and the aroma of melted cheese and pepperoni invaded the air.

In the reshuffling around the table, as people grabbed pizza and drinks, Jane ended up next to Zeke on the railing, who had cooled down and put his T-shirt back on. James was directly opposite them next to Cara, who, from her animated expression and puppy-dog eyes, whenever he spoke to her, confirmed Jane's theory that she definitely had the hots for him. She felt a sharp twinge of jealousy. Cara *was* extremely pretty, and she was wearing a tiny white tank top that clearly showed off her big boobs and toned, tanned arms. Her denim skirt was barely there. It looked like she worked out too so they could compare muscles, Jane thought grumpily.

There wasn't much room on the railing as they were bunched up next to Melany and Shelley, so she ended up leaning against Zeke's shoulder. He didn't seem to mind and put his left arm around her waist and munched his pizza with his right. She saw James notice but deliberately concentrated on eating her pizza and tried not to catch his eye. Whether it was the vibe of this place, or having Zeke show an interest in her, she suddenly felt rebellious.

'So where are you from Zeke?' asked James casually, looking over at them.

Zeke swallowed a mouthful of pizza and wiped his hand on his jeans before replying.

'Um—Kent, originally.'

'Oh wow,' said Jane, turning to him, 'I *thought* you sounded like a Brit. Whereabouts in Kent?'

'Sevenoaks. But I can't really remember it that much; I haven't been in the UK for about ten years. We moved to Hong Kong when I was thirteen.'

'What do you do?' continued James. He seemed to be intent on questioning Zeke. Jane narrowed her eyes at him, but he ignored her.

'I'm a TEFL teacher ... for now,' said Zeke. 'The pay's ok, and I can also do some online teaching while I'm travelling.'

'Sounds great. Hey, do you want a beer? Jane?'

Jane declined, saying she'd have a water, but Zeke took the beer James offered him.

'Thanks, who should I pay for my share of the food?' he asked.

'That's ok,' broke in blond-haired Mitchell. He'd been quietly munching his way through a box of pizza, and had come up for air. He wiped his mouth and straggly beard on a napkin. 'James gave me a bunch of forints and said it was on him.'

Jane looked over at James. Weren't they supposed to be conserving money? Why was he buying pizza for a bunch of strangers? She hoped he'd actually paid off his credit card with the money she'd given him.

She tried to catch his eye, but it seemed he was still in interrogation mode with Zeke.

'So, you live in Hong Kong?'

'Yeah.' Zeke took a swig of beer, and glanced around. Jane sensed he was getting annoyed with the Spanish Inquisition. He didn't ask James what he did or where he lived. Awkward.

'So how long have you been here?' she said brightly to Melany and Shelley to change the subject. James took the hint and started talking to Cara, who instantly perked up.

'We just arrived today like you,' said Shelley. She was pretty and slender with long, swinging hair and streaked blonde highlights. She wore thick-rimmed glasses that gave her an intelligent air. Whether or not she was, Jane was yet to find out. 'We were in Poland for a week—but we'd heard this hostel rocks, so we were super excited to stay here. Plus do some sightseeing, of course. From what we've seen just walking around, Budapest looks amazing.'

'Yeah,' said Melany. She had blonde streaks too, but a bobbed haircut and a heavier build, like her brother. 'Mitchell's friend stayed here over the summer, and he said the place went off.'

She lowered her voice. 'He didn't actually sleep in his own bed the whole time he was here.'

Shelley giggled and twirled her hair, glancing coquettishly at Mitchell, who was cramming the last cheesy slice into his mouth.

Good luck with that, thought Jane. She might have to drape herself in pizza to get his attention.

'So, what about you?' asked Zeke softly in her ear. Jane jumped, and blushed, thinking he'd overheard what Melany had said and was enquiring if she were into bed hopping. Then she realised he was asking her about work.

'Oh! I'm trying to get into freelance travel writing. But early days.'

'Yeah? That sounds great. Had any interesting clients?'

Jane smiled wryly, the Como fiasco springing instantly to mind.

'One or two,' she said vaguely. 'In fact, I'm speaking with a friend of James's in Bangkok tomorrow morning.'

'I know Bangkok pretty well,' Zeke remarked. 'My ex was from there.'

'Oh.' Jane was surprised at the sudden personal divulgement. 'Ah ... was she a TEFL teacher too?'

'Yeah, we went out for a year but only saw each other once a month—long distance never works.' He chugged back the last of his beer and changed the subject. 'Do you wanna head back down to the party?' He gave her hip a slight squeeze, which made her feel better about there being an ex.

Shelley and Melany were keen to go with them and Cara nodded her assent. James agreed somewhat reluctantly. Whether it was because he didn't want to be left alone with Mitchell or because Zeke had instigated it, Jane wasn't sure.

As soon as they reached the ground floor, the thumping amplified tenfold. James pushed his way through the dancers and headed to the bar with Cara and Mitchell in tow.

'What's with him?' shouted Zeke over the music and jerked his chin towards James's retreating back.

'He's fine,' shouted Jane in reply. 'Let's just dance!'

They plunged into the crowd, which seemed even more packed than before. Mitchell joined them soon after, which put a smile on Shelley's face. Ten minutes or so went by, and Cara came through looking miserable.

'He won't come and dance!' she shouted at Jane. Jane shrugged and kept dancing. What's his problem? she thought; he's the one who wanted to stay here and party. Finally, though, James's absence was getting to her so she called over to Zeke. 'I'll be back in a sec!'

Zeke nodded and gave her the thumbs up. Jane elbowed her

way out and went over to the bar, where she found James frowning into a glass of whisky.

'Hey, score. Who knew they had the good stuff here?'

He lifted the corner of his mouth in a small smile.

'What's up?'

'It's nothing.'

'Is it Zeke? It just sort of happened. I was looking for you and I bumped into him at the bar and we got chatting.' She left out the bit about meeting Zeke in the shower. No point in antagonising him further.

'He seems ok. I'm just tired.'

'Why don't you come and have a dance?' Jane persisted.

'I think I might head to bed.'

'It's only …'—Jane checked her phone—'11:30. It's early!'

'Hmm, it's not early. Dinnae forget you're talking to Rick tomorrow morning.'

'I haven't forgotten.'

'Ok.' He frowned.

'What?'

'Just ... be careful,' he muttered.

'You mean Zeke?'

'Forget it. Look, go and have fun. I'm just being an old fuddy duddy.'

'Yeah, they might chuck you out if you can't handle the pace.' Jane punched him playfully on the shoulder. 'I won't be far behind you.' She yawned loudly behind her hand. 'I'm starting to fade myself.'

'Ok, I'll just finish this drink and send my client another message.'

'It'll be fine.'

'Hopefully—I hate the fact that I owe you money. I'm going to tell him if he doesn't cough up within a week, I'll take him to court.'

'Really?'

'Aye, I found out how to do it when we were in the common room. It's pretty simple. You can just file a claim online. I hoped it wouldn't come to this, but he's brought it on himself.'

'Wow, good on you. I'm 100% behind that,' said Jane.

'And not biased at all, since it's your money,' he teased.

Jane pulled a face. 'You know what I mean.'

James laughed and some of the tension between them dissipated, to her relief.

'I'll see you later on then …' said Jane, turning to see where Zeke was.

James followed the line of her gaze and didn't say anything.

Chapter 23: Bangkok Offer

Jane had good intentions of going to bed, but the drinks kept flowing and they were all having too good a time to leave. Eventually, one by one, the others peeled off, admitting near exhaustion, until she was left alone with Zeke, who seemed to have boundless energy.

'Aren't you tired?' she called over to him. The music hadn't lessened in volume or intensity, and it was the early hours of the morning.

'Yeah, I'm knackered!' he confessed. 'Do you wanna head?' She nodded, and they threaded their way through the crowd, back into the main corridor and up the stairs to the first floor. There were a series of dim fluorescent strips along the ceiling that were giving out a weak glow.

Jane's ears were ringing, but it was mercifully quieter inside, with the music now just a distant muffled thudding.

'Which is your dorm?' she asked Zeke.

'Uh, I think it's the one at the end of the hall.'

'Don't you know?'

Zeke grinned mischievously. 'Well, I do, but I was going to say I forgot, so I'd have to sleep in yours.'

'Ha ha.'

'Is that a yes?' He inched closer until he was nuzzling her neck. He wasn't backward in coming forward, Jane thought, but they'd both had quite a lot to drink. The neck nuzzling led to kissing her on the lips and then, as things heated up, kissing her fervently with his tongue in her mouth. Somehow she ended up leaning against the wall with Zeke grinding his pelvis against hers and her groping his butt.

Eventually she pulled away gasping. Things were happening too fast, and she couldn't think straight.

'So, you wanna go in?' he said softly.

'Er ... it's not very private,' she said as an excuse. 'I don't really fancy everyone listening. And James is there.'

Zeke frowned. 'You're not with him though, are you?'

Jane didn't say anything and dug a hand into her skirt pocket to retrieve her key card. Zeke looked at her for a long minute and when he realised she wasn't going to change her mind, he shrugged as if to say 'your loss'. He tugged on her ponytail gently and said 'Catch ya later, shower girl', and sauntered off down the hall, flicking his hair back out of his eyes.

She hesitated, watching him walk away. Her lips were tingling and the rest of her was buzzing. Maybe she should go after him and pull him into a nearby storage cupboard ... Damn, she thought, shaking her head, how the hell did that happen? A few hours ago she'd been daydreaming about making out with James and now she'd just kissed and groped a complete stranger! She leaned against the wall feeling exceedingly drunk but surprisingly lucid. It was pretty obvious what was going on: human biology. James hadn't made a move on her even though they'd been alone in a luxury five-star hotel room, with whisky and wine to soften the mood. The most that had happened was a hug on the bed and hysterical giggling. So it was no wonder she was taking out her sexual frustration on another extremely attractive male. She hiccupped. It all made perfect sense …

At 7:30am Jane was rudely awakened by her phone alarm ringing in her ear from under her pillow. She turned it off and lay there in the gloom, trying to remember where in the hell she was for a moment. Then it all came flooding back: the manic dancing, the terrible beer—groping Zeke's butt in the hallway. She closed her eyes as her stomach roiled. Hearing faint tapping noises from above, she decided to climb up and see if James was in a better mood. When she swung her feet to the floor she had to laugh: she still had her shoes on.

James was surfing on his phone, and he started when her head appeared at the top of the ladder. 'Hi, it's me,' she said. 'I didn't mean to scare you.' She noticed he was wearing a black T-shirt. Not the Vans one though, it looked well worn. So much for catching him in bed with his T-shirt off, she thought. He'd covered all the bases.

'Hi, yourself.' He peered at her over his phone. 'Um … I dinnae mean to be rude, but have you looked in the mirror?'

'Not recently.'

He turned his phone camera to selfie mode and handed it to her.

'Oh!' Her mascara had pooled into black smears under her eyes while she'd been asleep, and her hair was still in its ponytail, but chunks had escaped and were standing up like a wonky mohawk around her head. Her eyes were bloodshot.

'God, I look like shite.'

'What time did you get to bed?'

'I don't know. It was pretty late.'

'Was everyone still there when you left?'

'Yeah, but we all left together.' *Don't* think about Zeke in the hallway, just don't! With an effort, she pulled her focus back to the present moment.

'How are you anyway? Still stressed?'

He nodded. 'A wee bit.'

She saw James's finely boned right foot poking out of the duvet near her head. He has nice feet, she thought, staring at the soft, creamy skin and well-shaped, narrow toes. Before she could stop herself, she reached out and touched his foot. He wiggled his toes at her, and she glanced across at him.

'What are you doing?' he asked, bemused.

'Uh, I could give you a foot massage, if you like. It'll help you relax.' She could hardly believe the words were coming out of her mouth. Zeke's attention last night seemed to have given her some sort of confidence boost. She waited to get knocked back but James, to her surprise, shrugged and went back to scrolling on his phone. 'If you want.'

Before he could change his mind, Jane hastily climbed up on the bed. She put his foot in her lap and looked at it. Now what? Vaguely she remembered reading a Cosmopolitan article about how to give someone an orgasmic foot massage, maybe she should try that?

Tentatively she started pressing into the ball of his foot with her thumbs, then moved down to stroke his instep, lightly but firmly. She could feel stiff tendons so she concentrated on those for a few minutes. Then she moved both thumbs to the bottom of his foot and pressed on his heel. She stroked lightly back towards the top and slid her thumb and index finger around the base of his toes and pulled gently on each of them in turn. Jane wasn't sure if what she was doing was really orgasmic but James didn't seem to be complaining. She noticed that he'd stopped scrolling and had lain back on his pillow.

'Is that ok?' she asked.

'Uh mmm,' he muttered.

'Give me your other foot.'

Silently he put his other foot in her lap, and she went through the same motions. She'd fantasised so much about getting intimate with him. Now here she was massaging his feet, which wasn't exactly romantic, but it was a relief just to be able to touch him finally ... she trailed her fingers over the top of his foot and up his ankle until she was massaging his lower calf muscle. James sighed. 'That feels great.' He now had his hands behind his head, his eyes closed and a blissful look on his face. It was making her flustered just watching him. The article hadn't mentioned the masseuse would start feeling orgasmic—she cleared her throat.

'Uh ... I have to go to the common room to chat with Rick. Did you want to talk to him when I'm done?' she managed.

James opened one eye and squinted at her. 'Aye. You might want to wash your face first though, otherwise he'll think it's Halloween.'

'Very funny.'

James was already in the common room when she walked in and busy assembling two bowls of cereal, fruit and milk from the provisions they'd bought yesterday. He was barefoot, and wearing butt-hugging ripped jeans and a white T-shirt. It was showing off his biceps and the light tan he'd picked up from walking around Barcelona. She gulped and mentally shook herself. Stop it! She needed to focus on this call with Rick, not on how unbearably hot James was. The orgasmic foot massage had clearly been a bad idea. She'd have to make up some excuse if he asked her for another one in future.

Jane logged into the video chat platform to wait for Rick to start the meeting. With the five-hour time difference, it was just before one in the afternoon in Bangkok. James was on the other side of the table, absorbed in typing something on his laptop. So, she munched on her cereal and jigged her leg impatiently. The minutes ticked by.

'He's late,' she said, finally.

James grunted. 'Sounds like Rick.'

Her white screen suddenly morphed into colour and she found herself staring at a friendly-looking guy in his early thirties. He was very tanned with shaggy blond hair, dark blond stubble, and a pair of startling blue eyes.

'Hello?' he said, squinting into the webcam. 'Is that Jane, James's friend?' She immediately picked up on his South London accent.

'It is, hello! James is here too. How's the weather in Bangkok?'

'Hot, as usual. Though we're due some showers later.' He panned his laptop around to show her where he was sitting. He was on shaded terrace next to a sunny open-air swimming pool with loungers around it. Rick brought the laptop back to himself, and she got a brief glimpse of yellow silk shirt and tanned hairy chest.

'Where are you guys again?'

'Budapest,' replied Jane.

'Yes, right, James did say. I'm not sure how much he's told you about what I do?'

'Nothing, really,' said Jane, 'Except that you own a content writing agency, and that you like to hang out in the jungle.'

Rick guffawed. He had very white teeth, with the two front ones slightly overlapping. 'Me Tarzan, you Jane. I like it.' Jane glanced at James, who just widened his eyes at her but didn't say anything.

'How much travel writing experience do you have Jane?' asked Rick, still chuckling.

'Not a lot.'

'What's your background then?'

'Um ... I've been working in accounting.' She was about to launch into a spiel about her partially completed degree and McDowd's, however, he interrupted.

'But you love to travel?'

'Yes.'

'Interesting, hmm ... it could work,' he muttered to himself. 'Look, so I'm operating out of Bangkok at the moment with a small team of local freelancers, mainly expat Americans who've escaped the nine-to-five. I've been focusing primarily on Asian travel destinations but I want to expand into Europe and that means I need a Head of European Operations. As of right this minute I'm thinking of you for the role.'

'Oh ... me?! Based on my complete lack of experience working for a content writing agency?'

Rick chortled. 'You're funny, Jane. Yes, I need someone who likes travelling but who's also good with figures. You seem to fit the bill.'

James was nodding enthusiastically at her. She tried to ignore him.

'Head of European Operations—that's a fancy title. So what are you called?' asked Jane, amused.

Rick thought for a moment. 'I'm the Chief Director of Asian Operations.'

'Just like that?'

He shrugged. 'Why not? I can make my own rules.'

'But there'll just be the two of us?'

'Yes, and the writers of course, but they'll come and go.' He sniffed. 'Freelance writers are notoriously fickle.' Jane huffed in mock offence.

'Can you tell me what I'll be doing exactly?'

'Basically, sourcing and maintaining a reliable pool of freelance writers living in Europe, matching them with client briefs, editing their work, managing client accounts, that kind of thing. I've got some billing practices in place to encourage prompt payment, but they don't always work if the client digs in their heels. So, you may need to be persistent in following up. I try not to work with problematic clients, but you get the odd doozy. I give them one chance, and if they screw me over, then they're gone.'

'Sounds like a good principle.' She raised her eyebrows at James, who looked sheepish.

'The tricky part is knowing what to charge them, so I make

enough money to pay you and the writers, and still make a profit, but I'll handle that side of things.'

'Um, speaking of which ...'

'I'll pay you a retainer,' he said quickly before she could finish.

'Will we have a contract?'

'Ah … sure. I'll send you something to look at this evening, and if you like it, just whack an e-signature on it and flick it back to me. Then I'll start feeding you through some small tasks to get you started. Don't want to scare you off or anything.' He paused for breath, frowning. 'Oh and I'll need some updates done on the website … is James …?'

'Right here and wanting to chat with you.'

'Great, thanks, Jane. Could you put him on? I'll be in touch later this evening with your "contract".' He laughed and shook his head as if this kind of formality was completely foreign to him, and he was more used to shaking hands over a Singha beer.

Jane moved over and James came round to her side of the table and was soon deep in a discussion about plugins and CSS edits. She rubbed her eyes. It was the quickest and most casual interview for the fanciest job title she'd ever had. And for some reason, Rick seemed to find her hilarious. She heard James ask him if he was ever planning on coming back to London and Rick saying something about having "met a Thai beauty" so she gathered he wasn't anytime soon. A few minutes later, James logged out and turned to her with shining eyes. 'Och that was productive! Two job offers out of one meeting!'

Jane was just about to ask him what he was doing with Rick's website when Zeke strolled into the room. He was freshly showered and wearing a grey muscle T-shirt and black shorts. He looked absolutely gorgeous. She stared at him wide-eyed, and he gave her a knowing wink, which made her cheeks burn, as she remembered the fevered kissing from last night. He grabbed an apple from the fridge and went into the courtyard.

James clocked the wink and frowned. 'Who does he think he is—Don Juan?' he muttered under his breath.

Chapter 24: Rudas and Ruin

Jane told the girls she was going to the women-only day at the Rudas Baths later on that morning and they all insisted on coming with her. The baths were a half-hour walk from the hostel over Elizabeth Bridge, on the Buda side, right by the river. The sun was out, and it was a pleasant stroll, but Jane didn't really feel like talking after the full-on night she'd had. She just walked along and listened to the other girls chat about people they knew back home.

When they reached the baths and went into the changing rooms, they were surprised to find women walking around in various states of undress—some wearing just bikini bottoms, others in one-pieces, others completely nude. There didn't seem to be any firm rules, so they weren't sure what to do. Cara, Shelley and Melany were all for going fully naked, while Jane was less certain about baring her flesh, even if it was women-only. In the end, she compromised by going topless but keeping her bikini bottoms on.

The Turkish bathing area itself had a series of pillared arches set around an octagonal pool. Above the pool was a domed ceiling with stained glass squares that shone like coloured stars. Half a dozen smaller pools with warm water of varying temperatures were stationed around the perimeter of the main pool. There was also a steam room and a sauna, plus an iced water bucket shower if you felt brave. At first, Jane was self-conscious, but she figured the others were more naked than she was, so she gave up worrying about it.

They tried out all the different pools but eventually ended up in the temperate main pool where they sat on the steps and chatted. The conversation turned to guys, and Jane was surprised to learn that the girls were staying in the same dorm room as Zeke. And his good looks, it seemed, hadn't gone unnoticed by them either. 'He's smoking hot,' said Shelley breathlessly. 'I wouldn't mind some of that.' She glanced sideways at Jane, as if to gauge her reaction. 'Though he *was* coming onto you pretty strong last night. Did anything happen after we left?'

Jane lay back on her elbows and tried to look nonchalant, as if hot guys being after her was an everyday occurrence. 'Uh, he may have wanted to come into my dorm. But it didn't happen. Besides, James was there.'

'What's the deal with him?' asked Cara instantly. 'Are you friends—more than friends?'

Jane wasn't sure what to say. If she said they were just friends, she'd give Cara the green light to pursue James, and she didn't want that. But she couldn't say they were more than friends because they weren't. 'Er ... it's complicated,' she said vaguely. 'He's been dealing with a bad breakup.'

Cara wrinkled her nose. 'I thought there might be something

going on. He totally wasn't taking the bait,' she said.

Jane peered at her across the greenish water. She could just make out Cara's large but pert breasts bobbing below the surface. Her hair was wet and scraped back from her pretty face and her lithe figure was taut. She exuded femininity from every pore. To be honest, thought Jane, if I had a body like that, I'd be using it as bait too. Maybe James was in the closet and just didn't know it.

After a while, they did the circuit of the smaller pools again, then came back to the main pool. She had to admit it was intriguing watching the Hungarian women interacting unselfconsciously with no men around. One young woman floated on her back with her breasts displayed like buoyancy aids while two others eased her around the pool by her shoulders and feet in slow motion. She could just imagine James's eyebrows raising skyward if she told him about *that*.

Cara and Melany jumped out at one point to stand underneath the bucket shower and take turns getting doused with iced water, which elicited high-pitched squeals each time and made Jane and Shelley laugh. Then they used the sauna and steam room. By this time Jane's fingers were thoroughly prune-like. Eventually they'd all had enough but pronounced it 'amazing'.

It was early afternoon by the time they were dressed and outside again, munching on snacks hastily purchased from the on-site cafeteria. The sun had gone in, and the sky was grey. A chilly wind whipped around Jane's damp hair, but she felt thoroughly cleansed and invigorated after last night. As they were walking back across the bridge, she started thinking about Rick's job offer and wondering what the pay would be like.

When they got back to the hostel, the girls went off to their dorm room to change and Jane went to hers. James wasn't there. She hung her bikini bottom over the rungs of the bunk ladder to dry and decided to make some notes on her laptop about the Rudas Baths while it was still fresh in her mind. The notes turned into writing a fair bit of the article as she got caught up with describing the baths, and the sights they'd seen yesterday. The House of Terror still wasn't her favourite place, but it made for interesting copy.

When she'd written as much as she could, it was getting on for dinner time. There was still no sign of James, and no texts. She shrugged. He was probably out with Mitchell. They'd mentioned going to a few of the Holocaust memorials. She knew Cara and the others were planning on going to a Chinese restaurant for dinner and out to a bar afterwards, and that she and James were welcome to come with them. They told her they'd invite Zeke if they saw him in their dorm, so with that in mind she decided to get changed into her black dress and put on some makeup.

There were a few people in the room, but they were still asleep, or had their backs to her, so she quickly took off her T-shirt and jeans and eased on the dress. Feeling brave after the baths, and to save on washing, she went without knickers and bra. Not that she could wear a bra with the dress anyway, the neckline was too extreme. She was just putting on some lip gloss when James walked in.

'Och, not the black dress. There's trouble.'

'You could just say I looked nice,' Jane pouted, her good mood deflating.

James glanced at her. 'You look nice. Getting dolled up for Don Juan?'

'No, I just felt like wearing it.'

'To a Chinese restaurant?'

'Oh, you heard about that.'

'Aye, Mitchell mentioned it.'

'Are you getting changed?'

'Nae, I'll just go like this.'

The Chinese restaurant was nearby which was good, as Jane decided to wear her black heels. Not that she felt her painful arches. When they'd walked into the common room to meet the others, Zeke had given a soft wolf whistle, so she'd floated there on a warm cloud of his approval.

At the restaurant he was attentive, getting her a drink, ordering dishes for them to share and making sure she had enough napkins. He was paying her so much attention, it was difficult for her not to feel flattered. James was practically ignoring her, anyway, focusing on Cara, who was glowing under his intense gaze (the one Jane had privately labelled his "panty dropping" look).

Cara was busy telling him about the baths and how they'd all been naked, apart from Jane who'd kept her modesty mostly intact. James caught her eye and raised an eyebrow, as she knew he would. He had a quizzical look on his face, and she wasn't sure what he was thinking. Probably that she was a prude. She was tempted to tell him she wasn't wearing any knickers at the moment just to shock him.

After the Chinese restaurant, Mitchell suggested they head to a nearby ruin bar that he'd heard good things about. 'What's a ruin bar?' Melany asked Jane as they walked there. James overheard and turned his head. He was walking in front of them with Cara.

'After WWII, the Jewish Quarter was derelict, until about fifteen years ago when locals started setting up pubs in the buildings. Now they're an attraction in Budapest ...' He trailed off, obviously realising he sounded like a history professor.

'You're so clever,' said Cara, gazing up at him adoringly. Jane rolled her eyes. The thought of hanging out in abandoned Jewish homes seemed somehow wrong, but she said nothing and just kept walking.

When they arrived, she had to admit the place was certainly eclectic; it was like an antiques shop had merged with a hardware store, and the owner had no interior design skills whatsoever. There was so much stuff! Silver disco balls, fluffy pink pom poms, electric guitars and what appeared to be knickers, dangling from the ceiling. All manner of paraphernalia was also affixed to the graffitied concrete walls: photos, old TVs, lamp wires and neon lights. A fair amount of people were milling around, drinking and laughing, and the decibel level had grown considerably, even in the few minutes since they'd walked in.

Mitchell immediately headed to the bar to get in some drinks, and soon everyone was clutching a tulip-shaped glass of clear liquid.

'What's this?' asked Jane, sniffing it. It smelt vaguely of apricots.

'Pally-lunka or something,' confirmed Mitchell. 'It was cheap. Only 900 forints, like three dollars a glass.'

'It's Pálinka, fruit brandy,' said James knowledgeably, 'a traditional Hungarian …'

'Yeah, yeah,' said Zeke, cutting him off abruptly. 'Bottom's up!' He clinked his glass with Jane's, and she took a large gulp, gasping as the fiery liquid raced down her throat. A warm glow settled into her stomach, and she finished off the rest.

James looked at her. 'You realise that's about eighty proof?'

'I'm fine,' said Jane, her forehead beginning to sweat. 'I can handle my alcohol.'

An hour later, she wasn't so sure. She'd had a G&T and a red wine, and now Zeke and Mitchell had just gone off to get in another round of Pálinkas. Cara was in the bathroom with Melany and Shelley. She noticed the room was swaying.

'I think you've had enough,' said James.

'I'm perfectly fine,' she slurred. 'I'll just hold onto this chair.' Jane swung her arm over the back of a tall-backed chair and leaned on it like a crutch.

'How's it going?'

'Bonny,' said James. He was drinking whisky, Jane noticed. Always the whisky. She wondered if Cara liked whisky ... James was talking but she couldn't hear what he was saying. There was a bright light winking off and on over his shoulder that was distracting her.

'Jane?'

'Huh?' She pulled her focus back to James with an effort.

'I said we have to talk about some stuff, but not while you're drunk.'

'I'm perfectly sober.'

'You're not.'

'Just say it.'

'Well ... how would you feel about ...' He faltered. She stared up into his face wonderingly, thinking he looked like an angel with the light shining behind his head like that.

'Feel about what?' she asked, her heart pounding. Oh God, he was going to ditch her again and go off with Cara.

'Here you go.' Zeke arrived back, interrupting the conversation. He plonked a full glass of Pálinka on the table in front of Jane, and James said instantly, 'I think she's had enough to drink.'

'Really? Well, she hasn't said so.'

James and Zeke locked eyes, and Jane instantly imagined two angry bulls pawing the ground with steam coming out of their nostrils. Zeke broke the staring contest first and gave an awkward chuckle. 'Fine, I'll have it myself.'

He tossed it back as if it were water and winced. 'God, that stuff's strong.'

James looked smug.

'What's going on here?' Cara had returned from the bathroom with the others and was staring at James questioningly.

James narrowed his eyes at Zeke and said to Cara, 'Jane and I are leaving. She's had enough.'

'I'm fine,' Jane protested, not wanting to be a party pooper. She stood up and let go of the chair. 'Look, see, I'm fine.' Her legs buckled, throwing her into Zeke, who grabbed her round the waist. Then there was a commotion as Cara and James tried to help. They propped her up between them, and they all stumbled out of the bar, everyone trying to look as sober as possible. Mitchell trailed behind, asking why they were leaving so soon.

James flagged down a taxi to take her back to the hostel, but when it pulled up Zeke quickly bundled her into back seat. 'I'll take it from here,' she heard him say to James. She didn't hear James's reply, but his tone sounded annoyed. Then she found herself sitting on Zeke's lap with her head out the window, a cold breeze rushing over her face and her hair streaming.

'Just in case,' he called out to her. 'I don't want puke on my jeans.'

Jane was mortally offended. 'I've never thrown up on anyone!'

'There's always a first time.'

'Whatever!'

Zeke grinned, running a warm hand up her thigh, and Jane suddenly realised she was showing quite a lot of leg. She brought her head in from the window and tried to pull her dress down, vaguely remembering she wasn't wearing any knickers. But Zeke pushed it up again.

'Come with me when we get to the hostel,' he whispered in her ear. 'I found a place for us to go.'

She poked his chest. 'You're a fiend.'

Zeke laughed. 'I am indeed. But you and your sexy dress are turning me on so it's not really my fault.'

Jane was glad to hear the dress was working on someone, even if it wasn't the person who it was originally intended for.

The taxi pulled up at the hostel and they got out, and then she was enveloped in heat and pounding dance music. The courtyard was going off as per usual, and Zeke yanked her through a wall of writhing, sweat-soaked bodies to dance. He was so close to her she could feel his breath on her face and the heat radiating off his body. He kept groping her hips and backside, and kissing her, which she didn't mind. But then, before she could stop him, he squeezed her breasts, which she was less happy about. She looked around to see if anyone saw. But the people nearby were just as intoxicated as they were and too busy getting it on with each other to care.

Then Zeke was beckoning her, so she followed him off to the side and up the iron staircase. She had some trouble walking up the stairs in her high heels and stumbled at one point, skinning her knee, but was pleased that she didn't feel a thing. Then they were at the top, and Zeke was elbowing his way through the crowd. They reached the other end, where there were fewer people, and he opened a nondescript door.

'Through here,' he said, stepping inside a dimly lit, spooky-looking corridor; she hung back and shook her head. Zeke grabbed her by the hand. 'Come on, it's fine.'

She trusted he knew where he was going, so she followed him in. He opened a door in the middle of the corridor and turned on the light. A bare, swinging bulb illuminated some kind of closet. It had a stack of old newspapers, a broken chair, a bucket and mop, and a single mattress propped on its end up against one wall.

'What is this place?'

Zeke shrugged. 'Dunno, but it's private, like you wanted.' He tugged on the mattress and it fell down with a whump, throwing up a great cloud of dust. Jane coughed. She was starting to sober up. And a quick fumble on a dirty mattress didn't really appeal.

'Er ... very romantic,' she said.

Zeke lay down on his side and patted the space next to him.

'Why don't you come in and shut the door?'

'I should text James,' she said, hesitating in the doorway. 'He's probably wondering where I am.'

'Nah. He'll be getting his leg over with Cara. She's gagging for him.'

'Oh.' An arrow of pain shot through her.

'Are you coming in or what?' Zeke sounded impatient. 'Look,

we don't have to do anything. We can just cuddle.'

Jane sighed. 'Fine.' She shut the door and took off her shoes and manoeuvred herself down onto the mattress, and into Zeke's arms.

'See, isn't this nice?' he whispered, running a hand soothingly over her hip and down her bare thigh. She relaxed and nestled into him. He smelt like spice and apricots. He started kissing her but all she could think about was James with Cara. The pain began physically manifesting itself as a series of pinpricks on her calf. It stopped and then she felt it again, higher up by her knee.

By this stage Zeke's breath was rasping loudly in her ear. He'd pulled her dress up and was feeling around between her thighs and grunting in approval because he'd discovered she wasn't wearing any knickers. But the pinpricks were intensifying to the point of being distinctly uncomfortable, so nothing he was doing was remotely pleasurable. She sat up and batted his hand away to scratch her inside thigh, which was now itching madly. Red lumps appeared.

'What's wrong? Just relax,' said Zeke, and tried to pull her back down onto the mattress.

'There's something biting me. Ow!' Now her hip was stinging.

'It's nothing, just forget about it.'

'No, it's definitely something. Ugh, I think it's this mattress— it's got fleas or bedbugs or something. They're all over me!' She scrambled to her feet pulling her dress down and scratching and rubbing at her skin, trying to stop the biting.

Zeke watched her, amused. 'I can't feel anything. Take your dress off properly and let me have a look,' he said, with a sly grin.

'Ah, I don't think so,' said Jane, she slapped at her head. 'Yuck they're in my hair now!'

'Shall we go down to the showers then? I'll soap you up and give you a thorough wash ...'

Jane stared at his smirking face and felt an overwhelming urge to see James.

'I need to find James ...'

'James again! You've got a thing for him, haven't you?' Zeke was scowling now.

'Um ... I think he's just got some hydrocortisone cream ... that's meant to help with bedbug bites ...'

'Of course, Mr Know-It-All would have. If he's so wonderful, why aren't you getting it on with him?'

'Don't call him that; ouch.' She rubbed her left eye. 'Look it's really bad. I'm going ...'

Zeke narrowed his eyes. 'He's got a small prick, hasn't he?'

Jane coughed. 'I don't know.' She put on her shoes and grabbed her phone. 'Look, sorry, I just ...' She couldn't actually be bothered explaining anything to him. She headed for the door, yanked it open, then stumbled into the hallway. Zeke yelled something after her that sounded like 'cock tease!' but she didn't care. Her whole body felt like it was one big uncontrollable itch, and she just needed to find James and smother herself in hydrocortisone.

When she reached the balcony and started pushing her way through, she noticed that people were giving her funny looks. She felt her cheeks; they were hot and lumpy. God, her face was blowing up like a balloon! The iron staircase loomed before her; she gulped. Just one foot in front of the other, she thought, don't trip or you'll break your silly neck. Halfway down her phone beeped. She stopped, hanging on to the railing, and checked it. James—wanting to know where the hell she was. She let out a sob of relief. A group of people came barging up beside her and she shrank back to let them pass. One guy openly stared. 'Jesus, what happened to you?!'

Miserably she scratched at her arm and kept going down. When she got to the bottom, she scanned the room, trying to see someone she knew. Her left eye had now swollen shut, which made her panic that she was going to go blind. She managed to send a text to James that she was by the stairs and to come quickly. She leaned against the wall shivering, and then he was there, saying nothing about how she looked or asking questions, just helping her back to the dorm.

Chapter 25: Buda

Upon hearing the word 'bedbugs', James immediately went out to a late-night chemist to get some antihistamine tablets. Jane popped a couple and conked out on her bunk.

When she opened her eyes, she was lying on her side, clasping an empty plastic container. Her left eye felt gritty and sore, though at least it was open again. She sniffed, and a hand came over with some tissues. Grabbing them, Jane wiped her nose. She turned over to see James, sitting beside her on the edge of the bunk. The light was on in the room, but they were the only ones there.

Jane sat up and the room spun dizzily. 'What time is it?'

'It's nearly nine.'

She looked at the container. 'What's with this?'

'I thought you might throw up.'

Jane groaned as bits and pieces of the evening started coming back to her. She prodded her face gently.

'Don't worry about it,' said James firmly. 'It's only a few bites.'

'I feel like the Elephant Woman! Is it really bad?'

'Och, let's just say you should avoid a mirror for now,' James said matter-of-factly. 'But it's better than it was.'

'Oh,' said Jane. She cringed, trying not to think about it.

'Why are you here anyway? Where's Cara?'

He frowned and shrugged. 'I dinnae ken.'

'What happened?'

'Nothing. Look, while you were out to it I checked us out of here and booked a cheap room somewhere else. I think this place is crawling with bedbugs. I've started itching myself.'

Jane sighed in relief, thinking she'd go with him to Timbuktu if he offered. But a cheap room sounded just as good.

'Thanks, I'm sorry for …'

'Dinnae worry about that now. Let's just get to the new place. We were supposed to check-in half an hour ago, but it should still be ok. I'll call a taxi to pick us up—where's your bag, in the locker?' Jane nodded. With James's help, she put on her trainers, and stood, leaning against the bunk taking small sips from her water bottle while he grabbed her stuff. She felt about a hundred years old, her body stiff, aching and so itchy.

'Ready?' asked James. 'I'll take your bag. Do you think you can handle your pack?'

'I think so. Just a minute.' She found a cotton scarf in her bag and wound it round her head like a hijab so that her face was mostly hidden.

Downstairs, the courtyard was flooded with people, and the thumping music disorientated her, making her feel sick again. The taxi was waiting for them, and the driver got out and helped James load up the boot with their bags.

Jane leant back on the cool vinyl seat and breathed a sigh of relief as they pulled away from the hostel.

'Remember how you said I could tell my grandkids about staying here?'

'Aye.'

'They don't need to hear about this bit.'

'Fair enough.'

The new accommodation was on the Buda side, in the hilly part of the city, so the taxi had to make a couple of switchback turns to get up there. Jane's stomach didn't take that too well, and she felt like she was going to be sick. She breathed deeply and tried to focus on staring straight ahead.

'Nearly there,' said James, getting out his wallet. The taxi stopped outside an austere rectangular building with a tall, ornate wooden door. James paid the driver, and he helped them retrieve their bags from the boot, and then drove off. It was a dark, moonless night with just one lone street lamp giving off a faint glow in the distance. James pressed the buzzer for the third floor. They waited. Nothing happened.

Déjà vu, thought Jane, tiredly. Why is there never anyone to answer the door in these bloody places? She sat down on her bag. At least James was here this time, so she wasn't in danger of being lured into some random Airbnb by a lurking Hungarian.

James tried the buzzer a few more times, then got fed up and said he'd ring the owner. He dialled the number and held the phone to his ear. Jane heard it connect and then a voice say something.

'Hello, it's James McAvoy, I made a booking …'

The voice said something abrupt.

'I know we're late. I'm sorry about that. Can we check in now though?'

He listened for a while, frowning and making faces. The person at the other end seemed to have a lot to say.

'What was that about?' asked Jane when he rang off.

'Och, her English wasn't too good. But from what I could gather, we were meant to check-in before 8:30. Now she has to come and let us in because she stays somewhere else.'

'Ah,' said Jane. Her eyelids felt really heavy all of a sudden, she couldn't seem to keep them open. She shivered.

'It shouldn't be too long. Are you cold?' He got her jacket out of her bag and helped her put it on.

After about fifteen minutes, which felt like an hour, a small red hatchback pulled up and a short woman in her forties with blonde hair scraped back tightly into a bun got out. She glared at them.

'You late,' she stated accusingly.

'Aye, sorry,' replied James in a placating tone. 'But we're here now.'

The woman sighed and pulled out a bunch of keys. She didn't look too happy about it, but opened the door and waved them in.

'Come!'

Thank God, thought Jane, and began to scramble to her feet. James lent her a hand to lever her up. They followed the woman into a pitch-black entrance way.

'No light. Use phone,' said the woman. She switched hers on and shone it upward, showing them a winding stone staircase with a black iron balustrade and thick, grooved wooden banister. Jane had never seen a spookier-looking place in her entire life. There were even stone gargoyles set into the wall. She gulped and gripped James's arm. He'd really outdone himself this time.

The woman started up the stairs, and James grabbed both their bags.

'Do you want to wait here, and I'll come back for you, or ...?'

'No way, José! I'm coming,' said Jane, fear spurring her into action. She took her phone out and turned on the torch so James, in front of her, could see where he was stepping. The woman went on ahead and they followed her more slowly, their footsteps echoing out into the cold, cavernous darkness.

Finally, they reached the third floor, and the woman opened an apartment door with another of the keys. She pressed a switch and yellow light flooded out into the landing. Jane was relieved. She'd been expecting kerosene lamps or umpteen candles that had to be lit.

The woman ushered them into a small entranceway with black-and-white lino and whitewashed walls, and shut the door. She bustled around behind the small reception desk, which had an iMac from the late nineties and an even older printer. She wrote the price of the room on a piece of paper and showed it to James.

'Only cash. No card,' she said and folded her arms impatiently.

'Uh, Jane, do you have any cash on you? I must've not read that part.'

'Yes, I think so.' She rummaged in her pack, and found her purse. She still couldn't see properly out of her left eye, so she handed it to James.

'Shite—ok, bad news. We're still short …' The woman was listening to all this and interjected.

'ATM down road. Do it.'

James glanced at Jane; there was no other option. 'Can she stay here with the bags?' The woman sighed heavily and nodded.

'Go now.'

'Hang on …' James checked his phone to locate the nearest ATM and showed Jane that indeed there was one in a small block of shops nearby. He gave her a quick smile and said, 'I'll be back soon' then slipped out the door and was swallowed up by the darkness. She felt a strange misgiving as he left her, like she was never going to see him again. Don't be daft, she thought, he'll be back in ten minutes.

Jane sat on the floor and leaned back against the wall and closed her eyes. She was starting to feel sleepy again from the tablets.

After a while she heard 'You sick?' She opened her eyes, and the woman was eyeing her warily. Jane nodded weakly.

'Ok.' The woman walked off and disappeared round the corner. Moments later she came back with a sturdy white enamel mug emanating steam that smelt like peppermint.

'Hot tea. You drink.' She handed her a small packet of biscuits, too.

'Thank you,' said Jane, thinking maybe she was actually quite nice. She drank her tea and ate her biscuits silently, while the woman pulled out a pair of glasses and did something on the computer. Then she seemed to want to chat.

'He boyfriend?' The woman nodded at the door.

'Oh ... um ... no ... friend,' said Jane, shaking her head.

The woman stared at her searchingly, and it felt like her black beady eyes were boring holes into Jane's brain. 'I see,' she said suddenly. 'I give bigger room, with double bed.'

She grinned, showing a set of stained crooked teeth. The smile, though slightly scary, did make her seem somewhat more human.

'Ah, ok,' said Jane wearily. At this point she just wanted something soft to lie on. She didn't care what it was.

The woman turned back to her computer, nodding and smiling to herself. Jane put her empty mug on the floor and closed her eyes again. She must've drifted off, as the next thing she knew James was shaking her awake and the woman was gone.

'Hey, sleepyhead.'

'Where is she?' mumbled Jane sleepily.

'Who?'

'The witch.'

James chuckled. 'I paid her the cash, and she was all smiles. She gave me the key and winked at me, then left. A very odd person. Come on.'

He hauled her up and they went down the short hallway to find the room. When he unlocked the door, Jane saw that the woman had indeed given them a room with a double bed.

'Huh, I was sure I booked a twin room,' said James, bemused.

'I think she upgraded us.'

'Weird, why did she do that?'

'I think she liked you,' said Jane, dumping her pack on the desk, which was the only other furniture in the room. 'Must've been the Scottish accent. Och aye.'

'Very funny. Which side do you want?'

Jane shrugged. 'I don't care. I just really need to go to sleep.'

Jane used the bathroom next door first. She had a quick shower to try and ease the itching, then put on a clean T-shirt and knickers. She got a shock when she looked in the mirror and saw her face. Her left eye was still puffy, and she had red swollen lumps on both cheeks, and up by her hairline. Definitely Elephant Woman material, and not ideal when sleeping next to someone you had the hots for, she thought grimly.

While James used the bathroom, she switched on the side lamp, turned off the main light and then got into bed. The sheets were soft and cool on her itchy skin and smelt comfortingly of flowers. She felt a wave of relief that she was finally lying down on a decent mattress and was out of the hostel, and any Zeke repercussions. James came in carrying his clothes and toiletry bag, wearing a T-shirt and boxers. She closed her eyes so she didn't see anything she shouldn't. He rummaged in his bag and produced a tube.

'Are you still itchy? I've got some hydrocortisone cream that might help.' He came over to the bed and handed her the tube.

'I knew you did,' said Jane sleepily. She sat up and dabbed some cream on the angry red bites dotting her arms and legs. She also rubbed a generous amount on her face. 'That's what I told Zeke.'

James came over to the bed and got in next to her. 'I assumed he was involved. Do you want me to put some cream on your back? You'll have to pull your T-shirt up.'

Jane obligingly rolled over on her side away from him and lifted her T-shirt.

'Jaysus!'

'What?!'

'The wee beasties have bitten you to pieces.' He smeared some cream on her back; it felt cool and soothing. And strangely erotic. She supposed it was because she was nearly naked and James was touching her, albeit in a medicinal way.

'Do you want to tell me what happened?' he asked.

'Not really—oh yes, there. That's really itchy.' He was covering a series of lumps on her hip with cream and he pulled the band of her knickers out slightly so he could reach the ones lower down.

James sighed.

'What?'

'I'm trying to be gentlemanly. But there's … er … nothing in the rule book about helping a woman with bedbug bites.'

She giggled. Eventually he was finished, and she reluctantly pulled her T-shirt back down. He reached over and turned off the light.

'I guess we should go to sleep,' he said.

'I guess.'

They lay there in the darkness, not saying anything.

'What happened, Jane?'

'I was up in a room by the balcony with Zeke,' she said eventually, knowing she owed him an explanation. 'He said he'd found a place that was private. Unfortunately, the mattress in the room was ancient and crawling with … well, you know.'

'Right. So, you were planning on sleeping with him.'

'I wasn't really planning anything. I was drunk. It happens,' said Jane defensively. He always took the moral high ground and acted like she was a naughty teenager. She felt so confused by him and tired. 'Please don't give me a hard time.'

James didn't say anything. She tried to touch his hand in the darkness, but he rolled over away from her.

Chapter 26: Full Scottish

The next morning, Jane woke to a steady patter of water which, as James wasn't there, she assumed was the shower next door. On closer inspection, from sitting up and pulling back the edge of the curtain, she realised it was lashing down. The first real rain she'd encountered on the trip since they'd left London, the day after the storm.

She lay back down in bed, feeling her face to see if the bites had gone down; they had slightly. Last night seemed like a dream. Did she really almost sleep with Zeke on a bedbug-infested mattress? Now she was ensconced with James in a room with a double bed, thanks to the witchy woman.

Jane heard him coming down the hallway and quickly shut her eyes. The door opened softly, and he edged in, thinking she was still asleep. He poked around in his bag trying to extract his laptop quietly but ended up making such a noise, dropping adapter plugs and various cords on the floor she had to laugh out loud.

He looked over when he heard her. 'Ooops, you're awake. Sorry.'

'Hard to sleep through that racket!' she teased. She watched him set up his laptop. He'd had a shower by the looks of it; his hair was damp. He noticed her looking at him and smiled. It was like the sun coming out. She breathed a sigh of relief he wasn't grumpy with her anymore.

'How are the bites?' he asked. 'The ones on your face look better.'

'Yeah, they're not as itchy. The cream really helped, thanks.'

'Nae bother. It's just in my bag, so let me know if you want it again.'

He nodded at the laptop. 'Rick's contract came through and a brief, so I thought I'd check out what he wants for his website.'

'Oh, cool. Did you ask for a contract too?'

'Nae, but he sent me one—I guess you set a precedent.' He opened his laptop and logged in.

Jane sat up and pulled the curtains to let in more light, but with the dark sky and the rain it was still gloomy in the room.

'You can turn on the main light if you want. I'm going to check my email, and see if he's sent me anything,' she said.

True to his word, Rick had sent through her contract too, attached to a lengthy email waxing lyrical about them working together. At the end, he'd inserted a GIF of Tarzan beating his chest, which made her giggle. She read briefly through the one-page PDF, and then read it again more closely.

'Are you happy with how much he's paying?' asked James when she didn't say anything.

'Yes; it's not a huge amount but it's regular money, and it's a good start. The rest of it looks fine.' She didn't say anything to him, but she felt mightily relieved that she now wouldn't have to live in a cardboard box and eat spaghetti out of a can. Money had been a major worry lately, especially since she'd taken a big chunk out of her savings to give to James.

'Well done,' he said, sounding impressed. 'You've landed two clients and you've only been freelancing for a few weeks. Some people would kill for that.'

Jane laughed, pleased at his praise. 'It's partly thanks to you, don't forget.' Then her stomach grumbled loudly.

James grinned at her. 'Wow, I heard that from over here!'

'I am starving,' she confessed.

'What's say we go out for breakfast to celebrate? I saw a cafe in the block of shops I went to last night. I can look at Rick's stuff this afternoon.'

Fifteen minutes later, they were seated at the cafe down the road, scanning the menu. It was a basic place, cheap but cheerful.

She ordered scrambled eggs on toast, with bacon, sausages and tomatoes, and James tried to order something resembling a full Scottish, minus the black pudding. The waitress didn't understand his accent and there was a lot of frowning and pointing to the menu on James's part, much to Jane's amusement.

'Who knows what you'll get,' she teased when the waitress was out of earshot.

'Aye, I ordered a hamburger in a cafe yesterday and got a meat patty in a napkin.' Jane cracked up.

Their breakfasts appeared quickly. So quickly that it was almost as if they'd been sitting under a heat lamp, but she was too hungry to care about salmonella. After munching contentedly for a few minutes, she started to feel human again.

'Thanks again for looking after me last night. Sorry if I interrupted anything with Cara,' Jane said, remembering Zeke's comment. If James wanted to hook up with her, she probably shouldn't be obstructive. She took a shaky sip of orange juice, and tried hard not to get emotional about it.

'Ah, no, you didn't,' James said, eyeing her juice. 'Can I have some of that?'

She gave him the glass, suddenly feeling like she wasn't getting the full story. 'Why, what happened?'

James drank some juice, then sighed. 'If you must know, she tried to kiss me in the taxi on the way back to the hostel, and I pushed her away. She stormed off to her dorm.'

Jane winced. Poor Cara. She'd warned her about James's emotional baggage, but she hadn't listened. And he'd rejected her. Yikes! Somewhat ironically, she realised that she was the one who'd slept next to him last night and now, here they were, eating breakfast together the morning after, but as what exactly?

She felt the silver question start to form in the air between them again; it was getting harder to ignore.

'So, are you still hung up on Kistella then?' ventured Jane tentatively.

James shrugged and handed her back the juice. 'Nae, I haven't really thought about her.'

'That's a good sign,' she said, feeling hopeful.

'Aye,' he continued. 'I'm thinking of doing some online dating, once I'm back in Edinburgh.'

Shite, Jane thought. If he goes online, he'll have women lining up halfway to Glasgow. Panicking, she said the first thing that popped into her head. 'You don't want to do that!'

James raised an eyebrow at her over his coffee cup. 'Why not?'

'Er … it's just not easy meeting someone decent online. People tend to be after one thing. Of course, if that's what you're after …' she added, forcing a laugh. Oh my God, shut up, she thought.

'Have you ever been out with anyone you met online?' He asked, eyeing her.

'Once or twice.'

'How did it go?'

'You don't really want to hear about it.'

'I do. I'm intrigued now.'

'Trust me, you don't.'

James laughed. 'That bad? Och, I'll take my chances, I guess.'

The thought of him scrolling through endless profiles of attractive women offering their wares was alarming. She noticed a slight smile playing around his mouth. Grrr, is he trying to rile me up? Fine, she thought … two can play at that game.

'I went out with this guy I met online, and he asked for a blow job in the pub toilet,' she said casually.

James choked on a mouthful of coffee. 'Seriously?'

She shrugged. 'As I said, people online tend to be after one thing.' (It had actually happened to Aimee, but he didn't need to know that.)

He frowned, his mind obviously chewing overtime on that nugget of information. There was a silence, and then sure enough the question came.

'So did you?'

'Did I what?'

'Give him one.'

She looked at him steadily, keeping her face deliberately blank and said 'What do you think?'

(As she remembered it, Aimee had called the guy a 'feckin' pervert' and thrown what was left of her pint over him.)

James looked back at her. His expression was a mixture of amusement and something else she couldn't quite read. She noticed he was gripping his coffee cup tightly and his leg was jigging under the table.

'Have you finished?' she said finally, breaking the tension. 'I need to start work on my article. And do you want this?' She offered him her plate with one sorry-looking leftover sausage. He stared at it and didn't say anything. Jane tried not to laugh.

Outside it was still pouring down, so they made a mad dash back to the apartment and stamped noisily up the dark staircase to the third floor. Jane said James could have the desk, so she sat on the bed with her laptop on her knees and attempted to concentrate on writing her article. But their conversation about online dating had effectively managed to get under her skin. Now all she could think about was him going on a date with a different woman every night, and all of them gagging for him. She sighed, and he glanced over.

'You all right?'

'Yes, yes, everything's fine,' she said brightly and pretended to tap away on her keyboard. 'What about you?'

'Aye, good, thanks.' She noticed his leg was still jigging under the table.

Finally, by mid-afternoon, she'd finished the article and was reading through it when James leaned back and stretched his arms above his head. He glanced out the window. 'It's stopped raining. I might go for a run.'

'Ok,' she said, still reading. He got up and grabbed something from his bag, and went out to the bathroom. When he came back in, she looked up and caught her breath.

He was shirtless, wearing only a pair of black Adidas running shorts and trainers, with his headphones hanging around his neck. It was the same gear he'd worn at her parents' place, but now she was getting the glorious frontal view. Seriously built biceps; broad, smooth muscular chest; six-pack abs and shorts that were so freakin' … tight.

Jane's vision blurred. She tried to speak normally without

sounding like a strangled cat.

'Are you going to be warm enough?'

'Aye, I work up a sweat pretty quickly. Thanks though, Ma.' He grinned at her. 'Right, I'm off, you ok here? I'll take the key.'

Jane nodded at her laptop. 'Yes, I'll edit this and get it off to Gemma. Have a good run.'

'Thanks, I'll see you later.'

He put his headphones on and left the room. Outside, she heard the main door slam shut. Jane fell back on the bed with a groan, feeling an exquisite burn start up between her thighs and slowly spread over her body. So much for other women gagging for it. There was no way she could be in the same room with him, let alone a double bed, especially now she knew how ripped he was. And the way the dynamic was going she was pretty sure he'd goad her to the point that she'd try and jump his bones. Then if he pushed her away like he did with Cara ...

She grabbed her phone and called Amber. Luckily, she picked up on the second ring. Jane didn't bother with niceties; there wasn't time.

'Ambs, it's me. Major problem.'

'Is it James?'

'How did you know?'

'Lucky guess,' said Amber wryly. 'What's he done now?'

'Long story short. James and I are staying in a room with a double bed. He just came in half naked, looking like a bloody Chippendale ... let's just say, my estrogen levels are seriously spiking right now.'

Amber giggled. 'Och, that good huh?'

'You have no idea. What am I going to do?'

'Sounds like he's going to get lucky.'

'No, no, no!' cried Jane. 'I can't lose it. If I throw myself at him and he rejects me ...'

'Why do you think he will? Maybe he's trying to get a reaction out of you by swanning around like that.'

'I don't know,' she moaned. 'Maybe, but it's also just his normal workout gear. I don't think he's doing it because of me.'

'Why don't you swan around half naked too and see what happens.'

Jane gave a choked laugh. 'Is that your best advice? I can't do that! Besides, he's already rejected someone—'

'Aw, who?'

'This girl at the hostel.'

'Was she minging?'

'No, she was actually gorgeous.'

'Och, he sounds really choosy.'

Jane groaned. 'Don't say that.' An image of Kistella—chestnut-haired, green-eyed and buxom—sprang to mind. 'There's only one thing for it.'

'You're going to jump him?'

'No—focus! I'll say I have to leave, that I sent Gemma my article and she immediately came back with another job to ...' Where should she say? Jane's brain whirred like a windmill, mentally flicking through European cities. 'Paris!' she cried triumphantly.

'So, you're going to lie to him?'

'It's not a complete lie. Gemma did mention something about going to Paris on the phone the other day.'

'James might want to come too.'

'No way,' said Jane confidently. 'He hates Paris.'

'Who the hell hates Paris?'

'James, apparently. He had a rant to me about it one time, it was pretty funny actually.'

'You could just stay and see what happens?'

Maybe—if she wasn't covered in bedbug bites and was feeling mentally stable—she could attempt some kind of seduction. But she knew she was completely on the back foot. Besides, she didn't want him to think he was a rebound after Zeke, and all she wanted was a quick fumble. He meant more to her than that. The whole situation felt incredibly volatile.

'I can't. I'm between a rock and a hard place,' Jane concluded dolefully. Amber sniggered, which made her start laughing hysterically. She gasped for breath and tried to calm down. 'I just need to get a hold of myself again, to get my head sorted. This is what we decided after Como anyway, that we'd have a flexible arrangement. So that if I got a job, I could take off, and then we'd meet up again afterwards. And I'll make sure from now on that we stay in separate rooms! It'll be fine. It'll work.'

'Well, if you're sure.' Amber sounded doubtful. 'So where are you going to go if it's not actually Paris?'

'I'll find somewhere. It's not a problem. I'll contact you from there, wherever it is. Look, I should go. He'll be back soon.'

'Ok, hen. Just please, be careful. If he finds out you've lied ...'

'I know,' said Jane. The last thing she wanted to do was hurt him.

James came in while she was packing and immediately wanted to know what was going on. The fact that he was flushed and sweaty and looked even more jumpable made her harden her resolve. He wasn't happy when she told him.

'Another one! Didn't you tell her we've got our own itinerary?'

'We still have,' said Jane, keeping her head down and packing determinedly. 'It isn't for long, and I'll meet up with you afterwards.'

'But why do you have to leave right now?'

It was a good question, but she had a ready answer. 'There was a cheap flight going there tonight so Gemma booked me on it.' She crossed her fingers. Please don't check it, she thought.

'I'll send you a photo of the Eiffel Tower.'

'Pffft, that eyesore,' he grumbled. But then gave her a halfhearted smile so she knew he was ok, or at least mollified enough to accept her explanation.

Chapter 27: Sant Agusti

Thanks to Google, Jane didn't have to think too long and hard about where she was actually going. On the way to the airport, she searched for cheap flights leaving from Budapest that evening and there was one scheduled for Majorca. It was perfect. She'd been to the capital, Palma, a few times. Plus, she wanted to relax and regroup so she could focus fully on Rick's job and get James to some level in her head (and loins) where she could handle being around him.

The budget hotel she'd hastily booked in the departure lounge was just west of Palma, in a small suburb called Sant Agusti. She liked the look of it because it was away from the main port and it had a pool, mountain views and was a ten-minute walk to Cala Mayor Beach. It also had over one hundred rooms, so she figured most people would be occupied with their own business. She could just sit by the pool and chill.

When she checked in, the friendly receptionist tried to sign her up for a multitude of activities, but Jane neatly evaded her efforts by saying she was planning on doing a lot of day trips. In fact, she slept in, walked into town to grab breakfast, then lazed on the beach until the sun drove her indoors. Then, after a leisurely lunch and a siesta, she headed out to the pool in the late afternoon to work, sunbathe or periodically take a cooling dip. It was bloody idyllic. Welcome to the world of freelancing, she thought, or being a 'glorified layabout', as her father had put it. She'd loved James's amusement when he'd been called that at the dinner table.

They hadn't spoken since she'd left Budapest, but the day after she arrived in Sant Agusti she'd emailed him a photo of the Eiffel Tower (and felt as guilty as hell about it). And a couple of times she'd started writing him a text but then quickly erased it. She didn't want him asking too many questions. But then he'd replied with a photo of Charles Bridge and a message saying he'd gone to Prague. And did she want to meet up there? Jane breathed a sigh of relief. It was all still fine.

Besides, she was busy. On the Thursday morning, Rick sent her an email with stuff he wanted her to do. Then another on Friday morning. He left her alone for the weekend. Then it was non-stop all through the next week. She'd get a notification around seven, groggily read the email, send a brief reply and promptly go back to sleep again. But he pretty much let her get on with it and didn't mind what time of the day she worked. It was so refreshing after the nine-to-five grind.

After a few days, she switched to working in the cool of the evening when the rest of the hotel was out at dinner. Sometimes she took a break at dusk and walked barefoot along the beach, now deserted by the day's sunseekers, for a change of scene.

Despite trying to detach herself, Jane ended up thinking about James incessantly. The way he bit his lower lip when he was concentrating on reading something. His long-suffering expression when she was being deliberately obtuse. The way his mouth twisted in a wry grin when she made him laugh. How on earth was she going to be around him in person and act normal? He was intoxicating.

Even more distracting were the constant daydreams she had about him while lazing by the pool on a lounger. It was always centred around the same scenario. Her lying on her side with her T-shirt pulled up and feeling him applying soothing cream to her itchy back. But when he finished, before she could pull her T-shirt down, his hand would reach over to stroke the soft curve of her breast. Or she was rolling over to face him and he was looking down at her breasts and saying, 'I'd like to rub cream on those' or something equally cheesy. Either way she was powerless to stop the fantasy unfolding, and usually became so hot and bothered by the end of it that the only thing that helped was jumping into the pool and doing a few laps. Then she had a vivid dream about him that muddled her brain even more.

It was the middle of the week and she'd been up late chatting with Amber. Things were going like wildfire with Colin now that she'd changed day care centres and his ex-wife and child were no longer in her face on a daily basis. She'd just come back from a week's holiday in Sweden with him, so she was bursting to tell her all about it.

On previous phone calls, Amber had tactfully avoided the subject of James, and Jane fleeing Budapest with her 'knickers on fire' (as Amber put it). But on this particular night, Jane was drinking sangria and after hearing about Amber's good time away, she was feeling sorry for herself.

'Maybe I should've stayed? Who knows, it may have been fine. What if he's found someone else?'

'Nae, it was the right thing to do under the circumstances,' soothed Amber. 'Even if he does happen to have a fling with some floozy—and I'm not saying he will!—he's mucked up in the head so you're better off out of it.'

Amber was right. It was best to play it safe. They still had months of travel to go. She had to control herself. After she hung up, Jane went to bed and fell into a sangria-fuelled doze. She dreamed she was at the Rudas Baths and completely naked but perfectly fine about it. She walked out of the changing room and into the domed area. James was lounging in the octagonal pool, with his hair slicked back. But he seemed to also be Zeke because he had a barbed wire tattoo on his left arm. As she walked down the steps into the steaming water, he raked his eyes over her body. Weirdly she didn't particularly mind but was more concerned that other women wouldn't want a man in the pool. She swam over to him and said sternly, 'You're not allowed in here; it's women-only day.' He just grinned at her lazily and said, 'How else am I going to see your sexy body?' But it sounded like something Zeke would say so she felt confused. Then a crowd of Asian women came bursting through the door and plunged into the pool together, creating a huge tsunami, and she was swept up to the domed ceiling on the crest of the wave towards the coloured lights. When she looked down, she couldn't see James. Then she felt like she was falling from a great height into the pool and woke with a start on her back with her legs in the air.

Maybe it was a sign he was thinking about her because that morning, when she went to use the ATM in town, she found two thousand pounds had been transferred into her account. Racing back to her hotel room, she breathlessly checked her bank statement online. There it was, J.H.McAvoy—two thousand pounds transferred yesterday. Go, James! So, he'd managed to get the wayward client to pay by threatening legal action. That always works, she thought, smiling to herself. She felt inordinately proud of him, and relieved that, at least on a monetary level, he was thinking of her.

The next day, out of the blue, Gemma rang her to say that she'd been networking with the tourism boards of several EU countries, and they'd all agreed to articles. The Budapest job had just been the tip of the iceberg. Jane listened, gobsmacked, as Gemma rattled off all ten countries she wanted her to visit: Estonia, Greece, Malta, France, The Netherlands, Germany, Portugal, Belgium, Cyprus and Finland.

'Of course, I'll pay you for all the articles, and I've even managed to wangle you some discounted accommodation and free city passes for transport and tours. The flights should be cheap enough if you get onto booking them asap and work out an itinerary for the cheapest route. It doesn't matter which order you do them in as long as it's in the next couple of months,' she said.

'Oh my gosh. It sounds amazing. Are you sure you don't want to do it?'

'To be honest, I'm burnt out. I need a holiday.' Jane giggled and Gemma realised what she'd said and laughed. 'Travel writing isn't a holiday! I just want to sit still and do nothing for a while.'

'I totally get that,' said Jane. She imagined jetting off every week to a new destination would take its toll eventually. It sounded glamorous, but it was still work. She was lucky that Gemma was doing all the hustling. She just had to do the travelling and writing part.

'So if I write the articles, what do you get out of it?' Jane asked curiously.

'Fresh content, backlinks, shares, likes, comments, you name it—all of that is gold. Plus, it frees me up to spend some time with my family. They haven't seen me for six months!'

'Aww, great! Well, I've got the next couple of months free before I'm due to head back to Edinburgh so it's perfect timing my end.'

Some of the countries that Gemma had listed were on the

itinerary she and James had planned. It was working out, she thought. Everything would slot in and they'd be able to get back to some kind of even keel. It would just take careful planning.

'I'm so glad I met you, Jane. You've been a real godsend, and your writing is just getting better and better, I hardly need to make any edits. And you're a lovely person to boot.' Gemma's voice wavered.

Wow, she sounds quite emotional, thought Jane. 'I'm glad I met you too. It's changed my life,' she told her and started welling up. Now *she* was getting emotional!

Before she rang off, Gemma said she had something else in the pipeline for her. 'It's an article for a hotel in Iceland, and I'm pretty sure they're going to say aye. I'll let you know, fingers crossed!' That sounded intriguing, but she couldn't spend time wondering about it. She had to talk to James to see if he was cool with the new itinerary, and then rework their spreadsheet for the next two months. And she had Rick's job to think about. Luckily, she'd just managed to get a couple of editors on board for his content so it freed her up to do some more travel writing. All she had to do was keep juggling all the balls in the air and make sure the clients paid their invoices on time so Rick could pay everyone, including her. If her father could see her now, would he still call her a 'glorified layabout'? she wondered. Probably, but she didn't really care.

CHAPTER 28: LEITH

Two months later

Jane arrived back in Edinburgh on a Saturday afternoon in the first week of December. It was a freezing, blustery day, and she caught the tram from the airport, then shivered on Princes Street waiting for the bus to Newington. Standing on board with her luggage, it felt like she was a tourist in her own city.

When she got to the flat, Aimee was there with the heating turned up full blast, the kettle boiling and a hot water bottle on standby for good measure. She'd also made her bed with clean sheets, hung up her clothes in the wardrobe and put out her knick-knacks that had been in a box in the storage cupboard.

Jane hugged her. 'What would I do without you?'

'Aw, nae bother. I wanted you tae feel it wiz yer room again. No that Johanna changed it much, but it's nice tae have yer own things around. Now lemme look at you.'

Jane laughed. 'It's only been three months, not three years!'

Aimee surveyed her. 'Och, but you do seem different. A wee bit older, maybe?'

'Older! I don't have grey hair, do I?!'

'Nae, you just seem surer of yerself. Of what you want.'

Jane looked away and didn't say anything.

She spent the next week settling in, and getting to know Trish, the new flatmate who had taken over Rebecca's room. Trish was also studying to be a nurse and was from Aberdeen. Aimee had been regaling her with tales of Jane's travels and the fridge was plastered with all the postcards she'd sent. Trish hadn't been out of the UK, 'apart from a family holiday to Spain eons ago,' she said, so she'd been eager to meet her.

'Yer so brave! Turning down a secure job and going off like that.'

Jane smiled. 'I had some help to start with. I don't know if I could've done it completely on my own otherwise.' She quickly changed the subject so she didn't have to think about James. But it was difficult *not* to think about him every time she walked past Costa Coffee and looked through the window—I was with him in there. We had coffee and talked about freelancing, he laughed at my jokes … he made me feel like I was special.

She'd managed to deal with it for the most part during the day when she'd been travelling, attempting to put on a professional face. But at night there had been distraught typing of draft emails and tear-stained hotel pillows.

Aimee hadn't mentioned his name as she knew it was a taboo subject. But on the Thursday of her first week back, Jane was downloading some travel photos from her phone to her laptop at the kitchen table. Aimee, walking behind her, happened to glance down at her laptop during the Barcelona download.

'Why are there heaps of dead gorgeous photos of you outside the Sagrada Familia?' she asked curiously. Jane shook her head and said 'James' and then couldn't speak because she was so choked up. Aimee said 'arsehole' and hugged her and she cried hot, messy tears onto her shoulder.

If she could turn back the hands of time, she'd do it all differently. She would've stayed in Budapest, confessed how she felt, taken the risk that his response would've been: 'Jane, it's just not going to work, I don't see you that way.' Then cried her heart out, left to go travelling on her own and eventually managed to get over him. He would've probably said they could be friends, to which she would've immediately replied, 'No—but thanks for the offer.'

It would've all been so much more dignified, perhaps even less gut-wrenching after the initial stab through the heart. But it was easy to say that now when she knew what the alternative was.

⊕

It had been Friday evening in Sant Agusti, her last night before she was due to fly to Prague and meet James. He'd agreed, somewhat reluctantly, to the revision of their own itinerary so Jane had spent all afternoon sweating over it, trying to include him as much as possible but keeping him at arm's length. A few of the tourism boards had provided discounted accommodation just for her which made it easy; James was forced to stay elsewhere. But in those cities, she'd suggested a range of options for him. In the other cities where they'd be sleeping at the same place, she'd recommended hostels with male and female dorms or cheap hotels with separate rooms, so that the double bed scenario couldn't happen again. It was a watertight, foolproof plan; not even a lawyer would find a loophole. Finally, she'd emailed it to him around four to approve so she could start booking everything.

He thought she was arriving into Prague from Paris so she'd also sent him bogus flight details. Luckily there had been a flight coming from Paris on Saturday, and the one she was actually on, from Majorca, landed an hour before the one from Paris. So, she had an extra hour to kill in the airport before meeting him in the city. Then there was the whole business of concocting a believable story about Paris. Things she'd done, things she'd seen. It was a complex operation trying to keep track of all the loose ends. But she knew once they were in Prague things would take care of themselves and she could just relax and have fun; things would be under control.

She'd been in the middle of packing when James rang her unexpectedly.

'Hey you—!' she said, surprised to hear from him.

But there was no friendly greeting in return and straight away she knew she was in trouble.

'You're not in Paris, are you,' he said flatly.

She sank onto the bed. Shite.

'No,' she said in a small voice.

'Where are you?'

'Majorca.'

'Feckin' Majorca!' Double shite.

'I know it looks bad.'

'You're feckin' right it does! I knew something was up when you left in a hurry. Why did you lie to me?!'

God, he sounded really angry. The ground opened up in front of her and she felt herself teetering on the edge, about to fall into a deep, dark hole.

'I ... I couldn't deal with ... stuff. It was all getting too intense, so I needed some space to get my head together.'

'But why lie about it? Why not just talk to me instead of taking off like that and feeding me a cock and bull story about going to Paris?!'

Because *you're* the reason things were getting intense! she wanted to yell at him.

'I thought I knew you. That you weren't a feckin' liar!!' She winced and held the phone away from her ear.

'James ... I'm so sorry.'

'Kistella was bad enough and now you're doing it too. It's Don Juan, isn't it? You've run off with him and didnae have the guts to tell me.' He gave a bitter laugh. 'That's why you've jacked up all these separate rooms on the new itinerary. It's so he can join you!'

'James, I haven't spoken to Zeke since that night at the hostel. I'm by myself. Look, I'll come to Prague tomorrow … I'll explain in person,' she said in a soothing tone, trying to calm him down.

'Tell me now. Why did you lie?'

'Uh …' Jane's mouth went dry. Her heart pounded. Tell him what exactly—that she couldn't be in the same room without wanting to rip his clothes off? That she was falling for him big time? She wanted to tell him the truth but was terrified he'd kick her to the kerb. He was so irate she didn't think he'd even believe her.

As the silence lengthened, she heard him sigh despondently, which was worse than the anger.

'And to think I was actually starting to trust you. This whole travel thing was a mistake—it's just been one thing after another, it's doing my head in. You're a feckin' liar and a troublemaker, like *her*.' She flinched, hardly believing he was tarring her with the same brush as Kistella.

'You can still trust me!' she said desperately.

'I don't think so.'

'James …'

'Have a nice life.'

'James!'

But he'd hung up on her. She remembered little else about the rest of that night because she was a mess. Numbing the pain with copious amounts of sangria and crying as she puked into the toilet.

Then ending up comatose on the bathroom floor, waking at some ungodly hour to crawl into bed, knowing that she wouldn't see him that day, or any other day.

⊕

Jane spent the weekend alone. Aimee had gone to Skye with a friend, Amber was visiting whisky distilleries with Colin in Speyside and Trish was on night shift. She didn't mind. The weather was terrible, so she just lay on the couch, ate a generous amount of chocolate, and watched rom-coms. She'd forgotten to buy tissues, so she had to make do with sobbing into torn-off wads of toilet paper when the main characters inevitably got together.

On Tuesday, Amber called to say hello, and to invite her out to dinner. 'There's a new restaurant opened up on The Shore. I checked out the website. It's lovely. Big picture windows facing out over the canal and booth seating. The menu looks yum too. How's Friday night for you?'

'Friday night's fine. Is it just you and Colin?'

'There may be one other person coming.'

'Oh—who?'

'Colin's brother, Keith.'

'Amber …' said Jane warningly. 'I don't want to be set up with anyone.'

'It's not like that! He's really nice …'

'Mmm hmm.'

'Anyway, you need to move on from Mr McAvoy. It's not healthy. It will do you good to meet some new men.'

'I don't think I can move on. I … I think I'm in love with him.'

It was the first time she'd actually admitted it to herself.

There was silence on the other end of the phone. Amber, for once, seemed lost for words. 'Aw, Janie,' she said eventually. 'Well, just come anyway, for a change of scene and to hang out with us. I'll see you Friday.'

Amber was right in one respect. She *did* need a change of scene. While she'd been travelling and on the go, she was moving from hotel to hotel, and from country to country every few days. Now she was working from home, it was different. She didn't have set hours but she still had to be disciplined otherwise she'd just lie in bed surfing on her phone and get nothing done. Aimee and Trish were often on night shift, so she was there by herself, which was fine. But she was starting to get depressed from the weather and about James, and she felt herself spiralling. Dammit, Amber was right about that too—it wasn't healthy!

With her wellbeing in mind, Jane chose her outfit for Friday night carefully. A halter neck jade silk dress that clung flatteringly to her bust and waist with a flared skirt that came to just above the knee. She'd seen it in a shop window in Amsterdam and immediately gone in and tried it on. It'd fit perfectly. This was the first chance she'd had to wear the dress, and she thought she may as well while she still had the remnants of a tan from Majorca. She decided to pair it with her favourite black heels, the ones she'd retrieved from Natalie. She also took extra time with her makeup, so it didn't look like she'd chucked it on in a hurry. She'd had a haircut earlier in the week so her dark-blonde hair, while still past her shoulders, had been trimmed and styled. At the last minute she decided to put her hair up in a low chignon, because it looked more elegant with the dress. She pulled out a few tendrils to frame her face and soften the effect. You'll do, she thought, looking at herself in the full-length mirror. Meeting Keith probably wouldn't be earth-shattering but it felt good to get dressed up and make an effort. She'd started getting used to comfy leggings and hoodies way too much!

Outside it was glacial with rain, sleet and a bone-chilling arctic wind. Welcome to winter in Edinburgh, she thought, glad she was bundled up in her thick black coat with a matching fur lined hood. Luckily the taxi down to Leith was toasty too.

Amber and the others were already seated when she walked into the restaurant, so she pointed them out to the maître d' and he said to go through. He took her coat to hang in the cloakroom and gave her a ticket. Amber was dressed up to the nines in a black cocktail dress and wearing full makeup, so Jane was glad she'd made an effort to look nice.

'Hi, Janie; wow, I love your dress!' exclaimed Amber when she saw her.

'Hiya! Thanks, you look gorgeous as usual.'

'Hello, Jane, welcome home,' said Colin, getting up to kiss her on the cheek. 'This is my younger brother Keith from Inverness. But don't hold that against him.'

Jane laughed and reached over to shake hands with Keith who smiled and nodded up at her but stayed sitting down.

She slid into the black leather seat beside Amber and looked around. They were in the middle of the restaurant in one of the curvy, high-backed booths that snaked the length of the long, narrow room. She and Amber were facing the bar area, which had well-stocked metal shelves and a busy barman. Behind them, a low black leather couch ran alongside a panoramic window frontage with more intimate table seating for couples. The place was humming and most of the tables were full. Opening week, she thought: time will tell.

Amber saw her surveying the decor. 'We were lucky to get a booth seat for four. But I guess they could've pushed two tables together.'

'It's cool. I like it. Vintage industrial with a sleek modern aesthetic,' she commented.

'Och, get you,' said Amber, handing her a chunky, leather-bound menu. Jane chuckled. 'I've described so many restaurants over the last couple of months I could probably write a review in my sleep!'

She opened the menu and flicked a quick peek at Keith over the top. He had the same stocky build, pleasant face and curly hair with a reddish tint as Colin, but a bigger nose and ears. He was wearing a three-piece brown tweed suit complete with a white business shirt and red tie.

She was willing to bet he had a flat cap somewhere around too. A real estate agent, perhaps? Looks-wise he wasn't doing anything for her but at least he was another Jamie lookalike. If Amber got sick of Colin, she could always make a play for his brother.

'How long are you in town for, Keith?' she asked politely.

'Just fer the weekend,' he replied. 'I thought I'd better visit ma brother tae see if he's still alive. No one's seen hide nor hair of him since he's been flitting around wi' the wee one.'

She took that to mean Amber rather than Hector. He had a thick brogue and Jane had to listen carefully to understand him. His next words to her were: 'You're no Scottish, are you, Jane?'

It sounded more like a statement than a question. Almost bordering on an accusation.

'How can you tell?' she said breezily. 'No, I'm from London.'

'And yer living here the noo?'

'For the meanwhile.' Is that ok? she felt like saying.

'Jane's just come back from a three-month trip around Europe,' piped up Amber. 'She went to ten countries!'

'Twelve actually,' corrected Jane. 'If you count Spain and Hungary.'

'Och, twelve countries! Was it an overdue holiday?' asked Keith.

'Work actually.'

'What do you do?'

'I'm a freelance travel writer and a content manager for a client in Bangkok.'

She decided Head of European Operations really was too highfalutin a title to mention under the circumstances.

'Sounds a lot more interesting than ma job by far,' Keith said with a self-deprecating smile.

'What do you do?' asked Jane.

'I'm an accountant.'

Luckily the waitress arrived then to take their orders, so she didn't have to reply. Grrr, she would murder Amber. Was she really trying to set her up with an accountant?! Keith seemed like a perfectly nice guy, but she would never get excited about someone who was an accountant. She tried to give her a kick under the table but Amber just smiled innocently and shifted her shorter legs out of the way. The topic of conversation changed to what Colin and Keith were planning to do on the weekend: a whisky walking tour that sounded more like a pub crawl.

'You girls are welcome to join us,' said Colin, but Jane shook her head. Then a discussion on the best Highland whiskies ensued. Please don't mention Glenmorangie, she thought, cringing.

After they'd finished their generous mains (her steak had been divine), everyone declared themselves "stuffed", so they decided to forgo dessert and just have a coffee each. Amber popped off to the ladies' and Jane checked her messages, while they waited for her to return. She seemed to be taking forever. Finally, she arrived back in the booth in a flurry of energy. She slid over to Jane so quickly she knocked into her.

'Are you ok?'

'James is here!' hissed Amber.

Jane frowned at her. 'Don't joke.'

'I'm not! Tall, dark—face like Adonis? It's him, all right! I had to hide behind a potted palm until they were seated before I could come back in.'

Jane felt like she was about to hyperventilate. James was here, in the same room? She clutched Amber as her stomach lurched.

'I think I'm going to be sick.'

'Aw, nooo, dinnae do that!'

She noticed then that Keith was watching them with a bemused expression and saw him nudge Colin. 'What's that aboot?' she heard him ask.

Vaguely she heard Colin's reply—'... the one that got away ... hasn't heard hide nor hair from him for two months ...'—and realised that Amber must have told him about what had happened. She closed her eyes, steeling herself against the memory of it. Their coffees arrived then, and she took a fortifying sip of her scalding cappuccino. Then Amber's earlier words registered.

'Hang on. Did you say "they"? Is he here with someone?'

Amber nodded, grimacing. 'A girl—they're over by the

window, to your right.'

'Oh God.' Jane turned her head and tried to peer over the top of the booth.

'Don't look! He'll see you!'

'What ... what's she like?' Jane asked shakily.

'Dark hair, pale, skinny, no boobs,' said Amber immediately. Not Kistella then. Hell, he was on a date with someone he met online! She drank the rest of her coffee in a hurry, burning the roof of her mouth in the process, but hardly noticed. It was fine—she could be here with him, sitting mere metres away, even if he was on a date. It was all just fine—Edinburgh was a small city. She was bound to bump into him at some point. She stared into her empty cup, remembering their meetup at Costa Coffee, and how much she'd liked him. How much she still liked him. A burst of determination went through her, or perhaps it was the caffeine hitting her system. Whatever it was, she knew she had to see him.

'I'm going over,' she announced to the table, hardly believing she was actually going to do it.

Colin gave a low whistle. 'You've got baws, lass.'

'Are you sure, love?!' We can just go. He hasna seen us,' said Amber, her voice a mixture of horror and concern. Then added quietly, 'Just to warn you. He looks *banging* hot.'

Colin overheard and frowned at her. 'Steady on.'

'Sorry, Colin, but he does. We're talking GQ magazine material. She needs to be prepared.'

Shite, Jane thought. She fumbled for her purse and applied some lip gloss and checked for mascara smudges under her eyes.

'How do I look?'

'Absolutely beautiful,' said Amber firmly, and gave Colin and Keith a fierce look. They nodded and murmured obediently that yes, she looked very bonny.

'Right, here I go.' She sat there unmoving, remembering the flinty anger in his voice, and how he'd called her a 'troublemaker'. She sagged. 'I can't do it. What am I going to say?'

Then Keith reached into his pocket and brought out a slim notepad and gold ballpoint pen and slid them over the table to her.

'Write on this, lassie,' he said to her gently. 'You can go over and say "hello" and "how are you?" then just give him yer note and walk away. Nae bother. Just say how you feel. Yer a writer, aren't you?'

She looked at the notepad; it had a header saying 'Strothers, Duncan & Co, Millburn Road, Inverness', which for some reason comforted her immensely because it made her think of meeting James at McDowd's.

Say how I feel in fifty words or less. No pressure, thought Jane. She'd written so many draft emails during the last two months, all variations of the same theme, that she was starting to think about writing a book entitled *Emails to James (unsent)*. There had been no eloquent way to explain her behaviour without revealing how she felt about him; it was a Catch 22.

Fuck eloquence, she thought now, looking at the notepad. She grabbed the pen and the words flowed effortlessly out of her and onto the paper. She knew exactly what she wanted to say. It was bold, it was raw ... Jane looked at what she'd written and gulped. God, was she really going to give this to him?!

The others had been watching on in silence whilst drinking their coffees. Colin muttered to Amber, 'I feel like I'm in *Notting Hill*.' Amber sssh'd him.

Jane tore off the piece of notepaper before she could change her mind and folded it tightly. Then said 'Wish me luck' and slid out from the table. Amber blew her a kiss and whispered, 'You can do it!', which gave her a confidence boost.

She adjusted her dress and started walking on quivering legs towards the half a dozen couples seated along the window, one of which she knew was James and his date. Thoughts began crowding into her mind telling her not to do it, that he was with someone, that he hated her guts. Don't think, she told herself, just focus on not tripping over!

Then, as she scanned the tables, she caught sight of him and her jaw dropped. Amber was right, he looked incredible. He'd had some kind of exotic makeover and was sporting a tan, as well as a short, spiky haircut, and even wearing a black suit jacket and open-neck white shirt that made him look like a freakin' male model. Jane moaned inwardly. Why couldn't he have had a few spots or have gained ten pounds? Even the onset of male pattern baldness would be helpful right now.

James was leaning in to say something to the girl opposite him and happened to catch sight of Jane as she stood there staring at him. They locked eyes, and she froze, her heart beating madly in her chest. She waited for him to frown, to look angry, but something even worse occurred. He quickly looked away and continued his conversation—like she meant nothing. After that, she knew it was pointless, but she still had to do it. She had no choice. He'd seen her now. If she turned around and went back, she'd look like a fool. Going up to him was the hardest thing she'd ever done in her life, but she plastered on a smile and walked over on shaking legs. Luckily, she arrived during a break in their conversation.

'Hey, James, I thought it was you! I was just here with some friends and thought I'd come over and say hi.' Even to her own ears it sounded rehearsed and completely unnatural. She felt a blush starting and blinked miserably. Just give him the note and get the hell out of there, she told herself.

James was staring down at the table, and didn't say anything. His silence was unrelenting. Wow, she thought, he definitely still hates my guts. Embarrassed, she turned in desperation to his date instead. 'Hi, I'm Jane. A friend of James's.' To her surprise the girl gave her a wide smile and held out her hand. She had long, black, curly hair, big dark eyes and beautiful translucent skin. She was wearing a silvery-blue silk top with batwing sleeves.

'Hello, I'm Lucy, his cousin. And I know exactly who you are, Jane! It's lovely to finally meet you.'

'Oh! Er ... likewise.' Jane was confused but relieved someone was responding to her. And Lucy was his cousin? Thank God she hadn't interrupted a romantic date. That would've been a nightmare.

'James! Shift over and let Jane sit down,' Lucy instructed. She had an English accent rather than Scottish, which intrigued Jane instantly. James hesitated but then sulkily inched over to make room for her.

'Oh, I don't want to disturb you ...'

Jane tightened her grip on the folded note in her sweaty hand. Should she just throw it at him and run? From James's reaction, it was obvious that he wanted her to leave. But Lucy didn't seem to notice James's stony silence or that he hadn't said a word to her yet.

'It's fine,' she said. 'We've just ordered and I'm sure they'll be ages yet. It's pretty busy. Anyway,' Lucy continued as Jane carefully sat down, 'so you're back in Edinburgh now, Jane? I think it's fantastic that you two went travelling together.' Then she peered at Jane more closely and smiled, saying, 'She does look like her, James. You were right!'

Jane looked sideways at James who was studiously ignoring her and buttering a bread roll. She saw a pink flush creeping up his neck. He's squirming, she thought. What exactly had he been saying about her?

'Lucy's just moved to Edinburgh,' he said pointedly, changing the subject. 'Haven't you, Lucy?'

Thank God, she thought, he's speaking. It was so good to hear the sound of his voice.

'Yes,' said Lucy. 'I moved up from Brighton last week and I don't know a soul apart from James. You'll have to give me your number, Jane, so we can do lunch and you can tell me more about your travels.'

'Um ... of course.' Bloody hell, she thought. Hadn't James told her about what had happened? Or had he only mentioned the fun times?

'What do you do, Lucy?' she asked politely.

'I'm a dress designer. Mostly independent but I sometimes work with chain brands. I'm hoping to take on some Scottish clients.' She ran an approving eye over Jane's dress. 'That is fantastic, I have to say. Where did you get it?'

'A designer shop in Amsterdam,' replied Jane. Gosh, listen to me, she thought.

'Oh, I love European designers! I'd be interested in getting your opinion on my latest sketches. I can tell you have a good sense of style.'

'Um, thanks,' said Jane. She was intensely aware of James's movements beside her. He'd finished eating his bread roll, now he was playing with the saltshaker. He was deliberately making it difficult for her, she thought, starting to feel annoyed.

Lucy was still talking. 'I mostly design evening wear because there's always a good market for it. And every woman needs a little black dress, don't you think?'

Jane couldn't help it. She glanced at James and saw the corner of his mouth twitching. She stifled a giggle, but Lucy picked up on it.

'Did I miss something? What did I say?'

'Nothing,' said Jane, trying not to smile. 'I totally agree with you.' She spied Amber and the others making their way over to the entrance. 'Ah, I should probably go. I think we're about to head off. But it was lovely to meet you, Lucy.'

'Here, Jane.' Lucy quickly handed her phone over so Jane could type her number onto the screen, which she did. Lucy seemed to have a knack for getting people to do what she wanted. Jane nodded in James's general direction. 'And it was great to see you again too, James,' she said politely. How the hell was she going to give him the note? she wondered.

'Who are you here with? Is that Amber?' he asked suddenly, looking over towards them.

Amber and the two guys had stationed themselves by the entrance. But they'd made it look totally casual, like they were just hanging out and chatting. She could imagine Amber hissing 'just look natural, everyone!'

'Yes, Amber and Colin, and Colin's brother, Keith,' she said nonchalantly.

'Is it a double date?'

She was surprised he cared. It was on the tip of her tongue to say 'None of your business' since he was acting so unfeeling towards her but there was something about the way he said it, so she relented and said, 'No, he's just here for the weekend visiting Colin. He lives in Inverness. He's an accountant.'

James glanced at her, raised his eyebrows and said, 'Ah,' meaningfully, which made her want to giggle again. She got up from the table and said 'Goodbye' and 'Enjoy your meal'. Then, before she could chicken out, she placed the note on James's bread and butter plate and walked off. She could sense his eyes searing into her back, but she just kept walking, unable to resist adding a slight hip sway for his benefit.

When she reached the entrance, it was just Amber waiting for her, and she was almost bursting out of her skin with curiosity. Jane grabbed her arm. 'Let's get out of here now!' She thought she might faint if she didn't keep moving.

Chapter 29: Clerk Street

Sure enough, Amber bombarded her with questions when they got outside, as she knew she would. 'How did it go? Was he surprised to see you? Did you give him the note? Who was the girl? Oh my God, I cannae believe you did that!'

Jane felt dazed, like she'd been slapped in the face. If someone had told her this was going to happen two hours ago, she wouldn't have believed it. She looked around for Colin and Keith. 'Where are the others?'

'Oh, they left to go back to Colin's flat. They asked me to say goodbye. Keith was pretty taken with you, I think. He kept saying, "I didnae think she'd do it and she did!"'

'I thought Colin lived in Ratho?'

'He's just moved in up the road.'

'How convenient,' said Jane.

'Yes, very,' said Amber coyly. 'But never mind about that. We have much more exciting things to discuss. Do you want to come back to my flat for a cup of tea?'

'That would actually be wonderful.' She was starting to crash from the caffeine and the adrenaline.

During the short walk to the flat, Jane filled Amber in on what had happened at the table; that the girl was James's cousin and that he'd hardly spoken a word to her, but yes, she had given him the note.

Ten minutes later they were lying back on the overstuffed couch in Amber's small flat on Commercial Street, big white steaming mugs of tea in front of them on the coffee table. Jane had taken off her shoes and curled her feet under her. She still had her coat on, waiting for the heating to kick up a notch. Amber didn't seem to feel the cold and was bare-armed and bare-legged in her cocktail dress.

'So how does it feel to see him again?'

'I don't know. To see him again like that out of the blue feels ... amazing ... sobering, and a relief. To be honest, I've been so afraid of bumping into him that at least I have now.'

'He had a good tan going on,' said Amber. 'Where do you think he's been?'

'No clue,' said Jane. 'He definitely didn't get that in Edinburgh.'

'His hair was shorter too.'

Jane laughed. 'I know, he looked bloody gorgeous. Damn him!'

'I told you,' said Amber grinning. 'So, what did you write in the note? Or shouldn't I ask?'

Jane shook her head and quickly changed the subject.

'Do you mind if I stay here tonight, Ambs? Aimee and Trish

are on night shift, and I don't want to go back to an empty flat.'

'Aye, stay. My bed's big enough for two.'

'Speaking of which, I'm assuming Colin won't be over tonight?'

'Naw, he said he's going to spend the weekend entertaining Keith. By the sounds of it they're going to be plastered for most of it.'

'Really? Keith seems so conservative. I can't imagine him drinking more than one dram.'

'Aye, but maybe underneath that tweed suit is a passionate Scotsman screaming to get out. I couldnae believe it when he gave you that speech about writing the note. He never says anything like that.'

Jane giggled. 'Maybe he should give up accounting and be a relationship counsellor.'

'Aye, he should!'

They stayed up talking until Jane felt her eyes start to droop. Amber hunted out a spare pair of pyjamas for her to wear. They fit ok apart from the bottoms, which came up to her calves.

'You short arse,' she teased.

'I'm the one who's normal height!' Amber retorted. She'd changed into a black silk negligee that didn't leave a lot to the imagination. Jane bet Colin loved that! Amber told her to help herself to her Clarins cleanser and moisturiser so she didn't have to sleep in her makeup, which was heaven. She even had a spare toothbrush so she could clean her teeth. Then they lay in bed with the lights out.

'Ambs?'

'Mmm?'

'What if what I wrote doesn't change anything?'

'Then at least you tried. What you did wasn't out of any intention to hurt him.'

'I just hope he understands that.'

'Och, it'll be ok,' said Amber. 'You'll see.'

Jane managed to make it through the weekend. On Saturday, Amber took her on an impromptu shopping trip, and on Sunday she went on a cold, rainy hike up Arthur's Seat with Aimee. But by Monday afternoon she was a bundle of nerves. She'd put at the end of the note that she'd be at the flat working during the week if he wanted to talk because she'd thought 'text me' sounded too casual. This way, a week was a firm deadline. If he didn't show, she could cry into her porridge and try to get over him. But it meant not slobbing around the flat in case he turned up, and not looking overly made up either. Trying to find the right balance of put togetherness was exhausting.

As for the other things she'd written in the note, she hadn't used the L word, but she'd said that she missed him and cared about him, and wanted to hang out again. There were also a couple of things she was now regretting because they were a bit … overzealous. She wasn't sure how he'd react. Hopefully he'd just brush it off as female hormones.

At five, Aimee went out to do some food shopping at the nearby Sainsbury's. Jane put her hair up in an after-work ponytail and was sitting in the lounge trying to read a book when the buzzer sounded. She almost jumped out of her skin. Quickly she took her hair down, fluffing out the kinks. With her heart in her mouth, she went downstairs to open the door. If it turned out to be Aimee without her key, she'd kill her. She poked her head out. There was no one there. Weird. She looked both ways down the street; there was just the odd passerby. Feeling relieved, she shut the door. She was about to go back upstairs when someone knocked. Bloody kids! she thought, frowning. Jane threw open the door ready to tell them to clear off, and found herself staring at James.

'Oh! Hello.' Her heart started hammering in her chest. 'Did you buzz just before?' she asked lamely.

'Aye, I did,' he replied, but didn't offer any explanation as to why he wasn't there when she'd opened the door the first time. He wasn't smiling but he wasn't frowning either, so she figured at least that was something.

'Ah, do you want to come in?'

He nodded, and she moved aside to let him through. Hell, he was here! She'd talked herself into thinking he wouldn't show up, so she didn't get disappointed. What should she do with him now? Tea, she thought, it has to be tea, so she ushered him into the kitchen.

'Have a seat,' she said, gesturing to the kitchen table.

James took off his puffer jacket and she noticed that he was wearing his black Vans T-shirt and jeans. The same outfit when he'd first come into McDowd's and flashed her a cheeky grin. Except he wasn't grinning now.

'I can make us some tea. Unless you prefer something stronger?' God knows I do, she thought.

'What have you got?'

She checked the cupboard. 'Aimee went to Skye last weekend and brought back some Talisker for the flat if you want some?'

'Peaty—' he said approvingly. 'Can I have both please: tea and whisky?'

Jane nodded. He didn't say anything else, but she could feel his presence behind her, and it was mightily distracting. When she turned on the tap to fill the kettle, she noticed her hand was shaking. While waiting for the tea to steep, she remembered that Aimee would be back any second. She had to get James alone.

'Um ... actually, do you want to go to my room with this?' He'd been in her room before. It wasn't a big deal. They'd sat in there going over the trip, her on the bed, him on the office chair by the desk. Now though, the statement felt loaded. But to her relief he nodded.

Jane gave him a whisky for one hand and a tea for the other and led him down the hallway. There was a slight panic before she turned her door handle that she'd left a pile of freshly washed underwear on the bed, but it turned out to be a false alarm.

She deposited her tea and whisky (she'd poured herself a double dram) on the bedside table and removed her jacket from the office chair for him. But he seemed to want to stand with his tea. Did that mean he wasn't staying long? She perched on her bed sipping tea and feeling incredibly nervous.

He looked around the room, and his glance landed on the desk and her laptop. 'So, you work in here?'

'Sometimes, or the lounge. Maybe the cafe down the road if I want to get out of the flat.'

'Right.' He walked over to the opposite wall, where she'd stuck some of her travel photos on a pegboard with drawing pins. 'Is this where you've been?'

'Yeah, I just printed out a few the other day.'

'I didnae think people printed out photos anymore.'

She shrugged. 'I guess I'm old-fashioned.' He didn't say anything, but she watched his eyes moving over them. They were mostly of scenery, but she was surprised when he picked out where they were.

'Athens, nice. And that looks like Berlin.' There was a shot of a cafe on the Champs-Élysées in Paris (she'd actually gone there a month later!) but he didn't say anything about that one. 'Where's that?' he asked, pointing to a blustery beach scene of a storm in progress.

She leaned forward to look. 'Um ... Cyprus.'

He nodded. 'Atmospheric.'

'It was.' She took another sip of tea. Ok, so we're just going to chat about travel stuff. That was fine, she could do that. Then he stopped and peered more closely. 'Hey, I took that one.'

'You did.'

It was one of the fifteen he'd taken outside Sagrada Familia, and it was her favourite. She'd grown bored because he was taking so long and had started doing silly poses. He'd zoomed up close and managed to capture her looking seductively over one shoulder at him and directly into the camera. She had a half-smile playing on her lips and the wind had tumbled her hair.

James looked at it for a long moment, and she squirmed, wondering what he was thinking. 'It's a good photo,' he said finally and sat down in the office chair, swivelling round to put his empty mug on the desk. He picked up the whisky glass and swirled the amber liquid before taking a sip.

'So where are you staying?' she asked politely. She tried not to stare at him, but it was difficult not to. He was rocking the short hair look.

'At Lucy's apartment in Leith for the moment. She rented a two bedroom, so I've got my own room, but there are boxes of dresses piled up in it.' He shook his head as if to say, women and clothes.

'I liked her,' said Jane. 'She was very ... forthright. I've never heard you mention her before though?'

'Her Ma is my Ma's sister. We never saw them much growing

up because they live in Brighton. Except for family reunions.'

'She seemed to know a lot about me.'

James shifted uncomfortably. 'Lucy has a big mouth.'

'Oh?'

He sighed. 'If you must know, when I first told Ma we were travelling together, she may have asked who you look like.'

'Huh?' Jane was confused.

'She's got this thing about people resembling celebrities.' Jane's mouth twitched. 'Aye, I know, ironic! Anyway, I was trying to think of a celebrity that she would know and who I thought you looked like ...'

'Go on ...' This should be good, she thought.

James rolled his eyes. 'I said you looked like a young Helen Hunt.'

Jane burst out laughing. 'I look nothing like her!'

'You do a wee bit, the hair at least. Anyway, Ma's obviously said something to her sister because now Lucy knows. Honestly, I can't say anything. Our family grapevine is worse than the tabloids.'

He leaned back in the chair, and it squeaked. Ok, so he's getting comfortable. Maybe he'll stay a bit longer, she thought, at least until he's finished his whisky. Their rapport also seemed to have picked up from the stilted one-liners at the beginning, so she was taking heart from that. She was just truly glad he was speaking to her again. No doubt the whisky was helping.

James now drank some more of the Talisker ten-year-old single malt and scrutinised her over the edge of the glass. 'So, who do I look like then?' he asked.

'Oh,' said Jane, caught off guard. 'Well, not James McAvoy obviously. I don't know—like no one.' Then she thought that sounded dismissive, so she added, 'No one I can think of at the moment anyway. But you look like you could be a celebrity ... with what you've got … going on.'

She waved a hand vaguely in his direction. He arched an eyebrow and she realised too late that she'd taken the bait. That he'd been leading her towards what she'd written in the note.

'What I've got going on …?'

'James …'

'Cannae find the words, hmm?' He took a familiar piece of paper out of his pocket. 'You were pretty explicit in here. Let's see now, what did you say ...' He opened the note and scanned it. 'Aye, these things I thought were particularly complimentary ...'

'Please don't …' she said, her face turning beetroot red.

'Quote "you're gorgeous, easily the best-looking guy I've ever seen in my life" unquote.'

She cringed, her face burning.

'And quote "you have a smoking hot body, and I had to leave because I wanted to rip your shorts off and jump your bones" unquote.'

Hell, she couldn't believe he was sitting here reading it back to her. Trust him to focus on that!

'I may have been high on caffeine at the time,' she squeaked. 'There were other less ... er ... teenagery things too.'

'Aye, quite a lot of descriptive words,' he said dryly. 'You're definitely a writer.'

He's enjoying this, she thought. Damn him.

'So, you liked it then?' she retorted.

He looked amused. 'No one's ever written me a note like that, not even in High School. It makes me smile every time I read it. In fact, I'm thinking of using some of it to spice up my testimonials: "Gorgeous James did a great job at designing my website, and he also has a smoking hot body."'

Oh God; she buried her face in her hands, embarrassed beyond belief. He thought she was a complete idiot!

'So, anyway,' he continued 'Aye, I liked the note and I'm very flattered. But unfortunately, we can't "hang out" as you put it.'

The weight of disappointment was so heavy that it crushed her vocal chords, and she couldn't speak. She died a little inside right at that moment. That was it then.

'In Edinburgh, at least.'

She lifted her head and looked at him bleary-eyed. 'Huh?'

'I'm going back to Bangkok but if you come with me, I *could* make time in my schedule for us to hang out,' he said lightly.

'Come with you to Bangkok ...?' she queried disbelievingly.

'If you want to. There probably won't be a spreadsheet with an itinerary like before. It'll be much more go with the flow. Maybe some communing with elephants ...'

Now she couldn't tell if he was being serious or not. She narrowed her eyes suspiciously.

'Is this another "travel companions" type arrangement?'

'Nae, I thought perhaps you could be something else this time. If you need a label—what about "girlfriend"?'

She stared at him, trying to make sense of what he was saying. 'You're asking me to be your girlfriend?'

'Aye.'

Jane searched his face to see if he was joking, but he gazed at her steadily without even the glimmer of a smirk. God, he was being serious! She clutched the bedside table feeling tremendously dizzy all of a sudden. James looked at her with a frown. 'Are you ok? You've gone really pale.' She shook her head, and he got up and put her whisky glass in her hand. 'Here have some of this.' She took a gulp and tasted the fire of Skye.

'Maybe I should go,' he said uncertainly.

'No, don't.' She grabbed him round the waist and buried her head somewhere in his midriff area. She could feel the soft brushed cotton of his T-shirt against her cheek, and beneath that the hard muscles of his abs. She closed her eyes tightly and felt his hand gently rubbing her back.

'Sorry, that was a bit mean,' he said, sounding contrite. 'I'm a wanker.'

She shook her head and said in a muffled voice, 'I wasn't expecting that. I was expecting, maybe, to just go for a coffee ...'

'I want more—'

The reality of James wanting more hit her again like a ton of bricks. It was momentous. She couldn't take it in.

'Though if you're not interested, I can always try online dating. I hear some of the women on there are really hot, and only after one thing.'

She looked up at him. 'I knew you were trying to rile me up at that cafe!'

James chuckled and sat down beside her on the bed. 'I may have been trying to stir the pot a wee bit.'

He flashed her a sideways glance, and she felt a frisson of electricity run through her body ... she swallowed and tried to focus on making conversation.

'So, when did you go to Bangkok? How did that happen?'

'After Prague. I was at a loose end, and got chatting to Rick and he invited me to stay with him. It was pretty relaxing. I spent a lot of time by the pool.'

'That explains the tan,' she said, 'and your hair's so much shorter.'

James smiled at her. 'Yeah, it was driving me crazy. Rick and I went to a Thai barber to get haircuts, and they did a bit of a hack job. It's grown out quite a bit.'

He ran a hand through it and the front part stuck up in spikes. She had to quell an urge to reach out and touch it. 'Rick was trying to be a good friend after ... what happened with us. Some of the advice he gave was helpful, but most of it was hopeless.'

Jane giggled. Rick must know the whole story then, she thought. To his credit, he hadn't treated her any differently. But it was weird to think they'd been talking about her, in Bangkok of all places.

James took her hand and looked at her. 'You should've told me how you felt when I called you.'

She shook her head. 'You were so angry, I was afraid …'

'I was angry because I was hurt and confused. I thought you were doing a Kistella on me … you wee eejit.'

Then they were lying on the bed with their arms around each other and she was trembling so hard she thought she might break into a thousand pieces.

'It's ok,' he whispered, rubbing her back. 'Just relax.' She breathed him in; his clean, fresh scent, and the whisky, calming her down. She could hear his heart drumming beneath her cheek.

'Déjà vu,' she said softly after a while. 'It feels like we're back in Barcelona.'

He stroked her hair. 'Mmm, I should've said something then.'

'Why didn't you?'

'Och, there was too much other shite going on. You with your blackmailers and me stressing about my finances. I thought I'd leave it to Budapest. But then you met Don Juan that first night. I was feckin' climbing the walls. I almost said something at the ruin bar but he interrupted that too.'

She shifted uncomfortably in his arms. 'I'm sorry. I thought you'd friend-zoned me.'

'Nah, I just dinnae want to get into your knickers like him.'

'But you do want to get into them a wee bit?'

He chuckled softly. 'Aye, and more ... if you'd like to. I'm assuming by what you said in the note about "jumping ma bones" that you want that too. But as to when it happens, well, that's a different conversation over another glass of whisky.'

Bloody hell, she thought, starting to tremble again. She felt him stroke her cheek, then suddenly they were face-to-face and his lips were inches apart from her own and his warm body was pressing up against hers. She could hardly breathe; her heart was thudding like a mad thing. Oh God, just kiss me, she thought.

Then James's pocket beeped loudly with a text and it poured cold water on the mood. He sighed and released her, lying back on the bed. 'I should probably go. That'll be Lucy. I promised I'd help her with her website right about now.' He sat up and checked his phone, then looked down at her, taking in her wide doe-eyes and flushed face. 'Bad timing.'

'That could quite possibly be the biggest understatement of the year,' Jane told him ruefully.

James grinned. 'Aye. Things were just starting to get interesting.'

Jane gulped. This was actually happening, she still couldn't believe it.

'Do you want to come round tomorrow night? I'll make lasagne. It's ma signature dish. Well, ma only dish. Plus, Lucy is dying to show you her sketches.'

'Ok,' she said, suddenly feeling shy.

He smiled at her. 'Walk me out?'

She nodded, so they went out into the hallway towards the stairs, and she heard Aimee doing something in the kitchen.

'Uh, ma jacket ...' said James, hovering on the landing.

'I'll get it,' she said and went into the kitchen. Aimee was washing up some dishes at the sink. She raised her eyebrows when she saw Jane and looked pointedly at the jacket on the chair—'James's?' she mouthed. Jane nodded and put a finger to her lips and jerked her head towards the hall. Aimee shrugged her shoulders and looked at her questioningly. And when Jane gave her the thumbs up and a big smile, Aimee's face erupted into a huge grin. She silently pumped one of her rubber-gloved hands in the air and soap suds went flying. Her grin was infectious and prompted Jane to quietly wiggle her hips in a happy dance.

Then she saw Aimee stop grinning and look past her shoulder. Jane slowly turned around. James was leaning against the doorway with his arms folded, smiling. 'I take it that's an "aye" for communing with the elephants then,' he said.

Chapter 30: Lucy and Lamplight

When she heard what happened with James and the ensuing dinner invitation, Amber squealed with excitement. Then she immediately booked Jane in with her beauty therapist in Hanover Street for the next morning. 'It's on me,' she said. Jane thought she was getting a relaxing massage and was disconcerted when she'd been shown to a treatment room and politely asked to remove her knickers. Amber had apparently booked her in for a "top and tail", which turned out to be a facial and a Brazilian.

Consequently, she was now lying on her back, naked from the waist down, with her feet in the air, while a girl about her age applied warm, gooey wax to her nether regions. There was a short wait for it to cool, then she said, 'This might hurt a bit.' Jane felt a tug and then a sensation like fire as the wax was ripped off. She gasped out loud, and the girl smiled sympathetically. 'It won't be so bad next time.' Jane grimaced thinking that this might be a one and done experience. She braced herself for the next onslaught and hoped the facial didn't involve any painful treatments.

When she rang her afterwards to tear a strip off her (so to speak), Amber just laughed and said she needed to be 'prepared'. Jane wasn't sure exactly what Amber thought she should be prepared for. James had invited her round to Lucy's flat for lasagne, not to get hot and heavy in the bedroom. If *that* did happen at some point she was already prepared. She'd been prepared ever since she'd decided to travel with him. And he'd more or less made it clear that he wasn't looking to rush into things.

More pressing was the current dilemma of what to wear. Dinner with a dress designer, plus the guy you were mad about who'd just announced he wanted to be in a relationship, required a certain outfit.

Luckily, she'd done some shopping in Paris and had bought some skin hugging, black tailored pants that looked great with her black leather, knee-high stiletto boots. She'd also bought a white off-the-shoulder top. For makeup she put on her usual mascara and blush, but added a slick of red lipstick. She left her hair down and brushed it so it fell loose and shining around her shoulders. Aimee gave her a wolf whistle. 'When he sees you lookin' like that he's gonna be gaggin' fer it.'

Jane laughed and shook her head. She shrugged on her coat and went to catch the bus down to Leith. It had been exactly twenty-four hours since James had dropped the bombshell on her, and the initial surprise and excitement had been replaced by jittery nerves. How would he act around her tonight in front of Lucy? Would they get to be alone together? What was the deal with Bangkok? She had so many questions whirring around in her head that she almost missed the stop.

James had texted her the address that morning and luckily the flat wasn't too far from the bus stop as she wasn't used to wearing such high heels. However, when Lucy buzzed her in, she did have to totter up four flights of stairs to the top floor with her pants chafing her tender crotch. Breathing heavily, she tried to compose herself before knocking but Lucy flung open the door.

'Hi, Jane!'

Jane managed a gasped 'Hello.'

'Sorry about the walk up. It's a killer, I know. Come in! Give me your coat, I'll hang it up.' When Jane took off her coat Lucy surveyed her. 'You look nice!' She was also wearing black pants, but with a pale-pink ballet-wrap cardigan over a white scoop-neck top. She'd plaited her long dark hair into a messy side braid. Jane wasn't sure how she managed to look both classy and casual at the same time.

'So do you,' said Jane, feeling suddenly fond of her. She gave her a small hug and handed her the bottle of red wine she'd brought with her.

'James is in the kitchen. Come on through.'

Jane followed her into the lounge. There was a doorway at the far end that she presumed led into the kitchen. She glanced around the room as she went. It looked like Lucy was still unpacking as there were a couple of boxes stacked in the corner. But she'd made it look homely already. There was a navy-blue roll-armed couch with a low, square coffee table in front. A white fluffy rug and a decent-sized TV and sound bar filled up the rest of the space.

A series of framed photos on the wall caught Jane's eye as she went by, and she couldn't help being nosy. It was a family gathering and everyone was dressed like they were at a Highland Fling. That must be one of the family reunions James had mentioned. She picked out a familiar figure at the end of a row and peered closer. Oh wow, James in a kilt. He looked at least ten years younger, and his hair was longer and shaggier than she'd ever seen it.

Tearing her gaze from the photo, she followed Lucy into the kitchen where she announced, 'Jane's here.' James was at the island counter chopping something and glanced up when she came in. Definitely much cuter now, she thought, staring at him, and more manly. He was wearing a dark-green shirt with the sleeves rolled up and showing a hefty amount of tanned forearm. The knife paused mid-chop as his eyes roved over her appreciatively. She felt like she was being undressed with his eyes. Then he simply nodded at her, said 'Hey, Jane, glad you could make it,' and continued chopping.

Jane was taken aback. She'd expected a warmer greeting than that by the way he was checking her out. Playing it cool for Lucy so the family grapevine didn't go crazy, perhaps? Well, she could play along. 'Hey, yourself,' she said nonchalantly.

'We'll sit at the counter and watch the chef at work,' said Lucy, hopping up onto a breakfast bar stool. She leaned over the edge of the counter, which had several bottles of alcohol at the end. 'What do you want to drink, Jane? I've got wine or there's some gin …'

'Ooh G&T, please, if one's going,' said Jane immediately. She followed Lucy's suit and levered herself up onto a stool. Now she could see James was chopping carrots.

'Jane loves G&Ts,' commented James, concentrating on what he was doing. 'It's all she ever drinks.'

'Rubbish,' said Jane, 'I drink other things.'

'Aye—Diet Coke,' he teased.

'At least I don't drink whisky all the time!'

She'd forgotten how much she liked bantering with him. Lucy handed her a tall G&T with ice and a wedge of lime. She'd made herself one, too.

'Bottoms up!' she said. 'Here's to good food (hopefully) and good company.'

'Do I get a drink?' asked James.

'You shouldn't drink and cook. We don't want a chopped-off finger in our food,' admonished Lucy. Jane giggled. But Lucy relented and poured him a small glass of the red Jane had brought.

'Sláinte,' said James, raising his glass to clink it with Lucy's then Jane's. 'Good company indeed,' he said and gave her a private wink. Jane looked away quickly, butterflies fluttering in her midriff.

'What *are* you cooking?' she asked, watching the muscles in his forearm flex as he chopped.

'Lasagne,' he said.

'I've never heard of carrots in lasagne before ...'

'It's a special Scottish recipe,' said James. 'Sometimes I make it with neeps. That's turnips for you English folk.'

Jane glanced at Lucy, who screwed up her nose—she tried not to laugh.

'Do you need any help?'

'Aye, you can be my sous chef if you like. The lettuce needs washing.'

Jane came round to stand next to him. With her stiletto boots on, she was nearly as tall as he was. He handed her a bunch of lettuce, then leaned in and murmured softly so only she could hear: 'Sexy boots.' She turned on the cold tap quickly, pleasure flooding through her. She wasn't used to James giving her compliments. It was both thrilling and alarming.

'I think that lettuce is well and truly washed,' he said a few moments later.

'Huh?' she said. 'Oh yes.' And the corner of his mouth twitched, as if he knew exactly what she'd been daydreaming about.

By the time the Scottish lasagne was eventually cooked, Jane was starving and looking forward to eating it, even if it did have carrots. They sat down for dinner in the nook off to the side of the kitchen and Lucy looked around the table. 'I feel like I should say grace or something,' but she settled for another toast: 'To family and friends.'

'To family and friends,' they echoed. 'And welcome to

Edinburgh,' added Jane. 'How are you finding it so far?'

'Cold,' said Lucy, doing a mock shiver. 'It's a bit of a shock to the system after Brighton.'

'You're brave moving here in winter.'

'She'll get used to it,' said James, handing Jane the salad.

'Easy for you to say,' Lucy said looking at him. 'You're going back to Bangkok after New Year's. Did he tell you, Jane?'

Jane took a generous helping of salad and avoided looking at James. 'Ah, yes. I know about the Bangkok part.'

But not when he was going, or anything else about it that may involve her. She also saw now that it was going to be awkward to scoot around the fact that they were a couple in front of Lucy. But she guessed he had his reasons for keeping it quiet. The thing between them felt so fragile, like a broken vase that had been glued back together.

Jane had taken off her boots, not wanting to mark the wooden floorboards. Now James, sitting across from her, stretched out a jeans-clad leg and brushed his warm bare foot against hers under the table. She jumped. He nudged his big toe against her instep, and she responded by running her foot sensuously along the top of his. He looked at her and rolled his eyes in mock ecstasy, and she had to look away before she burst into giggles. She sat up straighter, tucked her feet under her chair, and concentrated on eating the lasagne, which actually tasted pretty good. She nodded at her plate and gave James a thumbs up.

'So have you got any travel plans before Christmas and New Year's Jane?' asked Lucy.

'Nothing concrete as such, but there may be an article in the pipeline.'

'Oh?' Lucy looked interested.

'Gemma, that's the girl who gives me travel writing assignments, wants to have lunch tomorrow. She mentioned something about a review for a hotel in Iceland. It's for a resort just out of Reykjavik.'

'That sounds amazing!' exclaimed Lucy.

James raised his eyebrows. 'Any chance you'll need a professional photographer?'

Jane smiled at him. 'I could mention it to her.'

But Lucy clicked her tongue at James. 'That's a bit cheeky. Jane may not want you tagging along.'

There was a small silence as they both looked at their plates and didn't say anything.

'What's going on?' Lucy said, sounding confused.

'I may have asked Jane to be my girlfriend yesterday and to come with me to Bangkok. She may have been ... agreeable to the notion,' said James formally.

Lucy burst out laughing.

'What?' queried James, looking defensive.

'The way you said it just sounded funny. Like you're in an Austen novel.'

'Hmph,' said James. 'I suppose you'll tell your Ma now.'

'I won't say anything if you don't want me to, but you like her, she likes you—what's the big deal?' Lucy shrugged. 'I kind of guessed anyway by the way you talked about her.'

'Oh?' Jane pricked up her ears. 'Pray tell, what has the said gentleman been saying?'

James chewed on a forkful of salad stonily.

Lucy gave him a sly glance. 'Oh, I really shouldn't tell tales, but I think that said gentleman is *quite* enamoured. There's definitely going to be a lot of striding around to your flat in tight jodhpurs.'

Jane stifled a laugh. She noticed James's cheeks had gone slightly pink under his tan.

'Shut it, Lucy,' he growled. 'Everyone finished? Good!' He collected the empty plates and strode off to the kitchen pretending like he was indeed wearing tight jodhpurs. Jane and Lucy looked at each other and giggled.

Lucy poured herself more wine. 'I shouldn't tease him. But he gives as good as he gets. To new relationships,' she said, clinking her glass against Jane's. She seemed to like making toasts.

Jane cleared her throat. 'Did you ever meet Kistella?'

Lucy shook her head. 'No, but we were all glad to hear they'd broken up. I never understood why he got involved with someone like that.'

'If you saw her, you'd understand.'

'Oh?' Lucy mimed big bosoms.

Jane nodded and then got a lump in her throat. Her eyes started to water. She blinked them rapidly.

Lucy grasped the situation. 'I take it you're worried she's going to rear her pretty head.'

Jane sensed Lucy was on her side, so she didn't mind sharing a little.

'Yes, something like that.'

Lucy reached over and squeezed her hand. 'I think he's well over her.'

'Oh?'

Lucy nodded. She was about to say something else, but James suddenly appeared in the doorway holding a tub of Ben and Jerry's and an ice cream scoop. 'Dessert anyone...?' Then he saw Jane and Lucy holding hands and his eyes narrowed. 'I leave the room for two minutes ...' and they laughed.

'Just some girl bonding. Nothing that concerns you,' said Lucy, smiling at Jane.

After they had some ice cream, Lucy went to get her sketches and laid them out on the coffee table in the lounge. 'I want your honest opinion,' she said. 'Would you wear something like this or is it the ugliest thing you've ever seen in your life?'

Jane couldn't help but laugh. She was fast becoming a Lucy fan, not just because she was James's cousin. She said exactly what she thought, no holds barred. It was very refreshing. Jane sat on the floor by the coffee table and James lay behind her on the couch, reading something on his iPad. She felt content just to be near him—to know that he wanted to be with her. She tilted her head back to look up at him, and he met her eyes.

'All right?' he asked, smiling down at her. He brushed a strand of hair from her cheek, and she entwined her fingers with his.

'Perfect,' she said.

After she'd examined Lucy's sketches (most of which she'd told her she *would* wear), she went to the bathroom. When she came out, she heard a 'pssst!' from the doorway across the hall. She stuck her head in, and James grabbed her hand and pulled her into his bedroom. There was no light on, but the curtains were open and there was a street lamp outside splaying up a faint golden glow. He circled his arms firmly round her waist.

'This is all very cloak-and-dagger,' Jane said softly, looking up at him.

'I had to resort to covert measures to get you alone,' he said, grinning at her.

'I'm sure Lucy probably guessed what you were up to. She's not stupid.'

'I'm sure she wouldn't begrudge us a cuddle.'

'Well ... if you insist.' Jane relaxed into his broad chest and felt him stroke her back. She sighed. He was so lovely. He could have anyone he wanted, and he wanted her. She had been at the right place at the right time. He could've chosen another accountancy practice and another receptionist would be in his arms right now. It was a horrifying thought. She shuddered.

James hugged her tighter. 'Are you cold?'

'No, just feeling lucky to have met you.'

'I'm the lucky one—you're sweet, kind, smart, funny; I could go on ...'

Her heart melted. Thank God "troublemaker" wasn't in the line-up.

'Did I also mention you're feckin' hot?' he whispered in her ear.

She gulped. 'Ah no, you didn't,' she said lightly.

'You drive me crazy,' he whispered. 'I can't stop thinking about you ...'

Her breath quickened. Perhaps he didn't want to take it as slow as she'd thought? Maybe lasagne wasn't going to be the only thing on the menu tonight.

He took her hand and led her over to the bed to sit facing him. The golden light was falling on his face and highlighting his perfect bone structure. She reached up a tentative finger to touch his face.

'Do you know how gorgeous you are?'

'Someone told me recently I was smoking hot, but she may need glasses.'

Jane laughed at that, and gently traced his eyebrows, his cheekbones. 'I think I wanted to kiss you the first moment I saw you.'

James smiled wryly. 'Aye, me too. Pretty much from day one.'

Jane giggled. 'Maybe you should've just said that at Costa

Coffee. It would've saved a lot of time. "Och aye, hurry up and drink yer cappuccino lassie, I want tae give ye a kiss!"'

James laughed softly. 'Nice accent—but we should probably stop talking about kissing,' he said, staring intently at her lips.

Her insides somersaulted. 'Why?'

He sighed and ran his hand through his hair. 'Because I *really* want to kiss you but I'm worried that if we start, we won't be able to stop, things could get ... chaotic. And Lucy ...'

'Uh huh,' she said.

'We should take it slow.'

'Ah, yes. Sounds sensible.'

'So we should probably go back out to the lounge.'

'Probably.'

But Jane was getting flustered just hearing him say he wanted to kiss her. In a daze of longing, she ran her thumb over his bottom lip. He caught his breath and then reached up and guided her thumb into his mouth. He started gently sucking on it while gazing intently into her eyes. Captivated, she couldn't look away. She felt the tip of his tongue swirling around pad of her thumb and a hot wave of desire built and slowly washed over her body. Groaning inwardly, she reluctantly pulled it out of his mouth.

He gave her a lazy grin. 'Mmm, that was nice.'

'Too nice,' she said, trying to breathe. 'We should probably go out to the ...'

But he began kissing his way down the sensitive skin of her

inner arm.

'James ...' she protested weakly.

'I ken, I should stop ...' But instead of stopping, he laid her back gently on the bed, lifted her top up slightly and caressed slow circles on her stomach. His warm hand felt amazing. Jane sighed and closed her eyes. This was ok, she could handle this. Then he started exploring further up. Uh oh. If he went any higher, he'd soon be touching her breasts. If he did that, she wasn't sure if either of them would be able to control themselves; even if Lucy was in the next room.

As if he suddenly realised the same thing, James abruptly pulled his hand away from her.

Jane lay there breathing heavily, looking up at him, not sure whether to be disappointed or relieved. He rubbed his hand over his face and sighed. 'Sorry about that. I got carried away.'

She touched his leg. 'It's perfectly ok, but we really should go back out to the lounge.'

James shifted. 'Ah, you go on ahead, I might wait in here for a wee bit 'til things ... calm down.'

She giggled. 'Do you want some ice water?'

'Aye, you might want to bring me a bucket of it.'

Chapter 31: Movie Night

After that night, James cooled things right down, to the point where the pot of water was barely simmering on the stove. It was like he referred to the Scottish gentleman's rule book whenever she did something that might cause a hint of passion. She's giving me a come-hither look. What do I do? Answer: Dinnae (I repeat DINNAE) invite her into yer bedroom or touch her in any way that's inappropriate. Ye may hold her hand, but THAT'S IT LADDIE! Jane assumed he was trying to enforce the "go-slow" rule so things didn't get out of hand. It was driving her crazy.

In keeping with this chivalry, he'd started inviting her out on dates that only involved hand holding—to the movies, for a winter's stroll in the park, an intimate dinner at an Italian restaurant. Then, to her amazement, he even sent her flowers. She'd been on the phone to Amber at the time, bemoaning the state of affairs (or lack of them) when the buzzer went. Jane hung up from her and went to check who it was. Five minutes later, she rang her back.

'Guess what James just sent me.'

'A dick pic?'

Jane laughed. 'I wish! No, red roses.'

There was an envious silence. 'Gosh, that's romantic. I'm jealous, Colin hasn't even bought *me* flowers yet.'

'Don't get me wrong, it's lovely of him …'

'But …'

'But we're going to Iceland in a few days …'

(Gemma had given her the green light for James to come along as her "photographer" for the weekend though she'd been surprised at his existence.

'I didn't know you were seeing someone?'

'It's only just happened.'

'Ah,' said Gemma knowingly. 'Well, you should have a great time. Iceland is a beautiful place.' And then added 'Nudge nudge wink wink', which made Jane laugh.)

'I know he wants to take it slow but this is bordering on torture,' she said to Amber. 'I don't think I can just hold hands demurely in a king-sized bed.'

'You'd rather be rolling around in it?'

'Something like that.'

'Hmm, he's obviously gun-shy after the Kistella business. There's only one thing for it,' Amber said, decisively. 'You're going to have to help him get back on the horse.'

'You're right,' Jane mused.

'What are you going to do?'

'Uh, set the mood and see if I can coax him into the saddle?'

Amber chuckled. 'Sounds like a plan …'

That afternoon she rang James and invited him over after dinner to watch a movie—some historical war thing that she'd thought he'd like. Sure enough, he took the bait. Though he queried whether she would enjoy it and suggested they could watch something else if she didn't. Since Jane didn't plan on watching anything but him, she said it was fine, she'd suffer through it, which he laughed at. She'd made doubly sure that Aimee and Trish were on night shift. The last thing she wanted was them walking in unexpectedly if stuff was happening. That could be awkward.

James arrived just before seven. She gave him a hug in the entryway (that was apparently ok according to the rule book). He smelt delicious: Eau de James, she thought, feeling the usual tug of attraction whenever she was around him. They went into the lounge, and she turned on the TV and killed the lights.

'Cosy,' he said, smiling at her.

Jane smiled back innocently, and said, 'Do you want to lie on the couch? It's a more comfortable viewing position.'

James nodded and she breathed a sigh of relief. The first hurdle was over. Take that, rule book, she thought. For the first ten minutes of the movie, she endured a particularly violent opening scene by closing her eyes and just enjoying lying next to him. He had his arm around her, and she was snuggled into his chest.

James had immediately taken off his jacket and shoes when he arrived because she'd sneakily turned up the thermostat to the highest setting. Without him reacting, she managed to lift the edge of his white T-shirt out from his jeans and then rested her hand on his bare hip. The heat emanating from his smooth skin warmed her fingers. After a few minutes, and much inner contemplation, she tried moving her hand up further inside his T-shirt and lightly across his ribs. By this time his T-shirt had fully come away from the waistband of his jeans, so she trailed her fingers across the flat plane of his stomach. She felt his muscles twitch in response, but he didn't stop her. The guns had thankfully gone quiet and there was some kind of intimate scene going on between the leading actors. That could be helpful, she thought, propping herself up on one elbow and glancing at the screen. Then she noticed James watching her with an amused expression. The light from the TV flickered across his face.

'Everything ok?' he asked.

'Yes, fine.'

'We can watch something else if you want.'

'No, no,' she said quickly, thinking, the view's pretty good from here. 'If you don't mind me …' She nodded at her hand on his stomach.

'I guess it's ok. I'll suffer through it,' he said deadpan. She stifled a laugh. Emboldened, Jane continued lightly caressing his skin. She snuck a quick peek at him. He had his eyes closed so she took that to be a sign he was enjoying it. This went on for a while. Unfortunately, the guns were back but she tried to ignore them. Then, luckily, there was another, even more intimate scene between the leading actors in which they were kissing in a bunker.

Perfect, she thought. She held her breath and unbuttoned his jeans, waiting for the rule book to screech 'DINNAE LET HER DO THAT!' Sure enough, it elicited an immediate response.

'That's primed and loaded,' he said brusquely.

She giggled. 'It's hardly a deadly weapon.'

He arched an eyebrow. 'No?'

But from his unsteady breathing and the way he was looking at her, it seemed he wanted her to continue. So she unzipped his jeans partway.

'Is this ok?' she whispered. He nodded, so she slipped her hand inside his boxers, hardly believing he was letting her, and discovered "the weapon" which was, as he'd warned her, rock hard. Wow, she thought, feeling down further, Zeke got the small part wrong. She started to move her hand in the warm, tight space and he caught his breath.

'I can stop if you want?' she teased.

He looked at her, and she saw in the flickering light that his pupils had dilated so his eyes were almost liquid black. He shook his head slightly and responded by unzipping his jeans fully so she could get a better grip. He looked so turned on and adorable, she couldn't help it. She reached forward and kissed him on the lips. Immediately he pulled her to him and gave her a deep, searching kiss that involved quite a bit of tongue. As she'd suspected, he was a fantastic kisser, and her desire ignited like a rocket. The kissing got more frenetic and so did her hand movements. James was sweating profusely, either from the heat in the room or what she was doing to him, she wasn't sure which. The rule book had gone strangely quiet, to her relief. She tried to tug his boxers and jeans down further. 'Maybe take these off?' she suggested.

James immediately sat up and pulled everything down, then kicked it onto the floor. She started to touch him again, but he said 'Hang on' and whipped off his T-shirt and socks too. Bloody hell, she thought, getting an eyeful of his naked body, which was quite spectacular. Maybe this was the back page of the rule book, Jane thought—if she manages to get yer troosers doon, jist lie back and enjoy it laddie!

Jane noticed the leading actors were now engaged in a horizontal embrace minus clothing, not that she needed their help anymore. James was naked and stretched out full length on the couch beside her. She trailed a finger over his bicep and ran her hand across his smooth, tanned chest. God, he was heavenly. She bent down and tentatively licked and sucked on his salty nipple, teasing it erect. James jolted and gave a 'Mmm', so she kept doing that for a while then kissed her way across his chest to pay attention to his other nipple. She nuzzled his neck and kissed his cheek and then his soft lips. He rolled towards her and she slid her hand over the hard muscles of his abs, and then down further to continue what she'd been doing. She couldn't stop touching him—he was just too delicious. But James didn't protest. By the way he was biting his lip and groaning softly in pleasure, she had a feeling the rule book had been chucked out the window and wouldn't be interfering again.

It didn't take long for things to escalate to the point where he was moaning hotly into her neck; it was turning her on something chronic but she couldn't even take her T-shirt off. James seemed to be in the throes of ecstasy and Jane didn't want to ruin the momentum. She knew he had one foot in the stirrup, and it was spurring her on. Just as things began to get seriously steamy, and she was wondering if they should move it into the bedroom, his breathing started to get ragged. She slowed her pace trying to bring him back from the brink but he was too far gone. He tensed into her, let out a 'Uhhh' and shuddered; coincidentally right at the climax of the bunker tete-a-tete. It was perfect timing.

Jane had planned on them getting more intimate but honestly hadn't expected him to let things go as far as it had, or for him to completely lose it. So she was momentarily flummoxed. Then she noticed he was lying there, breathing heavily with his eyes closed and not saying anything.

'Are you ok?' she asked tentatively, removing her hand.

'Just give me a minute.'

He sat up slowly, pulled on his boxers and jeans and grabbed his T-shirt from the floor. He held it against his stomach carefully, and went out of the room. Jane started getting worried. Dammit, why couldn't she just be content with cuddling on the couch? She heard the bathroom door open and shortly after he came back in with his T-shirt on.

'Are you watching this?' he asked.

'No.'

He clicked the off button on the remote and lay next to her in the darkness.

'Your flatmates are working night shift, I take it?'

'Yes.'

'I kept thinking one of them was going to walk in on me in flagrante.'

'I'm sure they wouldn't have minded. You're pretty hot.'

He kissed her cheek. 'You minx. You planned that.'

'Moi?'

'Aye, you.'

'I may have engineered the setting, but I didn't expect things to, er, go off like that, pardon the pun.'

James chuckled. 'I may have been a wee bit … pent up.'

'But you're ok it happened?'

'Aye, of course, it was feckin' brilliant!'

'Thank God,' she said, relieved. 'I thought you might be annoyed at me.'

'Annoyed?'

'You know, for breaking the go-slow rule and all that.'

'Hmm, I think that ship has well and truly sailed.'

He hugged her and teased her about being a femme fatale and she knew things were still ok between them. Then they kissed and she didn't want him to leave.

'Can you stay over?'

'I'd like to but I cannae. I've got a tight deadline tomorrow and then we're away Friday.' He kissed the tip of her nose. 'Can you cope until then? We'll have more time.'

'I guess so.'

But she wasn't sure she could cope. When he left, they had another heated make out session at the bottom of the stairs, and it almost did her in. Her knees were so weak afterwards that she could hardly walk back up.

Then, when she was getting ready for bed, he sent her a text that said: *2nite was amazing xxx. Your turn next, J.* And a kissing face emoji.

God, she thought. What with the couch, the stairs and now the text, she was going to have to run an ice-cold bath.

After a sleepless night fantasising about what "her turn" might entail, she texted Amber in a panic the next morning saying she needed to buy some sexy lingerie—immediately. They met up after work and went to a specialty store on Princes Street. Having never bought anything remotely racy, she had no idea where to start, but Amber took charge, piling all sorts of garments into her arms. She decided to come into the changing room to assist.

'Amber, do you mind!'

'You'll need ma help. Trust me. Some of these things are fiddly.'

She tried on half a dozen pieces, each more revealing and

outrageous than the last. Jane surveyed herself in the mirror. She was wearing a black, strappy BDSM number. It looked hot, but also like she was trying too hard.

'I look like a desperate prostitute.'

'Och, is that a bad thing?'

'Maybe something a little less *Fifty Shades of Grey*.'

She took it off and tried on a white baby doll set. 'This is cute.'

'I think that may be bridal lingerie.'

'Oh.'

'I take it you managed to coax James into the saddle last night if you're rushing out to buy sexy lingerie today?'

Jane smiled to herself, remembering. She didn't give Amber any details, though, in case she mentioned it to Colin. She doubted that James would want Colin knowing he was "back on the horse".

'Let's just say we had a pleasant evening.' She tried on another piece. 'What about this one?' she said, surveying herself in the mirror.

'Aye, it's very you,' said Amber. 'Understated with a hint of sex maniac screaming to get out.'

Jane giggled. 'That's definitely the look I'm going for.'

Chapter 32: The Grotto

Jane thought things might be awkward between them when she saw him on Friday at the airport, but James was in fine form. Teasing her and being touchy feely. Once they'd boarded the plane, he held her hand and slowly stroked the back sensuously with his thumb and pretended to look out the window—it made her laugh but it was actually stirring her up quite badly.

She felt like she was having a steamy affair, escaping the gloomy UK for an exotic destination with her hot lover. Lucky for her though James wasn't married, or otherwise emotionally entangled. She'd been through that nightmare and was glad they were well and truly past it.

They still hadn't discussed what *would* be happening in Bangkok, which was why she hadn't said anything about it to Gemma yet. James was in go with the flow mode, but she needed something more concrete. Was he planning on them staying in cheap backpacker hostels? After Budapest she doubted it but James was unpredictable and liable to throw something completely out of left field at her, so she was determined to pin him down at some point this weekend.

'It's a pity that Lucy has only just arrived and we're going,' she commented, trying to ignore her growing arousal. 'I thought I might introduce her to Amber, just so she knows someone else in Edinburgh. And she's only just up the road from her.'

James squeezed her hand. 'That's nice of you. Lucy's pretty sociable so I'm sure she'll be fine, but it would be good for her to have someone to go to lunch or have coffee with.'

'As long as you don't mind Amber finding out all your family secrets,' Jane said slyly. 'Who knows what Lucy will tell her. Then Amber will tell me and we'll all know.'

'Hmm,' said James, looking worried. 'On second thoughts, maybe don't introduce them!'

The flight to Iceland took just over two hours and they arrived at Keflavik at around one in the afternoon. Jane stepped out of the double sliding doors at the airport and the frigid air immediately took her breath away. She scampered back inside and quickly put on a few more layers under her coat. Edinburgh was cold in December, but Iceland was positively arctic. James didn't seem to mind it. She gathered he was acclimatised from many Scottish winters.

They caught the bus to Reykjavik and then a taxi to the hotel which was around thirty minutes away. The landscape was dramatic; treeless and rocky with dark, brooding skies that threatened snow. It looked like there had already been a recent snowfall from the patches of icy white with bright-green moss peeking through. Jane started shedding clothing at a great rate of knots in the taxi as she was now overheating. She noticed James was busy taking copious amounts of photos through the window while there was still light. Since he was actually an awesome photographer, she'd had no qualms asking if he could 'tag along', as Lucy put it. Initially she'd thought it was weird that he'd never been to Iceland, as it was so close to the UK, but then remembered she'd never been to Stonehenge and that was practically a cardinal sin if you were English.

The Icelandic winter had just five hours of daylight so it was dark when they arrived at the hotel. It was a long, low-slung rectangular building on stilts with huge windows set along its frontage that looked out over a lake. The lobby was lit up welcomingly with strings of fairy lights and a white frosted Christmas tree.

'This place must cost a bomb,' commented James while they were waiting on a black leather couch to check in. Jane looked around at the stark but tasteful décor. It was all glass, wood and architectural nuances.

'It's not cheap,' she agreed and told him the cost of a standard room in pounds. James looked impressed. 'You've got the best job,' he said, which made her feel proud. 'It's Gemma,' she said quickly. 'She's the one bringing in the work.'

'Maybe you could be a Gemma too,' he said. 'You've got all the right skills, and you've written a heap of articles.'

'How do you know?'

'Because I've read them all, of course.'

She got a lump in her throat at that, so pretended to look out the window at the lake and didn't reply. When they finally got to check in, she introduced herself to the woman behind the front desk, who said she was called Estrid. She was tall and blonde with pronounced cheekbones, and was starkly attractive like her surroundings. She reminded Jane of a Scandinavian version of Francesca. Estrid gave a little spiel about how pleased they were to have her stay, and James too, she said, eyeing him up. Jane was used to James getting appraising looks from women by now; he didn't seem to notice or if he did, he didn't let it go to his head. She didn't really care, as long as she was the one he was kissing.

Estrid gave them brief rundown of the hotel's amenities and told her to please ask if there was anything further she needed. Then she handed her a folder with some basic information and a page of photos. Jane scanned it briefly and then read something about the outdoor silica pool that made her eyes widen.

'Um ... this bit here about swimsuits, is that right?'

'Oh yes. It's a natural pool, so it's a very delicate ecosystem. We don't allow swimsuits for hygiene reasons. We would, of course, expect you to use the pool so you have the full guest experience.'

'Are there separate female and male areas?'

'No, it's unisex,' said Estrid. 'I hope that won't be a problem?'

'Ah no, that shouldn't be a problem,' Jane said slowly, looking at a photo that showed the changing rooms were nowhere near the entrance of the pool. In fact, it looked as if they were inside the hotel!

'Er … can I wear a towel?'

'Unfortunately not,' said Estrid. 'The pool area itself is a no-towel zone. Just because people tend to leave them strewn about and it creates more work for the staff.'

Jane gulped. So much for the best job. Now she had to walk around starkers in front of James and God knew however many other males! She could sense James beside her, trying not to laugh. When they got to the room, which was amazing, she barely saw it. She dumped her bag and screeched, 'Bloody hell!'

'Did Gemma not mention that?'

'No!'

'Och, it'll be fine. There's probably no one staying here anyway. It's too expensive.'

'I'll just wear my bikini!'

'You can't, Jane, you heard her. It's a delicate ecosystem. And it's a no-towel zone.' James grinned at her.

She narrowed her eyes. 'You're enjoying this.'

He shrugged. 'I'm going to see you naked at some point this weekend. So what's the difference if it's in the pool or in here?'

'Oh, are you?'

'Aye, I am.'

He sounded so completely sure of himself that she had to

laugh, but her heart was pounding. Oh God.

'Maybe we should do the pool thing now and get it over with so you're not stressing about it all weekend.'

'Ok,' she said reluctantly.

'But check out the room first. It's crazy!'

He was right. They'd been given a corner deluxe suite with a super-high ceiling. The room was softly lit by hanging lights placed at various points, like small glowing planets. There were steps leading up to a wooden platform that had a California king with a gazillion pillows and white fluffy throw. It was bordered on three sides by square picture windows, each dissected with a big steel X. There was a separate lounge area with two sofas and floor-to-ceiling windows showing a view across to the lake. Outside, she could see that snow had started falling.

'Wow,' she said. 'What's the bathroom like?' She opened the door and her mouth dropped open. The entire room was decked out in black marble with silver fittings, and there was a huge Jacuzzi bathtub big enough for about four people.

'Forget the pool,' she joked. 'Let's just hang out in here.'

'Fine by me,' said James, standing behind her and looking over her shoulder. 'But you kind of have to ...'

'I know,' she sighed. 'Let's get the bloody thing over with.'

'That's the spirit,' said James cheerfully.

She felt like hitting him.

There *were* separate male and female changing rooms at least, so

James kissed her, said he'd see her in the pool, then headed into the males. Jane took off her clothes, underwear and shoes and stuffed everything in the provided locker. They'd been given wristbands at reception, which when held up to a small scanner on the door, locked or unlocked it with a whirring noise. She spent some time playing with that and fussed about putting her hair into a ponytail. You're stalling, she thought.

Her mantra of "don't think about it; just do it" wasn't helping. She considered what was scarier—walking across the restaurant to talk to James or walking out to a pool with him looking at her naked body? Perhaps the restaurant, she thought, at least now she knew he wanted to be with her. Hopefully he still did after he saw her in the flesh.

She'd just taken the requisite shower when an older lady in her sixties came into the changing room. Her skin was very tanned as if she sunbathed in the nude. She didn't seem to care that she wasn't wearing anything. Jane, on the other hand, quickly sat down on the slatted wooden bench to cover her bits.

The lady looked at her and smiled and said, 'Are you Jane?' with a German accent.

'Yes?'

'A nice young man sent me in to see if you're coming out?'

She sighed. 'Yes ... eventually.'

'He also said to tell you that he'll close his eyes.'

Jane laughed and then groaned. The woman grasped her

dilemma.

'New boyfriend? Hasn't seen you undressed before?'

She nodded.

The woman looked her over. 'You have a nice body. You have nothing to be ashamed of, especially at your age,' she said kindly. 'Perhaps we could walk out together?'

Jane sagged in relief. 'Thank you.'

Maybe she could orchestrate it so the woman walked in front of her, and she could scuttle along behind. She stood up and the woman ushered her towards the door before she could change her mind. Outside there was a corridor that led to the pool and, at the end of it, a glass-fronted swing door. The woman did something to a square panel and the door swung open for her and she walked through but then it shut before Jane could go through after her. She could see the pool through the glass door with a few people swimming about but no one was looking her way. She tried pushing the panel, but the door wouldn't open. She started getting heart palpitations, then realised that the band around her wrist activated it. There was a whirring noise and the door swung open. You can do this, she thought. She squared her shoulders and walked out into the bitingly cold air, trying to act confident like she did this kind of thing every day. The woman had disappeared into the steam, so Jane started walking around the edge of the pool.

Unfortunately, the small area she'd glimpsed through the glass door didn't give the true picture; the pool was quite full of people.

A lot of naked people. She gulped. It was also lit up with spotlights everywhere. How nice of them to do that, she thought witheringly. The lack of mood lighting would certainly be mentioned in her review. It had stopped snowing, but she was wet from the shower and the wind chill factor felt about minus ten. Her nipples were standing to attention like icicles—she *had* to get in the pool. Maybe she could just jump in on the side? But no, of course there was a sign saying "please use the designated entry steps" and reminding everyone it was a "delicate ecosystem", blah blah blah.

Jane deliberately tried not to scan the pool to see where James was. Following the signs, she reached the entry steps and was horrified to see half a dozen men in their thirties lounging about at the bottom. Obviously some kind of business group, or maybe a stag do?

As she watched, a girl about her own age, not unattractive but with very small breasts, came down the steps in full view of them. They gave her a once-over and then had an impromptu conference that involved nodding or shaking of their individual heads, hand gestures and cackling like a bunch of old women.

That got Jane riled up, so she put on her haughty look, determined not to let them bother her. As she walked down the steps into the warm, milky-blue water, she avoided looking at them but she could feel their brazen stares. Out of the corner of her eye she saw one of them nudge his mate.

'Cor, I'd like some of that,' she heard him say. British yob,

Jane thought, typical! She happened to see James directly behind them, who had of course been watching the whole proceedings with amused interest. She didn't wait around to see what the men's verdict was, she just swam over to the side of the pool well away from them. James came up behind her and pressed his body against hers.

'Cor, I'd like some of that,' he whispered in her ear, and she grimaced.

'Perverts.'

'Och, I wouldn't worry, there was a lot of unanimous nodding going on.'

She turned around so they were facing each other and put her arms around his neck. His hair was slicked back, and steam was drifting across the water. He snaked an arm around her waist and pulled her closer so her breasts were touching his chest.

'You are quite stunning,' he said.

'Flattery will get you everywhere.'

He kissed her tenderly and gently stroked the curve of her hip and the top of her thigh, which made her quiver. She saw over his shoulder that a few of the men were looking at them.

'Do you want to move somewhere else?' she said, feeling like they were putting on a show.

'There's a spot nearby that's not as public.'

'Great.'

She followed him as he swam over to a small, cave-like grotto set into the side of the pool. It seemed to be some kind of private enclosure, as it had a door you could lock from the inside, which James did. It wasn't completely black as there was a small soft light embedded in the ground making the centre of the milky water appear intensely blue, while the edges round the side of the grotto were dark sapphire. She could hear the lapping of the water against the wet rock and felt the occasional cold drip from the ceiling on her head. When she stood up, the waterline was just above her breasts, which she was glad of.

'That's better,' she told him. 'I didn't really enjoy being judged for having small boobs.'

He frowned at her. Uh oh, she thought. Sure enough, she got a lecture.

'Firstly, they're not small. And secondly, even if your breasts were the size of gnats, I'd still want you.' Jane giggled. He did have a way of putting things sometimes.

'Said no guy ever.'

'It's true.'

He put an arm around her waist to draw her closer. She felt him gently cup her breast and hardly dared to breathe as he stroked his thumb across her nipple, sending an intense dart of pleasure down her body.

'They're pretty exquisite, I have to say. And everything down here is doing my head in.' He reached down with the other hand to caress her behind. She looked at him. 'Uh ...' was all she could say. A pleasurable throbbing started up between her legs as he continued rubbing her nipple and caressing her backside. James saw the expression on her face, and chuckled softly. 'Maybe we should go back to the room?'

She shook her head weakly. The way she was feeling, she might have to crawl there on her hands and knees. He stopped touching her breast and traced a finger across her midriff tantalisingly. Then slipped his hand down further. Oh God, she thought.

'Is this ok?' he whispered.

'Mmm …' was as much as she could manage.

She twined her arms around his neck and he sucked on her bottom lip and teased her tongue with his. With him stroking, as well as kissing her, her brain started going haywire.

They floated over to a ledge running around the edge of the grotto where the water was shallower. She lay back on her elbows and they kissed while he caressed her breasts and lightly tweaked her hardened nipples. After all the build-up, she was seriously turned on just from him doing that but then he slid his hand down to stroke her again. 'You feel so nice,' he whispered, and slowly rubbed her *there* with his finger.

Jane groaned softly. He was making her so hot—if he kept that up, she was going to come unstuck in less than ten seconds. He'd think she was a lightweight. Maybe she could concentrate on Russian tractors or something?

She took a deep breath and tilted her head back to look up at the dripping ceiling and tried to control the arcs of excitement radiating from her groin. It didn't help that she could feel him pressed hard up against her thigh; it was making her feel even more aroused.

As if he knew she was fighting it, James took his hand away and kissed her. First softly, then deeper until he was sucking on her tongue and massaging her breasts while gently but firmly squeezing both her nipples between his fingers. She felt like a violin, with each one of her strings being sensuously tightened to breaking point.

Keeping one hand on her breast, his other crept back down again between her legs, rubbing and circling her. She tensed. It felt so good, oh God, she was going to lose it ... But he moved his hand away at the last second, caressing her inner thigh instead. Jane took a deep breath, and calmed down.

James shifted position so their slippery bodies were pressing together in the warm water. She ran her fingers over the taut muscles of his back and kneaded his firm butt with both hands making him groan. He hooked one of her legs up behind his hip and started doing something even better with his finger, while simultaneously rubbing with his thumb. Jane moaned in bliss. The Russian tractors by this point were seriously wavering. James started kissing her again; deep, urgent kisses that made her helpless with want. Jane gave up. She just couldn't resist him. He had her exactly where he wanted her. She let him stoke the fire, stroking and rubbing and kissing her until she was lost in it.

Just when she couldn't take any more pleasure, she detonated, arching into him and groaning as raw ecstasy crashed over her like a tidal wave, flinging her up and out of the grotto, and into the inky Icelandic sky.

Eventually she fell back to earth and found herself lying in James's arms as the warm, milky water rocked over her body. She could hear it slapping up against the sides of the grotto. He smiled at her and kissed her damp, flushed cheek.

'Was that fun?' he asked softly.

'It was freakin'…' she breathed, hardly able to speak.

James chuckled modestly.

'I think I'm going to have to focus on something a hell of a lot more boring than Russian tractors from now on.'

He frowned. 'Eh?'

CHAPTER 33: CORSET CONFESSIONS

James said he needed to swim around in the main pool for a bit, so he didn't 'shock the lasses' and 'make the lads envious' when he got out. Jane had snorted at that. But going back to the room first did give her time to pull herself together.

In the bathroom, she shakily brushed out her hair, cleaned her teeth and put on some lip gloss. She looked at her glowing face in the mirror, and blinked. Did that just happen? Maybe it was a dream? Her body was still throbbing from his touch, so she didn't think it had been. It had certainly surpassed any fantasy she'd had in the build-up to the trip: getting it on in a grotto—maybe she should use that as the title of the article?

Just thinking about it began to make her feel aroused again. So she put on the black lace corset she'd bought and the matching pair of skimpy g-string knickers, and looked at herself in the full-length bathroom mirror. God, the top half was pushing her boobs skywards and the bottom half left nothing to the imagination. Hopefully it was screaming sex maniac in a classy way.

In the room, Jane turned the dimmer switch down so the lighting was more intimate. There didn't seem to be any controls for heating, so she figured it must be centrally operated. It was warmish in the room but still colder than she would've liked. She tried to strike (what she hoped) was a seductive pose on top of the bed. But she kept shivering from anticipation and cold. So, she went and got into her winter pyjamas, keeping the lingerie on underneath. So much for seduction, she thought.

James finally came in wearing just a white towel slung around his hips and carrying his clothes. His dark hair was standing up in wet spikes and beads of water glistened on his tanned, muscular chest. He looked so heart-stoppingly sexy Jane almost whimpered. James paused when he saw her on the bed in her pink pyjamas. 'Are we going to sleep?' he asked.

'No, definitely not!'

'Whoa, feisty lass,' he said with a grin. He came up the stairs to the bed and saw her shivering. 'Are you cold? Why don't you get under the duvet?'

She hesitated and then said 'Ok,' because it *was* really cold. The window behind her seemed to be sucking the warmth out of the room. James dumped his clothes by the bed, lost the towel and they got underneath the duvet. He was radiating body heat, so Jane snuggled against him.

'You're so warm!'

'Aye, I had to spend quite a lot of time in the pool before I could get out. By the way, you might not want to mention what happened in the grotto for the article ...'

'Mmm, it might get more traffic if I *do* mention it ...'

She ran her hand down his thigh and felt the muscle tense, but he grabbed her hand before she could explore further.

He smiled at her. 'I was thinking we could order some room service first.'

Suddenly she was starving. 'Ok. Good idea.'

Perhaps she should order spaghetti and slurp it seductively if he was going to play hard to get?

James got out of bed, walked down the stairs and grabbed the room service menu off the sideboard where the phone was. Then he turned around and stood there, reading off items to her. She watched him with a smile, thoroughly enjoying the view. He didn't seem to mind being naked in front of her, though with a body like that, why would he?

After he'd ordered the food, and was back in bed, Jane got out and sat cross-legged on top of the covers and pulled the white, fluffy throw around her shoulders. Thanks to that little show, her estrogen levels were now spiking like crazy. If she stayed in bed she wouldn't be able to keep her hands off him. Perhaps this was a good time to do some digging.

'So, tell me about Bangkok.'

'What did you want to know?'

'Um, why you have to go back?'

'Ah, right. Well, Rick sorted out a work visa for me and I took out a lease on a flat in his apartment building, but I sublet it when I went to Edinburgh. The person who I sublet it to is leaving after

New Year's.'

'Can't Rick find someone else to take on the lease or sublet it to?'

'I dinnae want to burden Rick with having to do that. He's busy with his own stuff, and he often takes off to the jungle at a moment's notice.'

'Oh. So, I could get a visa too since I'm working for him?'

'That's what I thought, aye. It'll only take about ten days to process when we get there.'

'How long are you planning to stay?'

'The lease has another three months on it, so three months, I guess? We can see how it goes and if you like it. If not, I can sublet it again and we can go somewhere else, or back to Edinburgh. I ken you've got your own stuff going on. I just thought as it's the European winter you might enjoy going somewhere warm, and there's plenty of sightseeing we can do for you to write about. And Rick wants to meet his new associate, of course.'

'Warm is good if there's air con and a pool. And I do want to meet Rick ...' said Jane tentatively, wondering about the living arrangements. 'So, I'm assuming if you have a flat, I'd be staying there too and we'd effectively be living together?'

'Aye, effectively—is that ok?' She breathed a sigh of relief that hostels weren't in the plans.

'I guess I can put up with you. As long as you don't expect me to cook and clean and wash your clothes,' she teased.

'Nae, we'll get a maid,' said James.

'Oh.'

'I'm joking! I'm perfectly capable of looking after myself. Ok cooking is not really ma thing, but the food is so cheap there you can eat out or get it delivered.'

'It all sounds fantastic,' she said, smiling at him. 'From what Gemma was saying the other day, she's ok for content for the next few months. And, since I've never been to Asia, it would be good to branch out.'

'Phew,' said James, looking relieved. 'All of this is completely up for discussion by the way. I want you to be happy with everything, so please tell me if you're worried or stressed at any point. I'd rather you tell me, and we talk about it, than you skedaddling off somewhere.'

Jane nodded. 'I will.' Then remarked, 'Though I don't think I'd really want to skedaddle off somewhere if you weren't coming too,' and felt herself blushing. Why did she always feel uncomfortable saying this kind of thing out loud? Hopefully James wasn't into big emotional speeches because he probably wouldn't be getting one from her, unless it was in written form.

'So, if you'd rented a flat in Bangkok why were you in Edinburgh? Surely you didn't come all that way to be a dress model for Lucy?' she queried, trying lighten the mood.

Just then there was a sharp knock on the door and she had to answer it because she was the only one wearing anything. The waiter raised his eyebrows when he caught sight of James, bare-chested and gorgeous, with the duvet draped over his lower half.

Jane stifled a giggle, feeling like a wanton woman. She came back to the bed bearing a plate of pizza and a box of sushi. They munched in silence for a while.

'So?' Jane said, dipping a piece of sushi in soy sauce.

'So what?'

'Why were you in Edinburgh? A work thing?'

James swallowed a bite of pizza. 'Because of you.'

'Me?'

'Rick told me you were back, and he was sick of me moping around, so he told me to go and sort it out with you. I'd realised by that point that I overreacted, and I … I had feelings for you.'

Her stomach flipped. Feelings, she thought, what kind of "feelings" exactly? She knew it was more than friendship since he'd asked her to be his girlfriend, and that he was more than mildly attracted to her, but up until now he hadn't mentioned any "feelings".

'Oh,' said Jane. 'So, if I hadn't seen you at the restaurant, you would've texted or called me?'

'Probably, if I managed to find the guts to do it. I didnae expect you to be there; I got a wee bit freaked. Then you gave me that note, and I knew I had to see you because …' He trailed off.

'Because you wanted to get into my knickers …?' she teased.

'Nae, because …' James took a deep breath, 'I'm in love with you.'

Jane had been playing with her last piece of sushi, trying to decide if she wanted it or not, but when she heard that she almost dropped her chopsticks.

'It's probably *waaay* too soon to say that,' he said hurriedly, seeing her staring at him in surprise. 'But in the note, you said you missed me and cared about me, and it made me hope you felt like I did. I couldnae stop thinking about you in Bangkok, and wishing you were there too so we could talk and laugh and make jokes about things. The way you make me feel, it's crazy … I want to be with you all the time.' He smiled at her. 'Anyway, life's too short not to say it when you know.'

A warm glow settled over her. He felt the same way she did. She'd never had to worry about him going off with Kistella or Cara, or some random woman he met online. He was hers all along. Regret washed through her. She should've stayed with him in Budapest, then they would've had those two months together.

James was looking at her expectantly and her mind went blank. 'I …' she said, then stopped. Uh oh, she thought, frustrated. So much for getting off the hook when it came to emotional speeches. Where was Keith's notepad when she needed it?

'James, I want to tell you … things … I'm just useless at saying stuff out loud. I'll get my laptop right now and type you an email,' she said, attempting to make a joke.

'Och, that's ok.'

'It's not. I want to tell you.'

'Well, tell me what you like about me then.'

That's easy, she thought.

'I like your sense of humour. You have such a dry wit, you crack me up with the things you say. I like your intelligence, the way you're always researching stuff and wanting to know things—' God, she felt like she was giving a school speech. But James was nodding, which encouraged her.

'Your drive and motivation is inspiring. You've helped me so much with freelancing, especially when I had no idea what I was doing; you gave me the courage to take a risk …'—she was working up to it now—'Your kindness and patience, you try and talk sense into me even when I'm acting completely mental.' James laughed at that.

'I don't know, there's so much more, we'll be here all night …' she trailed off. Dammit!

James took her hand and squeezed it reassuringly. 'There you go, that wasn't so hard, was it?'

She gave a small laugh. 'Well, you did make it easy on me by going first. That was kind of an amazing speech by the way …'

He smiled but she saw disappointment in his eyes. Jane, you wimp, she thought, just say it, he loves you. She put her sushi box on his empty plate and moved it onto the floor. Then edged forward until she was straddling him. She twined her arms round his neck and buried her fingers in his damp hair. Her heart was practically jumping out of her chest.

'There's more.'

'Oh?'

'I love you so bloody much it's ridiculous!'

James sighed. 'Now *that's* what I wanted to hear.'

'I thought after what I did, I'd lost you. I was a mess.'

He shook his head. 'Och, it's ma fault. I should have realised why you left. I was just paranoid you didn't want me. If it's any consolation, I was in agony ...'

'Uh huh, lying by the pool and working on your tan sounds really agonising ...'

James chuckled. 'Ok, that bit was all right. But at night I was greeting alone into ma pad thai and wishing you were there to massage ma feet.'

'Ah, well, I'm sure I can give you another orgasmic foot massage. As long you take back what you said about me being a troublemaker.' She shifted her hips against his.

'I cannae do that,' he murmured huskily. 'You do like to push ma buttons.'

'Pushing your buttons is fun,' Jane said lightly. She shifted her hips again. 'You get this look in your eye like you want to put me over your knee and spank me. It's pretty hot.'

'Hmm, well, you're a wee mischief.'

She shifted her hips, slightly harder, and James groaned softly. 'You're killing me.'

Jane giggled. 'Not quite the effect I was after.'

He suddenly pulled her down on top of him into the mound of snow-white pillows and they were kissing urgently and she was frantically trying to get under the duvet with him; her hair flying all over the place.

'Hang on.' James was getting out of bed.

'What are you doing?' she asked, breathing heavily.

'I've, er, got some condoms in ma bag.'

'Ah, ok, we're having the sex talk. Have you got a bottle of whisky in there too?'

'Very funny.'

'Look, it's ok. I'm on the pill ...'

'I trust that you are. It's just to be doubly sure and all that. You dinnae mind, do you?'

'That's perfectly fine, my sweet.' Oh James, she thought.

He came back and dumped a pile of condoms on the nightstand.

'I've got some more if we run out.'

'Exactly how many did you bring?' Jane asked, amused.

'Erm ... about sixty.'

'Sixty!' she exclaimed. 'You do know we're only here for the weekend?'

'Aye, I just grabbed a bunch of boxes at the airport. I may have gone a bit overboard. The woman at Boots was looking at me like I was a sex addict or something.'

Jane spluttered with laughter. 'I'm flattered you think I have that kind of stamina!'

'You may surprise yourself, beautiful.' He drew her hair to one side and licked lightly down the entire length of her neck.

She shivered. Perhaps she should have that last piece of sushi to keep her strength up ...

James undid a few of her pyjama buttons and caught sight of the tops of her breasts spilling over the corset. 'Mmm, I'm not sure what's going on here but I like it.' He bent his head and kissed his way across her soft flesh. She sighed at his touch of his lips.

'It's just a little something I bought.'

James undid the rest of her buttons and ran his hand over the structured front of the corset. 'This is intriguing. I think I'm going to have to see the full effect.'

'If you must.'

She got up off the bed and shed her pyjamas.

'Jaysus, that's nice,' he murmured, raking his eyes over her.

Jane laughed. 'I was going for Raunchy Receptionist.'

He nodded slowly. 'Aye, it's certainly that—what's the back like?'

She did a twirl showing off the g-string knickers. 'What do you think?' By the sultry look in his eyes, she could tell exactly what he thought.

'Hmm, it's *very* alluring. I think you should hop back into bed immediately, Ms Receptionist. Otherwise, I think I might spontaneously combust, and it's all going to be over bar the shouting.'

'Oh really?'

James flicked the duvet cover back and her eyes widened. Whoa, ok, he wasn't joking.

She gave him an enigmatic smile. 'Your taxes look like they need *immediate* attention, Mr McAvoy. Unfortunately, all our accountants are busy right now. But I can sort you out myself.'

'Mmm, excellent. I'm looking forward to that.'

'I should warn you though, the methods I use are *very* unprofessional.'

He grinned and held out his hand to her. 'Unprofessional is ma middle name, sweetheart.'

'You do realise the way things are going, we may not actually get any work done in Bangkok,' whispered James in her ear.

It was late, the lights were out and they were spooning, watching the odd snowflake drift gently past the window. Jane was hoping the aurora borealis might make an appearance as Estrid had mentioned sightings during the week. The sky was now starting to clear so her eyes were peeled for a glimpse of it. She yawned and snuggled back into James's body, enjoying his warmth and his arms around her. The corset was in a tangle on the floor, she wasn't sure where. Things had become extremely chaotic ...

'It'll be fine, we'll just stick to a schedule. Work in the

morning; play in the afternoon. Or the other way round if you prefer?'

'After tonight, I think I prefer play all the time,' he murmured huskily, nuzzling her neck and running a hand down her thigh.

She giggled. 'Rick might have something to say about that. He'll be banging on the door.'

'Hmph, he better not be.'

She was quiet, thinking.

'So how hot will it be in Bangkok when we're there?'

'It's a slightly cooler time of year, but some days will still be in the high twenties, maybe over thirty.'

Jane gulped. 'So, I know there's a pool. Does the apartment have air con?'

'Aye, but it's a wee bit temperamental. One time it broke down and it was sweltering. I had to keep running ice cubes over myself to cool off.'

Hmm, she thought. Hopefully the air con broke down once or twice while they were there, James running ice cubes over her naked body sounded quite fun.

'I know you're not used to hot weather,' he continued, 'So if you can't handle it, as I said, we can go somewhere else.'

'Um, I'm sure I can handle it. I just did two months by myself in all kinds of weather, and without any other … issues.'

'Issues? By that you mean blackmailers, bedbugs and other kinds of crazy?'

'Yes.'

James chuckled into her hair.

'What?'

'For someone so sensible, you do seem to attract a lot of mayhem.'

'This time will be different.'

'Mmm hmm.'

She turned over and kicked him, and then there was a slight tussle that ended up with them kissing for quite a while, so he forgot about teasing her. For her own part, Jane wasn't worried. It was going to be a carefree three months of freelancing, sightseeing and making love (a lot) with James. It sounded bloody idyllic.

Besides, all the signs were there for it to run like clockwork: her instincts were giving her a thumbs up emoji; the travel gods were saying it was a go, and even the aurora borealis was now swirling greenly in the sky above them like a good luck portent. What could possibly go wrong?

ACKNOWLEDGEMENTS

Many thanks to my beta readers: Katie Griffin, Carina Barrau, Isabel Alcuaz and Ellie Race for their encouragement and feedback on my first draft. I'd also like to thank Elaine Seabrook for her diligent copy editing; Anita Saunders for her eagle eye proofreading; Estella Vukovic for her fab cover art; and Janis Wemyss for her Scottish input. Last, but definitely not least, special thanks to my partner and fellow globetrotter, Chris Lambert; you rock!

Thank You For Reading

I hope you enjoyed reading *Travel & Mayhem*. If you have a moment, I would be so grateful if you could leave an honest review on Amazon and/or Goodreads. Reviews are crucial for any author, and even just a line or two can make a huge difference. I genuinely appreciate your time and support!

Happy travels!
Angela X☺

Website: angelapearse.pub

Instagram: @angelapearseauthor